LINCOLN LIBRARY

February 2022

Tall Willows

A Ruth Willows Mystery/Romance

by PC Feather

Tall Willows

ISBN: 978-1-09837-579-9
ISBN eBook: 978-1-09837-580-5

for Frank Feather

Chapter 1

THE SLAP OF his dress shoes hitting the pavement quickened along with his breath. As Hector Alverez yanked on Golden Valley High School's small blue employees only door, the force of his pull almost sent the papers in his awkwardly held manila folder flying. Clutching at them like a newborn, he caught them, heaved a deep sigh, and stumbled through the door.

During summer break, the halls were unlit, and the main office glowed from a solitary, overhead fluorescent. The two secretaries' desks were unoccupied. One was neat and tidy. The other looked as though a twister had hit it, leaving scattered papers, files, and paperclips in its wake. Hector's gut sank when he saw the frosted glass windows of Principal Rodriguez's office were black. He turned when he heard someone fumbling under an old copier machine.

"Paper's jammed," a loud cheerful voice rang out. "Goes to figure. I try to get some work done when I can have the copier all to myself and the paper jams or the toner leaks or some other stupid problem."

Hector had no clue what to say to this creature; a woman clad in blue jeans, a grey hoodie, and oversized ball cap.

"I ... I ... I have an eight a.m. appointment with Principal..." he petered out. Her unexpected presence threw off his concentration.

"He'll be back any minute, honey. Rodriguez came in a little bit ago and turned right around. Said he had left somethin' at home. He told me to tell anyone lookin' for him he'd be back in twenty. Then my paper jammed, and I've been fiddlin' with this darn machine ever since." She pulled out a piece of crumpled paper and presented it as evidence to Hector.

"Will you gimme a hand, honey," she continued, "since you have to wait anyways? There's a box of colored copy paper in the storage closet. Trouble is, the lights don't work too good and when the door shuts, it goes pitch black in there. If you hold the door for me, I might be able to make some copies before the morning's over."

Hector didn't want to help, but she grabbed his arm and pulled him toward the door.

"I need to wait for Principal Rodriguez," he said.

"We'll be done before he gets back," she said, "the closet's just down the hall."

Hector distractedly dropped his thick manila folder on the nearest desk before she whisked him out the door.

She led him down the dim, locker lined corridors of the old high school. They turned a corner and entered a newer and brighter addition that offered a picturesque view of the Southern Colorado Rockies through oversized double glass doors. The school's football, baseball, and track fields stretched out until they touched the majestic mountains.

Hector paused in front of the doors to admire the beautiful scenery. He realized he had gone over the school's budget with a fine-toothed comb but couldn't recall spending reports for the athletics department. More money went to sports than math, art and, music combined. *It wouldn't be surprising if Coach Wayne got greedy, felt like he deserved a little more than everyone else.* Wayne would be the first person Hector looked into after he met with Rodriguez.

Hector looked at his watch, eight-O-five, now he was late for his meeting. "I have to go. I must speak with Principal Rodriguez."

From the stairwell, the woman called as she glided up the stairs, "The closet's just up here, honey. Besides, I don't see his car in the parking lot yet."

She was right. The principal's parking spot in the lot below remained empty.

"If you just hold this door for me, you can be on your way, and I won't bother you anymore," She called down from the top of the stairs.

Hector climbed the stairs and joined her outside a door. Black painted letters on it said DARKROOM.

"It's just storage now," she chattered. "The box of colored paper is on a shelf in the back. I'll hold the door open, and you grab it for me." She stood firm by the door, not moving to go inside.

Hector decided to get the paper so he could get back to the office and on with his meeting. His hand patted the wall for a light switch. He flicked it on. Only a dim red glow emanated from the back of the closet. He flicked the adjacent switch, and a florescent weakly flickered. Hector shuffled through the small cramped closet. He only saw old camera equipment and film developing chemicals.

"Ma'am, I don't see a box of paper," he called to her.

"I know it's in there! Check under the shelf!" she demanded, her voice taking on a distinct edge.

He didn't have time to protest. The lights went out; the door clicked shut, and the sudden darkness blinded him. He assumed he was alone in the pitch-black closet when the red light flicked on. A bright flash produced an ear-splitting sound. His thigh burned in intense pain. He grabbed his leg; it was warm and wet. *What the...* His mind raced. *Is this... blood?* Hector didn't have time to form another thought before the second bullet penetrated his skull.

Chapter 2

JOE CLIMBED OUT of his pickup, "We'll unload the horses here. I'll go find Shep."

"Sure thing, Granddaddy," Ruth answered. She jumped out and opened the ramp of the horse trailer. A myriad of thoughts churned in her brain. High school senior year would begin in less than two months, but she would take her first college final in less than two weeks. Now she'd been roped into performing at the annual Kiwanis Club benefit rodeo. *Why did I say yes to this rodeo? It's too much on my plate,* she thought.

Joe Willows was a consummate member of the Kiwanis Club and proud owner of Tall Willows Horse Ranch. An active and spry seventy-two years young, tall and lanky, his blonde hair had turned white, and his skin was tanned and weathered from seven decades of working out in the elements. Ruth's parents and sister had moved back to Colorado, nearly ten years ago, to help Joe run the family business after Grandma Loretta died.

As Ruth began unloading horses from the trailer, Joe and his old friend Shep emerged from the barn.

"Put'em in that paddock till everyone shows up, and we can decide who suits who best," Shep told Ruth. "You ridin' Blue?"

"Yes, sir."

"Some of the team'll ride our horses," Shep continued. "There's a beautiful black gelding brought in yesterday. It's the Silver boy's horse."

"Silver's, you say?" inquired Joe.

"Yup."

"That just might be one of our horses."

"When you see Kenny, you can ask him," replied Shep. "We might need only two or three of your horses, Joe. Can you stay and help me match up your horses with my riders?"

"Shep, I don't know a rodeo coach better than you, but I'd be glad to do what I can." Joe closed the corral gate, and they headed to the barn.

Ruth said, "If you don't need me, I'll take the shuttle over to main campus."

"I was hoping you could meet everyone and look at the schedule. We've only got three weeks to put this shindig together," said Shep.

"I have a class at eleven, but I can stay for a while." Ruth conceded.

"Thank you, dear." Shep gave Ruth a one-armed bear hug. "It's summertime, so tell me what you're doing taking a class here at the university. Did you graduate high school already?"

"My Grand-baby is not only beautiful but also brilliant," Joe beamed. With a mischievous glint in his eye, he added, "And you watch what you're doing, you sly old fox. You're old enough to be her father."

Ruth's porcelain skin flushed red. Joe knew teasing and compliments unnerved his granddaughter.

"You ignore that old goat and tell Uncle Shep all about it, Ruthie dear." He leaned his back against the side of the barn and wiped his forehead with a handkerchief. Nights were cool in the west, but by nine in the morning, July days were already hot.

"I'm in the College for High School Seniors program," Ruth explained.

"What does that mean?"

"I've gone beyond our high school's math and science programs."

"She gets that from her Daddy," Joe interjected.

Ruth continued, "I still have to take classes at high school, but I can take my math and science classes here at Southern Colorado University. Then I can apply those credits to whatever school I go to next fall. I'm taking Biology now so I can take math theories in the fall, then molecular bio in the spring. That'll give me a good head start for the programs I'm looking at for next year."

"Darlin' you're growin' up too fast! I remember when I first met you shaking in your brand new pink cowgirl boots."

Ruth hugged her adopted uncle, "Well, you were a lot bigger and scarier lookin' back then."

Shep laughed, "And you've grown a lot smarter than me. I'll have you on that bus in an hour, promise."

The radio blasted as they walked into the university's beautiful barn, "*... police still searching for local school official Hector Alverez. It has been three days since the recently promoted school official was reported missing by his family. Authorities...*"

"Stu, turn that danged thing down!" Shep hollered down the wide aisle, "We've got guests."

"Sorr-ry," Stu's singsong voice called as he stepped out of a stall with a pitchfork full of muck and tossed it into a nearby wheelbarrow. He quickly turned off the radio.

Stu and Shep had worked together for many years. Shep with his barrel chest, flaming red handlebar mustache and matching hair was the antithesis of Barn Manager Stu who was a thin live wire of a man. His skin was espresso brown, and his hair cut close to his head. He had a kind and gentle way about him that made animals feel safe and secure. Stu said hello to Joe and Ruth, then hauled the wheelbarrow out of the barn.

Shep turned to Ruth, "I need you to look at the schedule. It's posted outside the office. We'll do most of the work in the evenings, except for Saturdays."

Ruth nodded and took two steps toward the office when a gorgeous site stopped her in her tracks. A beautiful black quarter horse was led out of a stall by a tall, handsome cowboy.

"OOOHHH... He's beautiful," she gasped.

Joe and Shep eyed each other and couldn't help themselves. Shep chortled, "She talking about the horse or the cowboy?"

Ruth took a closer look at the young man holding the lead rope; *not too bad himself.* She gently lifted her hand to the horse's forelock as he dipped his head down for a scratch.

"Don't know if you recognize him, Joe, but this is Ken Silver," Shep said.

"I thought you looked familiar son, good to see you again," they shook hands. "Is this the horse your daddy bought off of me years ago?"

"Yes, sir," Ken smiled. "This is Remington."

"Well, he's a fine specimen. What have you been doing with him?" Joe asked.

"We did some rodeo in school and a lot of trail riding and camping," Ken said. As if on cue, Remington turned his face towards Ken for a kiss on the top of his soft nose.

Shep interrupted with another laugh and slapped Joe on the shoulder, "Now there's a cowboy for you. Not only takes his horse to school but kisses the horse instead of the pretty girl standing next to him."

Ken looked over his shoulder. Ruth had worked her way down the horse's flanks, around his hindquarters, and up the other side. He returned the appraisal he'd unknowingly received from her; she was a beautiful girl. She was tall and slender, and it was easy to fall into her aqua-blue eyes. Out from under her cowboy hat, wisps of white-blonde hair fell around the delicate features of her face. Her arms and legs were long and graceful as she gently stroked Rem. A half-cocked smile inched across his face as he thought, *what an appropriate name; Willows.*

"Ken, where are you putting your horse?" Shep's voice snapped him back to reality.

"How about in the little pasture near the barn?" Ken asked.

"That's good," Shep agreed, "it has a fence down the middle, close the gate and put Remington in the bottom half. Ruth, you put Blue in the other side."

Ken led Remington out the large sliding door at the end of the barn; Ruth headed out to get Blue.

Ken leaned against the gate, waiting for her as she walked Blue to the pasture. She got a good long look at him as she walked towards him. Back in the barn, she'd had to look up to see his eyes. They were warm and as brown as melted chocolate. His face was kind and strong. Other girls would ooh over his broad, muscular shoulders or coo at his deep dimples. They might drool at how his legs seemed to go on forever in those old jeans. She admired all that too, but she was more fascinated with his handsome face. His nose, of all things, captivated her. *It's straight, it's not too narrow or too wide; it's a very handsome nose!*

She led Blue into the small field, closed the gate behind her, and removed his halter. Blue immediately trotted over to a rack of hay and began munching. Remington was content doing the same on his side of the field.

"Guess they'll be all right." Ken walked toward her and removed his cowboy hat. He extended his hand to her, "We weren't properly introduced. I'm Ken Silver."

"Hi," she smiled and took his hand to shake it, "I'm Ruth Willows. Joe's my Granddaddy."

"Good thing he's your granddaddy. Thought I'd have to call you Grand-baby too." He kept hold of her hand.

"Only my Granddaddy gets to call me that, cowboy," she said with a wink.

"Then I'll have to find something else that suits you, Baby Doll." He returned her wink.

They held each other's gaze for a long, awkward moment. "I should have known," Ken finally broke the silence and his stare.

"What's that?"

"That Blue was a Blue Rhone. He's beautiful."

"Thanks." He let go of her hand, and they started back to the barn, "But I didn't name him cause of his color."

"Oh? Why then?"

"Well...it's stupid... but," she paused to decide if she really wanted to elaborate. "Well, there was an old TV show I watched when I was little. It was about this family, and they lived in the mountains and stuff. They had the prettiest white mule named Blue. I told everyone that I wanted a mule named Blue. Mom promised me a horse when we moved here and said I could name it Blue."

Ken laughed.

Defensively Ruth stammered, "Hey, I said it's silly..."

"I'm not laughing at you, Baby Doll," Ken smiled apologetically; "You're talking about The Walton's, right?"

"Yeah, I think that was the name of the show."

"I loved that show. I always wanted to be John Boy," Ken chuckled. "Well, I wanted to be the oldest, so my sister couldn't boss me around, and I wanted to be a writer."

As they walked back through the barn doors, Ruth asked, "And are you?"

"What?"

"A writer?"

"Well, sometimes I..."

Shep's whistling through his fingers interrupted Ken. The group of riders had arrived, and Shep called his meeting to order. "Every year, the Kiwanis Club holds a benefit rodeo. We help them out by doing the opening ceremonies each day and some demos. Everyone will ride in the drill team demo. If you did a demo last year, you can do it again. If you didn't, we'll find one for you to do.

"Some of our regulars are out of town for the summer, so we have a few ringers here to take up the slack. This here is Ken Silver," Ken tipped his hat, "Lynette Jones," she smiled, "and Ruth Willows," she smiled too. "And this gentleman here is Joe Willows," Shep nodded toward Joe, "he's brought us a few horses to use."

"Before you leave this barn this morning, I want you all to look at the schedule to see what you'll be doing and when I need you here to do it. If you have a problem with the schedule, tell me now... Derrick... not ten minutes before you're supposed to mount up."

A stocky boy with a round head of curly black hair grimaced when the guy beside him punched his arm.

"Also, before you leave this barn this morning, I want to know what horse you'll be riding. Mr. Willows has agreed to stick around and help out with matching you up with the best horse for your needs.

"Lastly, say hello to our new riders. I can attest that they are all very good at what they do; otherwise, I wouldn't have asked them to join us."

A tiny girl with short mousy brown hair, a little turned-up nose, and slightly bulging eyes bounced up and down in her seat trying to get Shep's attention, "Oh yes, please welcome a new member to our team, Miss Katie MacKay."

The pug-faced girl jumped up with a little pop and gave everyone a big wave, and "Hi ya!" Before she sat back down on a hay bale.

"Katie'll be joining the team this fall, and I thought it would be good for her to take part in this event too." Shep concluded, "Now go do what you need to do."

The crowd relaxed. Ruth said hello to Lynette. She didn't know her well, but she knew that she was Stu's daughter.

Derrick came over to introduce himself. Lynette looked at his extended hand, turned, and walked away. "Wonder what bug crawled up her ass and died." He said loud enough for Lynette, but not her father, to hear. He grabbed Ruth's hand and held it rather than shook it, "I'm Derrick Gills. Anything you need, little lady, you just let Derrick know."

Ruth bit her tongue hard. She didn't want to laugh, but she always found it amusing when a guy shorter than her called her 'little lady.' She managed a polite thanks before Katie, the pug, popped up beside her.

"Hi there. I'm Katie."

"I'm Ruth," She said, still biting her tongue.

Derrick grunted at the intrusion on his time and space.

"I'm so excited to be riding on the team this fall!" Katie began, "And even more excited to be doing demonstrations at the rodeo. When I was little, my folks took me to this rodeo every summer, and now I'm gonna be riding in it. It is so... so... so exciting!"

Derrick and Ruth stared in wordless astonishment at Katie. Derrick grunted, then turned and walked away.

Katie asked, "What are you goin' to be doing' Ruth? I show western pleasure and showmanship."

"Well, actually, I need to check the schedule." Ruth hoped their conversation would end when she walked to the board to study the schedule, but Katie followed.

"So, you don't actually ride with the team during school? I can't wait to meet everyone. I hope there are a few more girls on the team, but if all the boys are cute, maybe it's better if there aren't as many girls...." Katie chattered and giggled.

Ruth glanced at her watch, "Oh no, I'm gonna miss the shuttle!" she gasped. Katie didn't get a chance to finish her thought before Ruth turned on her heels and ran to Joe and Shep.

"Shep, the schedule's fine. See you tomorrow. Granddaddy, can I call you for a ride home after class? I came with you, and I don't have my truck."

"Anytime Grand-baby," he answered with a smile.

Ruth kissed him on the cheek, then fled across the dirt parking lot down and the lane to the shuttle stop.

Chapter 3

SHE'D INTENDED TO burn the car inside of Rocky's Junk Yard, but when she got there, the gates to the yard were locked. The sky was still light, but the street was deserted. She hid the.22 under the seat and doused the inside of the car with gasoline. She left the canister inside the car to burn.

She walked two blocks to the only biker bar in town. Mike's had a good crowd for a Tuesday. She sidled up to a few of the regulars she knew.

Her plan was simple. Have a drink, light up the car, and get one of these dolts to take her home before the sheriff showed up.

By nine-forty-five, she'd rounded up her ride, told him she was going to the bathroom, and to be ready for her when she came back. She'd jogged to the car, tossed in a lit Bic, and WHOOSH. Gasoline was a faster accelerant than she'd imagined, and the back of her hair singed as she fled the scene. The stench of burning chemicals filled her nostrils.

She had taken care of the school's new little bean counter, Alverez. She wasn't happy about that situation. Murder had never been a part of her plan. There was nothing she could do about it now. They would find him in due course, and no one would ever suspect her.

Now alone in the dark, with her second bourbon on the rocks, she replayed the events of the last five days through her mind. She took a long drink. Two decades of skimming and saving were on the line because of someone else. She had to make sure it would all be worth it.

If it hadn't been for her no-good drunk of a husband, she would have never been in this position. Her thoughts detoured from the last few days as old memories played in her head. Barely out of high school and pregnant by her boyfriend, she'd gotten a job at the school as a night janitor. How humiliating; she'd gone from the most popular girl in school to scrubbing its toilets.

She had the baby, yet she still worked. After a year of a soulless marriage, her husband was gone. He'd run off with some tramp. It wasn't long after she'd received word he'd been killed in a bar near Phoenix. No matter to her, he hadn't left her anything but funeral expenses. She'd realized it was time for her to take charge of her life.

She'd worked and went to community college and got a degree. That'd helped her move up the ladder of the school system. She'd found her way into an office as a go-for to Mr. Marty Alberts. She hated him, but she got to work during the day and wear nicer clothes. She could pretend to be respectable while sleeping with her boss for fringe benefits. *How else was a girl going to move up in this world?* And move up, she did. *Look at me now, in charge of so much! And a Ph.D. too, who'd believe it!*

She took another swallow of bourbon. *Marty Alberts - the mongrel.* He'd given her the idea to skim money off the expense reports all those years ago. As he'd moved up through the ranks, she had too. He knew how she supplemented her meager income and had looked the other way. He'd even showed her ways to do it more effectively. All he'd asked for in return was a quick roll in the hay.

All she'd asked of him was that he kept his mouth shut and not retired for two more years. That was all she needed, and she'd have enough to get out of this godforsaken desert and go somewhere tropical. It would have only been one more year if not for her worthless son.

Women and fast cars were his vices. He'd bought a sports car last Christmas, and it had set her back an entire year's worth of work. That would be her legacy to him, a fancy car. Once she was gone, no one would hear from her again, including her worthless son. She'd change her name and live the good life till it killed her.

She swirled the liquor in the glass and took the last swig. Trouble was, someone else would take Alverez's place, and soon probably. That meant that someone else would figure out what she was up to. She needed a plan, but she'd set her mind to that tomorrow.

Exhausted, she took three ibuprofen and went to bed.

Chapter 4

RUTH LOVED THE university's library. It had the perfect mix of modern and historical southwestern architecture. Study and meeting rooms were scattered throughout the building, but her favorite place was near the entrance. Ruth sat at one of the oversized wooden tables where she could look out the large windows, across the campus to the mountains in the background.

It took a little over an hour to finish her lab write up, but she wasn't having any luck with her research paper. Her brain had had enough.

One o'clock found her gazing out the windows, daydreaming about horses and sexy cowboys, and tall sexy cowboys on horses and all kinds of trouble she could get herself into when the gorgeous cowboy got off the horse and wrapped himself around her... *Why can't I get him out of my head! Only talked to him once! What's with me!* She exhaled a long deep sigh when she heard, "What's up, Baby Doll?"

She almost rocketed out of her chair when she turned her head and saw Ken seated next to her. She yelped, "You scared me!"

A bright smile showed off his dimples before he kissed her on the cheek, "Sorry." He studied her face, "Where were you just now?"

Breathing ceased for a long moment. Her heart raced, and her head went dizzy. *What the heck was that? OMG! Did he just KISS me?* She smiled and tried to compose herself.

"Well, I wasn't finishing my paper." She returned his gaze and was warmed by the soft brown of his eyes, "How about you?"

"Research. I've been collaborating with a prof from the theater department on a new play."

"Wow, so you really are a writer!" She hated that her voice sounded all flustered and breathy, but the lingering tingle of his stubble on the corner of her lips unnerved her.

"I try." He noticed her hair pulled up loosely to the top of her head. It made her neck look long and lean. "Mind if I join you, or do you prefer to work alone?"

"Don't mind," her voice kinda squeaked as she gathered her scattered notes and books to give him room. Her heart was racing, her hands quivered, and her face felt flush.

"I'll be back," he said, placed his worn leather book bag on the table, and disappeared into the stacks.

Ken's presence in the chair beside her was a major distraction. After an hour, she'd had enough of trudging through her paper. She put her head down on the table and groaned.

"What's the matter, Baby Doll?"

"I give up. I'm not going to finish this paper. I'll fail biology, and I'll have to think of something else to do with my life that doesn't require a college degree," she said with a resigned matter of fact-ness.

"Glad to see you're not overreacting. Can I look?"

"I'm not a very good writer."

"Well, I'm not a very good scientist, so we're even. What is it about?"

"The pros and cons of stem cell research; profitable frontier or moral catastrophe?"

"Whoa, did you come up with this little doozy of an idea?"

"Professor Ann gave us a choice of several thought-provoking topics, and this was the one I thought would be the...easiest," she replied sarcastically.

"I would hate to have seen the others." He leaned in close to her. Ruth could feel the warmth of his body permeating her skin. *He smelled of spice and spring hay.* Her daydream wormed its way back into her brain.

"Take a break and let me look at this."

She shrugged and smiled, "If you really want to."

"I could use a break from my own tedium."

Ruth wandered around the library while Ken read over her paper. She strolled back to him as he finished and gave him a sheepish grin, "Well... you think I'm a dolt?"

"Hardly. It has sound arguments; it's just unorganized. Let me see your outline."

She stared blankly, "I don't have an outline."

"What!" The exclamation produced a loud SHHHHHH from the librarian on duty. Ken continued in hushed tones, "How can you write without an outline? It's like trying to ride a bull without a rope. It's what holds your thoughts together; it gives you a place to start from and return to when you lose your way."

"O-Kay..." He was obviously passionate about outlines.

"Get your stuff. We'll go outside, where we don't have to whisper." With that, he shoved his notes into his bag and disappeared to return his books.

As Ruth collected her belongings, Ken stopped and watched her from between the stacks. *She's beautiful and brilliant. My God, her ideas in that paper are amazing. What is with me? I've met her less than a week ago, and all I want to do is kiss her; well, more than that—but I'd like to start there. God man, this is not a drunken frat party. Just what do you think she'll do if you go after her like an animal in heat?* He took a deep breath and tried to shake some sense into his head.

Grabbing her hand, he led her outdoors to a grassy spot under a tree.

"I'll take notes; you do the talking," he said and pulled a pad and pen from his bag. "Start with your thesis sentence and think of which point you want to prove first."

They worked for an hour before they were both tired. "I think you've just about got it now," Ken said, handing her the pad, "You'll just need to reorganize it according to your outline and tidy it up."

Taking the notes, she thanked him.

They sat side by side for a while in comfortable silence. The touch of his leg pressed against hers left her breathless. A breeze blew the hem of her gauze skirt over his leg, and he played with it between his fingers.

"Are you riding tonight?"

"Yes," she glanced at her watch, "oh no, what time is it? I gotta catch the shuttle. I parked at the barn this morning." She jumped up, "I wanted to eat, and I have to change..."

"Whoa, slow down, Baby Doll," he grabbed hold of her hand. "My car is here, I can drive us to the barn, and we can get something to eat. Unless you prefer the shuttle?"

Bewildered, she said, "I didn't think ... thanks!"

"Let's go then." Ken stood up. He slung his bag over his shoulder and took her laptop case in one hand. He pulled her to her feet with his other hand. Her heart pounded so hard in her ears she could barely hear him speak.

"What would you like to eat?"

★ ★ ★

They grabbed a quick burger, but they didn't have time to waste. The barn's parking lot was packed when they arrived. Ruth's truck was near the barn. Ken had to park at the far end of the lot. He held her hand as he walked her to her truck.

Perfect time to kiss her man, he thought as he leaned forward to put her laptop on the front seat. His lips were mere inches from her mouth when a voice shouted, "Ken, Shep wants to see you in the barn before you saddle up!" It was Stu. "Howdy, Miss Ruth," he added with a wide grin.

She waved to Stu, and Ken said, "See you inside." He managed a kiss on her cheek and jogged to the barn. Stu turned to go.

Ruth trembled as she slipped her jeans on under her skirt before sliding it off. *What the heck just happened?* she thought as she pulled on her socks and boots.

Stu was grooming Blue in a stall as Ruth walked in. He gave her a big grin and said, "I saw you were running a little late, so I brought Blue in for you. I've picked his feet and brushed him. Just saddle him up. I'll go and get Remington for Ken." Stu chuckled as he walked out. "Gal's got herself a beau."

"Thanks, Stu."

Blue's saddle and bridle were on the rack outside his stall. Ruth smiled as she tacked the horse in his stall. *Her beau? Was he? No - they hardly knew each other.* She walked out of the stall to grab the bridle. She was unbuckling the throat latch when she felt someone behind her. *Ken?* She felt a hot breath on her cheek. *What is he up to now?* Hands slid around her waist, and a warm, wet tongue penetrated her ear. *EEEWWW!*

A coarse whisper surprised her, "If you like that, you'll love what I can do to your..."

She spun around, dropped the bridle, and came eye to eye with Derrick. "YOU PIG!!!"

She raised her hand and slapped his face so hard his hat hit the ground.

He stumbled backward, rubbed his cheek, and hissed, "So ... you like it rough lil' witch?"

She clenched her hand into a fist, but before she could strike him again, he grabbed both her wrists and squeezed so hard her legs buckled. He jerked her arms over her head and smashed her wrist into the metal bars of the stall.

Ruth gave a pain-filled whimper. Blue kicked the wall of the stall, sensing Ruth's distress. Derrick had an evil look in his eye and a nasty grin on his lips. In a visceral reaction Ruth sank her weight down into her heels, and with all the power she could gather, slammed a knee into Derrick's crotch.

Derrick gave a long, loud agonizing moan and sank to the floor. Ruth rubbed her wrists and glared down at Derrick. Shep and Ken ran out of the office. The rest of the team soon followed.

"What the devil happened here?" Shep demanded.

Ken took hold of Ruth's hands and saw the redness around her wrists. He looked from her face to Derrick, writhing on the ground, back to her eyes again.

"What's going on? What're you doing on the ground, Gills?" Shep demanded again.

Derrick looked up at Ruth, tears streaming from eyes that reflected stone-cold fury.

"He must have tripped and fallen into the saddle rack, Shep." Ruth offered as an explanation, "I was in the stall with Blue."

Shep looked at her. He looked at the agitated horse. He looked at Ken cradling Ruth's wrists, "That the story you're sticking with Willows?"

She nodded. She was no snitch, and Derrick had gotten what he deserved.

He looked at Derrick, still in the fetal position on the ground, "That your story too, Gills?"

He tried to nod his head in agreement.

"Boys, take him into the office, get him some ice," Shep ordered. Larry and Clayton obliged. "Derrick, no riding tonight," Shep called after him, "you sit on the fence and learn the maneuvers from there."

Shep looked at Ruth. He quietly asked, "You okay?'

She nodded, yes.

★ ★ ★

Practice got underway. Derrick and his icepack made it outside and sat on the fence.

It was exciting to ride with eight other riders in the ring. She'd previously met the jokester duo Larry and Clayton, as well as a quiet and reserved cowboy named Jeff. Tonight she met Philippe, who was from Quebec, and Jesus from Albuquerque. They both seemed to be good, all-around cowboys.

Shep directed the drill team from the ground and occasionally reminded someone to leave room for Derrick. When Shep dismissed everyone, he asked Ruth and Jeff to stay to work on their demos. Ken hung back. Larry and Clayton stayed to watch too. Shep asked Stu to put a few calves into the staging area; he wanted Ken to do some roping.

Jeff's mastery of the lasso awed Ruth. He dismounted Bo and started out with the flat loop lift and then danced in and out of the Texas skip. Shep asked if Jeff could do a wedding ring while on horseback. He said he had never tried, but if Shep could find a rope big enough, he'd give it a shot. Stu went into the office to look for more rope, and Jeff remounted Bo.

"Ruth, what do you think you want to do?" Shep asked.

Before Ruth could answer, all hell broke loose. Bo reared, and Jeff, who'd been resting in the saddle, flew off the back of the horse. Blue spooked next, but Ruth stayed mounted when he jumped sideways. Over her shoulder, she saw several calves storm through the chute gate, pushed by an angry-looking steer.

The wind knocked out of Jeff; he was just starting to come around when the steer made a beeline for him. Ruth didn't think. She turned Blue in a tight circle and came around behind the steer as fast as she could. Swinging her lasso, she hoped the loop would be big enough in time. She hadn't quite got parallel with the steer's hind feet, but she threw the loop at its head before it could trample Jeff, caught its horns, and wrapped a dally around her saddle horn to take up the slack. As she sent Blue to the left, she felt strong tension on her rope.

Ken had thrown a trap for the steer's heels and caught him. Remington was briskly backing up to take up the slack. Jeff rolled to his feet and scuttled over to the fence as Larry and Clayton herded the calves into a tight group.

As the dust settled, the only sound heard was Derrick's raucous laugh. "Oh, man!" he guffawed, "The lil' twink got thrown off his horse like he never rode a day in his life. The looks on your faces were priceless!"

Ruth thought *I didn't knee him hard enough.*

Clayton and Larry were off their horses and ran to Derrick. Clayton, the tallest of the three, had Derrick by the collar and on his toes. Larry held Derrick's arms twisted behind his back.

"You moron!" Clayton screamed, "You almost got Jeff trampled."

"Get over yourself," Derrick snapped. Larry tightened the grip on his arm, and he winced, "And let go of me! It was a joke."

"That was no joke, you jackass," Shep stormed over. "Let him go boys, I'll take care of him myself." Shep took hold of Derrick's ear and threw him forward, "You get into that office before I kick your ass right here in front of everyone."

Shep was beyond anger. No one, not even Stu, had ever seen Shep this furious. Stu ran out of the barn when he heard all the commotion. "Stu, see that these cattle get put away. Each of you take care of your horses. I'll see you all Saturday." Shep headed for the gate. He turned and shouted, "Willows, Silver, good work. Looks like we found you a demo. We'll work you two together next week."

Ruth helped Larry and Clay pen the calves. Jeff and Ken put the steer away. Stu went into the barn and made sure Derrick didn't slip out while Shep walked off some of his frustration.

It didn't take long for everyone to untack their horses and turn them out for the night. Trouble was, no one wanted to walk into the barn to put their tack away. The group looked at each other and agreed that there was safety in numbers.

From the tack room, they heard snippets of Shep's tirade from behind the closed office door, "DAMN IDIOT ... WHAT WERE YOU THINKING ... EVERYONE INJURED ... PROBLEM, YOU COME TO ME ... RESPECT ... DON'T YOU LAY A HAND ON ... IF I EVER LET YOU RIDE ON THIS TEAM AGAIN ..."

"Man, he's not letting up," Larry ventured a whisper.

"THREE MONTHS BARN DUTY AND PROBATION ... IF SO MUCH AS A HAIR OUT OF PLACE..."

The five of them quickly and quietly exited the barn and made their way to their cars. Ruth's truck was the first one they came to. Everyone stopped and heaved a collected sigh of relief.

"I've never seen Shep lose it like that before," Jeff exhaled. "I've known Derrick to be cruel, but never as ... dangerous ... as he was tonight."

"I guess that run-in with the saddle rack really damaged his manhood, huh, Ruth?" Clayton teasingly chucked her arm.

"Guess it did." She answered, not sure if she was being held responsible for Derrick's action.

"Don't blame Ruth," Larry chimed in.

"I'm not!" Clayton defended his comment, "I'm sure he didn't get half of what he deserved." Clayton gave her a fraternal pat on the back. "I'd like to know what he said to you to make you kick him in the nuts."

They all stared at Ruth. She opened her mouth, looked at their faces, and said–nothing. She closed her mouth.

"I'm sorry, I don't want to repeat it," she said finally.

"Oh, come on. I'm sure we've heard it before."

"I'm sure you have, but it was embarrassing, and I'd like to forget about it."

"Understood," Clayton replied. She could tell it disappointed him not to have any juicy gossip. "Great roping. You saved Jeff's hide. Come on, Ruth, I'll buy you a drink to celebrate!"

Larry suggested, "Let's go to the Hangman."

Ruth, who had no intention of going out underage drinking, asked, "Why that dive?"

Larry laughed, "Cause it's Derrick's favorite bar, and he'll be pissed we went without him."

"Is he twenty-one?" Ruth questioned.

"Nah, but the Hangman'll serve anything that walks in on two legs. That's why he likes it," Larry explained. "You in Ken? Jeff?"

Jeff said sure, and Ken added a why not. Ruth told them to make it a boy's night out; she was going home.

They all went to their cars, but Ken lingered. He gently held her wrists and looked at them, "You okay?"

"Sure thing, Cowboy."

"Good ropin' tonight."

"You too."

They stood, gazing at each other.

Larry pulled up with the car window down, "Come on, Ken, kiss her goodnight and get a move on it," he shouted.

Ruth climbed into her truck before Ken could turn back to her. She rolled down her window, "G'night, Cowboy."

He'd missed his opportunity again. "Sweet dreams, Baby Doll."

She started the truck and drove away.

Chapter 5

RODEO PRACTICES CONTINUED. Katie flitted around Derrick and gave the stink eye to Ruth every chance she could. Ruth hung out with Larry, Clayton, Jeff, and Ken when there was downtime.

She and Ken never had a private conversation, and that troubled Ruth. He was gorgeous; he was working on his play; they flirted constantly, but beyond that, she knew very little about him. Not his favorite color or food. Nor his favorite movie or book. *What did he do when there was nothing else to do? How the heck old is he, anyway? Would he even want to talk to me if he knew I was still in high school?* That thought always made her nauseous.

Ruth aced her bio final and paper. To celebrate, Constance, her mom, made all of Ruth's favorites for dinner. It was a comfort to sit down to a meal with her family. Daddy, Ed, had a long story about his job at the state engineering department.

Constance continually reminded Ruth's younger sister, Grace, "no phone at the table! Talk with the family."

Unfortunately, as dessert was being served, Constance commented, "Joe, I can't believe you sat through this entire dinner and not one word about the rodeo."

"Well," he began, "I spent a few moments talkin' to Shep today. He said it seems to be going A-Okay. Wouldn't you agree, Grand-baby?"

Oh sure, Granddaddy's comment seemed innocent enough, but that twinkle in his eye told her he was up to something.

"It's going okay," she replied cautiously.

"Shep said there were a few problems the first day or so; had a few stallions... I mean cowboys butting heads, so to speak. But my Grand-baby seemed to help them work it all out."

"What do you mean?" Ed inquired, glancing over at Ruth.

"Seems that your daughter single-handedly stopped a cattle stampede before anyone got trampled,"

"It wasn't single-handedly, and it was hardly a stampede," Ruth defended herself against Granddaddy's hyperbole.

Ed, Constance, and even Grace wanted to know exactly what happened. Joe had the pleasure of telling his version of the story.

Ruth kept her comments short. "It wasn't like that at all. One guy thought it would be funny to let a few calves into the pen while everyone else was riding."

"What a stupid thing to do! I don't think that's funny at all." Constance was incensed.

"No one else thought it was either, Mom. We all left as Shep was in the office tearing into him."

"Anyone get hurt?" Ed asked.

"No."

"Did any of the calves get hurt?" Constance added.

"No, Mom, none of the calves got hurt."

Ruth was relieved Granddaddy omitted the kneeing Derrick in the crotch part from his tale. As Joe had put it, Ruth was the new sweetheart of the team.

"And speaking of sweethearts," Joe added as he put down his coffee cup, "I hear that my grand-baby has a beau of her own following her around the barn."

Ruth sucked in a breath. *I knew he was up to something!* She stood and calmly began clearing plates from the table in the vain hope that they would forget the comment if she exited the room.

Constance was too quick, "Ruthie, why didn't you say something? Who is he?"

"Don't know what Granddaddy's talking about."

"Oh?" Joe teased, "Stu said you two were kissin' in the parking lot the one evening, almost made you late for practice."

"We were not!" Ruth's face turned crimson. "He helped me carry all my junk to the car–that was all! I was almost late because I spent too much time at the library!"

The entire table stifled laughter as Constance asked, "Who is this young man?"

Ruth answered by exiting into the kitchen, so Joe happily replied, "The Silver's boy, Ken. Seems like a nice young man. Met him up there the day we dropped the horses off." No response came from Ruth when she returned. "As I was saying, Shep said they make a good team, and they're going to partner in the head and heels demonstration."

"Sweetie," Constance took Ruth's hand, "you're almost eighteen. You're free to date whoever you please. Donna Silver's my friend. I guess I never thought of her son and you together because he's been away at school for so long...maybe we should invite him over for dinner?"

"NO! No dinner, no inviting him over. Nothing is going on. Just leave me alone!" Ruth rushed out of the dining room, out of the house, and into the barn. She had no intention of returning until the conversation had been long forgotten.

★ ★ ★

The Kiwanis traditionally hosted a dinner-dance after the rodeo. Ruth changed from her riding clothes into a pair of snug-fitting jeans and a clean cowgirl shirt. Joe dropped her off in front of the Kiwanis recreation hall. "You go and eat and have a good time. Your daddy'll help me unload the horses. Your Ma and Gracie have been cooking all day, and they can't wait to see you."

Ruth found her way to the long tables of food where dinner was being served by volunteers. Chairs were packed in around small tables that filled the room. Bales of straw were piled up against one wall, adding ambiance and a rich, outdoorsy smell and more seating. At the end of the room, microphones and music stands waited on a stage. Men traveled in and out of the side door carrying large trays of chicken and ribs from the kitchen to the outdoor BBQ pit and back to the waiting guests.

She surveyed the crowd and spied Ken near the front of the food line. He waved her over. In one hand he held an empty white plate, the other he slipped around her waist. Smoothly, he bent forward and kissed her cheek. She was aware of the warmth of his body through her cotton shirt. *God, he smells good, like soap and fresh-cut hay.* A hot flush rose in her cheeks when she remembered they stood amid a room full of people.

Her eyes locked with the earthy green eyes of her sister, Grace. Two years apart, they were very similar looking, but Grace's long hair was golden brown and her eyes earthy green. She stared slacked jawed from behind the serving table filled with biscuits and rolls. Her long metal serving tongs held nothing but air as the roll she had been serving fell to the ground.

Constance whispered, "Gracie, pay attention to what you're doing!" Her eyes followed Gracie's gaze, "Oh Ruthie, there you are. Where's your plate, dear?" she casually questioned.

Ken handed Ruth his plate and grabbed himself another.

Constance looked over at the polite gentleman and said, "Why, Kenny Silver, how are you? I haven't seen you since you came home from school."

"I'm well, thank you, Mrs. Willows. How are you?"

"We're fine. Ruth, you were wonderful tonight, and so were you, Ken. You gave everyone a brilliant performance."

While Constance continued talking with Ken, Grace leaned over the table and whispered to her older sister, "Is that him?"

"Who?" Ruth tried to be cool.

"You know who!"

"We're... friends."

"You look like more than just friends!" Grace's stern whisper sounded a little jealous.

Constance plopped steaming vegetables onto Ruth's and Ken's plates, "You two go enjoy your dinner. I'll let you know when we'll be heading home, Ruth."

The room was packed. Others from the team were squished around a table near the stage. Thankfully Ken directed Ruth to an empty space on the bales of straw.

Ruth couldn't remember feeling so at ease with another person outside of her family, maybe her best friend Paloma, but definitely not any guy.

First, they talked about their shared passion for horses. Ken told Ruth about the summers he'd spent camping with his friend Greg, Remington, and a pack mule named Jack. Ruth envied being able to spend weeks in the wilderness with just Blue and maybe a friend, a special friend...

She didn't share Ken's fondness for poetry. He could go on and on about the symbolism and metaphor of one poem or another. Eventually, she conceded the beautiful cowboy poem he recited about a lone rider on the open range held some allure. The poem was humorous and melancholy and romantic all at the same time; Ken had also penned it.

He found her ability to comprehend scientific literature mind-blowing. That she had read the Encyclopedia for Western Botany was worthy of admiration.

The band was tuning up on stage when they finished their meal, and Ken asked if she wanted anything else.

"Something to drink," she replied.

"I'll get it," he said with a smile.

Ruth cleared their plates and headed to the ladies' room. Her stomach clenched when she saw Derrick coming towards her. He grabbed her arm and steered her against the wall.

"You weren't too nice to me when we first met Willows," he scoffed, "but play your cards right, and I might give you a second chance."

Anger welled up within her. She yanked her arm from his grip. "I want nothing to do with you, Derrick," she growled.

"The trouble with you, Willows, is you think you're too good for everyone. I'm not finished with you..."

Before he could continue, Ruth escaped into the ladies' room.

She almost puked, Katie was in there. "You and Ken look awfully cozy. I didn't realize you two were dating," Katie talked at Ruth through the mirror.

Ruth's head swam. First Derrick, now Katie. *Do these two have nothing else to do but keep tabs on me!* Pushing all her feelings aside, she sputtered, "Oh, we were just talking..."

"Good! I'll join you then. I'm so sick of Derrick's asinine behavior. He thinks he's God's gift to the universe or something. Ken is so much cuter and ... sexier. I'd much rather spend the evening with him... and you too." Katie flounced out of the ladies' room.

Ruth peered into the mirror and let her thoughts unwind. *What the hell just happened! Derrick - EW! And Katie? But Cowboy, do we look like we're dating? I mean, sure, we've been flirting nonstop for nearly three weeks. He wraps his arms around me and steals a kiss every chance he gets. He obviously likes me... And you know you like him, like really like him.* Admitting her feelings to herself, surprisingly calmed her. She took a deep breath, smiled, and marched out of the ladies' room.

She found Ken standing by the bales of straw with Katie. She sidled up to him.

"There you are," he sighed with noticeable relief. "I didn't know what you wanted," he offered a cold bottle of water.

She grabbed the bottle, "It's perfect, thanks."

Tables and chairs cleared from the dance floor, the band started with a set of country/rock songs. Ken slid his arm around Ruth's waist and pulled her in tight while Katie droned on about something.

"Excuse me, Katie," he interrupted, "Baby Doll, wanna dance?"

Ruth smiled and let herself be led to the dance floor. He led her through one brisk dance and then another. Then the band played one of those slow numbers where there's not much involved but swaying to the beat. She nestled into his chest and felt utterly enveloped. He gently kissed her temple. She smiled, snuggled close, and prayed she wasn't dreaming.

The loud twang of the guitar and the four beats of the bass drum let everyone know it was time to speed things up again. Ruth's mother tapped her on the shoulder and nearly brought her out of her skin.

"Ruth dear, I'm sorry, but I'm exhausted. I need to go home." Her mother stood on the side of the dance floor with Grace beside her.

Ruth stared at them as if they were speaking a foreign language.

Reality slowly seeped back into Ruth's brain, "Oh...oh, right." She hated the thought of leaving Ken's warm embrace.

"I can take Ruth home if she likes," Ken's brain was functioning a few steps ahead of Ruth's.

Constance looked into her daughter's face and remembered what it was like to be in love for the first time, "That's up to Ruth."

Ruth smiled and nodded.

"Don't stay out too late; you know your Granddaddy will be waiting up for you," Constance hooked Grace's arm and headed home.

The band turned up the volume a few notches. Ken took Ruth's hand and said, "Let's get some air."

They stepped outside onto a large covered porch that looked out onto a beautiful garden. Stepping stone walkways and various flowers, shrubs, and trees had been perfectly organized so different species would be in bloom throughout the year.

Ruth leaned against the banister. Western nights were cool, but Ken's presence warmed her. He turned her towards him, wrapped both arms around her, and kissed her–finally on the lips. Her heart pounded. His lips were warm and soft, but firm. She was sure that she was shaking; hopefully, he'd think it was from the chilly night air and not her nerves. As he pressed himself into her, a tingle traveled up and down her spine.

When he stopped, she had to remind herself to breathe.

"You okay?"

"Yes - very okay," she whispered.

Others came out onto the porch, so Ken and Ruth wandered down the wooden stairs and into the garden.

Ruth's mind raced as they walked hand in hand. *What do you say to a guy after a kiss like that?* Faint sounds of music wafted down on a gentle breeze, and they sat on a bench tucked into a small grove of spruce trees.

He kissed her again, this time much stronger than before. She welcomed his kiss. In fact, she wished he would have kissed her sooner and stopped her inane ramblings about edible flowers.

As he pressed his lips into her, his tongue explored her mouth. Fireworks went off through her body. Every nerve—every cell was being hit in rapid-fire secession by jolts of electric passion. Her mind raced on, over-analyzing the situation. *People do this all the time, right? It's kinda like a movie, right? It's not that unusual-even though I've never done this before. I mean, I've kissed before, but not like this. Am I doing it right? It's kinda gross if you really think about it. Duh - then maybe stop thinking about it. Good idea, I'll shut up now.*

The other half of her mind basked in every new and wonderful sensation. Everything in the world disappeared except them. They separated after a long while, and Ken swung his leg over the stone bench to straddle it. Between kisses, she raised a hand to caress his cheek. His recently shaved face was smooth and soft. Her finger traced his lips; those wonderful, delicious lips had just made her feel things she'd never felt before. Her hand drifted up, and she ran her fingers through his hair. He wore a hat when he rode, so it was nice to see and touch his wavy locks. She noticed a mist of perspiration on his brow. Her smiled widened at the realization that she had worked him into a sweat.

That smile was all he needed to spur him on. His hands, already on her thighs, slid back to her rump, and he pulled her onto his lap. She sat awkwardly on her one knee with her leg over his thigh. He started with his mouth at her lips and worked his way down, kissing and ever so lightly nibbling her neck. She shuttered, and her breath escaped in a sigh. He laughed softly, a self-satisfied throaty laugh, and he worked his way downward. His right hand eased around her ribs and lingered on her breast. The combination of sensations made her back arch as she gasped. Her heart raced, and alarms sounded in her head; this was too much, too fast for her. His fingers popped open the top snap of her blouse. Her entire body tensed as she realized where he was heading.

A whisper escaped her lips, "Whoa, Cowboy." She pulled back and sat back down on the bench.

"I'm sorry, Baby Doll," he whispered and relaxed his grip.

"I...I... I just..." *What the hell am I gonna say now? How about I've never had sex before, and this is not how I want to lose my virginity? Or maybe–I'm scared to death right now, and I think I might puke.*

"No explanation necessary. I apologize for getting carried away." He leaned forward and whispered into her ear, "It's just that I'm crazy about you, in case you hadn't noticed."

How could she help but smile? She kissed him sweetly on the lips and said, "Yeah, me too."

Ken swung his leg back over the bench. They sat side by side as he held her tight. Ruth nestled into him, soothed by the rise and fall of his breath.

The music had stopped. "Band must be on a break. Wanna go back and see who's left up there?"

"Not really," she smiled.

Ken was pleasantly surprised that she wasn't looking for an excuse to run back to the safety of a crowd after he had pushed her to her boundaries.

Eventually, she said, "I guess we've gotta go back, huh?"

"Yeah, come on, Baby Doll," he stood up, pulled her to him, and kissed her one more time. Ruth made the most of this kiss. They fell into a natural pulsating rhythm as moans of deep delight came from both of them.

He took a deep breath and squeezed her hand as they meandered along the path to the porch. "Next time you kiss me like that, Baby Doll, I might not be able to stop."

Next time! Woo hoo! He thinks there'll be a next time!!! She held his hand all the tighter, brimming over with excitement.

From the doorway on the porch, they saw the band packing up. The crowd had thinned. Ruth didn't feel like facing Derrick or Katie.

"I really don't want to go back in there unless you do."

"I don't need to."

"Do you mind just taking me home?"

"Let's go."

The radio was on when he started his Jeep. The dashboard clock read one a.m. The voice on the radio said it was going to be another beautiful day tomorrow. The story about the missing school budget coordinator only reminded her that her senior year was about to begin. *Oh, I wish it was over. I wish I could continue at the university full time and be done with high school. And now there's Cowboy–what's going to happen when he finds out about me?*

The Jeep crunched loudly as they pulled up the gravel driveway of Tall Willows. The front porch light was on, but none other. She got out of the Jeep. Ken flew around the car to meet her. He wrapped himself around her and spoke first, "We never talked about where either of us will be this fall."

"Oh, I'll be here, in town. University classes start this Wednesday." *I never mentioned that I'm also finishing high school, too!* "What about you?"

"I start a new job here next week."

"Wow, that's great!"

"But listen, I'll be out of town this week. I'm moving stuff out of my old apartment. My roommate Greg is moving out too. I have just enough time to pack-up and move before my new job starts."

"Okay." *crap... an apartment,* she thought. *Am I ready for a guy with an apartment? He'll never want to stay with me once he finds out about high school.*

"Maybe we could go out after I get back?"

She smiled, "Yeah," she answered before he kissed her long and deep.

Eventually, he walked her up the porch steps to the front door. Holding both her hands, he said, "Good night, Baby Doll." He kissed her sweetly on the lips, "Sweet dreams."

"Thank you, Cowboy," she replied.

"I'll call you."

"I'll be here." With that, she went inside.

Chapter 6

THE TORRES FAMILY had gone to Spain, and four weeks without her best girlfriend, Paloma, was pure torture for Ruth.

"Your family's outside of Barcelona?" Ruth recalled from her trip with Paloma two years before.

"The wedding's about an hour north," Paloma added, "Cousin Enrique wants to know why the beautiful blonde with the amazing eyes didn't come with us," Paloma told her over the phone.

"Isn't he the one getting married?" Ruth asked.

"That's what I said." Paloma answered, "But he said that for such a beautiful American, he'd forget he was married for one night."

"Gosh, sorry I missed that opportunity," Ruth quipped. "Don't break his heart and tell him I'm interested in someone else."

"You're kidding! You met someone? Where? When? Who? Tell me everything!"

"We rode together in the rodeo. His name is Ken. I call him Cowboy." Paloma squealed as Ruth continued, "He's very tall and very sexy, and...," Ruth whispered, "a really good kisser."

"Oh, my Gawd!" Paloma giggled. "Does he go to USC?"

"He just graduated from UC Davis..."

Paloma cut her off, "Ooooooo, an older man. Does he care you're in high school?"

Ruth was silent for a long moment. "I haven't told him."

"Ruth!" Paloma shouted, "What do you mean!"

"I haven't had the" Ruth paused, "... opportunity, yet..."

A commotion on Paloma's end cut their conversation short, and she promised to call when she got home.

Immediately Ruth's phone buzzed. She opened the message:

Hey Baby Doll, just got to the old apt.

Too much stuff. Packing is gonna be hard work.

Wish u were here. XOXO

Her heart cartwheeled inside her chest.

Hey Cowboy. Sucks to be you, I'm enjoying the day off. XOXO

My last day of summer, Ruth thought, Theories of Mathematics starts tomorrow. Taking part in "college for high school students" meant Ruth would attend high school every morning, and on Monday, Wednesday, and Friday, she would drive to SCU for her class. SCU classes started the week before high school, so she downloaded the rented math book and gave the syllabus a quick glance: mostly tests, but a research paper–*What kind of teacher gives a research paper in math?*

She soon found out. Professor Langley looked like Colonel Sanders in his seersucker suit and had the personality of a cardboard box. From day one, he droned on about the world's great mathematicians and the significance of their theories. Professor Langley presented calculations by writing the information on a dry erase board with his right hand and erased it with his left.

A week later, Ruth picked Paloma up for the first day of Golden Valley High School. They'd been friends since the day Ruth moved to Tall Willows. They had a lot of catching up to do. Ruth filled Paloma in on her new romance before they had to split for different homerooms.

"So he just got back from California. When do you see him?" Paloma asked.

"We're supposed to go out Saturday," Ruth giggled.

"And did you tell him you're in high school?"

"Not yet," Ruth admitted, "we've mostly been texting. I'd rather tell him in person."

They had similar schedules and reunited on their way to their daily second period AP English class.

"Did you see the new AP English teacher?" Paloma huffed as they took the stairs and dashed down the hall.

"Phew!" gasped Ruth, "What smells so putrid! Thank God I did bio this summer; I'd puke if I had to stay in this wing too long!" Then she added, "What happened to Mrs. Gills? I thought she taught AP English?"

"It's Doctor Gills now. You can't call her Mrs. anymore." Paloma had Gills for homeroom. "Dr. Gills hired a new teacher for AP English, and I heard that he's sick, like male model sick." Paloma continued, "Missy Fairchild has him for homeroom and was texting everyone about him."

"Well, if he's Missy's type, I'm sure he's not mine." Ruth scoffed.

The girls rounded the corner and entered the English room. Ruth first scanned the room for empty seats. Then she checked out the new teacher.

Ruth froze. The new AP English teacher was sick. Now she was going to be sick. Her stomach clenched, her throat tightened, she couldn't breathe. Someone shoved her forward as they walked through the door, but her legs wouldn't work. She had to leave. She still couldn't breathe. She had to leave now!

The new teacher was leaning against his desk. His long legs, stretched out in front of him, were clad in dark brown slacks. He wore a light blue button-down dress shirt and a tan blazer. He smiled that perfect smile of his as he looked at the piece of paper in his hand. *Probably the attendance sheet. Has he looked at it before? Does he know who's in his class?*

His smile faded when his eyes reached the bottom of the page.

Nope, he hadn't read it before. The realization on his face clear.

Ruth tried again to go. She couldn't make her feet move. She still couldn't breathe. She remembered her shoulders twisting, and when she saw the door, someone had closed it. She reached for the knob, but suddenly everything swirled in front of her eyes before it all went black.

★ ★ ★

"Ruth, Ruth dear, it's Mrs. Peters, the school nurse." she heard a woman's voice calling her name,

"Cowboy?" she murmured.

"It's Mrs. Peters, the nurse. You got quite a gash on your head when you fell. You hit the metal bookcase."

Ruth reached her hand up, but Mrs. Peters was holding something firmly against the side of her head. She tried to stand, but she couldn't get her body to cooperate.

"Be still dear, we're going to take you to the hospital; you might need a few stitches and a tetanus shot too. Your mother will meet you there. The ambulance is on its way." Mrs. Peters turned to Paloma, "Will you gather her things and carry them downstairs with her. I'm sure Mr. Silver won't mind if you're gone for a few minutes."

Ruth looked up and tried to focus on Ken. Their eyes met, and he was not happy. His face was white as a sheet; his eyes were frightened and angry. "I'm sorry," she tried to say with her eyes. She got no response from him. She opened her mouth and said as well as she could, "I'm sorry." He turned away without saying a word.

The nurse thought she was speaking to her, "Oh, there's nothing to be sorry about; accidents do happen."

The next thing Ruth knew, she was being strapped onto a stretcher, wheeled down the hall, down the stairs, and put into an ambulance. Paloma put Ruth's stuff on her lap and disappeared. The medics asked her all kinds of questions: did she know her name? Did she know the date today? Did she remember what happened? She didn't want to remember, but slowly it all came seeping back into her brain.

★ ★ ★

"Please, just let me take the GED test. I know I could pass it. I have all my college applications ready to submit. I'll submit them tomorrow. I'll get a job till next fall; I'll help out at the ranch more. Please don't make me go back to school." Ruth had been pleading with her mother since Constance arrived at the hospital.

"I told you I will not discuss this now. I want to know why you passed out. I don't want them sending you home if there is a more serious problem."

"I'm fine! I tripped, that's all. I was clumsy and tripped over my own two feet. Then I hit my head on a stupid old bookcase." Ruth's eyes filled with tears at the thought of the classroom that held the bookcase and the teacher that occupied that room. "And I want to talk about getting my GED, Please..."

Constance had never heard such desperation in her daughter's voice. "I want to know what happened today. Why such a dramatic change of heart?"

"It's not dramatic," she sniffled, "I've been thinking about it all summer. I just never said anything before."

A knock came from the door, and a nurse entered, "The doctor will be in to see you in a few minutes. He said to tell you that all your tests came back fine, and he'll be releasing you shortly. Mrs. Willows, I have some paperwork for you to sign at the desk if you'd like to come out and do so."

"Yes, thank you," Constance replied. The nurse exited the room. Just as Constance turned back to her daughter, there was another knock at the door.

Both assumed it was the doctor. Instead, Ken walked in, still dressed in his school clothes. Ruth's heart raced. If the nightmare of what happened in the classroom wasn't bad enough, this was so much worse.

"Ken, what a surprise!" Constance was glad to see him but was also a little confused. "How did you find out Ruth was here?"

"I wasn't sure... what the protocol was for a... student passing out in one's classroom..." he began his explanation with a strained voice, but he couldn't find any more words to complete his thought. He tried again, "So, I thought given the circumstances, I mean the history, I mean... the fact that..."

Constance's eyes widened to saucers and looked from her daughter to her boyfriend and back to her daughter, "Oh... Oh... OOOOOHHHH..." the reality slowly sank in, "Oh my... oh my, my, my... Oh, dear..." It made sense. She looked at her daughter; tears were silently streaming down her cheeks "Ruth why didn't you..." She looked to Ken, he was pale, "I didn't know that..." Constance's own chest tightened, "Oh dear ... The nurse has some papers for me to sign. I'll leave you two alone ... The doctor will be in, in a few minutes." She left the room quietly.

Ken just stood there staring at Ruth. He had never been so worried and so angry at the same time in his life. All he wanted to do was touch her and hold her and make sure with his own two hands and own two eyes that she was all right. Then he wanted to throttle her.

"Are you all right?" He managed in a cool voice.

She couldn't look at him. She tried to speak, but the words stuck in her throat. She nodded, yes. She managed a glance at him through watery eyes. The sweet, gentle man she knew wasn't there. In front of her stood a cold, guarded stranger. "I'm sorry," she sobbed.

He exploded, "Why the hell didn't you tell me you were only in high school? How old are you? Fifteen?"

The attack got her ire up, and she struck back, "Since when do recent college graduates teach high school AP classes?"

"Since I have a master's degree!"

Wow, a master's, I had no idea. "Well, how old are you to have a master's degree - thirty?" She knew there was no way he was thirty, but she wasn't fifteen either.

"I'm twenty-three; I'll be twenty-four next month. I went straight through from my undergrad into a master's program. You still haven't answered my question."

"I'll be eighteen in January. And my age didn't seem to matter that much the last time..." she couldn't continue.

Ken sank down into an orange plastic chair near the foot of the bed. He bent over, holding his head in his hands as he thought about what to do next.

"Does my age make that much of a difference?" she whispered.

He looked at her; she was beautiful, even with a massive bandage on her head and red-rimmed eyes. He thought about the time they'd spent together, how intelligent, strong, responsible, and self-reliant she was. Hell, most of the women I've been with aren't as mature. Slowly he shook his head, "You - are - illegal. Do you know how much trouble I can get into if I'm seen with you? Do you know how much of a shock it was, seeing you walk into my room today? You acted like you go to SCU."

"I DO go to SCU!" she defended herself, "and don't you think I was shocked too! Why didn't you tell me you are a high school teacher?"

"I was going to." Ken stood up, "Ruth, we can't date."

He'd never called her Ruth before; it stung as though he had slapped her in the face. She could feel the tears welling up in her eyes. Damn it, don't cry!

He could no longer look at her, "We need to forget that we ... once thought about... We can't have anything to do with each other, Ruth. That's it."

He walked out of the room without looking back. She held it together until the door clicked closed.

Chapter 7

SHE ENTERED HER house and locked the door behind her. The heat outside was stifling, and the A/C in that pathetic school was inefficient, to say the least. She drew the shades over the picture window overlooking the street and peeled her work clothes off as she walked to the bedroom for a robe. Her son wouldn't be home for hours if he came home at all—*time to relax.* First stop, the thermostat, *crank up the cool air baby,* next stop the kitchen, *time for a drink.* She stood in front of the freezer; *ah, that feels good,* she thought as the cool air hit her warm skin. She filled her glass with ice and went for the bottle of bourbon, but it was still empty-*Damn.* She opened the fridge and found some wine.

She walked back to the dim living room, sat in her favorite chair, and sipped her chardonnay. School was back in session, and no one had found Alverez - *yet.* It was inevitable they would. The hallway already smelled, but the first day had been the one she'd been dreading. Now she felt in the clear.

As she sipped, the cheap wine's bouquet assailed her nose. *A full day with staff and students present, and they were all too busy checking out the hot young teacher.* He oozed sex. The pheromone level in the teachers' lounge was high enough with him around. *When those school girls came in today, it went through the roof - One little twit even fainted.*

She thought about her relationship with her former boss, Alberts. He'd tried to break his promise to her to stay on for two more years. Now he was back as official bean counter until Alverez, or his replacement could be found. *Ha, Ha, Ha, you got what you deserved, sucker, and it makes my life a lot easier.* She wondered if Alberts would want to resume their weekly rendezvous. He had broken it off abruptly when he retired. It was no skin off her nose. She didn't really enjoy him all that much, but after twenty-two years of succumbing to his desires, she felt a little miffed that he ended it so hastily.

That didn't matter. She had to know how much money had she accumulated, how much more did she need if she left town suddenly?

She logged on to her offshore bank account. She had almost one million dollars tucked away. That was good, but *will it be enough to live off of the rest of my life?* She could live on a lot less in Mexico, but she didn't want to live like a pauper. She logged out of the offshore account and checked a real estate website. She owned a two-bedroom, one-bath bungalow in an old section of town. A few years ago, her house could have sold for two-hundred-fifty-thousand; but since the housing market crash, the website estimated her property as on-hundred-fifty-thousand. She made a mental note and hoped that a quick sale would probably get one-hundred-twenty-five-thousand.

Next, she checked her local accounts, three thousand in savings, and checking. That could get her to where she needed to go. Lastly, from the school's retirement fund, she could take a lump sum payment of three-hundred-thousand. Thank goodness Alberts let it slip about the loophole. Any district employee could receive a bump in pay and a higher percentage donated to their retirement plan if they held advanced degrees. It didn't matter what the degree was in or where the degree came from; Alberts' Ph.D. came from an online school. Nor did it matter the position one held; Alberts was a budget coordinator, not a teacher.

When she'd learned about the loophole, she searched Alberts' file and found the name of the online diploma mill he'd used. She filled out the appropriate paperwork and got approved for her online courses. *What a joke! A second-grader could have answered the questions.* What did she care? In five months, she went from an average community college graduate to holding a Doctorate of Philosophy. Her salary went up three percent, and her retirement contribution tripled.

By her calculations, she had one-million-three-hundred-twenty-five-thousand in assets. *Pretty good lady, but her goal had always been one-million-five-hundred-thoudans. Do I really need the extra?* She wanted it. *With Alberts back at the helm, I might get it.*

Maybe she could blackmail him? His infidelity wouldn't come as much of a shock to his wife. His "little woman" was the type that didn't care what her husband did as long as he paid the bills. There had to be another way.

She was restless, and she wanted to celebrate; the first day back, and no one found the body. *To Mikes!* She dressed in black leather pants and a black v-necked T-shirt, then put on riding boots and black leather jacket. She grabbed her keys and helmet, locked the door on the way out, and jumped on her bike. She loved the way the engine on her Ninja roared as she started it up.

Chapter 8

RUTH WAITED FOR her mother outside the main office for a meeting with the guidance counselor. Having just come out of the emotionally tumultuous AP English, Ruth would have rather headed home.

Miss Lana Laurence had been Ruth's guidance counselor since freshman year. Lana recognized Ruth as an exceptional student and pushed her to join the honors program. She'd also lobbied for Ruth to be one of the few students allowed to participate in the College for High School Seniors pilot program. As Ruth scanned the parking lot for her mother, she spied Ken taking the shortcut from the cafeteria through the parking lot toward his classroom. Her stomach lurched.

Her mother touched her shoulder, "Hello dear, are you ready?"

"Yeah, let's get this over with." Ruth led her down the hall to the councilor's office.

The door was open, and Miss Laurence welcomed Ruth and Constance with a friendly handshake and warm smile.

"It is so good to see you, Mrs. Willows. Ruth, how are you? I heard you had a little accident the other day. Are you okay?"

"I'm fine," Ruth responded, trying to suppress all thoughts of Tuesday. The school had been abuzz with rumors about the girl who swooned and fainted at the new teacher's feet. Ruth hated that kind of attention.

Lana began, "I received your transcript from the university, 'A' in your bio class, excellent job. I knew you'd do well. You're here today so we can make sure you have everything you need to graduate. Also, I want to talk about your college applications."

This cued Ruth to dig into her backpack and pull out a file with seven-color coded tabs; she placed it on Miss Laurence's desk. Lana added, "of course, if there's anything else you'd like to discuss, we can do that too."

"These are my college applications. I've chosen seven schools; they all have very diverse and very good biology programs. Most accept the Common App, but a few don't. I printed out copies of the essays I've written and attached them to the appropriate application. I need copies of my high school transcripts. I'm pretty much ready to submit."

"You're very thorough, Ruth. I will go through them just as thoroughly."

"Great," Ruth answered.

Lana took the applications and put them aside before she changed the subject, "Now we need to get you graduated from here."

"Actually, Miss Laurence, I have a question about that."

Constance rolled her eyes. She couldn't believe that her daughter was really going to try to go through with the harebrained scheme (*and all over a boy-well young man - well first love. Love could make a sensible person do stupid things.*)

"Yes?"

"I want to quit high school and get my GED."

Lana was taken aback, "Really, Ruth, are you joking?"

Ruth shook her head no.

Lana looked at Constance, "Do you support her in this Mrs. Willows?"

"No," Constance answered to Ruth's disappointment.

"I don't think dropping out of high school is a good idea, Ruth, in fact," Lana flipped through Ruth's college apps, "here ... and here ... and ... here too." She handed her several applications. "These universities will not accept a GED in lieu of a high school diploma."

Constance breathed an audible sigh of relief. Ruth looked at the label on each folder. She handed the files back to Lana with annoyed displeasure.

"Why would you even would consider dropping out? Is there a problem?" Lana looked at Constance, "Something medical? Or something... else?"

"I just can't stand being here anymore!" Ruth was up and pacing around the small office. "I just wish I was done with this place ... and these ... people..." she was upset, but she didn't want to say the wrong thing.

Lana interrupted, "Are you being bullied?"

Ruth took a deep breath. "No." She counted to ten, "I would prefer if I could just continue at the university level and be done with high school forever." She sat down in a huff.

Trying to put a positive spin on the conversation, Lana said, "Being ready to move on is a good thing. Look at you; you've already tackled your first college class successfully, and you've started your second class, right?"

Ruth countered, "This isn't about my ego. It's about...it's about being free of this...place."

"You have your college applications ready. You can submit early admittance. All you need to do is fill out your schedule here with one last requirement. In a few short months, you will be free of this place, as you put it."

"I thought all of her requirements were taken care of with the college classes," Constance queried.

"The school board requires four semesters of fine arts. Ruth has only completed two." Miss Laurence explained.

"Doesn't my AP English cover that? We read plays." Ruth protested.

"No, AP English is language arts. Fine art classes are in music or art. Do you play an instrument?"

"NO," Ruth replied.

"Do you want to perform with the choir?"

"NO."

"How about a theater class?"

"NOT."

"Well," Lana said as she read more of Ruth's file, "I see you've taken art classes with Mr. Kutwright in the past. You'll have to take two more semesters. Senior art class is Wednesday and Friday afternoons, period six."

"I'm at SCU every Monday, Wednesday, and Friday from one to three." Ruth reminded her.

"Hmmm, I knew there was something that created a conflict for you." Lana picked up the phone in her office and dialed a two number extension, "Hang on, I had an idea." She turned her attention to the phone, "Mr. Kutwright, this is Miss Laurence ... Do you remember the conversation we started yesterday?... Yes, the independent study..."

Lana continued her phone conversation; Ruth and her mother looked at each other. "I'm glad you have to stay in school," her mother said, patting her daughter's hand.

"I'm not," Ruth whispered back.

"Since I'm here, do you want me to talk to him? Maybe I can help smooth things over?"

"GOOD G ... MOTHER NO!" Ruth was repulsed at the idea that her mother would talk to a boyfriend – ex-boyfriend – not even an ex-boyfriend about their relationship, or lack thereof, and she was frightened her mother just might seriously try to do it.

Constance smiled a teasing smile, "Just offering."

Lana hung up the phone, "It's all set! The head of the art department, Mr. Kutwright, has agreed to allow Ruth to do an independent study." Reading from her notes, Lana continued, "The subject for this semester is digital photography. You'll learn how to edit photos using the graphics program on the school's computer, and you'll be expected to take photographs for the yearbook as well as newspaper."

"What! I can't do all that! I have classes and papers to write and ..." Ruth protested.

"Ruth, you don't exactly have a full schedule, you're here for three hours every morning, and you only have one class at SCU three afternoons a week. That leaves you plenty of time for this independent study."

"What exactly do I have to take pictures of?" Ruth was suspicious.

"Well, Mr. Kutwright will fill you in on those details, but I assume that if someone needs a picture for a story in the school newspaper, you'll be able to do that."

That didn't sound too bad, Ruth surmised.

"And of course, there's football games and pep rallies and dances," Lana continued in wistful remembrance.

"No, I hate those things! I really hate those things!"

"Then don't graduate," Miss Laurence snapped back. "I'll give you the papers for dropping out of school right now. You're old enough to do it with or without your parents' permission. And you can have these essays back because I won't need to review them." She held the college folder mid-air, but Ruth didn't take it. "Mr. Kutwright is being very generous and taking time out of his own schedule to allow you to do this. Please, at least, appear to be appreciative."

"Yes, ma'am. I will be. I am."

"He has time to get you started this afternoon. He's waiting for you now."

Constance thanked Miss Laurence for all her efforts. Ruth headed off to find Mr. Kutwright.

She went directly upstairs and turned down the hall past the science rooms. She halted before she turned the corner and looked through the glass window into Mr. Silver's room. She prayed he wouldn't glance in her direction. *He's smiling. He seems happy and excited to be teaching. Like the day he helped me ...* a lump formed in her throat. *Does he ever smile in my class? I can't remember seeing a smile on his face. Then again, I try not to look at him.* She got lost looking at him. It felt like it had been forever since she had seen him–the real him. He moved with ease in front of the class. As he wrote on the whiteboard, she realized he was explaining how to write an outline. *Figures!* She laughed softly. For a brief moment, all the stabbing pains from her throat to her guts faded away, and she was just standing there looking at her Cowboy.

"Ruth, what are you doing here? It's after one o'clock." Paloma came walking up from behind.

Startled, Ruth was happy it was Paloma. "My mom and I had our appointment with Miss Laurence. Now I have to go and find Mr. Kutwright."

"I have my appointment with Mr. Hunt tomorrow," Paloma recalled. "Why are you looking for Kutwright?"

"Independent art study."

"Wow, cool," Paloma seemed envious, "What are you studying?"

"Digital photography."

"Hey, did you know that the newspaper is looking for someone to be their photographer?" As much as Ruth loved horses, Paloma loved the newspaper business. She wanted more than anything to be an investigative reporter. Paloma was disappointed she hadn't gotten editor of the school's paper for her senior year, but she was still a senior staff writer, and she had her own blog on the school's website.

Ruth mumbled, "You're looking at her."

"What?"

"You're looking at her."

Paloma began jumping up and down, squealing, "Yea! Yea! Oh, Ruth, I know you'll just be great! We'll have so much fun this year together! You can come to the paper's meetings and plan articles and...."

The door from the English classroom opened. Ken poked his head out and said, “Ladies, do you think you can keep it down? We are having class inside.”

Ruth cringed; the stabbing pains instantly reappeared. Paloma bubbled over, “So sorry, Mr. Silver, but the paper finally found a new photographer! You know Ruth Willows, don’t you? She’s in your AP class with me!”

Ruth turned, looked at Ken, and grimaced a half-smile at him.

“Good for the paper,” Ken gave Paloma a wink, “but please keep it down.” He closed the door and returned to his class.

“Missy was right; he is so sick,” Paloma sighed.

“I’m gonna be sick if I hear one more girl fawn over some guy just because he’s twenty-three, good looking, and he’s forced to talk to her daily.” Ruth started for the art room.

“How do you know he’s twenty-three?” Paloma hurried after her.

Shoot, now what do I say–cause that was his reason for breaking up with me??? “Just a guess,” Ruth lied, “what difference does it make anyway?”

“Just because you have some gorgeous cowboy in love with you doesn’t mean the rest of us can’t have some eye candy to fantasize about.” Paloma’s words cut Ruth to the quick, and it showed on her face, “What’s wrong, Ruth? Is it your cowboy?”

“Yeah, we had a one-sided conversation the other night. He decided that we shouldn’t see each other anymore.”

“Oh no, Ruth, why didn’t you tell me?”

“What’s to tell? He doesn’t want to know me anymore because I’m still in high school. Hooray for being a senior.”

They arrived at the art room and saw Mr. Kutwright was in the middle of an energetic explanation. He waved them in.

They found an empty table and chairs and sat. Students stood at easels, surrounding a bowl of fake fruit. Paloma continued where they had left off. She whispered, “Ruth, I am so sorry. He sounds like a ...jerk.”

"Yeah, well...he has his reasons."

Paloma gasped, "He dumped you, and now you're defending him?"

"I'm not defending him," she whispered, "what did I expect when I met him at SCU? I hate it, but I see his point. The whole thing sucks."

Mr. Kutwright came over to the girls, "Hello there, Ruth, Paloma. I'll be with you after I set up the next still life." He turned his attention to the fake fruit.

"P, shouldn't you be in class?" Ruth asked.

"Study Hall. Dr. Gills gave me a pass to work on paper articles whenever I have a free period. Speaking of which, I have a great project for us to work on."

"What could that be?" Ruth was wary of what Paloma might have in mind.

"I need a great article, something different, something everyone will love."

"Right..."

"Well, what's the one thing every senior and junior and even a few highly motivated sophomores is worried about?"

Ruth sneered, "I don't know, what to wear to the prom?"

"Ha, Ha, hilarious. No, really think. What does everyone get all anxious about?"

"I don't know."

"Everyone worries about what school they are going to next, right! How do you pick a college? How to choose the right one? Well, I figure that I should ask the people who have already been there–our teachers–right! I want to interview as many teachers, from as many different departments as possible, and get their insights."

"That actually sounds like a good idea," Ruth admitted.

"And now you, my dearest friend, can accompany me and take pictures of each teacher I interview."

"Yippee for me!" Ruth was sarcastic.

Mr. Kutwright walked over to the girls, "Are both of you doing this independent study?"

"Just me, sir." Ruth volunteered.

"I'm here for moral support," Paloma cracked, "and to discuss my idea for a great newspaper article. By the way, Mr. Kutwright, may I interview you? At your convenience, of course."

"Yes, but later, okay?" He turned to Ruth. "Do you know anything about photography?"

Ruth shrugged, "Nope."

"You soon will!" he chuckled. "Give me one more minute, and we'll get you started." He walked to the other side of the room and pulled an oversized book off of his bookshelf. He gave the class a final set of instructions and told them to continue working until he returned.

He handed the book to Ruth, "Flip through this book. It will give you a few basic ideas of how to set up and frame a shot." Ruth smiled at him. "It's my personal copy, so I'd like it back when you've finished with it. Oh, and there'll be a test on the material."

"Of course, thank you," said Ruth.

"Do you have a good camera?" he asked Ruth.

"My cell phone."

"No, that won't do." He thought for a minute, "Randall used the school's last year ... and when he graduated he put the camera ..." He went to a closet and rummaged through boxes and bags, "No, no, not in there." He went to another cupboard and rummaged through those boxes. "No, not there either. There's only two other places it could be, in the newspaper office with Mrs. Gills..."

"You mean Dr. Gills," Paloma chimed in. Mr. Kutwright raised one eyebrow and continued, "Unless Randall took it home with him, it might be in the darkroom. It's across the hall; let's look there first."

They crossed the hall to the little closet marked DARKROOM. Mr. Kutwright turned the doorknob, "Humph–locked. Let me grab my keys." He walked back to the art room.

"This place stinks more than I remember," gagged Ruth. "What have you been doing in Chemistry?"

"Nothing yet," replied Paloma, "And it doesn't smell half this bad in the chem. lab."

Mr. Kutwright returned with his keys jangling, "There should be something you can use in here."

He opened the closet door, and the strangling odor overwhelmed them. Paloma gagged and fled to the girls' bathroom. Ruth covered her nose and mouth, as did Mr. Kutwright. He reached his hand around the wall to flick on the lights. The florescent slowly flickered on, revealing what remained of Hector Alverez.

"Oh, my God!" Ruth shrieked and staggered backward till her back slammed into the lockers on the opposite wall.

For a moment, Mr. Kutwright froze, staring at the corpse, then slammed the door and locked it. "Ruth, stay right here, don't say anything to anyone. I'm calling the sheriff," He pulled a cell phone from his pocket. "If anyone asks, tell them I'm in the main office."

Ruth was shaking uncontrollably as Paloma returned pale, "I'm sorry, that smell and the school's lunch just didn't mix. Where's Mr. Kutwright?" Ruth's eyes were as wide as saucers. "Ruth, what? You look like you've seen a ghost!"

"Worse," gasping for air, Ruth whispered, "d.d.d.d.dead.... b.b.b.b.body."

★ ★ ★

A young officer from the county sheriff's department was the first on the scene. He cordoned off the hallway with bright yellow DO NOT CROSS tape. Ruth and Mr. Kutwright were asked to wait within the limits of the yellow tape. Paloma was excused but gave her name and phone number to the officer.

The bell rang, signaling the end of the school day. Students poured out of classrooms and were detoured away from the scene. Now shaking from the adrenaline rush, Ruth gave a quick call home to tell her family she'd be late. She continued to hold the phone to her ear to avoid questions from the crowd.

As the milling students thinned, more officers arrived along with the Sheriff. They all placed handkerchiefs over their noses and mouths, "All right, Tommy, opened it up." Sheriff Davis ordered.

With Mr. Kutwright's keys in hand, the young officer opened the door. Ruth held her breath.

"Close it up. Anybody been inside?" Davis asked.

"Not since I've been here," answered Tommy.

"What about these two?" Sheriff Davis indicated Ruth and Kutwright.

"They said they opened the door and turned on the lights but didn't go in."

"Well, that's good," Davis looked at an older officer next to him, "John, call the medical examiner. Nobody touches this room till we get some evidence." Sheriff Davis looked at the two civilians again. "Tommy, anyone take their statements yet?"

"Not officially, sir. I was the only one on the scene till you got here."

"Come on, then, you're with me." They walked over to Ruth and Kutwright. "Howdy folks, I'm Sheriff Davis. Sorry, you folks had to find this, but we appreciate you not touching anything and calling us. This is Officer Clark. We'll be taking statements from each of you. Let's start with this young lady, Tommy." The three of them ducked out from under the tape. Davis called back to the remaining two officers, "No one touches anything. I'll be back in a moment."

Ruth followed the lawmen down the hall to the first empty classroom. Ken walked down the hallway towards them. He called out, "Uncle Bob, you checking up on me or something?"

Sheriff Davis returned the jibe, “Hey Kenny boy, gotta make sure you stay out of trouble.” The sheriff gave his favorite nephew a warm, welcoming handshake and pat on the shoulder. “I almost forgot you work here now. How’s it going?”

Ken looked past his uncle and saw Ruth. The blood drained from his face, and he stepped to her, “What happened?”

“The little lady here found a dead body,” the sheriff answered for her.

“Who’s? Where?” Ken took hold of her hands, “Are you all right?”

“I’m fine, Cowboy.” She smiled. She didn’t mean to call him that, not in public, especially not here, but she’d never called him anything else.

Ken didn’t realize until he heard it how much he missed his moniker.

“I take it you two know each other,” Sheriff Davis injected.

“Uncle Bob,” Ken held Ruth’s hands because if he let go, she might slip away for all eternity, “this is Ruth ... Ruth Willows.”

“Oh yes, Ruth, a pleasure to meet you. I know Joe and Ed, and Kenny speaks highly of you too.”

She looked up at Ken and smiled, “Oh, he does.” It was fun to hear his uncle call him Kenny, to know that he had talked about her, and they weren’t only a figment of her imagination.

They stood there for a long moment and looked at each other. He wondered *does she know how much I just want to hold her right now. Hold her and kiss her and not let go of her?*

Sheriff Davis cleared his throat, “We need to get your statement Ruth,” He held the door to the classroom open for her. “Feel free to stick around Ken, I’m sure Ruth won’t mind the wait so much if you’re here to keep her company.”

Abruptly the moment ended, “I’m sorry... I can’t stay.” He released her hands. “Good to see you, Uncle Bob.” He looked at her again. She felt as if a solid metal door was slamming close between them. He turned and left.

The heaviness that made it hard to breathe squeezed her chest as she watched Ken's long, lean figure walk away. She turned and followed the sheriff into the classroom to give her statement.

Chapter 9

SCHOOL BUZZED WITH gossip for several days. News outlets confirmed the body in the darkroom was that of Mr. Hector Alverez. Sheriff department vehicles greeted students one morning. Ruth and Paloma were called down to the office.

The main office was busy doubling as a holding room for interviewees for the sheriff. The two secretaries, Lezza and Carol Ann, were at their desks, busy with their usual duties and acting as liaisons between school personnel and the police.

Carol Ann had taken charge of the chaos. She was neat and organized, and efficient; her apparel and desk reflected that. In her late forties, her brown hair was trimmed attractively above her shoulders. She wore comfortable, conservative clothing that gave her an air of authority. She had no problem giving out orders and deciding where the sheriff should conduct the interviews and which staffer should be called when.

Lezza was Carol Ann's opposite. Also, over forty, she was a perpetual wild child. Her desk was known as "the disaster." It was a wonder that she could accomplish anything in the clutter that surrounded her. Somehow she always got her job done. She was attractive, but she had a hard edge to her looks. Lezza's hair was buzzed short in the back with long strands hanging down to her chin, and her outfits were borderline professional.

Paloma watched the two secretaries while she and Ruth waited to be called. Ruth flipped back and forth through a notebook.

"Whatcha doin'? Big math test?" Paloma asked.

"If only," answered Ruth. "We just got our math final assigned to us; it'll count for half our grade."

"Your final? It's only the second week of classes?"

"It's our third week of class, and it's a research paper due instead of a final test." Ruth clarified.

"How do you do a research paper in a math class?" Paloma asked.

Ruth shook her head, "So far, the whole class has been about mathematicians. I figured we'd have to do a biography on one of them."

"Could be interesting, could be boring," Paloma surmised, "but not too horrible."

"If it were only that easy. We actually have to take real-life data and then apply two theories from two different mathematicians to the data. Then compare and contrast the results."

Paloma exhaled in hushed tones, "That sounds annoying. What's your plan?"

"I don't know!" Ruth moaned. "I guess I should find some data to work with."

"Your Granddaddy has a business. Can you use his books?"

"Not really, we're supposed to use public data."

Both girls sat in silence for a moment, then Ruth asked, "How's your article coming?"

"It's really cool! I can't wait till the Thursday morning newspaper meeting. Oh, you've gotta come, Ruth, now that you're the photographer."

"Do I really?"

"Yeah, it will be great! You'll get to know everyone, and you'll get different assignments depending on which articles are approved."

"What do you mean?" asked Ruth.

"We have two editors. They decide which articles get published after they're written. First, Dr. Gills has to approve which articles we work on. Technically, I shouldn't have started my interviews yet, but I just couldn't wait."

"How many have you done so far?"

"Six–and I need you to take their pictures..."

"I know–no camera till they process the darkroom," Ruth shrugged.

Paloma continued, "I've written the first four. I think I might have enough to do a series. Like one or two interviews in each edition this year." Paloma thought for a moment, "You know, I was doing some research, comparing salaries of different jobs, and I read that our school district gives bonuses to teachers with advanced degrees."

"Yeah, well, that sounds typical."

"Maybe you could use that for your paper."

"What do you mean?" Ruth asked.

"What if you looked at the school's budget with different amounts of teachers having different degrees? Like if there were no advanced degrees versus all teachers having advanced degrees."

Ruth thought, "Yeah, I need a little more than that, but I could use the school's budget and teachers' salaries and maybe other expenses as well.... that kind of stuff should be public information, right?"

"I think so," answered Paloma. "Maybe ask Lezza or Carol Ann if..."

Officer Clark interrupted and led them to a small room where the Sheriff was conducting interviews. With nothing new for them to add, it was over in moments. Both girls headed for the door. Sheriff Davis handed Ruth his card and said, "If you think of anything else you'd like to add, please don't hesitate to call."

Carol Ann intercepted them at the door, "Girls, Principal Rodriguez would like you to stop by his office for a moment." They walked back into the main office, and Lezza told them to go on in.

"Hello ladies, sit down, please," the principal said in a mild tone. He was a tall, good-looking man with tanned skin and prematurely grey hair. He kept his square jawline clean-shaven and wore wire-rimmed bifocals. "I just wanted to thank you for all your cooperation, and I'm sorry you two had to be the ones to find Mr. Alverez. I don't know what I might be able to do for either of you, but if you think of anything that could be helpful to you, please don't hesitate to ask."

Paloma spoke up first, "May I interview you for my newspaper story?" She explained her premise.

Mr. Rodriguez chuckled. "Not what I had in mind, but sure. Just talk to Carol Ann and find a suitable time for both of us."

He looked at Ruth, "Anything I can do for you, Ruth?"

She hesitated but explained her predicament with her math paper. "I wouldn't want to use anything that contained information about current employees, maybe some budgets from ten or fifteen years ago."

"It's a little unusual, Ruth, but let me see what I can do. I believe most of that information was made digital a year or two ago." He picked up the phone and called the secretary's desk. "Speak to Lezza on your way out. She'll get you what you need."

Ruth and Paloma thanked Principal Rodriguez and left his office. Paloma made her appointment to interview the principal. Lezza promised Ruth her info and added, "Ya gotta give me a day or so to get it. With all this hullabaloo going on here, I hardly have time to breathe. Try back on Thursday or Friday."

★ ★ ★

Paloma dragged Ruth, with a camera in hand, to the newspaper meeting Thursday morning. The newspaper staff, about thirty-five students, sat in chairs and on tables in the newspaper office. Surprisingly, rather than Dr. Gills entering, Mr. Silver entered the room as the bell rang.

"What's he doing here?" Ruth whispered in Paloma's ear.

"Gills wasn't in homeroom this morning. Ms. Laurence said she had car trouble."

"You couldn't tell me this sooner?" Ruth was agitated.

"What difference does it make?"

Paloma was right. What difference did it make? No one, not even her best friend, knew the stabbing pain she got in her gut every time she saw Cowboy. No one knew how her heart fluttered, and her mouth went dry, and she felt like she was going to explode or implode or both.

"What is your problem with him anyhow? You hardly know him, and you've seemed to just hate him from the first day of school." Paloma chided her. "He's nice, and he's a good teacher."

"Yeah, whatever."

Ken introduced himself, "I'm filling in for Dr. Gills. She should be here later today. I'll pass your notes on to her. I'll let your editors handle business as usual, and I'm here if you need me."

The two senior editors, Jenny and Brad, discussed ideas for articles. Paloma gave a full rundown of her idea for her "How to Pick the Right College for You" article. Both Jenny and Brad thought it sounded great, Ken liked it too. Of course, Paloma asked Mr. Silver if she could interview him, and he said yes. Much to Ruth's chagrin, Paloma introduced her as the new photographer, then asked Mr. Silver when she could do the interview.

"I can talk with you at lunch, Paloma." He smiled and gazed at Ruth, "Do I get my picture taken too?"

The bell rang. Ruth grabbed her backpack, said, "I have a class," and left.

★ ★ ★

Ruth arranged to do most of her independent study on Thursdays for a double period after lunch. Having only gotten her camera that morning, she hadn't taken any pictures, but she'd brought in a file of photos her mom had taken of her during the rodeo. She used these to learn how to use the editor program, make corrections, add fancy graphics, and the like.

By the end of the school day, she'd had enough of staring at images on a computer screen. She saved her work on the removable drive, collected her bags, and went to find Paloma to go home.

As the girls strolled along the sidewalk toward the parking lot, Paloma spotted Ken and flagged him down. "Mr. Silver, Mr. Silver!" she called to him, jumping up and down, waving her arms while Ruth's insides cringed. "Can we get that picture of you for the paper now?"

"Do I look good enough for a picture?" he teased.

"Oh, Mr. Silver..." Paloma giggled. Ruth looked at her friend, *Good God, is she blushing? Don't tell me she has a crush on him! GEEZ - What else do I need!* "Come on, Ruth, take his picture."

Begrudgingly Ruth pulled out her camera, thought about the angle of the sunlight hitting his face - *that nose, those dimples, his eyes–I wish I didn't exist-* and took several quick shots. "All done," she said.

"Let me see," requested Paloma, and both of them leaned over Ruth's shoulder to look.

"Miss Torres, we need to speak NOW! I demand that you stop harassing the staff of this school..." Dr. Gills' shrill voice startled the trio. Ruth jumped back and lost her footing on the curb. Paloma grabbed the camera out of Ruth's hands before it hit the ground, and Ken reached out for Ruth, caught her by the arm and the waist, and pulled her into his side.

In an instant, they were transported back through time to only a few weeks ago when they'd spent the evening talking and dancing and holding and kissing.

Dr. Gills stared at them and scolded Ruth, "Miss Willows... MISS WILLOWS, you may let go of her now, Mr. Silver." He loosened his grip, but not his gaze.

Dr. Gills continued hounding Paloma, "How dare you invade the privacy of the teachers and administration of this school with your puerile ideas of what is proper reporting. I forbid you to continue this excuse of an article!"

Paloma was mortified; her bright and sparkling personality deflated quicker than a popped balloon. "But... but... but... everyone said they liked the idea..." she whimpered.

"I don't care what they told you, I'm telling you to stop this badgering or not only will you never write for this school newspaper again, you can forget any college reference from me or any member of this staff!"

"I think it's a good idea." Ken tried to interject,

Dr. Gills interrupted him, "I didn't hire you to think, Mr. Silver!"

"Then what did you hire me to do?"

Gills was visibly flustered, "I didn't hire you to take over the paper duties for me. You are here to teach English classes."

Tears welled up in Paloma's eyes; it embarrassed her to being reprimanded in front of another teacher and a friend. She didn't understand why Dr. Gills was so unreasonable.

A black convertible Dodge Viper with the top down pulled up to the curb with a loud squeal. A young man with black curls revved the engine and sniggered, "Well, well, if it's not the two lovebirds. Whadaya doin'?" Eyeing the camera still in Paloma's hands, "Taking engagement photos? Send me one so I can throw darts at it."

"Derrick!" Ruth and Ken hissed.

"What on earth are you talking about, Derrick?" his mother demanded.

Ruth gasped as her brain made the connection. *Of course, Derrick Gills and Dr. Gills,* she'd never seen them together and never thought about them being related.

"Lil' Ruth and Kenny here, the two little Sweethearts of the Rodeo. They had everyone thinking they were so innocent, but we know better, don't we, Willows?"

Ken stepped in front of Ruth as if to shield her from an invisible force.

Paloma, who was more confused than anyone, managed, "You're wrong. They barely know each other."

"Oh, they know each other. Intimately wouldn't you say, Silver?" Derrick took in the scene, "Wait, what the hell are you two doing here, anyway? This is high school, not... Oh, wait!" Derrick burst into irrepressible laughter, "You've got to be kidding... This is too much..."

"Derrick, Mr. Silver is the new teacher I hired, and Miss Willows is a student." Dr. Gills turned to Ken, "Mr. Silver, is there something going on between you and Miss Willows?"

"Ruth and I were partners in the rodeo this summer. Our families have known each other for a long time, and we became close friends, but we have not had any type of personal relationship since school began." Ken was emphatic in his clarification.

Ruth was fit to be tied at having her character defamed, "Thought you were still on probation and barn duty Gills. Shep give you a day off?"

"That old man can suck my co..."

"Derrick!" his mother interrupted, "That will be enough of language!"

"I couldn't care less about college rodeo. I'm going big time–PBR–that's for me. One of their scouts saw me at the rodeo, and now he's courting me! Even gave me this pretty little car to borrow while my Mom's car is in the shop." He turned to his mother, "Come on, Ma, let's get going. I got places to be and things to do." He revved the Viper's engine again.

Dr. Gills' eyes darted between Ken and Ruth, "Mr. Silver, I will deal with you tomorrow and Miss Torres," she turned to Paloma, "mind what I had to say to you as well." Dr. Gills climbed into the sports car and sped off with her son.

Ruth, Ken, and Paloma stood staring at each other, speechless. Ruth felt as if someone had sucked all the air from her lungs. Ken remembered the knot in the pit of his stomach, and Paloma's head was spinning.

"Who was that ... that ... creep?" Paloma asked.

"That was Derrick. I told you about him... the one I slapped..."

"So it's true?" Paloma gasped. "Ruth, you and..." she looked like a small child who had just been told her pet had died, "you and Mr. Sil..."

Ruth nodded her head, "Most of what Derrick said is... was true."

"You never told me! How could you! I'm your best friend!" Paloma shouted at her. "All the times I went on and on about Mr. Silver this and Mr. Silver that, and why you don't give him a chance, and why do you dislike him... You must think I'm an idiot!"

"I'm sorry, Paloma...," Ruth pleaded.

"I asked her not to say anything to anyone, Paloma, even her best friend," Ken spoke up. "I don't want to lose my job." He looked at both girls, then turned to leave.

Ruth called out to him, "Cowboy..." he turned back, locked eyes with her, and shook his head before she could utter another sound.

Ruth and Paloma watched in silence as Ken crossed the parking lot, got into his jeep, and drove away. Paloma handed Ruth the camera and began walking.

"Where are you going?" Ruth ran after her.

"Home."

"My truck is here. I'll drive you."

"It's not far," Paloma said, "I'll walk."

★ ★ ★

Friday morning sucked. The sky was uncharacteristically grey; it reflected Ruth's foul mood. Grace refused to ride to school with the "girl who fainted." Paloma had not waited for Ruth's ride to school either. *Fine be that way*, thought Ruth, *take the crappy bus.*

First period's Current Events class held an avid discussion about the body of Hector Alverez and the local paper's reporting. The Sentinel stated the ME would not release a complete autopsy report for several weeks. It also reported the body had been untouched; the victim's keys and wallet with cash and credit cards were still in his pocket. The class was eager to hear Ruth's tale of discovering the body - again- but she couldn't add anything to the paper's story.

Out of the frying pan and into the fire, thought Ruth as she entered second period AP English. Paloma sat on the opposite side of the room from Ruth. Ken was even cooler and more remote than usual. Ruth thought it pathetically sad that the highlight of her day would be Colonel Sanders' math class. That thought reminded her she had not yet stopped by the school office to pick up her math paper data. When the bell finally rang to end second period, Ruth shot out of English and down to the main office.

She was standing in line waiting to speak with Lezza when she noticed the school's music department's head, Mr. Bowman, sitting at Carol Ann's desk.

He was a huge guy, at least six foot six inches tall, with a fifty-inch chest. He had a soft heart and a coffee cup always in hand, but he was no pushover. He shot straight from the hip and didn't take any malarkey from anybody.

Today he looked like a man on a mission. His fingers flew over the keys of the computer. He was on the phone, taking down notes on post-its. He slammed the phone down on the receiver.

Simultaneously, Carol Ann emerged from Principal Rodriguez's office, and Ken walked in through the main office door. Carol Ann spotted Mr. Bowman as he defiled her pristine desk. "Mr. Bowman, what on earth are you doing?" she shouted.

"I'm looking for my tuba!" Mr. Bowman shouted back.

"Well, it's certainly not in there! Let my desk be!" She ran to him and tried to pull his massive frame away from her sacred space.

Meanwhile, Ken crossed to Principal Rodriguez's door. Rodriguez showed Ken into his office but added, "Could you please keep the shouting down?" His secretary's behavior stunned him. He noticed Ruth waiting in line, "Ruth, could you come in here a moment," Rodriguez's voice was so kind that butter could have melted in his mouth. His eyes told a different story.

It was Ruth's turn to talk to Lezza. She just wanted to get her papers and leave, but she really didn't have a choice.

Principal Rodriguez had two chairs facing his desk. When Ruth entered, Ken was pacing between the desk and one of the chairs.

"Ruth, I wasn't going to involve you with this conversation," Rodriguez started, "but when I saw you, I thought you should have the chance to speak for yourself."

Ruth hadn't the faintest idea of what the principal was talking about, but she knew it couldn't be good. She stood behind a chair, her hands gripping its back, girding herself for what was to come next.

"Please, both of you relax. I am not accusing either of you of anything. I just want to get the facts. With the publicity over Mr. Alverez, I'd like to nip this in the bud before it goes any further."

Ken spoke, "Nip what in the bud?"

Principal Rodriguez continued, "I received an anonymous letter this morning. It gives details about an illicit affair between a student and teacher at this school." He cleared his throat. "It involves the two of you."

Ruth's heart sank, *no this cannot be happening, this cannot be happening.*

Ken's face went pallid, and his voice was tight, "May I see this letter?"

Rodriguez handed the letter to Ken. He read it and handed it to Ruth.

She read it twice.

Dear Principal Rodriguez,

I am writing because I am concerned about a situation of which I have recently become aware.

I have witnessed blatant and public sexual contact between Mr. Ken Silver, a teacher at your school, and Miss Ruth Willows, a student. I am sure that Miss Willows is not an adult and most likely under the age of consent, whereas Mr. Silver is an adult and a teacher.

I have seen the two of them parading through town together, accompanied by kissing, groping, and other lewd acts that should have been reserved for a more private and appropriate time.

I believe this type of relationship is frowned upon by the school itself and our great state's laws.

I find it to be a terrible crime when a grown man preys upon such a young victim.

I hope you can put a stop to this indecent behavior.

Ruth shook from both rage and fear by the time she handed the letter back to Mr. Rodriguez. "It's not true, not true at all..." her voice shook too, trailed off.

"Ken?" Rodriguez addressed him.

"Anyone capable of reading the newspaper would know both Ruth and I rode in the town's rodeo this summer. And yes, we paraded through town, on horseback in front of at least a thousand spectators."

Ken continued, "On a personal note, Ruth is a very good friend. Our families have been friends longer than she and I have been alive. BUT in class, we are student and teacher, period."

Rodriguez studied them. Finally, he took the letter and put it through a shredder beside his desk. It hummed, and the letter was gone. "I choose to believe the two of you over an anonymous letter. Do you know who would want to disparage or embarrass either of you?"

Ruth couldn't speak. She was still shaking, now more so from the relief that Ken would not be losing his job.

"Does that really matter?" Ken replied.

"Not as long as I don't hear any more about it." Rodriguez added, "Thank you both for taking the time to discuss this. Please use extreme caution when dealing with each other, particularly here at school." The conversation was over.

Ruth and Ken left Rodriguez's office, shutting the door behind them. As Ruth was about to say something, hoping to ease the tension between them, Ken rolled his eyes and, in a barely audible whisper uttered, "I wish I'd never..." He stopped mid-sentence when he saw Ruth's eyes upon him and the look of horror on her face. He clamped his lips tightly shut and stomped off. Ruth's world crashed down around her.

The office had emptied of everyone except for the two secretaries and Mr. Bowman, who still argued over the tuba. Ruth leaned her butt against the counter that separated the office staff from the visitors and doubled over, hands on knees, breathing heavily, trying not to throw up. *Why can't they shut up!*

"When's the last time you saw the tuba?" That sounded like Lezza.

"Gills used it as a prop for the spring musical–The Music Man," Bowman growled. *Gills - Did that woman have her fingers in every department in this school?* Ruth wondered.

"Maybe it's still in the prop closet or backstage," Lezza again.

"No, it was supposed to be sent out to Garcia's so they could fix a valve," Bowman was almost screaming.

"Mr. Bowman, we really don't know where it could be." Carol Ann offered.

Mr. Rodriguez emerged from his office under a full head of irritated steam. "I've heard enough! Bill and Carol Ann come into my office. Lezza, please find Dr. Gills and Mr. Kerr. They're responsible for the drama club; ask them to join us, will you?"

Lezza was heading out of the office door following the principal's orders when she spotted Ruth.

"Ruth, are you okay?" Lezza paused to check her.

"Honestly, I don't feel so good."

"Do you need some help to the nurse's office or bathroom?"

"No, I'll be fine," Ruth whispered and straightened herself.

"All right then." Before she left, Lezza remembered, "I have the information you asked for. It's in the manila folder on top of my desk. Just go ahead and grab it before you leave."

Lezza hurried out, and Ruth rounded the counter to Lezza's desk. There must have been fifteen manila folders scattered across her desk, along with yellow and blue and green folders and binders and paper-clipped papers. The first three manila folders had students' names on them, none of which were hers. Ruth opened another folder, but it contained requisition forms. Her head spun, and her mouth was watering. Any moment what was left of her breakfast was going to be on the floor. She put her hand down on the mess to steady herself, which caused an avalanche of papers and folders to come sliding down onto the floor. *No, no, no, not now.* She did her best to scoop up everything and put it back in the same order from which it had fallen.

She saw a thick manila folder and flipped it open. The first page read **District's Budget 1999**. She flipped through the next few pages and saw more of the same headings for subsequent years. *This must be it.* She picked up the folder; it was a lot thicker than she had expected. Folder in hand, she flung her backpack over her shoulder and fled to her truck.

Her truck was parked close to the main entrance, close to where the Derrick incident happened. The thought pushed her over the edge. She flung open her truck door, threw her bag, camera, and folder onto the floor, and vomited what little breakfast was left in her stomach onto the ground.

With the pressure of keeping it all inside removed, Ruth not only lost control of her stomach but her emotions as well. She crawled into her pickup, locked the doors, and sobbed uncontrollably, an ugly cry filled with self-pity and rage. She laid across the bench seat as a movie of the past three months played in a continuous loop in her mind. *It's not fair,* was her mantra. *It's not fair that we hardly got to know each other; it's not fair that we don't even get a chance; it's not fair that my best friend hates me because I couldn't tell her the whole truth; it's not fair that I have the worst senior year in the world's history; it's not fair that it hurts so much.*

A bell rang; she heard voices, so she stayed close to the seat. She laid there for a long time, just listening. Listening to her heart beating, to the sound of traffic passing on the road. No birds sang. No wind whispered through the trees; all was still. Ruth tried to think, *what do I do now? I can't go on like this. This is not me. I am not a fainting, throwing up, crybaby. I've never acted like this before, and I can't stand myself. But I don't know what to do...*

A bell rang again. More voices and shuffle of foot traffic broke the silence. *What would happen if someone looked in and found me?* She wondered. She looked at her bags, strewn on the floor of the truck. *Shoot, I hope I didn't break the camera.* She reached forward and straightened the mess. The huge file she had taken from Lezza's desk came to hand. *I'll deal with that another day, she thought,* feeling like Scarlet O'Hara, and neatly tucked it into her bag. She grabbed the camera and sat up. The parking lot was again empty. She looked in the rearview mirror; *Ugh, what a mess.* The small amount of makeup she wore had either been cried off or smudged into a brown mess around her red, swollen eyes.

She pressed the power button on the camera. *Well, at least it still turns on.* She adjusted the view screen to a better angle. It showed the last pictures she took–Ken. She deleted all of them, except for one. It was a good picture, even if looking at it made her gut wrench.

She switched the camera from view to shoot; *better make sure I didn't crack the lens or something.* It seemed to work. There wasn't much scenery to take pictures of in the parking lot; just a brick wall of the theater. She took a few shots, anyway.

Ruth spotted a man and a woman walking down the sidewalk. They were too far away to see who they were, so she used the zoom lens. Mr. Bowman and Dr. Gills. *Wonder if they're still looking for that stupid tuba? Like anyone could really lose a tuba.* Without thinking, Ruth snapped pictures of the unlikely couple as they walked down the sidewalk and into the back of the building. Afterward, she looked at the camera and thought - guess it still works. She turned off the camera, put it safely away, and lay down on the seat again.

She closed her eyes and slipped into a half-dream state. Pictures of Ken danced in and out of her mind; the picture from the camera, how handsome and proud he'd looked on Remington, the image of his face after they'd kissed, the look in his eyes when he said, I wish I'd never met you...

Another bell and she sat bolt upright. The grey clouds had dispersed and white fluffy pillows dotted the blue sky. A ray of sunlight stung her already sensitive eyes. People moved all around her truck, but they didn't matter. All she could see was Ken's face saying those awful words, repeatedly. She couldn't believe she had tears left, but what she had silently poured from her eyes.

A loud banging on the door shocked her back to reality. It was Paloma and a guy Ruth didn't know. Paloma shouted at her as she pounded on the window, "Ruth, Ruth, open up, Ruth!"

Ruth couldn't open the window because she didn't know where her keys were. She fiddled with the locks and opened the driver's side door. "What?" she asked in a dazed voice, tears still on her cheeks.

"It's almost three o'clock. What are you doing here?"

Ruth looked at her with a puzzled expression.

Paloma continued, "Didn't you have a math class today? Did you come back for something?"

Ruth inhaled a gigantic breath, "Oh, NUTS! I totally forgot math class!"

"How could you forget math class? You're sitting in your truck! What have you been doing for three hours?"

"Three hours?" I've been here for three hours? Her eyes burned, and the warm tears dripped onto her lips.

"Ruth! What's wrong? What Happened?" Paloma turned to the guy standing next to her and said something Ruth couldn't hear. He grabbed her hand, gave her a quick peck on the lips before he walked off. Paloma returned to Ruth and said, "Where are your keys? Give them to me."

"I don't know..."

"Slide over and give me your bag," Paloma demanded, and Ruth obeyed. "What the hell happened to you? You're a mess."

"Ken said he wished he never met me."

"No way, Ruth! I watched him today in class. He adores you! He never took his eyes off of you."

"Not after what happened today. I don't know how I'm ever going to face him again."

Paloma fished the truck keys out from Ruth's bag, turned over the engine, and pulled the truck around to a shady spot.

Paloma opened the windows and said, "All right–TALK!"

Ruth did. She told the entire tale while Paloma listened.

"Gills! I betcha she wrote the letter to Rodriguez. That woman is nuts! She cornered me in homeroom this morning, started screaming at me like I was a mass murderer or something. I had to tell three people what puerile and jejune means."

"I don't even know what jejune means, and I got a 735 on the critical reading section of my S.A.T.S," Ruth confessed.

Paloma smiled because this was the Ruth she knew and hadn't seen in the last three weeks.

Ruth asked, "Why do you think it was her? It could be anyone who saw us at the rodeo."

"Who really cares if you two ride horses together! That has nothing to do with this. This is personal. She told Mr. Silver yesterday that she would deal with him today, so... she did."

"But why slander us?"

"Cause she knows it's not far from the truth–right?"

"I don't get it. What does she have to gain? She hired him–why try to get him fired or jailed?"

"Well," Paloma thought for a moment, "from what you said, the letter was so obviously bogus that she knew Rodriguez would never believe it, yes?"

"Yeah... maybe."

"So there was really no threat of him getting fired. It did what it intended to do, which was to put doubt in Mr. Silver's mind about ever being with you."

"But why?"

"First off, I think she's batty. Second, she probably wants him all for herself."

"Ewwww, that's gross. She's old enough to be his mother."

"Well, add cougar to the list of her abnormalities. I'm telling you, Ruth, every female in this school is gaga over Mr. Silver whether they're fourteen or forty. Maybe you can't see it because you're too close to the situation, but he has quite a following. Dr. Gills is trying to remove her biggest competition."

Ruth shook her head, "I don't know... But, speaking of gaga-just who was that young man kissing you beside my truck, young lady?"

Paloma giggled, "Scott."

"Ooooohhh... Now it's your turn. Talk." Ruth smiled again, feeling more normal with her best friend back.

"Senior, artist, met him while I was in the remedial art class, and he was in the back working on a big painting."

"Yes... and..."

"And we're going out tonight, and I'll tell you more tomorrow."

"Well, we better get you home then so you can get all gussied up for your big date."

"Want me to drive?" Paloma asked.

"Yeah, sure."

Chapter 10

THERE WAS AN industrial-sized coffee maker in the staff lounge, and she always enjoyed one last cup after the students had gone home. Especially after a day like she had today.

She liked the staff room when it was empty. She searched for sweetener, but the supply cupboard was empty. She dug through her purse to find a packet. *Nail file, comb, lipstick, loose change, sweetener, what's this?* She held a small plastic vial filled with white powder. *Oh, I forgot about this.* GHB–She'd gotten it from Critter, a regular at Mike's, ages ago, but never had tried it. She slid the vial into her cleavage. *This is not the place to get caught with drugs.*

The door to the staff room opened and closed. A familiar voice spoke, "I've been looking all over for you."

"Well, you caught me," she joked, turning around, "one last cup of coffee."

"More than coffee." Bill Bowman retorted.

"Excuse me?" *He couldn't have seen the vial,* she thought.

He had a peculiar look on his face, "We're going to finish our conversation from earlier."

"Are you still going on about that ridiculous tuba? I have NO idea where it could be." She sipped her fresh brew.

"You know damn well what happened to it! You can lie to everyone else, but you can't lie to me!" Bowman came close and towered over her, ever-present coffee mug in hand.

This wasn't a situation she had foreseen; *oh, I hate having to improvise.* "Mr. Bowman, are you threatening me?" She batted her eyelashes, "or something else?"

"Cut the crap. Do you know how I spent my free period this afternoon?"

"No, but I have the feeling you're going to tell me." She took the coffee mug from his hand. "If we're going to have some sort of knock down drag out, you might as well join me." She rinsed the mug out at the sink and asked which blend he preferred.

"Morning roast." He mumbled, a bit thrown off his stride.

"Mmmmm, you like it strong. Black, sugar, cream?"

"One sugar, no cream, please."

She kept her back to him while the coffee brewed. *What am I going to do!* She knew the bible-thumping family man would never look the other way of her little indiscretions. *Maybe he needs a minor indiscretion of his own. I'm not above murder. Why not throw a little blackmail into the mix?*

She unbuttoned the top button of her blouse and pulled out the vial of GBH. *How much did Critter say to use?* She'd gotten it such a long time ago. *Was this vial good for three doses or six doses? Bowman's a BIG boy; I'll just use it all.* She emptied the drugs and the sugar in at the same time, stirred, and handed the mug to Bowman.

"Sit, Bill. Let's talk this out," She was as sweet as pie as she rested her rump on the arm of a chair.

Bill Bowman did not sit. He took a long drink of his coffee to prepare for his diatribe. "I spoke to Wally at Music World," he looked at her pointedly; she continued to look at him innocently. "There was a bill of sale for my tuba. Appears Wally got it into his head that the school wanted to get rid of that fine instrument." She still would not satisfy him with a reaction. "Whose name do you think was on that bill of sale?"

She continued to smile as she walked over to him, pulled him down into the armchair, and repositioned herself on the arm. "I know whose name is on the bill of sale," she whispered into his ear, "and Wally is an idiot writing down my name. Now, is that all you're worried about? We can get you another tuba, silly. It might take a week or two to submit all the paperwork, but we can get a brand new one if you like."

"That's not the point!" he protested.

"What's the point then?"

"Concert band starts rehearsals next week. I need that tuba NOW! second," she started running her fingers up and down his shirt sleeve and across his shoulders. It unnerved him. "Second, I spent my free period this afternoon locked in my office, going through the last seven years of purchase orders for the music department."

"Mmmmm, locked in your office? That sounds kind of naughty. Were you alone?" She was stroking his neck and ear.

"Yes, damn it, I was alone!" He tried to brush her away, but she held on to his hand instead.

She remembered that GHB made the user open to suggestions, "You don't really want me to stop touching you, do you, Bill?"

"No, but where was I?" He swigged more of his brew and tried hard to think. "Ah, I found that in the seven years I've been head of the music department, there have been gross misappropriations of funds. I've never got all the copies of music I ordered. If the department paid for seventy-five copies, I'd get forty. Where did the extra money go? And that's not the only thing..."

"I know all about it, Bill." She interrupted his thoughts and began loosening his tie, "It's not a big deal. Haven't you always got what you needed to run your department?"

"Mostly... I guess..." he was starting to fade.

"Now would you like to give me what I deserve, Billy?"

"Yes, I would..." He was ready.

"Why don't you take me to your office where we won't be interrupted, and you can show me all the bad things you've found out about me? Then we can work out what kind of punishment you should give me." She stood up and took his hand. He still held his mug of coffee, "Go on, drink up, so you don't spill." He obeyed.

The band room and Bowman's office were located behind the theater. By the time they reached the hall that led into the music room, Bowman was in a dead out run. He dragged her through the empty band room into his office. With one arm, he flung everything from the top of his desk onto the floor. He threw her on top of the desk. In one swift move, he proved that the drugs had taken their full effect. She screamed, not with delight but from pain. Her body was not prepared for his onslaught. His speech slurred, but he laughed at a joke he'd made about her scream being soprano.

He continued his assault, her teetering on the edge of the desk, him with his feet planted on the floor. He collapsed on top of her, and it was over. Now she needed to make him realize what he had done, how he had betrayed his wife and family. She needed to show him how everyone makes mistakes and how they could come to an understanding.

Instead of waning, the effects of the drugs got stronger. Bowman straightened, headed to the other side of his desk, and sat in his chair. He looked at her as though he'd just realized she was there. He stood and pulled her over the desk, ripped her blouse open, and sent the small fake pearl buttons flying. Then he dragged her to the floor between the desk and chair; he raped her again.

Bowman sweated profusely. His breathing hitched into an irregular rhythm. His pace built faster and harder. She tried to pull away from him, but he held her fast.

Bowman began convulsing. She screamed in fear as he collapsed on top of her. All was quiet. With a herculean effort, she rolled him over and scrambled up.

The small office looked like a cyclone had hit it. *It must be after four. It won't be hard to sneak out. Everyone should be gone.* She rearranged her clothes as best she could. Most of her blouse buttons were gone.

She sat in the chair and looked down at Bowman. *I never knew he had so much rage in him. Maybe it was the drugs. What should I do now?* She had the feeling he would not remember this, and if he couldn't remember raping her (twice), what good would blackmail do? She studied him on the floor.

Oh my God, is he still breathing? She started to panic. She got down on her knees and put her ear to his chest. She didn't have any medical training, but anyone could tell that his heartbeat was irregular. He barely drew a breath, and the pulse in his neck was weak.

She knew she should call 911. Bowman would not survive if she didn't. The idea struck her. If she called the ambulance, they might be able to save him. If she just left him here, he would probably die. *How bad would that be? Obviously, some hanky-panky had happened, but no one would know with whom.* Her blouse's buttons were all over the place. She could get rid of the blouse. She definitely had left DNA evidence behind, but she could ... *always admit to being raped, too afraid to report it, and leaving the room before he went unconscious. Yes, that would work! That would take care of the tuba situation too.* She had already told Wally that Bowman had told her to sell the thing. *With him out of the way, who could contest it?* But why would Bowman make such a big stink about it in front of half the staff? She had to think ... *Because she wouldn't add sex to his list of demands. She would say that he made her sell the tuba and misappropriate funds, but when she wouldn't have sex with him, he threatened her and eventually raped her. PERFECT!!!*

Now, to tie up any loose ends. She picked up the empty coffee mug with a tissue from a box. She didn't want anyone to know that she had given him the drugs, so she wiped it out and smashed it on the floor with the rest of the chaos. She hadn't touched much, but she wiped the desk and chair down with more tissues just to make it harder for anyone trying to lift prints. She stuffed the used tissues into her bra and was good to go.

What about him? He was still breathing. How long would he last? She had no idea about overdoses. *What if one of the janitors or security guards finds him before he dies?* She paced around the small room. *If I hadn't gotten rid of the gun, that would have been a simple end to it... I could hit him with something. I don't know if I'm strong enough to do any good.* And then her eyes fell upon the chair. On it was a pillow decorated with music notes.

She grabbed the pillow, sat on his chest, held the pillow over his nose and mouth, and closed her eyes. *Oh, God, how long is this going to take!*

His arms thrashed from the elbows down only. His legs shook. She tried to keep steady pressure on his face; she didn't want this to take any longer than necessary. He was in terrible shape, so there wasn't much fight left in him. Two minutes seemed to last forever. After he was gone, she wiped the spit and mucus off the pillow and onto his shirt and placed the pillow back on the chair. She checked again. He was definitely dead. She pushed him under the desk as much as she could. He was too big to fit, but the longer it took for someone to find him, the better.

She used the bottom of her blouse to open the office door and turned around. The place was a mess, but Bowman couldn't be seen at first glance. She locked the door from the inside, slid out of the office, and closed the door behind her.

She tucked her button-less blouse into her skirt and headed to the parking lot. *Damn! I need a drink!*

Chapter 11

SATURDAY, PALOMA ARRIVED at Ruth's house with a laptop and overnight bag. She had a research project planned for them. When Joe offered to take everyone out for ice cream after dinner, they all piled into the car.

Kids from school were crowding Archer's Cream Shoppe. After they were served, Grace wandered off to talk to friends, and Ruth and Paloma joined a group of their classmates.

"What's up?" Paloma asked in her usual perky style.

"Haven't you heard?" Carla, first clarinet, was visibly shaken.

"Heard what?" Ruth interjected.

Carla's voice quavered, "They found Mr. Bowman."

"I didn't know he was missing, just his tuba." Ruth snorted.

"He's not missing. He's dead!" Carla sobbed.

"What happened?" Paloma gasped.

Dwayne, a trombone player, put his arm around Carla and continued her story, "He didn't show up for marching band, so we called assistant director Ms. Stack. Bowman's wife showed up, saying that he hadn't come home yesterday."

Ruth's stomach knotted as the picture of Bowman and Dr. Gills flashed in her mind.

"The sheriff," Dwayne continued, "and the groundskeeper found him locked in his office, curled up on the floor, dead."

"I saw the room, it was a disaster! Stuff thrown everywhere! But the sheriff yelled to get the kids out because he was half-naked," Carla found her voice to add the gruesome detail. The group collectively cringed.

"Did they say how he died or when?" Ruth asked.

"Nope, we were just told to go home."

Ruth gave Paloma a look that meant that she had something to add, but not here.

★ ★ ★

"You girls were awfully quiet on the ride home," Constance commented as they entered the house.

"We have some homework to do. Guess we just started thinking about it," Ruth lied. Bowman would be all over the news by the morning, and she needed to think before she said anything. "We're gonna get ready for bed and try to do some work before we fall asleep," Ruth added as she and Paloma went upstairs.

Sleep was the last thing from the girls' minds. "Weird about Bowman, huh?" Paloma powered up her laptop.

"I've got something weirder," Ruth showed the pictures of Bowman and Gills to Paloma.

"When did you take these?"

"An hour or so before he died."

"What?" cried Paloma.

"Ssh, keep your voice down. I have to think about this before I say anything to anyone else."

"What are you talking about? You gotta go to the sheriff. Look who he's with!"

"I know, but I don't want to say anything, especially to my family."

"Why?"

"I took these pictures accidentally when I was in my car ... crying. I don't know if Cowboy and I will ever go out again. I don't want anyone in my family to hold it against him that he made me cry for hours because he said I wish I never met you..."

"He wouldn't say that. You heard wrong." Paloma protested.

"He did," Ruth argued back, "but that's not the point. I can't say I took these pictures without telling everyone why I was there. I was supposed to be in math class."

"What are you going to do?"

"Don't know. If the sheriff suspects foul play, then I'll have to say something. If they rule it an accidental death, or a suicide, or natural causes, I'll keep my mouth shut."

"Speaking of Gills being a creep," Paloma changed the subject, "I need your help."

"What are you planning?" Ruth was cautious.

"There's something wrong with her, and we're going to find out what it is."

"How do we do that?" Ruth scoffed at her.

"It's too hard to spy on her at school."

"Maybe she has nothing to hide?" Ruth suggested.

"I've been in her homeroom and on the newspaper for four years. She's never been warm and fuzzy, but she ripped into me for two days over my article idea. Believe me when I tell you something is going on. Tonight we're going to find every scrap of information on Dr. Elizabeth Gills we can."

Ruth looked at Paloma like she had a screw loose.

"Come on, Ruth. She has it in for you and Mr. Silver too. That was nasty to write an anonymous letter to Rodriguez."

Ruth nodded in agreement, then shook with disgust.

"And now you have what is probably the last picture of Bowman alive, and who is he with?"

"Okay, okay," Ruth conceded, "But what are we looking for?"

"Not sure, but I'll know when we find it!"

★ ★ ★

Ruth was in the AP English room. Cowboy's desk was covered in dozens and dozens of cupcakes, each with a little candle on it. *Stupid Missy, there should only be twenty-four of them. Why did she bring so many?* She looked around the packed room. From freshman to the lunch ladies, every female in school stood in the classroom singing Happy Birthday, dear Cowboy...

"Wait!" she shouted above the din, "Only I call him that!"

Through the classroom door rode Cowboy on Remington, "Why aren't you singing Ruth? You're the only one not singing."

"Why should I sing? You wish you never met me."

"That's not what Paloma says," he remarked.

Suddenly she didn't care who was watching, she pulled him off of his horse and said, "I'll give you something better for your birthday," before she kissed him.

Dr. Gills grabbed her and shrieked, "You're not old enough. He needs a real woman!"

Mr. Rodriguez appeared and yelled, "You told me nothing was going on between you–now look at you!"

She looked down at herself. She was naked, *OH CRAP! Why does this always happen to me?*

Ruth sat bolt upright in bed. Slowly she realized it had been a dream and gradually, last night flooded her mind. She and Paloma had spent hours searching websites, looking for information on Gills. It was after midnight when Paloma's tenacity and perseverance paid off. The county's website had provided the link to teachers' performance reviews.

Ruth looked over at Paloma. She was curled up on the top of the bed. Her laptop gripped tightly in her arms. Ruth looked at the clock, seven-thirty. She got quietly out of bed and tipped toed around to her best friend. She eased the laptop out of her grip.

Paloma resisted, cracked one eyelid and in a hoarse voice whispered, "Ruth, I did it, I did it."

"That's good P, go back to sleep."

"I found it. She's a fake. It's not real."

"What time did you come to bed?"

"Three, maybe four."

"Go back to sleep, and tell me in a little bit, okay?"

"Okay," Paloma drifted back to sleep as Ruth covered her with the comforter and set her laptop aside.

By ten-thirty Ruth finished her barn chores. Paloma had rejoined the land of the living, dressed, and packed.

"Do you mind taking me home, Ruth? I need to do more fact-checking before I decide what to do with this information."

"Yes, I do mind. My mom's making a big brunch for you. Second, I want to know what's going on, what did you find, what's not real?"

"I don't want to say anything until I check the details."

"Don't you dare try that with me," Ruth warned. "You know about Cowboy and me, and I want to know about you and Dr. Gills."

"All right, we'll eat, we'll take a walk, and then you'll take me home?"

"Deal."

Brunch was delicious. The subject of Mr. Bowman surfaced, but since no one was in band, it quickly faded. Afterward, Ruth and Paloma struck out to their old treehouse on the edge of the woods. The old platform Ed built in a giant cottonwood tree had weathered the years well.

"You were still awake when I found the website with all the teachers' info, right?" Paloma asked.

"Yes. I now know Cowboy's birthday is October sixth."

"I found out Gills received her undergrad degree from Green Brook."

"What's Green Brook?" Ruth asked.

"It started out as a junior college, but in the early eighties, it was awarded its accreditation as a four-year community college."

"Okay, so for undergrad, she went to a community college."

"She started teaching in the elementary schools, and she worked on her masters at a local branch of the state university. That took her another five years. After she got her master's, she began teaching at the high school."

"Long time to get a master's. Was she doing it part-time while she taught?"

"I don't know," Paloma answered, "What's interesting is just one year ago, she applied for funding to further her education and receive her Ph.D."

"So you're saying it took her five years to complete her masters but less than a year to get her Ph.D.?" Ruth caught on.

"Yup. And the coup de grâce is that her Ph.D. is from an online university–I think the name is Universal University."

"What's Universal University?" Ruth felt clueless.

"It's one of the facts I need to recheck, but I am ninety-nine point nine nine nine percent sure that it is a diploma mill. I'm not even sure if it's an accredited institution." Paloma beamed when Ruth's mouth gaped. "I also did a quick scan of other teachers, and if I'm right, I've found four others who have degrees from the same online school."

"This is unbelievable Paloma, what are you going to do?"

"I'm not sure. I want to recheck all my facts. Then, hopefully, I can get the right person to listen to me. I'm going to email you all my findings, just in case."

"In case what?"

"In case my computer crashes, and I lose all my info. In case Gills catches wind of what I'm doing and something nefarious happens to me."

"Paloma, don't say that!"

Paloma smiled, "At least now I know one thing."

"What?" Ruth asked.

"I know why she canned my story."

"That's what this all really comes down to, isn't it?"

Paloma squirmed, "It was a great idea for a story."

Chapter 12

AFTER SUFFOCATING BOWMAN, she left the school unseen. She headed to the liquor store, bought a supply of bourbon, and went home to soothe her misery.

She didn't feel too bad the next morning, so she burned the blouse and tissues in an old can outback. Luckily, her son wasn't home. She'd been doing fine until that night when the ten o'clock news led with the story of Bill Bowman being found dead in his office. Hearing it announced out loud hit her harder than she'd expected. She'd changed from her sweats into one of her black leather biker chick outfits, hopped onto her Ninja, and took off to Mike's.

She hadn't been back since the night she'd torched Alverez's car. All the regulars were there, and one new guy. A skinhead, but cute. Tall, muscular, young; *why did everyone seem to be so young lately?*

"Yea, I come down from South Dakota. Looking for work," he told her, but he'd asked a lot of questions—too many questions for her liking.

Hours later, she cracked open one eye. *Ow... light hurts.* She looked at the clock. It was spinning and out of focus, but it looked like it said ten-forty-five. *What day is it?* She had to think long and hard, but she knew she was in her own bed and was fairly certain it was Sunday. She'd never gotten that drunk two days in a row, ever before. *Why did I do shots? Why did I kill two men in cold blood?... Necessity.*

Her head felt like railroad spikes had been driven through it and left there to rust. Her mouth felt like it was stuffed with cotton. Her first attempt to get up told her that her body wasn't about to cooperate with her intentions of rising and shining. She drifted back into an uneasy sleep. It was past noon when she awoke and forced herself into the shower. While the hot water enveloped her body, she thought about Bowman. If she hadn't sold that tuba, he wouldn't have had to die. But when Wally had offered her six thousand dollars for a used instrument, how could she have passed that up?

She got out of the shower, and her son walked into the bathroom, "You ever hear of knocking?" she scolded as she wrapped herself in a towel.

"It's not like I haven't seen you naked before."

"It's called respect. Heard of it?"

"Whatever." He had obviously just gotten up himself and lifted the toilet seat to pee. She left the bathroom to dry off and dress in her bedroom.

When he finished, he followed her to her room, "I need some money." He looked around the room for her purse.

"Go get a job."

"No, really, Ma, I need some green."

"No, really, go get a job." She looked at him; he looked just like his father at that age. Behaved just like his father too. She wouldn't be surprised if one day he suffered the same fate as his father. "I'm finished with you. You've got six months. You hear me SIX MONTHS. I'm putting this house up for sale. You need to get yourself a job, a place to live, and a life."

"Yeah, right, whadda you gonna do if you sell this house?"

"Don't you worry about me. I know how to take care of myself. You don't. Now get out of my room and let me get dressed!" She shoved him out of her room and closed the door.

Well, I guess that's that. I've got six months, and then I move on with my life. Even though her body still felt like crap, it felt good to make a decision and have a plan. *I'll retire as soon as the house sells. I'll keep a low profile till then, make do with the money I already have. Mexico, here I come.*

Chapter 13

SOON AFTER BOWMAN'S body was discovered, the authorities released the autopsy and ballistics reports for Hector Alverez. Alverez's death was deemed a homicide.

Authorities had not released Bowman's findings to the media, so the public was doing a lot of speculating. A forensic team had worked on his office. Everyone knew someone had trashed it and that they found him under his desk undressed from the waist down. All the paper revealed was that Bowman's death was considered suspicious.

As they walked into AP English, Paloma asked, "Ruth, it's been three weeks. Are you going to say anything about those pictures of Gills and Bowman?"

"I don't know. I know Gills is no angel, but it's a big leap to go from a fake diploma to murderer."

"Yeah, but the sheriff's department is asking for anyone with information to step forward."

"Ugh. Alright, I think I still have Sheriff Davis' card."

Paloma asked, "Have you been reading what I've sent you?"

"Every word, and I'm saving it on a flash drive, so there's an extra copy. Paloma, what you've found is extraordinary. You've got to go public with this story and not the school's paper or blog."

"I have to find the right venue; otherwise, all my work will be wasted. Do you think the sheriff would have any interest in it?"

Mr. Silver closed the classroom door.

★ ★ ★

Ruth's appointment with Sheriff Davis was for twelve-thirty on Tuesday during his lunch break.

She walked into the lobby of the sheriff's department. A sign directed her to pick up a phone and dial 0; she did. She told the voice on the other end she had a meeting with Sheriff Davis and the voice told her someone would be with her shortly. The lobby was a plain white room with the sign and phone, two plastic chairs, and a locked door leading to the sheriff's department's inner workings.

The door opened. A tall, good-looking officer with a buzz cut asked her to follow him. He looked familiar, but she couldn't place him. He led her down a hall to a door that read Sheriff Davis.

The officer knocked on the door, and a mumble came from the other side. The young man opened the door. Davis was on the phone, but he waved for them to enter as he finished his conversation.

As he hung up the phone, he said, "Well hello there, Miss Willows. Thanks, Tommy."

"Oh my gosh, it's you, Officer Clark?" Ruth was a little taken aback, "Last time I saw you, you had hair."

Tommy turned beet red all the way to the top of his shaved head. Sheriff Davis answered for him, "Officer Clark's been on special assignment." Tommy left. "Now, what can I do for you, Ruth."

"I'm not sure how to begin. I have two items to discuss with you. The first one, it might be a waste of time, I don't know..."

"Well, spit it out," Sheriff Davis advised as he dug into his bagged lunch.

"I accidentally took a picture of Mr. Bowman shortly before his death. He was walking through the parking lot into the building where his office is, well was, whatever."

"All right, and why would this be significant?"

"He was entering the building with Mrs. Gills, head of the English department."

"I see." Davis thought for a moment and took a bite of his sandwich, "And how did you accidentally take this picture?"

"That's kinda a long story. Let's just say that I was in my truck getting ready to leave. I was checking my camera to make sure I hadn't broken it cause I dropped it on the floor of the truck, and so I snapped a few pictures, and they happened to be in some of them."

"So if you were leaving, this was around three o'clock?"

"No, it was earlier than that. I attend a math class at the university, so I usually leave the high school by noon."

"So this was at noon then?"

"No, sir, it was later than that. I had been sitting in my car for a while."

"What time was it exactly when you saw Bowman and Gills together?" Davis was a kind man, but his patience was wearing a little thin.

"I'm sorry, but I don't know the exact time. It was between twelve-thirty and two-thirty."

"How darn long were you sitting in your car?"

"Paloma found me just before three o'clock."

"Found you? What were you doing in the parking lot of the school for two hours?"

Ruth cringed.

"Were you alone?" Davis continued his questions.

"Yes, sir."

"Do you want to explain yourself?" Davis' voice sounded irritated.

"Do I have to?"

"If you want me to believe you!" Davis took a breath, "Start from the beginning, Ruth, and try to keep to the facts, okay?"

She went through the story of Derrick and how he ran into Ken, Paloma, and herself in the parking lot the previous day.

"How did I know my nephew's name would turn up in this?" Davis interrupted, and he offered Ruth one of his homemade chocolate chip cookies.

She told him about the letter and the meeting with Mr. Rodriguez.

"I still don't understand Ruth. If Rodriguez told you and Kenny not to worry about the letter, why were you in your truck for such a long time?"

"I was just... upset... and being... stupid." was all she would say. "I lost track of time, and I missed my math class, which I didn't realize until Paloma banged on my window."

"You must have been mighty upset." Davis raised his eyebrows and looked at her. She was staring at her hands in her lap. He'd seen that look. She was embarrassed, and she was trying to keep her emotions from getting the best of her. "What did my nephew do to upset you so badly?"

She looked at him with surprise, and then tears filled her eyes. The last thing she wanted to do was to blubber to Ken's uncle,

"It was stupid," she said as she blinked back the tears. Davis said nothing; he just continued to watch her. "He kinda... as we left Mr. Rodriguez's office... said he wished he'd never met me."

Davis furrowed his brow, "Ouch, that musta hurt."

"Yes sir, it did." She regained some composure and sounded very matter of fact.

"I assume you have these pictures with you?"

She handed him the camera. The first picture he came to was of Ken. The next was of Bowman and Gills.

"Well, it's no smoking gun, but it raises a few questions. You wouldn't happen to have a copy of these, would you?"

Control regained, Ruth pulled out her flash drive, "I do, as well as my next piece of business."

Davis raised one eyebrow and plugged the drive into his computer. Ruth launched into her next story. She went right to the facts, "Mrs. Gills' Ph.D. is fake, gotten from an online diploma mill. There are one hundred and ten teachers at the high school; seventy-five have advanced degrees. Out of that seventy-five, nine teachers had masters and or doctorates that are from online schools. There are six staffers; three cafeteria workers, two secretaries, and one janitor who had received advanced degrees online. Some online schools are legit; some are questionable. Paloma has the facts to support her findings. The calculations at the bottom show how much this potential fraud is costing taxpayers."

Sheriff Davis studied the information on his screen, blew out a long whistle, and rubbed his head. "When do you ladies have time for all this?"

"It's mostly Paloma's work. She had a personal interest in it."

"As sheriff, I don't have the authority to bring charges against these people. But I know someone who can help."

"Who?" Ruth asked.

"José Pluma. He's a reporter. The best one I know, and more importantly, the only one I trust." Ruth listened to Davis's instructions, "Take his card and give it to your friend, Paloma. I'll give José a call to let him know what's going on. I think he'll find this a fascinating story. In the meantime, don't either of you say anything about this to anyone. Do you understand me?"

"Yes, sir."

"I mean no one. No playing Nancy Drew and Bess Marvin." Ruth fervently nodded her head in agreement. "You did the right thing coming here. I don't want you thinking you two should take the matter into your own hands."

"We won't, sir."

"And as for that nephew of mine," Sheriff Davis wiped his hands on a paper napkin and came around to lean on the front of the desk. He studied Ruth again for a moment. "When I saw you in the rodeo, and he told me who you were, I could tell from the look in his eyes that you are mighty special to him. The two of you are in quite a predicament right now, and it can't be easy for either of you." Ruth didn't know how to reply to Sheriff Davis, so she just nodded and let him continue. "I don't have any sage advice for you," he shook his head. "He's a fine young man. Sometimes people don't always say the right things or what they mean to say in the heat of the moment. Be patient is all I can say."

Chapter 14

PALOMA WATCHED THE man with curly grey hair and goatee exit the elevator and cross the lobby of The Sentinel toward her. José Pluma gave her a firm handshake and the five-dollar tour. She was beyond thrilled to be in a real newsroom. When they finally sat in his cubicle, he couldn't help but interview her, "What draws you to journalism? Why would you want to be a reporter?"

"I've wanted to be an investigative reporter since I learned about Woodward and Bernstein and the Watergate scandal. I mean, the whole Deep Throat thing sounds like something out of a spy novel."

Pluma replied, "I'd have half a mind to walk you out of this building right now if I hadn't already read your work."

Paloma's heart sunk as Pluma continued. "This job isn't about being glamorous. It's about research, and double and triple-checking facts, interviewing people, diving through archives, and rechecking the facts.."

Only momentarily deflated, Paloma defended herself, "You asked me what drew me into journalism. Well, learning about those reporters during Watergate fascinated me and made me want to learn more. And everything I learn about reporting only makes me more excited and more interested in pursuing it as a career. I don't think it's glamorous, but I think it's important... and exciting."

Pluma studied her for a long moment, "Duly noted." He continued, "So tell me why you decided your teacher, um, Dr. Gills, needed your investigative prowess?"

Paloma launched into the story of Gills and the berating of her newspaper story, "After knowing her for four years, I knew something was up with her, so I decided to find out."

"Ideas have come from stranger places," Pluma grimaced and continued, "Now, your piece is good, but I can't run it as it is. Your investigation is incomplete. We'll need more sources to corroborate the information. I make sure I have all my ducks in a row before I run a story with my byline."

Paloma nodded, not at all sure what to say.

"I could see expanding this investigation to include the entire school district and retired employees." he continued. "I would name you only as an anonymous source. I don't want you to have any more trouble in school. Feathers could get ruffled, things could get ugly,"

"Oh," Paloma was a little stunned, "I didn't think about that."

"If you want to walk away from this story, I understand. I promise to do my best. It's a story that needs to be told. If you want to see it through, you'd have to be very tight-lipped. I could take you on as an unpaid intern if you think that would be interesting."

★ ★ ★

"That's so great, Paloma! Are you going to do it?" Ruth squealed as they walked out of school Thursday afternoon.

"My parents weren't too excited, but I reminded them a job like this would look good on my college apps."

"I am so glad I have mine done," Ruth interjected.

Paloma continued, "So as long as I keep my grades up, they said okay."

"I am so proud of you." Ruth asked as they got in her truck, "When do you start, and when do the articles come out?"

"I'll call when I get home to tell him I can do the internship. The first article should run in a few weeks."

★ ★ ★

A week after the university's midterms were midterms for the high school. Teachers were to inform all students of their midterm grades.

White slips were passed out at the end of AP English. Ruth saw a note in Cowboy's handwriting, 'Please see me after class.' She was stunned. There was no grade on the little black line where the 'A' was supposed to be, just his note.

Paloma waved her white slip of paper like a flag to get Ruth's attention. She saw that Paloma had an 'A.'

Paloma waited for Ruth to flash her paper back. One look into Ruth's eyes, and she grabbed the paper for herself. A look of puzzlement washed over Paloma's face as the bell rang and the class exited.

"What do you think this means?" Paloma whispered. They both noticed that Missy and two of her friends were hanging back as well.

"I don't know," Ruth whispered back.

"Are you doing badly in here?"

"I don't think so," Ruth shrugged. "Guess I'll find out."

Paloma mouthed, "Call me later," as she left the room.

Ruth nodded and walked up to Ken's desk.

Ken looked up at her and then to the three girls hanging by the door, "Ladies, I don't have time to chitchat today."

"Okay, c'mon Ruth, we'll walk down to lunch." Missy flashed a bogus grin.

Surprised that Missy actually used her name, Ruth said, "No thanks, I go off campus after this class."

"We'll walk you downstairs," Missy insisted.

"Ladies, I'd like a moment of Miss Willows' time, if you don't mind," Ken interrupted. As the threesome sauntered out of the room, Ruth overheard Missy snidely remark, "I can't believe the brain bag is failing."

"Is this about my grade?" Ruth asked.

"Just a minute," Ken stood, crossed to the open door, and closed it. He chuckled, "You would not believe the things those three tell me in their writing assignments. Sometimes I feel more like I'm reading their diaries rather than grading a paper."

Ruth was in no mood for small talk, even if it was an interesting tidbit. "I have a class after this," Ruth announced.

"I'm aware of that."

Ken walked back to her and pulled an empty chair next to the far side of his desk, facing him. "You can sit if you like."

"I'd like to know my grade." Ruth was antsy, but she sat.

He sat, "Oh, it's an 'A' I think; I can look it up."

Even as she wrestled with anxiety, it felt normal to sit and talk with him.

"If this isn't about my grade... then why did you ask me to stay?" Ruth tried to stay focused.

He took a deep breath, "I need to talk to you."

Oh no, a terrible thought flashed through Ruth's head, *he's seeing someone. He's dating someone and feels like he has to come clean with me before he can move on. Oh no, I really don't want to hear this.*

"I didn't say what you thought I said," he began.

"Who is she?" She talked over him.

"What did you say?" Ken looked at her, confused.

"What did I say? What did you say?" She replied.

"I didn't say what you thought I said."

"You didn't say what I thought you said?" she repeated. "Did you not say what I thought you said just now or was that something I thought you said before that you didn't say?"

Ken was flummoxed. "Can we start this conversation again?"

"Please," she agreed.

Hidden by his desk, he took hold of her hands. "You told Uncle Bob I said I wished I never met you. I'm not sure what possessed you to talk to him about...us...but I never said that. I would never say that. I'm hurt you would think I would."

"But I heard you. The day we left Rodriguez's office, I'm sure you were angry Gills wrote that letter, so I understand ... but I heard you."

"What does Dr. Gills?... Never mind. I said I wished I'd never, but it wasn't about you." He looked her straight in the eyes, leaned forward, and whispered, "I wanted to say I wished I had never taken this job. I held my tongue because I didn't want my boss to hear."

Shocked, she asked, "But... but why?"

He interlaced their fingers, "C'mon Baby Doll, if I wasn't teaching here, we wouldn't have all these... complications. I took this job for the money, and believe me, after six years of school, I need it."

"But what would you've done?" she asked, relishing the feeling of his touch.

"I had two offers; one from here and one from St. Joseph's Catholic. I went to St. Joseph's. I would've liked to teach there. But here I get twice the money; there I get twice the work."

There were so many things she wanted to say to him, but all that came out was, "I...I... I didn't know. I thought you hated me for almost getting you fired... and..." she trailed off.

Ken loved it when her hair was down and fell over her shoulders. She was so beautiful. He could see faint freckles on her nose. He wanted to kiss her pink, moist lips. It'd seemed during the last nine weeks and five days since he had last kissed her (but who's counting) that "they" had been just a dream. But now, he knew his feelings were as real as could be.

A bell rang, interrupting their connection.

Ruth jumped, “I have to go.” She scrambled to untangle herself from her thoughts and jumped to her feet.

“I have a class coming,” he said.

Students were at the door. Ruth pushed past the underclassmen as she left, wondering what had just happened.

Chapter 15

THE STORY BROKE on the first Friday of November. The news of teachers with bogus diplomas spread like wildfire.

José Pluma's digging had identified several teachers, cafeteria workers, a retired supervisor, a night janitor, and both main office secretaries who had received one or more dubious online diplomas and were benefiting financially from the questionable degrees. Names were named, flashed across television screens, and raked over the proverbial coals of the news cycle.

State police were called to the school to remove news crews vying for a glimpse of anyone connected to the story. High school classes were canceled until Monday. Employees named in the scandal were directed to take six days' vacation until the next school board meeting.

Ruth had said nothing to her family about her or Paloma's part in the saga. Constance and Joe were having their midmorning coffee break when Ruth returned home.

"My goodness Ruthie," Constance loved a juicy news story, "I can't believe the news today. Did they really need to send you all home?"

"Television news crews were pretty persistent. They had to be thrown off school property."

"Do you know any of ... those people–the ones they're all talking about?" Constance sounded a little star-struck.

"Duh... yeah. I know them, except for the night janitor. I see them every day. I mean, it was Paloma's beef with Mrs. Gills that started the whole thing in the first place." Ruth casually replied.

Constance and Joe stared at her. The information was a bombshell. "Ruth, what do you mean?" her mother's tone turned serious.

"Oh, I'm so sorry," her apology was sincere, "I forgot you didn't know."

"Maybe you better explain Grand-baby."

She told them about Paloma's story for the school newspaper and how Dr. Gills had debased her. She confessed that the night Paloma had stayed over was the night they'd begun their research on Dr. Gills.

"That's it, no more computers, or cell phones or electronics in yours or Grace's bedroom! How am I supposed to know what you're up to? How am I supposed to protect you from predators when you have all those electronics behind closed doors?" Constance exclaimed.

"I'm a little old for doing my homework on the dining room table."

"You most certainly are not!"

"Calm down, Connie. Be proud of your girl." Joe interjected.

"I am proud of her, but I had no idea of what was going on right under my own nose."

"It's not like we were dealing drugs." Ruth protested. "I couldn't say anything because Sheriff Davis told us not to breathe a word to anyone. José Pluma didn't put Paloma's name in the article to protect her."

"The Sheriff told you not to say anything? Doesn't that prove that what you were doing was dangerous?" Constance was getting more incensed with each explanation. "How did you get so friendly with the sheriff, anyway? Do you have his number and call him up every time you have a problem?"

"As a matter of fact, I do," Ruth answered.

"Since when?"

"Since I found a dead body in school!"

That statement hung in the air for a while, and the three of them just looked at each other.

"She's got ya there, Connie," Joe felt the need to point that out.

Constance went to her daughter and put her arms around her, "I'm sorry, Ruthie. I'm shocked you had anything to do with this. I wish you would have trusted me, us, your family enough to have said something. We would never betray your confidence."

"You're right, Mom, I should have."

"It scares me to think you and Paloma are doing something that could get you hurt," Constance continued. "When you say that people want you to keep quiet for your own protection, that doesn't make me feel good."

"I didn't think of it like that," Ruth admitted.

"And I'm sorry that you had to find that poor man, dead in your school ... to find that in school... it's unthinkable."

"It's not the dead body that's so bad," Ruth looked at her mom and then Joe, "it's the who did it that bothers me."

★ ★ ★

With nothing to distract her from the inevitable, Ruth finally opened the manila folder to begin her math paper.

"Ugh, how much data did Lezza give me?" She ran her thumb over the thick edge of the papers.

She looked at her cell phone. *I wonder what Cowboy's doing?* Not that she could call him. Mom and Granddaddy were doing something with the horses. Daddy was at work.

"For crying out loud, Ruth," she said, "just get on with it!"

She opened the folder. The first page's heading read District's Budget 1999, followed by a spreadsheet four pages long. The next heading read District's Budget 2000; it was followed by another four-page spreadsheet.

She flipped through the years 2001, 2002, 2003. *This has got to be more than enough data,* she thought. She removed the years 2000 through 2003, closed the manila folder, and set it out of her way.

She looked over the spreadsheets. Each department had its own budget and pages giving detailed spending reports. It wasn't surprising that all the departments spent every cent of their budget. Quite a few departments had gone over budget. Several departments had gone way over budget. Ruth got out a pencil and notepad and went to work playing with the numbers.

It was five-thirty before Ruth knew it. Grace and Constance were downstairs, and Daddy would be home soon. As for her paper, why was nothing ever easy? There were no organizational problems this time–like it had been when Cowboy had helped her. Her mind wandered back to that day in the library; *that was the first time he'd kissed me and held my hand.* She could still feel the touch of his lips on her cheek. *That seems like years ago...*

This paper was the issue now. She'd chosen two theories that Professor Langley had discussed in class; one involving probability and one using inferential statistics. Her idea was to use both methods to predict how much the budget would grow for the next year. Considering that the data was old, and she didn't really need to predict anything, the calculations should have been the easiest part. They weren't. No matter what she tried, the numbers didn't... well... they didn't add up.

A car door slammed. She looked out her window, five till six and completely dark, winter was just around the corner. Daddy was home. It was time to join the family.

After dinner, Ruth asked, "Daddy, Granddaddy, can you help me with something?"

"Sure, honey, what is it?" Ed answered.

She asked them to wait, and she returned with her data, outline, and pad of scratch paper. She explained the assignment, walked them through her outline, and then got to her problem.

"It doesn't matter what kind of calculations I do. These numbers are just not right. I've tried different trend analysis, and it comes out wrong. I mean, I have the budget for the next year in front of me, so I know it's wrong. It's like I'm missing a huge piece of information or every year more money goes missing."

Joe waded through her work. "You know, Grand-baby, most of this is way beyond me. I used to do my own books before your mom came along, but I think I can still balance a ledger sheet."

"I haven't done these sorts of stats for a long time, but I'll give it a try," Ed added.

She watched them for a while, then she wandered off. They were still at it when she returned, "Have you two come up with anything yet?"

"Yeah, neither of us wants to go back to school," Ed answered.

"Thanks, Daddy. How about anything that can help me?"

"Well, you're right, something is amiss. But I couldn't tell you what," Ed's analysis didn't help much.

"When you forget all those fancy equations and whatnot," Joe continued for his son, "and just balance it all with simple arithmetic, it doesn't balance correctly. Now, these budgets are so old, who knows what's missing. You could be missing an entire page of spending that we'll never know about."

"Your Granddaddy's right, honey. Your calculations seem fine. I think it's your data that's flawed."

She looked at her father and grandfather, "What should I do? I had a hard enough time coming up with this idea for a paper. I don't want to start all over again."

"Who said you had to start all over again?" Joe put his arm around her, "just make up what you might be missing."

"What," she cried, "No, it's supposed to be real data. I can't make stuff up."

"Fine then, I will." Joe offered.

"Look, honey," Her dad tried to convince her, "it is real data. You said that all these budgets had been transferred to computer a year or two ago. It's very likely that some miscellaneous expenses or whole pages never got entered when they typed in the data. No one is going to audit budgets from twenty years ago, and quite frankly, I'm surprised they even bothered inputting them."

"I guess Colonel Sanders won't know if I make up two or three entries that cover the differences." Ruth gave in.

She thanked and kissed her Daddy and Granddaddy, picked up all the papers, and put them away.

★ ★ ★

The November Board of Education meeting was Standing Room Only. The room overflowed with concerned taxpayers and the media. José Pluma had arrived early. Paloma and her father sat next to him.

In typical board fashion, they began the meeting twenty minutes late and blamed it on the crowd. They announced they would adjourn at ten p.m. sharp, regardless of how far they got into the agenda. This caused quite an uproar. Hecklers were told they would be removed if they didn't sit down and shut up.

Slowly and methodically, the board slogged through its agenda. It wasn't until nine-forty-five when the subject of employees possessing fraudulent degrees was addressed. The attorney for the board stood and addressed the crowd with a prepared statement.

"He basically told everyone that they weren't going to do anything about it!" Paloma screamed into the cell phone from the passenger seat of her father's car.

"How can they do nothing?" Ruth was flabbergasted.

"The statement said that the school district and the Board of Education took these allegations very seriously and needed to do their own investigation to determine the validity of the charges." She read to Ruth from her own notes.

"Is that it?" Ruth was incensed.

"Mr. Pluma said it was typical. No one wants to be blamed for letting the situation get this bad. We'll keep up the investigation and the media coverage. Everyone gets looked into now; the BoE, school superintendent, attorney, everyone. Hopefully, something will be resolved before the end of the school year."

"June—you're kidding!"

Chapter 16

THE WHIRL OF excitement named Aunt Celia arrived for Thanksgiving. Aunt Cee was full of laughter and fun and surprises By Saturday afternoon Ruth was a little anxious, "Mom, I love Aunt Cee but..."

"Yes..."

"I need to get some schoolwork done."

"Okay."

"The university's library is open late tonight. I need fewer distractions for a few hours."

"You better go while Grace and Cee are digging through closets, or you'll never get out of here."

Ruth grabbed her laptop and left.

A few dozen people occupied the library. It reminded Ruth of the summer. She claimed her favorite table and went to work. By six-thirty p.m., she had finished her math paper. She added an extra page to each expense report that totaled the amount missing from each budget. All the calculations worked out nicely, and she thought her paper did an excellent job illustrating her knowledge of the theories she'd chosen.

She didn't feel like leaving. She moved to a big, comfy chair and pulled out her copy of Hamlet. She leafed through it, hoping for an idea for her English paper.

As she scanned the paperback, she remembered scenes from the film they'd watched in class. It had been a long film. Cowboy still ignored her even after their little midterm chat. Her mind began to wander. The movie, class, Cowboy... he'd moved his chair to the corner of the classroom where she and Paloma sat. She'd pretended that they were on a date when he sat next to her. *I'm such an idiot.*

But the paper, the movie... she liked it when they all died. She felt Hamlet got what he deserved. He'd been betrayed, but he was such a histrionic brat. *How else could it end? If I feel sorry for anyone, it's Ophelia. She got used and abused by everyone. She truly loved Hamlet. Then he crushed her like a worthless piece of paper...* There was her paper! She grabbed her notepad and feverishly scribbled ideas. Once she had her thoughts down, she organized them into an outline. *Curse him and his outlines.*

Ruth wanted to reference a quote she'd remembered from Macbeth, so with notes in hand, she went to the stacks where Shakespeare's works waited. She grabbed The Complete Works of William Shakespeare, sat on the floor, and began leafing through it.

She didn't know how long she'd been sitting there when a voice whispered in her ear, "Are you conquering the Bard's entire library in one fell swoop, Baby Doll?"

Cowboy's face hovered mere inches from hers. He knelt on the floor beside her, "I love the plays, but I'm not partial to his sonnets." He ran his finger over the book and her fingertips. "I much prefer John Donne's view on love-or Bobby Burns, if you'd like more lusty poetry."

Shocked at his proximity, she blushed at him, unable to speak. A heavy, sweet scent was on his breath.

He picked up her notepad and whispered the first line, "The Plight of Ophelia."

She whispered back, "Please don't. You'll get the paper when it's finished."

Ken's head swam with the liquor he had drunk that afternoon. It swam with her sweet scent and the hundred things he wanted to say to her. Her lips were so close, he felt he couldn't breathe again unless he kissed her. He relinquished the notepad and brushed his lips past hers.

"I've never read Bobby Burns," she said, flustered.

At that moment, she didn't care if she read anything ever again. If he didn't kiss her, she was going to explode. *Maybe I should kiss him? No, I can't...*

Her internal argument was moot. He gave in first and kissed her softly on the lips.

The rush of emotions almost brought tears to her eyes. He looked at her and kissed her lips again. Reality melted away. They kissed long and deep before an annoying voice jerked them into the present.

"My God, Kenny! I leave you alone for one minute, and you go snoggin' the first coed you find with a book of poetry in her hand." A beautiful redhead with bright green eyes snapped, "If I'd have known you were that eager, we could have left that reception, and I would've read you poetry naked." Her shoulder-length hair bounced in soft waves with her apparent irritation.

Ken got to his feet with a surly look. Ruth looked up at the beautiful stranger. She was dressed to the nines.

Ruth looked at Cowboy. He was dressed up too. *They must be on a date.* She was panic-stricken. *Why the hell did he kiss me if he's with another woman?* She felt that sickening pain return to her stomach.

"Knock it off, Ellie," was Ken's terse response. He took Ruth's hands and helped her to her feet. He held her hand as he said, "Ruth, this is Professor Ellie Pearson. She teaches in the theater department. We're co-authoring the play I told you about." He looked back at the redhead, "Ellie, this is Ruth Willows." No further explanation of their relationship was offered.

"I spent the last three hours getting you good and liquored up so I could take advantage of you, and this is the thanks I get? Did you know she'd be here?"

Ruth stammered, "I was working. I didn't know you were on a date..."

"We're not," Ken said flatly.

Ellie huffed.

"We attended a faculty reception for a visiting playwright. One who will be judging our not yet finished play in a competition very soon." He glared at Ellie, then turned to Ruth. "Ellie is an old friend,"

"I am not an old friend," Ellie quickly corrected him, "I am a friend he has known for a long time."

"Ellie and my sister were best friends growing up. Ellie is like another sister to me."

"You really know how to sweet-talk a girl Kenny." Ellie sidled up beside him, not acting at all like a sister. "I have the DVD I wanted you to see. I'm ready to go unless you want to go on," she chucked her head towards Ruth, "a bit longer."

"You can come with us if you like," Ellie offered to Ruth, "we'll just be watching this and bickering like an old married couple."

Ruth's mind raced. She didn't understand where Ellie was coming from. And what was with Cowboy? He was either boiling hot or ice cold. "No, thank you," she answered politely, "I have...things...people...to get back to."

Ellie shrugged, "Suit yourself," and she trounced off.

Ken looked into Ruth's eyes, still holding her hand. For the first time, she didn't want to kiss him. She was exasperated. He took a step forward, but she stepped back. She held his gaze. Shocked, he dropped her hand and walked away.

Ruth picked up her notepad and re-shelved the book. She made sure Ken and Ellie had left before she went back to get her bag. By the time she packed up her belongings, she was shaking. She grew angrier with each passing moment. *He always manages to turn his back and leave me to pick up the pieces by myself. I bet anything that he'll ignore me in class on Monday.* It felt like pieces of her soul were being torn apart. *Ha, she thought, the plight of Ophelia – the plight of Ruth is more like it.*

Chapter 17

THE DECEMBER'S BOE meeting was again packed by an extra-large crowd of concerned citizens, Paloma, her father, and Pluma. After a month of terrible publicity, all eight board members, along with the superintendent of schools, head of teacher's union, and a representative from the state board, decided to deal with the problem head-on rather than sweep it under the rug. The state board representative stated their position and concerns.

Paloma took notes as the woman from the state spoke.

- State board governing body...
- This issue is out of the scope of this board...
- Not in the position to tell districts how to negotiate union contracts...
- Can only recommend disciplinary actions since no law was broken...
- Slight concern that the district would support non-accredited institutions...

Blah, Blah, Blah, thought Paloma, *how much rhetoric can one person spout?*

Next up was Superintendent of Schools, Dr. Hulls. Paloma had done her research on him. He'd attended two public universities. They were real schools and real degrees. Much of what he had to say was more of the same, but Paloma made a note of:

-Need to clarify the contract to state that only accredited school diplomas will be recognized.

The principals rose next: Mr. Rodriguez from the high school and the principals from the middle school and elementary school all spoke of the high-quality work they received from their employees regardless of where they received their education. The temperature went up a few degrees when board member Sally Mitchell spoke up. Seems she had done some research on her own. Paloma put exclamation points and stars next to Ms. Mitchell's name in her notes. Mitchell said that she had recently attempted to get a degree from the same website the majority of employees had used.

"Turns out," Ms. Mitchell had a sassy twang as she flipped her short strawberry blonde hair from her eyes, "that for as little as five hundred dollars can get myself a Ph.D. based on my life experience. Now, do you think, Mr. Rodriguez, that I should receive the same monetary rewards as someone who studied and worked for their degree all because I know how to fill out a reimbursement voucher and type my address into a computer?"

"I'm not here to make that call, Ms. Mitchell. I am here to stand by my staff and vouch for their abilities to do their jobs well." Rodriguez retorted.

The board made two decisions: one to form an ad hoc committee to study all the ramifications of paying employees for degrees earned from non-accredited schools, and two that all current employees with questionable advanced degrees would be subject to a salary rollback. The money would be held in escrow until the committee's recommendations could be reviewed, and a final decision could be reached. The ad hoc committee had until the June board meeting to present their findings.

"The board acted surprisingly straightforward," José Pluma commented. Paloma scoffed, to which he explained, "The fact that they rolled back salaries pending investigation is nothing short of a miracle. Political machinery at any level moves slowly, and I think the June time frame is reasonable. Plus, it comes after April's elections. This decision will put a damper on some of the negative publicity they've been receiving. But it won't slow us down," he gave her a wink.

★ ★ ★

Missy Fairchild organized a Christmas party on the last day of AP English. There was a Yule log cake to eat and mulled cider to drink. Mistletoe was hung and most of the girls tried to get caught under it to see if Mr. Silver would follow the accustomed kiss; he did not. Ruth refused to be blindfolded for the game of blind man's bluff. Missy was displeased when others didn't do as directed.

"God Willows, if there's not a pony ride involved, you don't know how to interact." Missy taunted.

Ruth looked at Missy, dumfounded. Even Missy's minions were startled. Missy continued, "We just got the invitation to her Grandfather's stupid Christmas open house. My parents forced me to go to that broken down excuse for a farm once, and there was little Ruthie leading pony rides."

"Miss Fairchild, what an ugly remark," Ken had worked his way between the girls. "I've known Joe Willows since I was younger than you. He is a respected leader of our community and a generous man. His horse ranch is a beautiful facility. I'm usually out of town for the annual event, but I think it would be a treat to be invited."

Missy looked at Mr. Silver slack-jawed. Not only had she not intend on being heard by him, but she couldn't understand why he'd have such a strong opinion.

"Well," she tried to compose herself, "I guess if you're into that sort of thing."

"Considering that one of my most beloved friends came from Tall Willows ranch, I guess that I'm into that sort of thing," Ken replied.

Ruth blushed. She knew he was talking about Remington, but she imagined one of his most beloved friends also meant her.

Ken continued, "And Miss Willows here is one of the most accomplished horsewomen I have ever had the pleasure of riding with." He shook his head at the pettiness of the girl and turned to address the entire class, "Thank you all for a very lovely Christmas Party. Now let's clean up. I will wish you all a wonderful break, and I'll return your Hamlet essays to you before you leave."

Ruth and Paloma cleaned up after themselves, and when the bell rang, they grabbed their papers and hightailed it out of the classroom.

"You're done for this year, aren't you?" Paloma said to Ruth as they made their way to Ruth's locker.

Ruth smiled, "I guess I am. U.S.C.'s break started last week," she took out her winter jacket and tossed two binders into the locker, "And I won't need these till next year." She gave her English paper a quick glance. It had a large 'A' written on the front, and she showed it to Paloma before shoving it into her backpack. "So, you're going to your Grandmother's house when?"

"We leave tomorrow. But I promise I'll be back for your birthday." Paloma gave her best friend a hug, "I'm sorry I'm gonna miss your Granddaddy's open house. I always think it's a ton of fun."

"It won't be the same without you, but maybe I'll be lucky, and Missy will show up."

"I've never known her to be so nasty," Paloma mused. "What's wrong with her?"

"I don't know. I just can't wait to be done with this place and these people for good."

Alone, Ruth started the truck. As it warmed, she took the English paper out of her backpack to see if Ken had written any comments about her work. The first page had the 'A.' The second page had one typo circled–*oh well*, the last page had a paragraph handwritten in blue ink. She smiled smugly; he had to have been impressed with her well thought out ideas and strong, opinionated style. Her smile turned to a sneer as she read through his comments. She couldn't believe it, so she read through it again. *Son of a ...* escaped her lips. *How dare he!*

She tossed the paper aside and pulled out of the parking lot. His words kept going around and around in her mind as she drove; Interesting P.O.V.... Have you no compassion for Hamlet?... Can't you understand his plight?.... Do you think he wanted to behave as he did?... Wasn't he just as much of a pawn as Ophelia?... Excellent argumentative style, but one-sided. *Jackass, I was trying to prove a point!*

She turned on the radio to clear her mind, she couldn't find a station she liked. She tried to think about getting ready for Christmas; that didn't work either. No matter what she thought about, her mind kept returning to Ken. Ken and the Christmas party, Ken and Missy, Ken and paper, Ken and library, *Ken and his sanctimonious attitude, damn him!*

She cut off an oncoming car as she made a left into Tall Willows ranch. The other driver blew his horn, but she barely heard. It was going to be a miserable vacation.

Chapter 18

CHRISTMAS WAS WHITE, but Ruth's mood was dark. Her emotions swung wildly. She either wanted to explode from resentment, or she wanted to disappear into a puddle of sorrow and heartbreak. She kept to herself as much as she could.

The annual open house was two days after Christmas. Both the house and barn were open to friends, neighbors, and business associates. Over the years, Joe's party had grown into a large and lavish production.

Ruth was proud of her family and their farm, but she couldn't keep the sound of Missy Fairchild's voice out of her head. Why did that cow belittle her family and their livelihood? It made Ruth furious. She looked down at the old paddock boots she wore, caked with mud, and thought about prissy Missy and the other girls who would have spent the day getting their nails and hair done to attend a party.

By three o'clock, the first wave of visitors had gone, and the second wave arrived. Joe and Constance spent the first three hours in the barn welcoming guests (mostly vendors and potential clients). Grace and Ed kept the warm cider going and the plates of cookies full. Ruth kept the kids busy and happy with rides and feeding their two ponies, Nutmeg and Buttons treats. As the crowd changed to local business associates, Constance and Grace went inside to manage the festivities in the house.

By five o'clock, Ruth was alone in the barn. Her dad came out to help her close up and make sure the horses were tucked in for the night.

As they walked across the frozen gravel toward the house, Ed put his arm around his daughter and said, "Thank you, sweetheart."

"For what?"

"For all the hard work."

Ruth just shrugged.

"What's the matter, dear?" Ed asked.

Not a subject she wanted to discuss, she replied, "Oh cold... tired, I guess."

Ed smiled, "Get inside and wash up. Your mother has outdone herself this year with the spread she's preparing."

As they climbed the stairs to the back porch, they met Donna and Frank Silver. Ruth's heart stopped; *Cowboy's parents.* The Silvers were friends with her parents and came every year to the open house, but Ken had never come with them. Why was her heart so disappointed he wasn't tagging along with them now?

"Hello, Donna, Frank, Merry Christmas," Ed greeted them.

Constance opened the door, "Merry Christmas, you two. Oh, Donna, thank you for letting me borrow your chafing dish; I made more than I thought."

Everyone was ushered into the warm kitchen. Ruth left her boots and hung her jacket on the hook. Ed and Frank quickly left the kitchen while Grace whirled around, placing food in serving dishes. Ruth let the heat wash over her. The women's conversation washed over her too.

"How was Christmas, Donna? Was everybody home?"

"Kathleen and her husband and the kids were here; they left this morning."

"Aw, that's too bad. We would've liked to have seen them," Constance said as she warmed Donna's chafer in water.

"Well, the baby's still little, and I think they feel more comfortable at home for now."

"How old is she?"

"She'll be three months next week and already spoiled by her two big brothers."

"What about Ken?" Ruth's mother glanced at her daughter to see if she was listening.

"He went on that ski trip anyway," Donna said, sounding slightly annoyed. "I know he's been going since college, but with his job, he'll only be gone for a few days. I really thought he might just stay home for once."

"When will he be back?" Connie asked.

"He said he'd see us on Wednesday. I told him I'd make plans for New Year's Eve if he got home in time."

Constance looked at Ruth, standing with her eyes half opened in a half-sleep stupor, "Ruth, are you all right?"

Her mother's voice woke her, "Just warming up. Didn't realize how cold and tired I was."

"Please wash up and change. The next crowd will be coming soon."

Ruth breathed in deeply, and the delicious smells of the kitchen registered for the first time. She realized she was famished.

Constance and Donna left the kitchen with trays of appetizers in hand. Ruth shuffled over to Grace to see what she was plating. "What's in these?" She asked, plucking a stuffed mushroom off a tray.

"Sausage," Grace answered, "and don't eat them all. They're for the guests."

"I've been out in the barn all day. I'm starving to death," Ruth popped another mushroom in her mouth. "These are good," she mumbled with a full mouth.

"Thanks. And that's redundant; starving already means you're dying."

"It's an idiom," Ruth added, "idiot."

"You're mean when you're hangry." Grace chided, "At least wash your hands." Grace picked up the tray and left the kitchen.

Ruth perused the other trays of food. As she sampled, she thought about skiing and what it would be like to be alone on a snowy slope with Cowboy.

"Ruth, your sister said you're in there eating," Constance cracked open the kitchen door. "Go up and change!"

Her daydream vanished. She popped a few more delicacies into her mouth and moseyed out the door.

Ruth paused at the foot of the stairs. Her mother and Donna were like two peas in a pod as they laid out food and chatted. Her father came up behind her mother, slid an arm around her waist, and kissed her cheek before joining Frank for a drink.

Joe joined Ruth as she took in the scene.

"You better hurry up. The party's going to start without my best girl."

Ruth gave him a weak smile, "Why didn't you remarry after Grandma Loretta died?"

The question gave Joe pause. Finally, he answered, "Lottie was the love of my life, from the first moment I laid eyes on her. No other woman ever made me feel like she did."

Ruth nodded. "But don't you ever want... someone... So you're not lonely."

"How can I be lonely when I have you," he wrapped his arm around her, "and Gracie, and your mom and dad. Look at all the folks in this house. I'm blessed to have all of you."

"K, Granddaddy," Ruth returned his hug and climbed the stairs.

She walked out of her mud-soaked jeans as she closed her bedroom door. Her attempt to peel off her hoodie and turtleneck simultaneously resulted in her arms being stuck straight up and her head caught in the bulky fabric. Some piece of clothing was stuck, and the more she tried to extricate herself, the tighter the tangle became. Her feet no longer knew where to fall, and her left foot planted itself on something hard and slippery. It took only a moment for her to realize she'd stepped on the pile of binders and folders sitting at the foot of her bed she'd meant to put away all break. The moment took too long. Her body automatically placed weight on the foot, and the binders started to slide. It took her no time to go ass over tits, land flat on her back, and scatter the binders and papers.

Ruth groaned. At least on the floor, it was easier to remove her tangled tops. Once freed, she raised her head and looked at the scattered binders. She gave them a good hard kick to teach them a lesson that scattered them even more.

The floor was hard, but it supported her weight nicely. Her thermals were still on, so even if she never got up again, she wouldn't freeze. She was too tired to do anything but lay still. In the stillness, the empty feeling in the pit of her stomach arose. She'd been trying to quell it for weeks. It scared her. It frightened her more than anything had ever frightened her before. It felt like it would consume her entirely, and if it did, what would be left of her?

Her mother knocked and open the door. "Ruth, I'm ready to serve dinner." she peeked in and saw Ruth on the floor, "Oh my goodness, are you all right!"

"I fell."

"How? Are you hurt?"

"No, I'm fine. I tripped on my books."

"Everyone is waiting for you to eat," Constance said.

"Start without me. I'll be down in a minute," Ruth assured her mother.

Constance closed the door, and Ruth slowly sat up. She didn't feel like joining the party. Instead, she got up and gathered her old notes. *Do I need to keep them? I have everything on my laptop*. She emptied the binders and threw the papers away. The only item that remained was the folder of data from the math project.

As she picked up the manila folder, the pages cascaded out, falling around Ruth's feet. *Nooooooo!* Tired and now cranky, Ruth sunk back to the floor and leaned against her bed.

She took a deep breath and promised herself a hot shower just as soon as she picked up the file.

Ruth began to gather papers. She didn't intend to put them into any order. *There must be twenty years of budget reports here–why would Lezza give me so much*, she wondered. She had worked with four years from the 2000s, but there were reports up to the present day.

As she gathered papers, she noticed that not only were there reports, but analysis too. Someone had done the same work she had done for her math final. *Is this why Lezza gave me so much stuff? Because someone else did the same paper before?* Now she had to organize the reports. As she got closer to the present day, the analysis became more detailed, more specific. She recognized the math theories and the equations, but it no longer felt like a student's work.

Whoever had crunched these numbers had come to the same conclusion she had; something didn't add up. Each year the total was off by more and more. They had circled the differences in red pencil. When Ruth added up the total, the amount of discrepancies equaled eight hundred fifty thousand dollars.

With all pages reordered past to present, Ruth tried to slide them back into the folder. Something's still in it. She peered in to find a personalized note pad. She picked it up, read it, and screamed.

The top of each page read: From the desk of Hector Alverez.

Chapter 19

IT WAS NEW Year's Eve and the eve of Ruth's eighteenth birthday. She was not in the mood to celebrate.

It had been four days since she'd found the dead man's notes. She hadn't said a word to anyone. Instead, she'd placed the entire package in a large envelope and put it between two oversized books on her bookcase, where it would stay until she could decide what to do.

Grace had an invitation for New Year's Eve. Their mother wanted the family to be together for Ruth's birthday, but even Ruth pleaded Grace's case to go.

"My birthday is January first, and it's not at midnight. Why should Grace be stuck here?"

"Fine, but Ruth, you're eighteen. You should get together with all your friends." Her mother paused. "At least call Paloma and ask her to come over."

"Paloma went to visit her grandmother in Las Cruces; she'll be back tomorrow. I don't want a big party. It's not like turning eighteen is going to be some life-changing event. I'll still have to go back to high school next week, and then I'll start my next class at the university the week after that, and everything will go on just the same as always." She put on her hat, wool coat, and gloves, "I'm going to check on Belle. I'll be in the barn if anyone wants me." She grabbed some books and left out the kitchen door.

Constance turned to Grace. "You heard your sister. Tell your friend you can stay the night," She was glad at least one person in this family would enjoy New Year's Eve.

Ed and Joe walked in from the barn. "My word, it's bitter out there!" Joe exclaimed. "That mare would have to pick a night like this to go into foal."

"Is there a problem, Joe?" Constance asked.

"Not for the mare, but I'd like to know when the foal is born so I can have the heat on for it. I'd like to make sure it's dried out and doesn't catch cold."

"Ed, did you pass your daughter on her way to the barn?" Constance asked.

"Yes," he replied, "she had a stack of books and said she'd watch Belle. Wish I knew what's bothering her."

"You know, and I do," scoffed Joe, "it's that Silver boy. One day they're dancing and kissing and having a good time; the next day, he's her teacher, and she's been in a funk ever since. I'm getting tired of it myself."

"Oh my, I almost forgot. Donna Silver wants to know when Belle goes into foal. She wants to come over." Constance went for the phone.

"Tell her to get that son of hers over here too," Joe added in a murmur, "kiss some sense into that daughter of yours."

Constance had the phone in her hand, "Joe, we can't interfere ... Oh hello, Donna ... It's Connie ...."

Joe sat at the table while Ed went to the oven to see what was cooking for dinner. It was only five o'clock but black as pitch outside.

Constance put her hand over the receiver and asked, "Donna and Frank have dinner reservations and want to know if we'd like to join them. Seems like their son made it home from his ski trip but is in a similar funk to our daughter."

"What about all this food you cooked?" Ed asked, eyeing roast pork.

"I can put it away for tomorrow," Constance replied.

"You two go on. I want to keep an eye on that mare. Tell Donna to send Ken over. I'll need an extra set of hands if that foal gets into trouble."

"Joe, don't meddle."

"Just tell her, woman!" Joe insisted, "I'm not as young as I used to be. I might need some help." He knew that comment would unnerve his daughter-in-law just enough to make sure Ken came over.

Constance finished her conversation with Donna. "We'll drop Grace off at her friend's, then swing by and pick up Donna and Frank. That okay with you, Ed?"

"Whatever you say, my dear. Am I okay like this?"

"Absolutely not! Put on something nice. They have seven o'clock reservations. I better get myself ready too." Constance looked Joe straight in the eye, "Ken has been living in their guest house. Donna will ask him to come over to help with the foal." She shook a finger at him, "You better know what you're doing."

"Stop wagging your finger at me, woman, and go get ready," Joe teased, "I'll take care of the kitchen–and the two lovebirds too," he added when she was out of earshot.

By six o'clock, Ruth wandered into the kitchen. Her mother said they'd probably be home before midnight. Grace said a cheerful Happy New Year. Ruth watched the three of them go.

"Looks like just you and me, Grand-baby." Joe hugged her. "Let's sit down and eat." He handed her a plate filled with the dinner her mother had cooked and joined her at the kitchen table.

They ate in silence for a while, then Ruth said, "Do you think Belle will have the foal tonight?"

"What condition was she in when you left?"

"Restless. She keeps looking at her belly."

"She'll probably foal tonight." He looked at his granddaughter. He remembered when she arrived ten years ago. "Guess if the foal is born on your birthday, you have naming rights."

"You think so?" she said with a faint smile.

"Don't see why not?" He pressed her a bit, "Guess that's one good thing to come of an eighteenth birthday?"

Her smile disappeared. "Tell me what's wrong, Grand-baby."

"It doesn't matter. There's nothing anyone can do anyway." She cleared the table.

"There's always something you can do..."

"No, there's not." She heard a car drive in on frozen gravel, "Thanks for having dinner with me. I'm gonna check on Belle." Ruth quickly wrapped herself against the cold and headed back to the barn.

Joe sighed; *what am I going to do with you, child?*

A few moments later, there was a knock at the kitchen door. Joe was putting away leftovers. "Come on in," he called.

Ken entered, looking not much better than Ruth. "It didn't look like anyone was up front, so I came around back."

"That's fine. Come on in and sit down. Would you like something to warm yourself up a bit? You look half frozen."

"No, sir, I'm fine."

"Really?" Joe left a very pregnant pause in the conversation to see if Ken was going to be any looser lipped than Ruth. From the lack of response, he didn't think so.

"You sure I can't get you something to eat? I know your folks are out having a fancy time. I'm just putting dinner away."

"No, that's okay."

"Coffee?" Joe offered.

"No."

"Something stronger? Whiskey? Get you through a long night."

"No," Ken chuckled slightly.

"Granddaughter?" Joe had to throw that out.

Ken was speechless.

Joe looked at the mortified expression on the young man's face and chuckled. "Oh, I wish old Shep was here to see the look on your face."

Ken loosened his coat and removed his hat and gloves. He dropped into a chair and let Joe enjoy the moment. Ken asked, "How's the mare?"

"They're both in the barn."

"Both?" Ken didn't understand.

"Belle and Ruth. Belle is the one having the foal, and Ruth is out there hiding from the world."

"Oh," was all Ken could muster as a response.

"Dog-gone-it now!" Joe was losing his patience. He pounded the table with the palm of his hand, and Ken jumped in his chair. "I've had enough of this moping around. You're keen on my Grand-baby, aren't you?"

Ken sat up straight and looked Joe directly in the eye, "Yes sir, I am, but..."

"Well, I'm pretty damn sure she's been mooning over you for the past three months."

"She hasn't..."

"Of course she has! Are you going to be a man and do something about it?"

"I'd like to, but my job ..."

"What's a job got to do with it?"

"I'm her teach..." Ken tried to explain, but Joe was not about to listen to any excuses.

"I know all about that, and I think it's a big load of horse manure."

Ken looked at him as if he were insane. Had he never heard of child predators or registered sex offenders? "Losing my job and going to jail is a big concern of mine, sir." Ken put it politely.

“Why are you planning on doing something illegal with her?” Joe asked pointedly.

“No, sir. But the school has policies in place to prevent this sort of relationship and...”

“That school has bigger problems to worry about than if an English teacher is eating dinner with his adult girlfriend and her family.” Joe eyed Ken, “You do know it’s her eighteenth birthday tomorrow, don’t you?”

They looked at each other across the table. It was nice to know Joe seemed keen on the idea.

Joe piped up before Ken could say anything, “I didn’t say you should parade her around that school of yours for crying out loud, but if both of you are this ... outta sorts, what do you have to lose?”

“Her parents? Do you ... Would they...?”

“Don’t you worry about Ed and Connie. They love her. They want her to be happy.”

Ken smiled. Then he added, “Ruth’s not too happy with me these days...”

Joe rolled his eyes, “When that foal is born, I want to make sure it’s warmed and dried. The barn is warmer than outside, but it’s cold in there for a little one.” Joe pulled two small, powerful electric heaters from a closet in the kitchen. He handed both to Ken, “Take these out to the barn and set them up but don’t turn them on yet. That mare’s better off with it on the cool side until she’s finished.”

Ken put the heaters down, buttoned up his coat, and put on his hat and gloves. Joe continued, “I have some things to finish up in here, then I’ll be out to take a look at her. If anything happens with the mare, come and get me, understood?”

“Yes, sir,” Ken replied.

“That mare should be fine on her own, but I’d like to be there once she presents.”

“Understood.” Ken picked up the heaters and marched off to the barn.

It was only a few hundred feet to the barn, but it might as well be a few hundred miles as far as Ken was concerned. *Might be better off if it was a few hundred miles. At least I'd have the opportunity to freeze to death.* He glanced back at the house and spotted Joe looking out the kitchen window. He quickened his pace to the barn.

Ken got into the barn and shut the door tight behind him. Ruth was camped out on several bales of straw two stalls down from Belle. Her coat and hat were on, and an old wool blanket was wrapped around her legs. She looked miserable. Books were scattered about, a magazine was opened on her lap, but the light was so dim Ken wondered how she could read.

He walked quietly to her. Casually he said, "Hey, Baby Doll."

She didn't know what to say. The first moment she saw him, her heart soared. This is what she had wanted. To see him here, to hear him call her Baby Doll, to feel the warmth of his body next to hers. She wanted to spring to her feet and fly into his arms ... but then her heart sank. *Why bother. It's just not worth the effort. We'll just go back to the same old same old next week when break is over.* No, she couldn't do it anymore. The pain in her chest was too much. A lump rose in her throat. She prayed she wouldn't start crying, not again, not now. She managed a "hey" and went back to the magazine.

"Joe asked me to bring out heaters for the foal." He got no response from her. "How's Belle doing?"

She looked up. "See for yourself," she croaked.

Ken went over to the mare. He placed the heaters down by the stall door. The mare laid on her side, her breathing slightly labored, but she popped up when she saw Ken. He gave the mare a gentle pat on the forehead and walked back to Ruth.

"You wrapped her tail?"

Ruth nodded.

"Any sign that she's ready?"

She was afraid to speak, so she ignored him.

"Joe wants to know..."

"So go look and tell him," she curtly replied.

Ken sat down on the bale next to her, "I want to talk to you first." He removed his gloves and grabbed for her hands.

"Leave me alone, please," she tried to pull her hands away, but he caught them and wouldn't let go.

"You're freezing; go into the house to warm up."

"No, go away." She was trying hard to hold on to what little composure she had.

"Baby Doll .... I..."

"Stop calling me that!" she shouted, the mare neighed, and the first tears started to fall. "You can't just walk in here and call me that..."

"I miss you," he brought her hands to his chest.

"You see me almost every day."

"That's not what I mean, and you know it," he was beginning to sound irritated.

She got up to leave. The blanket and magazine fell to the floor.

Ken pulled her back, "Please talk to me, don't just walk out," he sweetly pleaded.

Angrily she shot back, "Why! Are you the only one who can do that?" She sank back onto the bale and muttered, "I can't do this anymore."

The words hit him like a ton of bricks. His memory flashed back to how he walked out of the hospital. He had been so angry with her. He had walked away from her time and again. Every time he found himself close to her, he'd turn his back on her. He was miserable. He looked forward to seeing her each day, and then he hated himself for letting her walk out of his class without acknowledging her.

Ken wrapped her in his arms. She buried her face in his chest. After a moment, he whispered into her ear, "I'm sorry. I'm so, so sorry. I wish you could forgive me for being such a... jerk. I miss you. I miss talking to you, and I miss touching you. I miss kissing you, but mostly I just miss being with you."

She looked into his eyes.

He continued, "I've treated you terribly. I'm sorry. I haven't done much else right lately either. I can't keep pretending that I don't care about you."

Ken went on, "I need to see you, and I don't mean in school. I want to find a way that we could be ... together. Maybe I can come over here? We can hang out, watch a movie, trail ride, just ... anything you'd like."

Her breath shook as she spoke, "What about your j... j.... job?"

"It goes against school policy, but right now, I don't care. Being here with you has felt more right, more real to me than anything else has felt in months."

She put her hand to his cheek; he turned his head and kissed her palm. He missed her touch more than he'd realized.

"Would you mind if we could only be together like this? I can't take you out to dinner, or to the movies, or the prom ..."

"I don't want to go to prom. I don't want to go to another high school function as long as I live. Well, except graduation."

"It will have to be a secret. We must be very careful. It's not the way I want things to be, but I don't know what else to do, and ..."

She reached up and kissed him, long and sweet, on the lips. When she finished, she said, "I understand, Cowboy."

"Oh, Baby Doll ..." and he kissed her again, more demanding and deeper, and again.

Ruth found him even more delicious than the first night they'd kissed. This was nowhere nearly as awkward as the library incident. She was sure of herself now; she knew what she wanted, and she knew he wanted her just as much in return.

As they clung to each other, both realized it was the first sense of peace that either felt in quite some time.

Ruth was startled out of her dreamlike state by an odd noise. "What was that?"

"Nothing, Baby Doll," Ken hummed.

"No, it was something." She stood up as she suddenly grasped what was going on, "Belle!"

In his own euphoria, Ken had forgotten all about the mare. Ruth was at Belle's stall. The mare was lying down, but her hindquarters faced the stall door. From under her tail, a whitish membrane bulged. Belle grunted, and the membrane burst, expelling a copious amount of liquid.

"Her water broke! Run! Get Granddaddy!" Ruth had seen a few births before, and she knew that it wouldn't take long now. She also knew if there would be a problem, now would be the time for one.

Ken took off for the house, and Ruth got an extension cord for the heaters. Belle was on her feet, pacing in a circle. Ruth kept looking for the first sign of two tiny hooves.

A blast of cold air at the back of her neck told her that Ken and Granddaddy arrived. Joe had clean towels in his hands, which he laid over the stall door.

"How she doing?"

"Her water broke, but that's it. You don't think there could be a problem, do you?" Ruth asked.

"Give her time. If she starts pushing hard and nothing happens, I'll check her out." Joe leaned back against the opposite stall wall, and Ken stood behind Ruth with his arms wrapped around her shoulders. She held on to his hands. Joe glanced over at them and smiled.

"You two doin' okay?"

Ruth blushed her trademark blush, and Joe laughed. Ken answered, "Yeah, we're doin' all right now."

Belle delivered her foal quickly, to everyone's relief.

"Turn on those heaters," Joe directed.

The newborn wriggled on the stall floor, trying to free itself of the amniotic sac. The reclining mare raised her head and gave the small creature a sniff.

"Normally, I'd let the mare do this, but it's so cold I want to dry this baby off," Joe whispered and took the towels into the stall. He removed what was left of the sac and gently rubbed the little thing dry.

"It's a filly," he announced. "What you going to name her, Ruth?"

"I don't know," Ruth thought for a moment and took a long look at the tiny animal, "Her daddy has an N name. Maybe ... New Year's Star. We'll call her Star."

"What time is it?" Joe asked.

Ken looked at his wristwatch, his arms still holding on to Ruth, "Eleven-O-five."

"Well, not midnight, but it's still New Year's." He turned to the mare, "You did a good job, Belle." She sniffed at the towels, then turned to tend to her foal. A foursome walked into the barn. "Donna, you missed it again," Joe announced.

"Oh no, you're kidding," Donna sighed, "when did it happen?"

"About thirty minutes ago." Joe wiped his hands on his pants.

"See Frank," Donna chided, "you had to have that second cup of coffee." She peered into the stall. "What did she have? Are they okay?"

"It's a filly," Joe answered. "They're both fine. I told Ruth she could name her since it is her birthday too."

Donna fixed her eyes on her son, holding on to a pretty young woman, "Were you two here?"

Everyone's attention turned to Ken and Ruth. Ruth attempted to loosen Ken's grip on her, but he held tight. *I hate it when people look at me like this.*

"Yep," Ken answered cheerfully with a cheshire grin, "We saw the whole thing, didn't we, Baby Doll?"

You had to call me Baby Doll in front of them? Ruth smiled and nodded. After an uncomfortable silence, Ruth finally asked, "How was dinner?"

Constance answered, trying to conceal a smirk, “Oh, it was lovely. Wonderful food and wonderful company. And since I am not dressed for barn work, I’m going into the house. Donna, Frank, what can I get for you?”

Joe piped up, “It’s New Year’s Eve. We all need a drink.”

“What do you got that’s good, Joe?” Frank asked.

“Just got a bottle of brandy for Christmas,” Joe answered.

“I’ll get out the snifters,” Constance’s voice trailed behind as she left the barn. The others followed.

Joe turned to Ruth and Ken, “Close up the barn. That little one ought to be dry enough for now. Unplug the heaters, but leave the heat lamps on.”

“Sure thing, Granddaddy,” Ruth said. Finally freed from Ken’s embrace, she bent down to turn off the heaters.

Joe advised, “We’ll expect you inside shortly.”

Ken took the heaters and extension cord to the office while Ruth picked up her books and took her blanket into the office too. He grabbed her and kissed her again.

When he stepped back, she said, “You know I embarrass easily, don’t you?”

He kissed her again, “Are you saying you’re embarrassed to be seen with me?” He feigned insult.

“You know what I mean.” She tried to push away from him, but he would not let her go. “I just don’t like being ... smirked at.”

“It worked out for the best–didn’t it?” Ken defended himself. “I should ask your parents if they mind me hanging out here all the time now.”

“All the time?” she smiled.

“As much as you’ll have me, Baby Doll,” he kissed her again.

“And you had to call me Baby Doll in front of everyone!” she scolded him. He gave her a big grin, flashing those white teeth and deep dimples at her. She said, “Are you always going to be this much trouble?”

"I sure hope so." He kissed her one more time. "Come on, we better get into the house before your Granddaddy sends out a search party."

Chapter 20

RUTH REMEMBERED EXAMINING everyone's shoes. Ken was wearing cowboy boots (of course); she just had on fuzzy socks. Her mom had on a pretty pair of heels that looked like black velvet. Granddaddy had slipped into his slippers, but Donna had a fantastic pair of snake-skin booties.

Ken's arm was wrapped tight around her waist, and his voice was strong and confident, "I deeply care about your daughter Sir. We'll have to be extremely cautious."

"You need to respect the fact that Grace is sixteen, and this is not a dorm. I don't want anyone walking in on you two in any compromising positions." She wasn't looking at her mother, but Ruth could feel Constance's eyes upon her.

Oh my God, Ruth suddenly realized she was talking about SEX. It hadn't dawned on her till this moment. *Ugh, what a uncomfortable thought to wake up to on New Year's morning.* Her mother had always been open. The two of them had had many sex talks growing up, but *EEWW, EEEWWW, EEEE-WWWW!!! She assumes we're going to have sex and talked about it in front of everyone.*

Which led her to wonder just what did Cowboy expect? They had kissed–a lot–but *how long would that last? When would he want–expect more? Maybe dating a guy six years older is a mistake?*

Ruth looked at the clock; nine-thirty. Her cell rang. She picked it up and stared up at the ceiling, "Mornin' Cowboy," she was smiling down to the tips of her toes.

"Mornin' to you, Baby Doll-Happy Birthday."

"Thank you."

"Did I wake you?"

"No. But I was laying here thinking about you."

"What a coincidence, I was thinking about you too. So what do you plan on doing today, birthday girl?'

"Well, nothing special, really. Mom invited you for dinner, right?"

"I'll be there. But is there anything you'd like to do before that?"

"I hadn't thought about doing anything, really. Got something in mind?"

"I have lots of things in my mind, but this is your day," he replied.

"I didn't want to celebrate… until last night. And ... it already was a very nice celebration ... you and me...and..." she let her thought trail off.

"Are you asking for more of the same?"

She felt him grinning right through the phone, "That would be nice."

"All right, but I have an errand first."

"Oh, all right," she tried not to sound disappointed.

"I don't know how long it will take. I'll call you when I have a better idea, Okay?"

"Whatever you say, Cowboy."

They said goodbye and hung up.

She had barely dressed when Paloma called, "HAPPY BIRTH-DAY!!!! How are you?"

"Thanks. Good. How are you?" Ruth wondered how she was going to tell Paloma about Ken.

"You sound different! What's wrong?"

"Nothing's wrong. Where are you?"

"We're on our way back from Grams. We should get home around three. I promised my mom I'd help her with the unpacking. Is it okay if I get there closer to five?"

"We'll light the bonfire when you get here."

"Listen, Ruth, I was thinking... you should have a party–it's your eighteenth birthday! Let me invite just a few people."

"NO, YOU CAN'T," Ruth cut her off.

"Just Scott and a few friends," Paloma tried to convince her.

"No, Paloma, you don't understand–you can't ask anyone to come over."

"What about Scott? He's been kinda mad that I've been out of town."

"No, not even Scott. Paloma, I am dead serious. If anyone besides you shows up, I will not open the door. Do you understand me?"

"But Ruth... I thought you liked him"

"That's not the point. Paloma, promise me."

"Okay... okay."

"Really promise me, say I Paloma Torres promise to not invite anyone to Ruth Willows house tonight. And I Promise to come alone."

Paloma repeated the promise to Ruth.

"You'll understand when you get here."

"Yeah, sure. I hope you know what you're missing, Ruth."

"I won't be missing anything."

★ ★ ★

"I'm about done and headin' your way, Baby Doll." When Ken called, it was almost noon.

"It's warmed up a lot since last night. Wanna trail ride?" Ruth asked.

"If that's what you'd like. Should I bring Rem over?"

"You don't have to if you ride one of Granddaddy's horses."

When she answered the front door, her heart nearly stopped at the sight. There stood her Cowboy. He had an old pair of brown leather chaps slung over his shoulder and a well-worn pair of boots in his hand.

He gave her a peck on the lips and said, "Happy Birthday, Baby Doll."

She smiled and said, "Thanks! Ready to ride if you are."

He set down his boots and chaps, took her hand, pulled her in close, and backed her up against the wall. He pressed himself against her and kissed her deeply.

"Who's at the door?" Grace's voice came echoing down the hallway.

Ruth drew back from the kiss, took a deep breath, and answered, "It's Ken."

Grace found them decently apart. Grace called out to her mother in the kitchen, "It's Ruth's boyfriend."

"Let them be Grace," Constance called out, but Grace stood rooted, smiling broadly at her sister.

"Hello Ken," Constance called out. "Sorry for shouting, but I've got my hands full at the moment."

"Could you use some help?" he called back to her.

"No thanks, Grace is my sous-chef today." Constance hoped this would remind Grace to come back to the kitchen and give the couple some privacy.

Grace turned and flounced back down the hall to the kitchen.

"Are we ready to ride now?" Ruth asked Ken.

"Aren't you curious about what I was doing today?" he asked as he fished a thin, white box out of the pocket of his down vest.

"I figured you'd tell me when you were ready," she returned, but saw the box, and her heart fluttered.

He walked into the parlor, placed the box, tied up with a light green ribbon, on the coffee table, and sat on the couch. Ruth slowly walked over and asked, "For me?"

"Does someone else here have a birthday today?"

"Do you want me to open it now?"

"I think now would be good."

She sat down, untied the ribbon, took off the lid, and revealed a velvet jewelry box. Inside, a delicate silver rope wound around the velvety clips three times. Clinging to the chain lay a charm of two silver horseshoes. Silently, she removed the chain and held it high in the air. It shimmered like a tiny waterfall in her hand.

"Well?" asked Ken, his heart pounding, waiting for a response.

"It's so...so...beautiful." She turned to him, kissed his cheek, looked into his beautiful brown eyes, and kissed him on the lips.

"Are you going to try it on?"

The rope was long, so she put it over her head, and the horseshoe charm fell between her breasts.

"You got this today? How? It's New Year's day," She asked as she beamed.

"Look at the charm."

She held the two linked horseshoes.

"Turn it over," he prompted.

She did, and she saw each horseshoe bore a tiny inscription; one said B.D. the other C.B. She looked at him with moist eyes and held the charm tightly in her fist.

"A friend is a silversmith," he explained. "I called him this morning and convinced him I had to have this today. I wanted the chain long enough so you could always wear it, but no one could see it if you didn't want them to."

She was speechless. She slid onto his lap, wrapped her arms around his neck, and held him tight. "Thank you. It's wonderful. Thank you," she whispered into his ear.

He was pleased she liked it. He held her for another moment before saying, "Are you ready to ride now?"

Dreamily, she loosened her embrace, "Yeah, let's ride."

★ ★ ★

They returned before sunset and had just enough time to take care of the horses and check in on Star before dinner guests arrived.

"What's on the agenda for tonight, Baby Doll?" Ken held her hand as they walked toward the house.

"We make a bonfire. Then we eat dinner."

"And how big does this shindig get?"

"Just a few people, Shep and his girlfriend Nancy, a neighbor couple, and ..." she looked at him out of the corner of her eye, "Paloma."

"Well, I expected her," he smiled. "Have you told her anything yet?"

"No, not yet. She's been at her Grandmother's since Christmas. I made her promise not to show up with any unexpected guests." Ruth shrugged her shoulders. "Are you going to be okay with her here? She can keep her mouth shut. No one knows that she's the anonymous source behind the whole fake diploma story."

"She's known about us since that day with Derrick. Besides, if she says anything, I'll give her an F before I get kicked out on my butt," he flashed a wicked grin.

★ ★ ★

Most of the guests were outside at the bonfire when Paloma arrived. She looked upset as she entered the kitchen.

"What's wrong?" Ruth was concerned.

"I just had a big fight with Scott. He was furious when I uninvited him. He said I wasn't much of a girlfriend, what with being away the whole Christmas break an' all."

"I'll tell him tonight was all my fault," Ruth promised.

"You would do that?" Paloma asked.

"I am the one who uninvited him."

Paloma sighed a heavy sigh as she sunk into a kitchen chair, "I don't know if he's worth the bother. Ever since I took the internship, he's all bent out of shape, accusing me of 'working for the man.' I mean, he's happy if I'm cooing over his work, but he's never says anything good about mine. And let's face it, I've been working on a pretty high-profile story."

Ken, who'd heard her from the hall, eased up behind Ruth and slid his arms around her waist. "Sounds like he's jealous and afraid you'll lose interest in him if you get interested in other things."

Paloma shrugged, about to respond when she realized the comment hadn't come from Ruth. She looked up to see Ken with his arms snug around her best friend, their faces beaming. Paloma shrieked and scrambled to her feet, "Mr. Silver! What are you doing here?"

Ruth burst into a laugh.

With a giggle, Ruth said, "Paloma, this is Ken. Cowboy, this is my best friend, Paloma."

Ken relaxed his grip on Ruth, took Paloma's hand, and after a polite kiss on the back of it said, "Haven't we met before?"

Paloma retrieved her hand and said, "You're both nuts."

Joe called from the back porch, "Got the bonfire going Grand-baby, what you still doing inside?"

"We're comin' Granddaddy!"

★ ★ ★

Ruth had a very happy birthday bonfire and dinner while trying to keep up with Paloma's questions about her and Ken.

By ten-thirty, the festivities wound down, and Ruth asked Paloma to stay for a few more minutes. "I have something important to show you.".

Ken and Paloma sat on opposite sides of the room. Both look uncomfortable when Ruth came into the parlor holding the envelope with the Alverez file. She looked at them and shook her head with a wry smile.

"I'm sorry! I've known him as a teacher before I knew him as your boyfriend." Paloma defended herself. Ruth went pink at the word boyfriend. "It's gonna take me a while to get used to it."

"Make sure you keep it to yourself while you get used to it. No sudden outbursts, or we'll be in big trouble." Ruth reminded her.

"I promised you I won't say a word." Paloma pledged, "What's in the big envelope?"

"It's the file Lezza gave to me for my math paper," Ruth explained as she sat next to Ken on the couch. "I was about to throw it away when I noticed some...additional information."

Paloma was straining forward in her chair to see better, "What kind of information?"

"Come over here, and I'll show you both, but don't touch it."

Paloma joined Ruth and Ken on the couch. Ruth carefully opened the envelope and slid out the manila folder. She opened it to the first page.

"When I was working on my math paper, I only looked at the first dozen pages. I found the data was flawed. It showed there was a significant loss for three years in a row. Dad and Granddaddy thought it was just missing information. When I went to throw the folder away, the papers fell. When I picked them up, I noticed these." She held up Alverez's calculations. "They looked so much like my notes, I thought another student had done the same paper. But then I realized that the calculations went all the way up to last year. I went through them. I was right; money is actually missing from the budget."

"How much money are you talking about, Baby Doll?" Ken asked.

"According to this data, over the last twenty years, nearly a million dollars is missing."

"What!" both Paloma and Ken cried.

"That's not the best." Ruth flipped all the pages over to reveal the personalized notepad from Hector Alverez.

"Oh, My GOD!" Paloma exclaimed as her hands flew to cover her mouth.

"You've got to be kidding!" Ken raked his hair.

Ruth nodded her head.

"This is why he was killed!" Paloma quickly jumped to the conclusion.

"I don't know," Ruth answered. "I mean, I guess it could be-right? All I know is that I took this folder off of Lezza's desk. I don't even know what I should do with it."

"You're gonna take it to the sheriff," Ken pronounced.

"I should, but after last time, I feel kinda foolish."

"What last time?" he asked.

"With the Bowman pictures?" Paloma interjected.

"What are you talking about?" Ken questioned.

"Cowboy, it's a long story," Ruth held his hand again, "Let's just say that I inadvertently took pictures of Bowman and Gills, and I gave them to the sheriff like it was a big deal, but now I realize it was probably nothing."

"Pictures?" Ken stared at her with a blank expression. It was getting late. He sighed, "Okay, we'll save that story for later. But this... this is... evidence."

The clock in the dining room was chiming eleven o'clock when Constance wandered into the front room. "Oh, I didn't know you three were in here. I thought everyone had gone home."

"I am about to," Paloma yawned, "sorry, Ruth, but I'm exhausted."

"Don't be," Ruth hugged her best friend, "I'm so glad you came." She added under her breath, "Are you all right with this Cowboy stuff?"

Paloma giggled, "Couldn't be happier. Happy Birthday, Ruth!"

"Paloma, are you okay to drive?" Constance asked.

"I'm fine. After a week on the air mattress, I can't wait to sleep in my own bed."

Paloma said goodnight and headed home. Constance said goodnight and started up the stairs.

"Mom," Ruth called, "thank you for a wonderful birthday."

She came back and kissed her daughter on the cheek, "You're welcome, sweetheart. I love you." Constance smiled at Ken, "Good night, you two."

Five more minutes, and I'm going home too, Baby Doll." Ken wrapped his arm around her.

Ruth put all the papers back into the folder and the file back into the envelope just before Cowboy began kissing her. It was after midnight when Ken pulled himself away and headed home.

Chapter 21

THE SECOND DAY in a row, Ruth's phone rang at nine-thirty a.m. She'd just finished morning barn chores. "Morning, Cowboy, you just getting up?"

"Nah, been up for a while. How about you?"

"Morning chores. Belle's being great about letting us handle her baby."

"Do you have to work all day today?"

"I took Grace's morning shift so she could go to an art class. I guess I could guilt her into doing the evening chores for me if something important came up."

"Something important has come up. We have a one o'clock appointment."

"For what?" her heart fluttered at the same time her stomach lurched, not sure where the conversation was headed.

"Just talked to my Uncle Bob. He wants to see that file of yours."

"Oh, no, Cowboy, you didn't. I don't want to talk to the sheriff. I'll just embarrass myself again."

"This is a murder investigation; you have to do this."

Silence came from Ruth's end of the phone.

"Baby Doll, are you still there?"

"I'm still here."

"I'll take you to the sheriff. Then if they don't arrest you..."

"Thanks a lot!" she interjected.

"How about dinner and a movie?"

"How are we gonna do that? We can't go out. It's risky enough being together at the sheriff's department."

"Anyone who sees us at the Sheriff's department has bigger problems to worry about. We'll get take out for dinner, and we can go back to your house and stream a movie."

He heard a long, exasperated sigh coming from the other end of the line.

"I'll take that as a yes. Pick you up by twelve-fifteen. Is that enough time for you?"

"Yeah, I'll explain the whole thing to my family."

"They don't know?"

"No. And the last time they found out I was behind a breaking news story they didn't know about, they were pissed."

★ ★ ★

Showered and changed, Ruth grabbed the Alverez file and headed downstairs. It was lunchtime, and the men were in the kitchen. "Connie just called and said they'd be home soon. You want me to make you a sandwich too, Dad?" Ed asked his father.

"Sure, any of that good ham left?" Joe answered.

"Daddy, Granddaddy, I need to talk to you," Ruth interrupted their exploits into the culinary world.

She sat them down at the kitchen table, laid out the file, and told them the whole story. As she finished, Ken knocked on the kitchen door.

"Come on in, son," Joe called to Ken, "Grand-baby here just told us you're taking her down to talk to the sheriff."

"Yes, sir. I think that file might have some bearing on the Alverez case," Ken answered.

"I think you're right," Ed agreed, "I just can't believe it's been in Ruth's hands all this time."

"At this point, I want to get rid of it," Ruth said as she put the file back into its envelope.

"Ready to go, Baby Doll?" Ken asked.

"Yes." She turned to Ed, "Daddy, will you explain this to Mom? I thought she'd be home by now."

Ed said, "I'll tell her all about it."

Joe interrupted, "You two not going to see a judge while you're down at the courthouse, are you?" Joe chuckled at his own joke.

Ed tried to ignore it.

Ken went pale.

Ruth just rolled her eyes and marched out of the kitchen with Ken in tow. That made Joe laugh all the harder, especially when she almost collided with Constance and Grace as she stormed through the door.

"Hello," Constance jumped to the aside, "where are you two off to?"

"Daddy'll explain!" Ruth shouted from the porch steps. "Grace, you have my barn duty tonight." Then she added, "And try to ignore Grand-daddy's lack of humor!"

Joe continued to laugh.

★ ★ ★

Officer Clark escorted Ruth and Ken to a conference room furnished with several hard plastic chairs around a large table.

"Hey, nice hair," Ruth reached up and rubbed her hand over his new flat-top style, "it's growing back."

"Yeah," Tommy rubbed his head after her, "I might keep it short for a while."

For some reason, Ruth's mouth decided to continue speaking, even though her brain told her to shut up. "No one can run their finger through your hair if it's too short."

Tommy locked eyes with Ruth and turned a deep shade of red. Looking for another place to gaze, he came to Ken's face. Ken set his jaw and clenched his teeth, and Tommy went white. "Yes, ma'am," he mumbled, looking at the ceiling. In an attempt to regain his composure, Tommy said, "Sheriff Davis will be in, in a minute." He turned and left the room.

"What was that all about?" Ken's teeth were still clenched.

"Huh?"

"Do you always flirt with deputies?" he continued.

"I wasn't flirting! The last time I was here, his head was shaved. We talked about it. I wasn't flirting!" Ruth defended herself.

Ken grunted.

"Cowboy, are you jealous?" Ruth grinned.

"Don't be absurd," he protested as the door swung open.

"Howdy Ruth, Kenny," the Sheriff greeted them with a handshake and a big smile. "Thank you for coming down here today. I hear you have some mighty important evidence with you, Ruth."

"Yes, sir. Here you can have it." Ruth shoved the envelope at Davis's chest.

"Let's all sit down for a moment and talk about it. I'm sure there's a good story here, and I love a good story."

On Davis's heels was a very authoritative woman in a fitted grey pinstriped suit. In her late thirties, her dark hair was cut pixie style. She wore only enough makeup to look feminine, and her only jewelry was her wedding band.

Sheriff Davis introduced her, "This is detective Pamela Ramos of the state bureau of investigations. She's a good friend and colleague, and

I've asked her to come down and take a look at this file of yours. This kind of work is right up her alley."

Detective Ramos gave a quick nod to Ruth and Ken and sat down to work. She pulled out a digital recorder and spoke her name, date, location into it. She said that she was interviewing Ruth Willows and Kenneth Silver in the presence of Sheriff Robert Davis on the matter of possible evidence relating to the murder investigation of Hector Alverez.

With all that done, Davis said, "All right, Ruth, show us what you brought."

Ruth opened the envelope, removed the file, and quickly told her story right up to the busy office when she picked up the file."

"And this was the file you took?" Detective Ramos asked.

Ruth nodded.

"So, you've had this file since September. Why wait till January to turn it in?"

"I didn't know what it was till the other day." Ruth continued her story, where she found the calculations were coming out wrong and finished with realizing what the file really was just before she threw it away. Ramos let her finish with few interruptions, but when she was done, the questions began.

Two hours later, Detective Ramos was still questioning Ruth. Ruth had been patient and answered everything to the best of her ability, but she felt like a broken record. Several times she had to quell the urge to pick up the digital recorder and play back her answers to the detective. When Ramos asked her to review her statement again, Ruth stood up.

"What's wrong, Ruth?" the longtime silent sheriff asked.

"I'm leaving."

"Oh, you need a break? Okay, we can stop for a few minutes." Davis said.

No," Ruth clarified, "I'm leaving."

"You can't," Ramos exclaimed.

"Am I under arrest?" Ruth questioned.

"Not yet." Ramos tried to sound intimidating.

"When I am, I'll come back. But now I'm leaving"

"Ruth!" Ken whispered.

"What?" She replied indignantly, "I've answered all of her questions... twice! If she wants to hear the answers again, she can play them back on that little recorder of hers." She turned to Davis and Ramos, "Instead of asking me the same questions, you should go over the data in this file and figure out who embezzled a million dollars from the school district."

Davis gave Ramos a sharp look and shook his head.

She grimaced and mumbled under her breath. Ramos gave Ruth a stern look and said, "Make sure Sheriff Davis can contact you in case we need further information."

Ruth gave her an incredulous look. "Sheriff Davis has been able to contact me since the day I found the body of Hector Alverez." She turned to Davis and finished in as polite a voice as she could, "I could have very easily thrown this file away, and no one would have known that it ever existed. I didn't have to bring it in here and spend the last day of my break being interrogated like I was the suspect."

Ken jumped up, took Ruth's arm, and interrupted her diatribe, "We'll get going now."

Sheriff Davis opened the door and said, "I'll sign you out. I'll be back in a minute. Pam, why don't we talk in my office?"

Davis walked them out of the building and into the covered parking structure. He put his hand on Ruth's shoulder and said, "Thank you for coming today. We'll need some time to go over that file of yours, but I think it's something significant."

Ruth gave him a weak shrug.

He continued, "I know Detective Ramos can come on strong, but she's one of the best. I feel like this case may be out of this department's league, and I wanted to get Pam's perspective on it." Ruth clenched her teeth and glared. "You did the right thing, Ruth. Remember, if you need me for anything, don't hesitate to call–all right?"

Ruth nodded. Davis said goodbye to his nephew with a handshake and a clap on the back.

Ruth turned to open the door of the jeep. Ken slid his arm around her. She stepped away, "Not here, Cowboy, someone may see."

"We're in an empty parking lot, Baby Doll," but he eased back. "Hey, you did a good thing today. Now it's over, and you never have to think about it again." He got no response from Ruth. "You know what they say..."

Ruth grunted.

"No good deed goes unpunished."

"Yeah, well, that's the truth." She wasn't amused.

"Hey, you ready for dinner?"

Chapter 22

BRIGHT SUN REFLECTED off thick frost, and the world sparkled.

"God, it's beautiful, isn't it?" Ruth proclaimed as Paloma climbed into the warm truck.

Paloma eyed Ruth, "Where is Ruth Willows, and what have you done to her?"

"What!"

"You haven't been this chipper since... you won the tenth-grade science fair and got a brand new microscope."

"Portable electronic microscope, thank you," Ruth's grin stretched from ear to ear. She pulled the car out of the drive.

"Cowboy, sure put a smile on your face."

"Yes, me and Cowboy, and the sheriff and the Detective had a really hot time," Ruth told her the saga of the interrogation.

Paloma prodded, "How was the dinner and movie part?"

Ruth smiled, "Oh, that was ... fine. We never got to the movie part." She kept a straight face as long as she could before she burst into giggles.

Paloma gasped, "Did you two...you know....so soon?"

"No!" Ruth exclaimed.

"What happened?"

"We hung out. We ate Chinese, we talked, we kinda just chilled."

"Nothing juicy?" Paloma frowned, "What did you talk about?"

"He forced me to tell him," Ruth was finding it hard to admit, "the entire story of how I took pictures of Bowman and Gills."

Paloma thought for a moment. "Oh my, you mean the whole I wish I never met you... crying in the car... thing. How did he pry that out of you?"

"Chocolate."

Paloma cocked an eyebrow.

With a smirk, Ruth resumed, "He just slowly, seductively, fed me truffles till he wore me down."

Paloma swallowed, "Where'd he get truffles?"

"They were a Christmas gift from... Missy," Ruth chortled.

"That's priceless," Paloma crowed. "Anything else fun?"

"I told him I was a virgin," Ruth said flatly.

"Why did you do that?"

"I figured, why not? I mean we were, kissing, you know, and I wanted him to know that I wasn't used to, well, you know, going all the way..." Ruth stammered a little, "But I told him it was because I had never wanted to 'be' with anyone, and things might be different now."

"I'm almost afraid to ask," Paloma said. "What did he say?"

"He said he understood, but that he was definitely not a virgin."

"Did he say how much of not a virgin he was?"

"No. He said he's had an occasional girlfriend, but that he mostly played the field."

"How far did things go?" Paloma sounded like an investigative reporter.

"Well," Ruth squirmed at the uncomfortable question, "we were enjoying each other a lot."

"Yeah," Paloma was hanging on her every word.

"I mean, I was really enjoying it. And I don't know if I would have gone all the way right then, but I was definitely willing to go further ... when he just stopped."

Paloma's face deflated. "What? What did he say?"

"He said it was late and time to go," Ruth shrugged.

"Was he not into it?" Paloma questioned.

"He felt like he was into it. I mean, I thought I could tell what was going on, ya know? All his working parts seemed to be working."

Paloma just looked at her. "Maybe he just wants to take it slow."

Ruth pulled into the parking lot, turned off the truck, and changed the subject. "What happened with Scott?"

As they crossed the parking lot into school, Paloma explained, "We fought ... We made up. It was nowhere near as romantic sounding as your weekend, but we went for ice cream. We also agreed to go over our schedules so we could make time to see each other. By the way, I'm going to be at the paper four days a week after school, so I guess I'll have to drive my own car starting Wednesday."

"Aw, I'll miss you. But four afternoons a week and you made up with Scott - that all sounds good," Ruth said.

It didn't take long to get back into the routine of school. By the end of the week, Ruth's homeroom teacher asked her to report to the office. As Ruth walked down the dreary hall toward the office, she daydreamed about Ken. The memory of his cologne on his freshly shaved face made her smile. She looked into the large office windows and saw her Cowboy standing at the copier.

"Well, looks like someone had a delightful break," Lezza chirped as Ruth leaned her elbows on the counter.

Before Ruth could answer, the buzzer for the delivery door buzzed.

"Hold on, I gotta get that door," Lezza jumped up and went to Carol Ann's unoccupied desk. She checked the monitor and buzzed the delivery guy in. “These office supplies are a month late. They never got ordered when we were furloughed and...”

Before Lezza could finish her complaint, Principal Rodriguez’s office door burst open, and Carol Ann rushed out.

“I gotta get someone from the school board on the phone; this is getting ridiculous,” Carol Ann spat out and headed to her desk.

“What can I do for you, Ruth?” Lezza approached her from the opposite side of the counter.

“I need to sign some forms before the university’s classes start next week.”

A delivery guy propped opened the office door and piled boxes in the narrow walkway beside the counter.

“You can’t leave those there!” Carol Ann shouted at him as one hand covered the receiver, “It’s a fire hazard to block a walkway!”

“Bring them around to this side of the counter,” Lezza suggested. He almost knocked Ruth over with his first load. “Come to my desk, Ruth. Carol Ann, will you hand me those financial release forms from the university?”

Carol Ann held out a folder as she spoke with a school board member. Her words were clear. “It might be disrespectful, but the students in her class are refusing to call her Doctor, and she’s becoming violent about it... She threw something... No, no, I don’t think it hit anyone. But one of the students is in the principal’s office complaining ... Yes, she’s in there too... She wants to call the sheriff... No, the student... Yes, yes, all right... I’ll transfer you.”

“Ruth, these are the papers you need to sign.” Carol Ann handed the file to Ruth.

Leaning over to sign her name Ruth exclaimed, “Wow, Lezza, your desk! It looks amazing!”

It was neat, clean, and well organized.

"Glad you like it. I can't find a damn thing anymore–pardon my French."

"What inspired you to...to...reorganize?" Ruth ventured to ask.

"They ordered me to." She shot a look over to Carol Ann. "It seems our temp didn't like her working conditions when she filled in for us and went crying to her uncle on the board. I was told to clean it up or not come back."

"After our pay cut," Carol Ann interjected, "I don't know why we came back!"

"I told you before, Car, I have half a mind to submit my retirement papers today. Let this school fall apart. See how much I care as I'm vacationing in Florida."

"You know as well as I do..." Carol Ann's thought was interrupted when Principal Rodriguez's door swung open.

Paloma emerged first. Her face was red. She flew out of the inner office and ran to the first phone she saw, which was on Carol Ann's desk. She placed both hands on the receiver but didn't pick it up.

Everyone heard Principal Rodriguez's quiet voice, "Elizabeth, calm yourself. We don't want this to go any further–do we?" he finished with an air of warning.

When the principal emerged everyone, except Paloma busied themselves. Lezza and Ruth fiddled with the papers she needed to sign. Ken collected his copies and made ready to leave. Carol Ann rummaged in a drawer.

"Paloma," Principal Rodriguez walked over to her, "let's take a walk. Oh, Ruth, how are you?"

"Good sir," Ruth replied. She saw Cowboy give her a quick wink from behind the principal's back, and she tried to suppress a grin.

"How did that math paper of yours turn out? Did you get the information you needed?"

"Yes, sir, it turned out fine. Got an A," Ruth answered.

"Good, glad to hear it. Come on, Paloma, let's go see if the vending machines have anything good today." He held the office door open for Paloma. The delivery guy took advantage and pushed his hand truck in with his last load of supplies.

Ruth handed the signed papers back to Lezza.

Lezza held up a yellow file. "That reminds me, Ruth, I found this when I was cleaning up my desk. I'm surprised you brought it back."

"Brought what back?" Ruth was puzzled.

Elizabeth Gills stepped out of the principal's office, poised to speak, but Lezza continued to Ruth, "Didn't you use this for that math paper?"

Ruth wasn't sure what to say. Her brain swirled with a flood of disjointed information, including her recent visit with the Sheriff, and her stomach rolled.

"Yes, I used..." she stammered, took a step backward, and teetered over a newly delivered box of paper. She fell in slow motion. It would have been funny under different circumstances. She landed on Ken, who was passing by her as he was leaving, taking him to the ground with her.

"For crying out loud, Willows," Gills bellowed from Rodriguez's door frame, "You are the most graceless, awkward child I know. And you make too much of a habit of landing on Mr. Silver, regardless of how well your families know each other."

"Betsy, it was an accident!" Lezza defended Ruth.

Ruth was mortified and outraged simultaneously.

Ken whispered into her ear, "Are you all right, Baby Doll?"

She nodded her head and said loud enough for Gills to hear, "I'm so sorry! Are you okay?"

"I'm fine," he answered with a smile and gave her a small push up. He stood and, while looking straight at Gills, said, "I'll see you in class-Miss Willows." He gave her a wink, picked up his papers, and left the office.

Every eye watched him leave and close the door behind him.

"Twenty years younger, and I'd like to fall into his lap," Lezza fanned herself with her hand and batted her eyes at Carol Ann.

"Twenty years nothing, I'd fall into anything of his right now," Carol Ann countered. Both secretaries broke into a cackle.

"You two better not let anyone hear you, or you'll be out on your ears for sexual harassment," Gills scolded.

"Betsy, you certainly have a bee in your bonnet today," Carol Ann chided back. "Ruth, really, are you okay?" Carol Ann inquired.

Ruth nodded, blushed, and said, "Really, I'm fine."

"So, did you take the information I printed out for you or not?" Lezza directed the conversation back to the previous subject.

Ruth nodded and tried to think of a way out of this bind.

"But you say you never took this yellow folder. It's been here on my desk for you."

"I took the manila folder you told me to grab."

"Manila? No, I put it in this folder."

Carol Ann spoke up with authority, "What was in the folder you took, Ruth?"

"Just some really old budgets, like twenty years old." Ruth sheepishly answered.

"That's not what I printed for you at all," Lezza said. "I got you teacher salaries from as far back as I could get them. That's what you asked for."

Ruth didn't know what to say. Lezza, Carol Ann, and Gills stared at her. She shrugged her shoulders, "I...I... I'm sorry? I guess I took the wrong folder."

"What else was in the folder, honey?" Carol Ann asked in a soothing voice.

"Nothing. Just a few old budgets. I didn't even use the whole thing. I just took the first three years off the top to compare spending practices."

"How big was the folder?" Lezza sounded a little panic-stricken.

"Not big," Ruth tried to downplay what she knew was an essential piece of evidence. "It was just a few really old budgets and spending reports. They weren't even complete; I had to make up numbers for departments that weren't listed."

"That doesn't sound like anything I've ever seen before. Have you ever seen old reports like that, Carol Ann?" Lezza, definitely worried, looked to her companion.

"I have no idea where something like that could have come from." Carol Ann replied. "Ruth, you better bring it back in ASAP. God help us if something important goes missing, we'll all be out on our ears, and with no severance package to boot."

"I don't know where it is." Ruth was trying not to sound panicked herself.

Gills was still stood in the inner doorway, making disparaging tsking sounds.

Paloma and Rodriguez returned. "Paloma, the bell's going to ring soon. Go to class and forget about all this for now. Try to have a good day. We'll take care of your cell phone. I'll speak to your parents and explain what happened."

Paloma and Ruth gravitated towards each other. "Yes, Mr. Rodriguez," Paloma answered.

Rodriguez continued with drill sergeant like focus, "Carol Ann, get Miss Laurence to cover for Elizabeth. Elizabeth, I just got a message from Superintendent Hulls. He'll be here any minute. Let's get your story straight." They disappeared into his office.

Ruth and Paloma made for the door, but Lezza's voice stopped them, "Ruth really, I need to get that file back. I don't want to be fired over this."

Ruth nodded as the first-period bell rang. Both girls shot out of the office and headed to class.

"What was that all about?" Ruth clung to Paloma's arm as they hurried down the hall. "What is going on? You looked terrified when you flew out of Rodriguez's office?"

"I refused to call Mrs. Gills, Doctor in homeroom today. Apparently, I'm not the first student to recognize the irony of the situation, but I was the first to say it to her face. She's been hearing mutterings in her classes since the story broke. I'm so used to referring to her just as Gills, especially at the paper, that missus slipped out. She got annoyed at me and demanded that I call her Dr. Gills in front of the class. I couldn't do it. When the rest of the homeroom started chanting Mrs. Gills, Mrs. Gills she threw a fit. Actually, she threw a paperweight."

"At you?" Ruth's eyes were as big as saucers.

"No. It was more towards the heater. The metal vents have a huge dent in them."

"What did she say to you?"

"She wanted me to apologize for being impertinent, but I wasn't impertinent! At first, it was an accident, but let's face it, her name is still Mrs. Gills, and she is not a doctor, and I see no reason why anyone should call her Doctor."

"Did you say that to her?"

"Well, only after she threw the paperweight. And I was very polite; I was not impertinent!"

"Oh, Paloma!" Ruth was still agog looking at her, "How did you end up in Rodriguez's office?"

"She grabbed my arm and dragged me down to the office, threatening to get me expelled. When we were in front of the Principal, I took out my phone to call the sheriff, and she took it and threw it across the room."

"You were going to call the sheriff?"

"She was losing control, and Rodriguez wasn't doing anything."

"You were pushing her buttons."

"I don't think I said anything wrong."

The bell signaling the start of first period rang. Paloma mouthed, "What about you?" as she headed across the hall to her class.

Ruth whispered, "I'll tell you later," and she went into History class.

AP English was only two doors down from history. Ruth grabbed Paloma in the hall after class and led her close to Ken's desk so he could hear the conversation.

"You know that math paper I had to do last semester?" Ruth began, "When Lezza cleaned her desk, she found the folder of data she had printed out for me."

"I thought you took a folder from her desk for your paper," Paloma played along.

"It must have been the wrong one. Now Lezza wants me to bring the folder I took back, in case it was something important, but I don't know where it is."

Paloma's jaw dropped as she understood the magnitude of the situation. "What are you gonna do, Ruth?"

Ruth glanced at Ken, who was listening as he glanced at his class notes. "I said that I didn't know where the folder was. I don't know what to do since I don't think I have it anymore."

"Must call Uncle Bob," Ken said out loud as if he was writing a note to himself. Then he looked up at Ruth and Paloma, "Would you ladies kindly take your seats?"

★ ★ ★

Much to Cowboy's frustration, Ruth didn't call Uncle Bob.

"They're just worried about losing their jobs," Ruth said of the two secretaries, as she and Cowboy stretched across the sofa in the Willows' family room. "If there's anyone I don't trust, it's Gills. Did you hear what she did to Paloma?"

"Did you hear how belligerent Paloma was to a teacher?" Ken retorted.

"I don't remember Paloma throwing anything at Gills, or dragging her down the hall, or breaking her cell phone," Ruth defended her friend.

Ken hugged Ruth tightly, "We need to not discuss school, and you should call Uncle Bob."

Ruth huffed out a sigh.

Chapter 23

***SATURDAY.* SHE GROANED** and rolled over. *Why not just lie in bed all day? Because if you don't get out of bed, nothing will get done, and you'll never get to your beach house in Mexico.* She groaned again.

The house would be on the market in March. She had spent most winter break getting rid of unnecessary stuff. Her original plan to arrive in Mexico with little more than the clothes on her back had been rethought since the pay decrease, and who knew what would become of her retirement plan.

She padded down the hall to the bathroom, and the house was silent. She hadn't seen her son for days, a week even.

As she showered, something nagged at her, but she couldn't put her finger on it. It had begun last night and kept her from going out and enjoying a Friday night at Mike's. The hot water rushed over her head and down her body; she closed her eyes and tried to organize her thoughts. Since he was MIA, she'd clean out her son's room.

She turned off the shower and dried off. She wondered what would become of her boy.

The nagging feeling returned as she sat on her bed. The image of a blond college girl her son had briefly dated ran through her mind. Then, behind closed eyes, that image changed to another young blonde–*Willows! That's what's been stuck in my craw!*

Yesterday's scene in the office flooded into her consciousness, and it didn't sit right with her. *Why be so cagey about a folder? What was really in the one she took?*

She needed to think. *The girl took the wrong folder; let's assume that was an accident. She said it contained old district budgets. How did that get into the office? Could Hector Alverez have brought in the file? Because if he did... this could be bad.*

Was Alverez carrying anything with him that day? She just couldn't remember. She had had her head stuck under the copier, pretending to fix it. *I didn't get a good look at him when he walked in the door. He hadn't had a briefcase or a laptop, I would have found that. But he had wanted to see Rodriguez about the budget. He could have had paperwork with him.* And once Rodriguez knew, it would finish her.

Images of her face as a mug shot floated through her brain; she pounded her fists on the bed. *Keep on track! What if Alverez brought in a manila folder of budgets and had ... placed it on the desk... and it had got lost with all the other folders! That had to be it! The sheriff's department had concentrated on the crime scene; they'd never searched the office. If that Willows girl hadn't taken it, it would still be where Alverez had left it.*

What should I do? She wished she knew what was in it. *The only way to do that is to get it back. How?* She could ask. She doubted that would work, but she'd try. *If the girl doesn't hand it over, what then?* She'd have to take it.

Breaking and entering seemed minor next to murder when she thought about it.

She finished dressing and went straight to her computer. It took her no time to log into the school's account and find all the student emergency information. She learned Ruth lived at Tall Willows Ranch, a business owned by Joe Willows. Her mother Constance worked for the ranch, and her father Ed worked for the State in the engineering department. Ruth had a younger sister, Grace, also in high school. She copied the ranch's address and all the phone numbers listed.

Next, she Google mapped the ranch. She studied both the roads and the satellite images. By the time she gathered all the information she'd thought useful, it was afternoon. She decided that a little bike ride was in order. She headed straight for Tall Willows.

Large fir trees framed the driveway's entrance, but she missed the sign that said, Tall Willows. When she realized her mistake, she made a U-turn. A black jeep wrangler wanted to make a left into the drive as she made her second pass, so she couldn't stop and look. She lowered the dark visor on her helmet and sped past the waiting Jeep. The road widened. She pulled over and turned off her bike. *This isn't going to be easy. There are too many trees to get a view of anything from the road.* She made three more passes, hoping for inspiration before she headed home.

★ ★ ★

She wanted to go back to the ranch early Sunday morning, but the weather had turned snowy and icy overnight; too dangerous to take the bike. Instead, she went back to the computer and printed satellite images of the buildings at Tall Willows. She packed a compass, flashlight, binoculars, and an emergency window breaker into an old backpack so she'd be prepared when her opportunity arose.

The week was slow going. Work was tedious. Try as she might to get out and do some surveillance of the Willows Ranch after school, the early sunset and waning moon didn't help.

She was ready to burst from frustration by Friday, so she had the Willows girl summoned to the office. She took Ruth to a small room used for private conferences.

"Ruth dear, you remember the conversation about that folder you accidentally picked up?"

"Yes," Ruth replied cautiously.

"Well... have you had any luck finding it?"

"No," Ruth was careful.

"Don't you think it's a rather important item you need to bring back to the school? I wouldn't want anyone to accuse you of stealing."

"I didn't steal anything!" Ruth could hardly believe what she was hearing, "I took the folder I was told to take."

"I think it's time you brought it back. I'm sure you don't want anyone fired. Why don't you bring it back, and no one will say anything more about it?"

"I'd like to... but... I can't," Ruth had an answer planned.

"What do you mean?"

"I mean, I don't have it. I threw it out when I cleaned out my backpack for the new semester."

"Are you sure?"

"Yes. I threw it away."

"Could you have left it in the recycle bin? I know your family has a business; did you leave it in your family's office? Or..."

Ruth cut her off, "I didn't leave it anywhere! I threw it away in the garbage. I don't have it. I can't bring it back. I didn't know I needed to bring it back!"

Ruth swung open the door, "I'm sorry. I have to go, I have a biology class, and I need at least half an hour to get there."

She watched Ruth's blonde hair fade into the sea of students before the door swung closed. She didn't believe that girl's story for a minute. *I'll just have to go and see for myself.*

★ ★ ★

Saturday dawned bright, clear, and cold. This was it, a three-day weekend for M.L.K. day; she had plenty of daylight for surveillance and a good possibility that the family would be away because of the school break. She dressed in warm coveralls; *I look so androgynous;* she thought as she glanced at herself in the mirror. She told herself it was for the best, grabbed the backpack she'd prepared, and hopped onto her bike.

She made it to Tall Willows before nine a.m. and did several passes before deciding on the best place to park and enter the woods. She knew that the trees were only two-hundred feet deep from the road and open space lay between the tree line and the house from her maps. She'd chosen a point on the north side of the property where the trees came the closest to the house. She parked her bike between two firs. Her heart pounded loudly in her chest. She moved slowly through the woods till she reached her spot.

Her vantage point gave her a good view of the back of the barn to the left. To the right, she had a good view of the front of the house. She pulled out a camouflage tarp, covered herself, and got her binoculars ready.

Activity was in full swing. She made out two people moving in and out of the barn, surrounded by too many horses for her taste. With binoculars to her eyes, she spotted Ruth and a man, maybe her father or grandfather. It was hard to tell since they both dressed in Carhartts and knit hats; she only recognized Ruth because of the long blonde braid that hung down her back.

She watched them work for a while. She was surprised by a car pulling out from the back of the house down the driveway. She tried to get a look at the driver, but the angle on the sun prevented her from seeing much. She made a note of the car; a dark blue - Chevy Tahoe.

As she watched the car disappear, she realized more cars must be parked on the other side of the house. She got out her maps and tried to find another point that would give her better views of the back of the house. A few hundred feet to the south, the tree line was a little further away, but a small hill might conceal her and give her a better view.

Carefully, she made her way south and settled in again. She had a small glimpse of the drive and a glorious view of the back of the house, barn, and yard. She saw vehicles parked in a carport. Best of all, she could see the backdoor to the house.

First, she noted the parked vehicles; an older green Ford Ranger, a newer red Chevy Silverado. *The girl drives that green one to school.* A flash of light alerted her to someone coming down the driveway. The Tahoe had come back and parked next to the Ford. A woman drove, and a girl with darker hair sat beside her; *Mother and sister, I presume.*

Her stomach growled, and she looked at her watch - twelve-thirty. Her legs were frozen, and she was getting hungry. Another flash caught her eye. The black Jeep Wrangler pulled around to the back of the house. A man clad in jeans, winter coat, and cowboy hat crossed to the house.

This man walked directly to the back door of the house, but he knocked and waited. It looked like Ruth answered the door, and they seemed to be a little too close for too long a time for her to be saying hello to her daddy. She'd forgotten that she held binoculars in her half-frozen hands. By the time she raised them to her eyes - *too late, he's gone inside. But it looks as though little Ruth has got herself a lover. She didn't seem the type, too prissy, but I guess there's someone for everyone.*

★ ★ ★

Most church services began by nine o'clock on Sunday mornings. She forced herself to get to Tall Willows by eight-thirty a.m. She pulled her bike snuggly between the fir trees and trekked to her hiding place on the hill. She'd hardly settled herself when four people appeared–one man, one woman, and two girls. She pulled the binoculars from the bag and focused on the man; He looks like the grandfather. Regardless, there should be another man in the house. She wondered where he could be.

The dark blue Tahoe pulled away, and she sat and sat and sat. *What am I waiting for? I don't know where the missing Willows is, but if he ain't home, I should take advantage of this opportunity.*

She worked her way through the woods and came out on the drive-way. She left her tarp on the ground and stepped out into the drive. She hadn't gone three steps when she heard the sound of gravel crunching. *They can't be back already!*

She grabbed the tarp, flew back into the woods, and took cover behind a fallen tree. She held her breath as the car, a white four-door sedan with an official-looking seal on the door, passed. She lay there till the crunching of the gravel stopped, and the racing of her heart slowed.

Cautiously, she made it back to her hill. The white car was parked in the carport. She pulled out her binoculars to study the emblem on the vehicle. It was the state seal. The words under it were difficult to make out, but it seemed to read Department of Engineering; *daddy's home.*

Annoyed that someone always seemed to be in the house, she rethought her plans. She got back to the road and hopped on her bike. As she pulled onto the shoulder, the black Jeep Wrangler drove into the ranch, this time pulling a small horse trailer. *The boyfriend is back.* She lowered her visor and waited until the Jeep was out of sight before she departed.

★ ★ ★

Monday came, and her last chance to study the Willows family. It snowed overnight, so she took her time heading out to the ranch.

She had her routine down; back the bike between the two fir trees, then head to her lookout point. The house and grounds were again lively with activity; horses in the fields surrounding the barn and in distant pastures, vehicles, including the black Jeep, were parked out back. Horses whinnied, and voices cracked the silence. She scanned the yard, and to her dismay, four people moved toward her, sleds in hand. She looked down her hill and spotted tracks made from a morning of sled riding.

They're coming up here! She scurried backward on her belly as fast as she could to the tree line.

The first person making it to the top must have been Ruth's younger sister because she wore a dark braid down her back. Next one she'd know anywhere, *Torres, that snotty little pain.* Then Ruth came into view. Finally, would be the boyfriend, she assumed. He crested the hill, but she was too far away to see his face. He had a familiar look to him, *must be a kid from school.* The first two girls hopped onto their sleds, and he gave them a push down the hill. Then, alone with Ruth, he pulled her into his arms for a blistering kiss. *WOW!*

She dug out her binoculars and focused on his face; who was this young Romeo? *My, My, My, My, MY!* She could hardly believe her eyes. She bit her gloved finger to keep herself from squealing. *Mr. Ken Silver, if you stick that tongue of yours any further down her throat, you'll pull out her tonsils.* She gawked at the kissing couple. *So your families have been friends for a long time–is that your story?*

The other two girls made it back to the top of the hill. This time all four of them mounted their sleds and sped over the crest and out of sight.

She was giddy with her new information, but what to do with it? As quickly as she could, she made it back to her bike and sped away.

★ ★ ★

She sat quietly in the staff lounge and sipped her coffee. Everyone had babbled about their long weekend. Ken had said nothing about frolicking at the Willows ranch with his student. She snickered at the thought and waited for an opportunity.

He graded papers as the crowd in the staff room thinned.

"You know Ken," She interrupted him, "I'm surprised you didn't come in here with a story of some exciting trip you took last weekend like everyone else did. You're the youngest teacher. I thought you'd be out having adventures."

He looked up from grading papers and shrugged, "You got me. I'm just a boring guy." He went back to grading.

"I don't believe that for a minute. A handsome young man like yourself! I can't believe you're not out enjoying the nightlife every chance you get. Heck, when I was your age, I don't think I ever slept."

"My horse takes up a good bit of my free time."

"A horse!" she laughed, "I thought you were going to tell me that you have a young lady that keeps you occupied."

He wasn't sure how to reply. No one at school had ever talked to him about personal matters, and he'd been glad about that.

He eyed her, suspiciously, "Are you asking me if I'm available?"

That caught her off balance. Her face went flush. "Well... I was... only wondering... um... because... I have a niece..."

"A niece?"

"Yes, beautiful. Smart girl. I thought the two of you might get along..."

"Well, I'm flattered, but I'm seeing someone."

"Oh really, who is she?" this should be an interesting answer, she thought.

"We met at SCU. I'm working on a... project, and she's a senior," he answered.

Knowing the truth, she kept her gloat to herself. "Are you at least going to do something fun with her this weekend?"

He didn't really want to continue this conversation. He had to finish it somehow. "We're going to a horse auction. We're helping a friend."

"That's your idea of exciting? Honey!" An undeniable look of disgust flashed across her face.

It was his turn to laugh, "Nothing like a road trip with my gal and a bunch of horses to make me happy." He gathered up his papers, "Gotta teach class," he announced, happy to go.

Oh, you go right ahead and teach your class Mr. Silver; she thought as an evil sneer spread across her face.

Chapter 24

THE HORSES HEADED to the auction were loaded into two trailers, one pulled by Joe's truck, the other by Ruth's. Ken found her sitting behind the wheel, heater blasting, and eyes closed. She didn't look too ready to head out.

He opened the driver's side door, "Slide over, I'll drive."

"That's not your job description today; you're a wrangler, I'm a driver," she said sleepily.

"You can barely keep your eyes open. Now slide over." He pushed her over with his hips as he slid behind the wheel. She grunted nonverbal complaints but buckled her seatbelt and curled into a ball.

"I left early last night 'cause we had an early start today. Did you sleep at all last night, Baby Doll?" he asked as he slowly followed the other truck down the drive.

"I tried, but it was after two the last time I checked the clock, and then I got up around four."

"What kept you up so late?"

She mumbled something incoherent.

Joe's truck stopped at the end of the drive.

"What d'you say?" He glanced at her, then turned his eyes back to the horse trailer in front of him.

"I fell asleep right away, then I had a dream, and I couldn't sleep after that," she explained quietly.

"Hold on a minute, Baby Doll." Ken held up one hand.

Joe was stopped for an unusually long time. Wanting to see if there was a problem, Ken opened the truck door. A blast of icy air hit him when he stepped out. He saw Joe had his window open and was talking to a guy on a bike. It was the same black cycle with the green flames that he'd seen before. Ken got back in and closed the door, "Your Granddaddy's talking to your neighbor with the cool bike."

Ruth opened her eyes and turned her head towards Ken, "What neighbor with a cool bike?"

"I don't know," Ken answered. "It's the same bike I've seen driving past your place. I figured the guy must live around here."

"I don't know anyone with a motorcycle." She looked at him sideways. "The kids down the road have dirt bikes... they're not supposed to ride them on the road."

"Well, I've seen that bike almost every time I've come here. It's a really cool, black Ninja with green flames–kinda hard to miss, you know?"

"I guess?" Ruth knew little about motorcycles and was too tired to think about them.

Joe's truck and trailer pulled forward, and Ken and Ruth followed. As they made the turn onto the road, the bike was still on the shoulder. The rider had the dark visor of the helmet down and had a map in a gloved hand. Ruth stared; *it's not that bright out to have your visor down. And what's the need a map for if he lives around here?*

Ken pulled her out of her thoughts as they headed down the road, "So tell me about this bad dream you had."

"Oh..." she sunk back into her upright fetal position, hugging her seatbelt, "It wasn't really a bad dream... It was more, just... animated."

"You mean like cartoon animated?"

"No, I mean..." She knew what she meant, but she didn't want to come out and say it. "It was the kind of dream when...you can...feel everything going on in your dream in your actual body, you know? And when you wake up, it just... stays with you... and you can't get rid of what was going on."

"So what was going on in this emotional dream of yours?" he smiled light-heartedly.

She let her head fall down to the door, "Nothing, it was nothing. I just woke up and couldn't get back to sleep."

Ken thought in silence before a twist of a smile crossed his lips. He held back a laugh as he said, "So you're saying it was an erotic dream?"

She squeezed her eyes tightly and mumbled, "Maybe -Yes."

He blurted out a laugh, "That's why they invented cold showers, Baby Doll."

"Oh, shut up!" she snapped at him, "I didn't need a cold shower!"

He slid his hand across the bench seat and stroked her leg as he continued to tease her. "So what did you do to get yourself to sleep? I hope you were thinking of me while you were doing it..."

"Leave me alone," she pushed his hand away. "I hate you!" came blurting out of her mouth.

This made him laugh all the more, and he likewise blurted out, "No, you don't. You love me!"

The words hung in thick, uncomfortable silence between them.

She never meant to say I hate you, but she was not about to be the first to say I love you. His silence made it all the worse.

Ken followed Joe onto the deserted highway and set the cruise control.

"I didn't mean to say I hate you, Cowboy. I'm sorry," she said with a crack in her voice.

"I know." He reached for her hand. "You're tired. Close your eyes, get some sleep. We have a long drive."

With her seatbelt still on, she laid her torso across the seat and rested her head on Ken's leg. He slid off his down vest and covered her. He draped his arm along her body.

As she drifted into sleep, he lost himself in thought.

He'd known lots of girls... lots. A wide smile grew across his face as he remembered a whole stretch of one-night stands after he got his first apartment. There were a few he had dated for a short stretch. But he'd never told any of them he loved them. He'd made a conscious decision a long time ago that he would never utter those words until he had found the one.

What's your problem, man? You've dated her for barely a month, and - love - is what you're hung up about–you're ridiculous! Yes, but you've known her for longer than just a few weeks. Ha, six months is a blink of an eye in a lifetime. But she's different. You haven't even slept with her. Not while she's my student. It's absurd enough this seeing her only at her house bullshit. I shouldn't say shit - her family is overly accommodating. They put up with me always being there. Anyway, I asked for it! For crying out loud, I asked her father for permission to date her and told him I cared deeply for her–where the hell did that come from? I'm not saying I don't. Just what on earth possessed me to say such a thing?

He felt the rise and fall of her breath as she slept, and his arm rested on her side. *Is this really worth it? Am I happy?* He thought back to last fall. *That was hell; seeing her every day, and I didn't even treat her with respect.* He was ashamed of his behavior. *Yeah,* he smiled despite himself as he stroked her hair; *I'm happy. Would I change anything? Well, this being her teacher throws a wrench into things. But then again, it's also forcing me to be–a better person... So what's really eating you?*

The words - *What Comes Next?* popped into his brain with no prompting. *Nah, how can I be worried about that? There are too many ifs in life to worry about what comes next. And why should I? I'm a young guy with no responsibilities except to myself–and my horse. Anyway, she's just a girl. No, she's not just any girl - she's a very special girl... and then again without any warning,* his brain said–*and I do love her, and I want her to be the one...*

Ruth stirred in his lap. He didn't want to disturb her, but he prayed she'd wake so he'd have someone to talk to aside from his crackpot self. She breathed deeply, stretched, and slowly sat up. She blinked at the brightness of the day.

"I guess I fell asleep," she moaned. "For how long?"

"Oh, bout an hour," he smiled.

"That long?" she whined. "I'm sorry."

"I'm not. You needed it."

"How are you? Do you need a break or anything?"

"I'm fine, Baby Doll. How are you?"

"Better," she gave him a weak smile. "How far do we have to go?"

"I guess about forty-five miles. This road is winding, and the wind has picked up, so Joe has really slowed down the pace." He asked, "What time does the auction open?"

"It starts at nine, but buyers can look at the stock starting at eight-thirty You know Granddaddy has to be early for everything." Her last remark had a biting edge to it.

"You told me you argued with your family yesterday, but you didn't say why. Wanna tell me about it?"

She took a moment before she began. "What am I doing every single time you come over?"

"Waiting for me with bated breath?" he grinned.

She rolled her eyes at him. She leaned over and kissed his cheek. It was a little rough from not shaving, but he was warm and inviting, and she let her lips linger. "Aside from that, what else am I usually doing?" She didn't wait for an answer, "I'm working in the barn! No matter what we plan to do, you spend the first hour helping me muck out stalls, prep grain, clean waters, work a horse, whatever. And why am I always out there?" Another rhetorical question, "Because Grace is always off at an art class or something, and I have to do her work for her."

"The deal is that we are both supposed to work in the barn, and we get to do other things. Like, I used to get money for show entries, now it's gas money to drive to the university. For the last few months, Grace has just stopped coming out to the barn. I've had to pick up her slack, and she just stays inside and paints and draws and signs up for art classes and does whatever she wants."

"Granddaddy was pissed when he found out that Mom had to take her to an art symposium in Denver yesterday. She signed up for it without checking to see if anything else was on the calendar."

"Yesterday morning was the last straw. Mom and Grace weren't leaving till noon. Did I get the morning off? No, Grace hid out in her room pretending to pack while I worked. She'd been packed and ready to go for the last week."

"When she came moseying out to say goodbye, some muck missed the wheelbarrow and hit her."

"Oh, Baby Doll, you didn't," Ken exclaimed.

"It only got on her shoes. Anyway, you shouldn't wear big fuzzy boots into a barn if you're afraid they'll get dirty!" Ruth continued, "Grace started throwing a hissy-fit."

Ken was laughing to himself. Grace was a lovely girl, but she was definitely higher maintenance than her older sister.

"She ran screaming to Mom and Dad, who told her to clean her boots off and not to go in the barn if she didn't expect to get a little dirty."

Ken sounded disappointed, "Where was the big fight?"

"Oh, it came next.They all came into the barn to yell at me but I told them I was tired of doing all my barn work and all her barn work. I reminded them that even if I spent time with you, I always put in six hours of work before you show up."

"Then I asked Granddaddy how many people he was planning on hiring to fill in for me when I go to school next year so that Grace could continue to sit on her delicate little be-hind and do nothing but draw pictures all day."

"Did you say that?" Ken gasped.

"Word for word."

"What happened then?"

"Not too much. Mom and Gracie took off. Daddy and Granddaddy told me to finish loading the trailers with hay, and then I could be done for the day. You came over, and that was that."

Ken was not sure of what to say. He wondered just what Joe and Constance would do with Ruth gone next year. He wondered what he would do with her gone next year too. "Have you submitted your college apps?"

"Early action, nothing binding."

"Where did you apply?"

"Northwestern, Rutgers, UC Berkeley, Colorado State Ft. Collins, and Penn State Plus, since I've got A's in my first two classes at the USC, they offered to matriculate me, but I didn't officially apply to them."

"Wow, I'm impressed," and he was. "Those are notable schools. You have any preferences?"

"I've been comparing Biology programs. Colorado State has a fascinating School of Natural Sciences. They have a zoology program, and they offer interesting research projects for both undergrads and grad students. As a matter of fact, there's a graduate research project going on right now that I would love to be in on."

Ken blew out a jovial sigh, "You haven't even picked your undergrad school, and you're already thinking about grad student projects?"

"Well... there's a lot to consider..." There was a twist in the pit of her stomach, and she blew out a sigh, "Any thoughts?"

"Ooh, Baby Doll, this is your decision. I can't get involved with it."

"But..." she wasn't sure how to ask what she'd been thinking, "if you're involved with me... doesn't that kinda make you a part of my decision?"

He grabbed hold of her hand, kissed her palm, and held it tight. "I am so happy being with you. But I can't ask you to base your entire future on me, right now, any more than you would ask me to base my entire future on you." He looked at her as best he could while keeping an eye on the road and trailer in front of him. He could tell by the tension in her body she didn't like the direction of his speech. "I'm not saying that you should go to school and forget about us–I'm not. I'm saying that this has to be a selfish decision on your part. You need to do what is best for you. You understand?"

He still held her hand, and she nodded her head in agreement as she stared straight forward.

"We have cell phones, text messages, social media. Wherever you chose to go to school, we'll keep in touch. The further away you are, the less we'll be able to touch physically," he kissed her hand again, "but whenever you want me, you'll be able to get a hold of me."

★ ★ ★

"That's why I wanted Connie here," Joe explained over a late lunch. "She's great at watching people's reactions and wheedling information out of them. I wanted to see the look in Shane King's eyes when he looked at our colt, but I was too busy talking to that man who wanted the mare for his daughter."

"Shane said he thought he looked like a real nice young horse, Dad," Ed interjected.

"You gotta know the difference between what he said and what he meant." Joe stirred his coffee, "I'll ask Connie to call him about the supplement he was telling me about. See what she can get out of him."

Ed glanced at his watch and said, "Connie and Grace should be home soon. We should get a move on it too, Dad."

"Yup, I'm ready to go." Joe agreed.

"I'll take my cake with me," Ruth offered. "I know trailers need to be cleaned out."

"You stay and finish your dessert, Ruth. Grace has had herself quite an expensive weekend. She's more than capable of changing her clothes and cleaning out the trailers," Ed said as he rose from the table.

Ruth's eyes popped, and she looked from her Dad to her Granddaddy to Ken in shock. Ken gave her leg a squeeze under the table.

Joe pulled out a wad of cash and laid some on the table, "This should cover the food. Make sure the waitress gets a good tip; I want to be able to come back here the next time I'm in town. Grand-baby, this is for you," he handed her several folded bills.

"No, Granddaddy, you don't have to."

"I most certainly do. You made quite a point yesterday. I can't just expect Gracie to want to work as hard in the barn as you do. I probably will have to hire someone to help out next year. But for now, you deserve this."

"Thank you, Granddaddy," she said, accepting the money.

Next, he handed a similar fold of bills to Ken, "Son, this is for you. Thank you for your help today. I couldn't have done it without you here."

"No, sir, I can't take it."

"Nonsense, of course, you can."

"I came because I wanted to. I wanted to see what this sale was like."

"Well, you worked hard, and you deserve to be paid," Joe insisted.

"Come on, Dad, let's go," Ed called to his father. "We'll see you two at home," he added. "Your trailer is empty. Be careful of that wind shear on the highway. I have my cell on if you need anything."

"Yes, Daddy," Ruth smiled.

★ ★ ★

The sun had disappeared behind the peaks when Ruth and Ken pulled into Tall Willows. Red and blue light lit the landscape that was in no way related to the sun.

"Oh, My God!" Ruth shouted as she took the bend in the drive and saw the source of the lights. As they came to a halt, Ruth flew out of the door, leaving the pickup and trailer in the middle of the drive. Ken parked the trailer before joining Ruth and Ed along with Officer Clark beside the two sheriff department cruisers whose lights continued to flash.

"Everyone is fine, Ruth. Grace and your Granddaddy are in the barn doing evening feedings," Ed held Ruth's shoulders to calm her. "Someone broke into the house, that's all. Your mom noticed it when they got home. She called me, and I told her to call the sheriff. They stayed at the neighbor's till Sheriff Davis check it all out and made sure the coast was clear."

"W... wh... wh... why did they break in? Did they take anything?" Ruth stammered.

"That's what your mom and the sheriff are trying to decide now."

"Ruth," Constance called, "I think you better come in here."

The whole gang followed Ruth onto the porch.

Sheriff Davis said, "You all can come into the kitchen. Most of the disturbance seems to have taken place upstairs."

Stunned, Ruth walked in, following her mother and the sheriff. He was right; the kitchen and family room looked normal. A crunching at her feet startled her. She looked to see the glass on one of the sidelight panels of the door broken.

"That's how they got in," Davis explained when he saw Ruth eyeing the door.

"Wasn't hard to reach in and unlock the door after they broke the glass."

She followed Davis and her mother, but she passed the stairs and walked to the other rooms in the house. The dining room looked untouched. The usually tidy parlor had de-shelved books and scattered papers from the desk on to the floor.

"Up here, Ruth," her mother called from the top of the stairs. She followed her mother's voice. When she reached the top of the stairs, she saw her mother and the Sheriff standing in the hallway between her and Grace's rooms. She peered into Grace's room first. It was disheveled like the parlor. A few scattered books and papers about, but nothing destroyed, just gone through.

She turned her head to her room. She longed for a hot shower and her comfortable bed. The thought quickly vanished when she saw the state of her room. Her mind took it in, in slow motion, and she heard someone scream.

Before she knew it, both Ken and her father were behind her, Ken's hands firmly on her shoulders. She was having trouble catching her breath. The screaming was getting annoying; suddenly, she realized the horrible noise was coming from her. She clasped her hands over her mouth to try to stop.

They had destroyed her room; not a shred of anything left in place. Books and papers were scattered, even the bookshelf overturned. Her school bags ripped open. Her drawers flung open and the contents tossed aside. Her bed had been torn apart; bed sheets ripped and mattress slashed.

Her knees buckled, but something, someone held her up. Ken. Next, he handed her a brown paper bag and told her to breathe into it. A chair was placed behind her, and she was told to sit.

Several minutes passed before she could breathe normally. She felt like she was waking from a horrific dream, except the all too actual image was right in front of her face.

"Ruth," Sheriff Davis spoke to her, "we need to know if anything was taken."

"I don't know where to start," Ruth whimpered.

"Did you have anything hidden in your room that someone might have wanted?" He whispered into her ear, "Did you have anything illegal... drugs, something?"

She shook her head, "No, nothing, honestly, nothing like that." Her voice petered out as she thought, "I mean, I gave you the pictures... and I gave you the... Oh, my God! The folder! I gave you the folder from Alverez!"

"That was my first thought," Davis assured her. "Did you make any copies or leave anything out."

"No... No," she said, thinking. "I did my math paper on my computer, but I gave you the whole ... Where's my computer!?"

She rushed into her room. She pushed clothing aside and started looking under her books. "I keep it on my bookshelf," she cried. "I keep it charging when I'm home. Here's the plug, but I can't find my computer!" She tried to upright the bookcase, but the solid wood was too heavy for any one person to lift by themselves. Davis joined her, but even after they uprighted it, her laptop was nowhere.

"All my school work was on it," she had tears in her eyes. "A... a... a paper for English, all my bio notes, and two labs that I was in the middle of writing up. I never use the cloud 'cause I don't trust it. Now I'll never get all that work back. I'll fail... I'll never get to college." She slumped to the floor, amid chaos, with tears streaking down her cheeks, fretting about school work. *You dope, she thought, be glad you're alive, be happy no one's hurt, stop crying over school work!* She couldn't.

Constance came in and guided Ruth out of her room. Constance looked at Davis, "Sheriff, I assume you'll want to ask some more questions, but can we do it downstairs in the kitchen?"

"That's a fine idea."

It was a little easier for Ruth to get control of herself in the kitchen, but she couldn't shake the feeling of betrayal and defilement the intruder had brought.

There wasn't much that either she or Ken could tell Davis that he didn't already know. They had left early that morning for the auction, and the only thing that appeared to be missing was her laptop.

"Did you ask the neighbor if he saw anyone?" Ken asked.

"Tommy went door to door, but these homes are pretty remote," Davis answered. "It's not like they can see each other's front door."

"What about the guy on the bike?" Ken asked again.

Ruth rolled her eyes. *What was it about guys and motorcycles?*

"What bike?" Davis asked his nephew.

"Every time I come here, I pass the same guy on a bike. He was at the end of the drive when we pulled out this morning. Joe talked to him. I assume he's a neighbor," Ken answered.

Davis sent Tommy to get Joe while he questioned Ken about the bike.

"It's a black Kawasaki Ninja. The guy who rides it isn't too big. I've never seen his face, always has his face shield down. But the bike you can't forget."

"Why's that?" Davis asked as Tommy, Joe, and Ed entered the kitchen.

"The Ninja is a cool-looking bike in its own right, but this one has an insane custom paint job: green flames front to back. Looks really wicked, ya know." Ken had a lusty glint in his eyes as he described the bike.

"You talking about that fool of a kid on the motorcycle this morning?" Joe broke into the conversation.

"Yes," Davis replied, "did you speak with him?"

"Sure did," Joe sat in a chair beside Ruth, "said he'd lost his friends. He was trying to decide if he should head up to the highway. Tried to use his cell, but cell phone coverage can be spotty out here at best. I asked him not to rev his bike till we passed."

"And this guy, you saw his face?"

"Nah, never saw his face, kept his face guard down. I just assumed it was a young guy." He looked at Ruth, "He didn't have a very deep voice, but you don't think of young girls out on motorcycles at five a.m., do you?"

"And you're absolutely sure you didn't know him?" Davis asked Joe, and he shook his head no.

"What about the bike?"

"Never saw that before either, Sheriff."

Davis pushed away from the table to stand. "Thank you, folks, for all your cooperation. I'm sorry I couldn't be of more help to you. Ruth, please let me know if you find anything else missing."

He shook hands with Ed and Joe, and Constance. He put his hand on Ruth's shoulder, "I'll keep in touch. I'll send a patrol unit around to keep an eye on things out here. Don't worry." He clapped his nephew on the shoulder and left the kitchen, followed by Officer Clark.

Ed and Joe returned to the barn. Constance put her arms around her daughter. "Ruthie, why don't I make up the couch for you tonight? You can't sleep in your bed even if we clean up your room. We'll get you a new mattress tomorrow. I'll help you straighten everything up in the morning. I don't think it's as bad as it looks."

"Thanks," Ruth sighed. "But what am I going to do about my laptop? I had so much on there!"

"I'm sure if you explain it to your teachers, they'll give you some time to make up the work."

"We'll get a few copies of the report from Uncle Bob to explain what happened," Ken interjected.

Constance patted her daughter's back and said, "I'll go get what we need to make up the couch," and went upstairs.

Ken slid his chair next to Ruth's. "Do you want me to stay with you tonight, Baby Doll?"

She looked into his eyes, "No. I don't think I'm going to school tomorrow, but you still have to go to work. No one invaded your home."

"Are you afraid they'll come back?"

"No," she thought for a moment. "I'm mad! I should have just taken that file back to school when I realized what it was, then none of this would have happened!"

"You're wrong! You did the right thing giving it to the authorities." He took her hands in his.

"Yeah, cause that worked out great!"

"Well, maybe you also should have told the sheriff that the secretaries asked you to bring the file back," Ken suggested.

"Right, I'm sure Carol Ann and Lezza broke into my home today. They're just trying to not get fired. You know, I wouldn't put it past Gills to do something illegal to get what she wants. And I bet Derrick loves zooming around on a stupid motorcycle."

"I think you're wrong about Gills ..." Ken said as Constance reappeared with bedsheets and a blanket.

"I'll leave these for you, Ruth," she said, eyeing the obviously bickering couple. She placed the bundle on the couch before she left.

Ken and Ruth sat in silence, staring at each other with frustration in their eyes.

"Well, if you don't want me to stay, I'd better go," Ken said with a bit of a huff. "I have a staff meeting in the morning, but call me if you need me." He kissed her forehead before he stood to leave.

She sank back into the kitchen chair and watched him in silence as he put on his down vest and cowboy hat. "Night, Cowboy," she offered quietly.

He returned to her and took her in his arms. He kissed her face and finally her lips, "Night, Baby Doll. I'm sorry this happened. I'll talk to you tomorrow."

Chapter 25

THE OFFICE PHONE rang, "Hello...."

"Well, Tootsie, so glad you answered the phone. Makes things much easier when I don't need to be transferred around to find you."

The voice cut her to the quick.

"Albee...," she took a deep breath and tried to compose herself, "long time no hear."

"How's life been treating you, Toots?"

"I'm still working," she said through clenched teeth. "How's early retirement?"

"Well, it really wasn't all that early, you know. I'd put in my time."

"Funny, I thought you still had a year or two to go." Her voice was acrid.

"Now, now Tootsie, don't get yourself all worked up over nothing. You know I've been called back to active duty since Alverez bit the dust."

"Yeah, I know."

Dr. Marty Alberts was done with the pleasantries and cut to the point, "We need to talk, now. Would you like to know who's been leaving messages for me all day? Detective Ramos of State Bureau of Investigations... the name ring a bell with you, Toots?"

"No, it doesn't," she answered coldly. The office was relatively empty - *but he doesn't know that.* "Yes, and students are coming in as I speak, but I'd like to discuss this with you another time."

"Don't you dare blow me off like that!" he bellowed into the phone. "I'll be glad to give this Ramos a full account of your past twenty years of bilking the system for all it's worth. Then I can wash my hands of you for good!"

Terror sent a shiver through her heart, "No need to be hasty. I'm sure we can sit down and talk this out. Please hold a moment."

She hit the red mute button before he could respond. She ran her fingers through her hair and tried to think. *I gotta find a way to stop him.* It was nearing two-thirty; she couldn't leave for at least another forty-five minutes. She glanced at the calendar and tore off January. *It's February, for crying out loud!* She took the phone off of mute and spoke before he had the chance, "Sorry about that, busy time of day. It's Thursday. Does that still mean bridge night for the wifey pooh?"

"Don't call her like that!"

"Well, is it or not?" she met the anger in his voice.

"It is, but that doesn't mean a thing..."

This time she cut him off, "It means same time, same place, just like old times."

"No!" he shouted into the receiver.

"Yes," she insisted coldly and calmly. "I'd like to discuss this as much as you, but I cannot do it here and now."

He was silent on his end of the phone.

"Albee," she whispered in a singsong voice, "just like old times... we never really said goodbye properly. We'll have a glass of wine, we'll talk, and then all will be right in the world. You can go back to the little woman with your hands clean of me."

"And Detective Ramos?" he asked with a childlike quality to his voice.

"We'll decide what to do about the detective. You can return the call first thing in the morning."

After a long pause, he answered, "I can only stay for an hour."

"Whatever you say, Albee honey."

★ ★ ★

It was a beautiful drive to Alberts' cabin, especially in the winter when pristine snow covered the ground and the bare trees showed off the dramatic mountain vistas. Cloudy, cold, and unusually damp, it was nearly dark at four o'clock. *I want to get home before the ice storm hits*; she thought as her headlight caught the moisture in the air. If all went as planned, she'd be home in time for the news.

She went through her mental checklist as she steered her bike through the winding mountain pass. Before she'd left her house, she made sure her Swiss army knife was in her pant's pocket. There was a bottle of chardonnay in her backpack. She'd tossed in a flashlight and a pair of latex gloves. Finally, she'd gone to her medicine cabinet and found the bottle of Ambien she'd removed from a friend's medicine cabinet not too long ago. *Ten mg was the standard dose, so might as well try thirty.* She'd grabbed three tablets, crushed them to a fine powder with the back of a spoon before securing the dust in a small vial.

That should do it. Yeah, but do what? That was the real question. She told herself that this meeting's purpose was to talk, but she wondered just how far Alberts would push her. She'd put her future on the line twice already. She would not let him screw up her life now that she was so close to getting everything she wanted. She told herself the pills and knife were just a precaution, but she knew she'd have no love lost if Albee ended up dead. Bowman's and Alverez's deaths were nothing personal, just a couple of loose strings. Alberts' was different. He'd manipulated and used her. She didn't like him, but it hurt when he said their deal was over. She wondered if she would have a sense of satisfaction when the news reported his death.

She chuckled to herself; *well, I guess I've made my decision. Third times a charm, isn't that what they say?*

The driveway was muddy when she pulled up to the log cabin. She parked her bike to the side of the porch. She stepped carefully as she approached the porch steps, but it was hard to avoid the soft squishy ground. Almost five o'clock, she had a few minutes to prepare before Alberts arrived, and she wanted everything to be perfect.

She grabbed the spare key in the porch lamp, then let herself in. It took just a moment to turn on the lights, remove her boots, and unpack her backpack. She'd wrapped the bottle of wine in a towel. She got out two glasses from the cupboard and opened the bottle. She hid the vial of sleeping powder in her cleavage for easy access. Next, she built a small fire in the fireplace, and with half a glass of wine for herself, she stretched out on the couch to wait for her former paramour.

Dr. Alberts arrived precisely at five. He made his customary three-point turn in the drive to turn his car around before parking and getting out.

The door flew open. "Toots, where are you?" he roared.

She raised her head lazily from the couch, "Here I am, Albee, come and join me." Butter would have melted in her mouth as she smiled and swirled the half glass of wine, beckoning him to her.

"Don't tell me you're looped already," he grumbled.

"Oh Albee, don't be so cranky," she took his arm, guiding him to the couch. "Have a glass of wine and tell your little tootsie what's troubling you."

"What's troubling me?" he shouted incredulously, "What's troubling me is that I've got some detective breathing down my neck!"

"What does he want?" she asked as she sat him down next to her on the couch.

"It's a she! And SHE wants to ask me a few questions about Hector Alverez and about how we do the accounting for the school! She seems to think there might be a discrepancy in the books and wants to know what I know about it."

Her mind went momentarily blank before it raced; it confirmed her worst fears. Someone–some detective–looked over the books, found the numbers off, and connected the bad books with Alverez's death. How long would it take for her name to be brought into this mess?

Obviously, the file the Willows girl took from the office came from Alverez, and she had enough brains to find the accounting errors herself. She did her civic duty and handed the file over to the authorities rather than just minding her own business. *I'll deal with her later. First things first.*

"Are you listening to me!" he bellowed at her again.

"Sorry, Albee. I got lost in my thoughts for a minute," she softly apologized.

"Couldn't have gotten too far," he sneered.

She hated his condescending attitude and his snide remarks, but she kept calm and walk to the kitchen to pour him a glass of wine. Her back to him, she added her own little kicker from the vial.

She sauntered back and handed him the glass, "Take a drink, Albee honey, before you give yourself a stroke."

He obliged.

"Now, what have you said to this detective woman?"

"I haven't spoken to her yet. Haven't you been paying attention?" he growled.

"Well, what do you want to tell her? Do you want to admit knowing that there has been a little skimming going on?"

"Ha, a little!" he snorted.

She ignored him and continued, "Or do you want to play dumb and act like you do not understand what she is talking about?"

He looked at her seriously, "I don't think that's going to work this time, Tootsie. We're talking about an investigation on the state level."

She looked into his eyes. He didn't look like he would regret spilling her secret. "Are you going to name names? Are you going to tell them it's me who's been stealing from the district?" She sipped her wine before her voice could break.

"I don't want to, Toots; I just don't see any other way out. Maybe you can pay back the money, and they'll let you off with parole. The jails are overcrowded these days. They don't want to put anyone away they don't have to."

"P...P... Parole?" was all she could get out. He was going to do it. He was really going to sell her down the river to save his own skin. "What about you? Won't they want to arrest you since you knew what was going on?"

"You got a point there. I better call my attorney before I talk to that detective. I won't say a word till I have a signed deal." He put down his wine, only half drained, and pulled out his phone.

"Oh Albee," she flung herself onto him. "Isn't there another way?"

"Can you come up with something?"

She took the phone out of his hand and replaced it with the wine. "Hold me," she begged, "hold me and let me think for just a minute. Finish your drink while I think."

He knew his lawyer would be in the office till seven, what was five minutes more or less. He finished his wine as she clung to his chest.

The fire in the fireplace burned low. "Have you thought of anything yet," he finally asked after a long silence. His hands wandered to the soft leather of her bike pants.

"Give me another minute. I'm trying," she said through clenched teeth.

"Answer a question for me, Tootsie."

"What's that?"

"What do you know about Alverez?" he asked with one eyebrow cocked.

"I'd never met him," she answered dryly. "You hired him. You should have known him."

"Oh, I knew him," he agreed. "The guy was a straight arrow. He wouldn't have let anything get by him."

"Is that why you hired him, Albee? You figure that he could put a stop to me?"

Alberts laughed, "That would have been a gas to see you two go up against each other. He was little and quiet, but he was persistent. Just like you, but you're not so quiet."

She clenched her jaw. He was on her last nerve, but she was determined to stay calm. "What did you think would happen, Albee honey? Alverez would turn me in, and you'd find my money while I was in jail? Then you and the wittle wifey would get off scot-free."

"I never thought that far ahead, Toots. I just figured Hector would keep you in line while I enjoyed my retirement."

The P.O.S. never thought that far ahead! It's just a game to him? Well, it's not a game to me, you s.o.b.

"Albee, what did you tell the old ball and chain to get out of watching her play bridge tonight?"

He was getting sleepy and starting to fade, "They were playing at her partner's house... Told her I was checking on the pipes..."

"Well, you're looking kinda sleepy," she picked up his phone off the coffee table, "you better tell her you're gonna sleep here."

"No, no, no," he mumbled, "gotta go home. Gotta call Ramos..."

"I'll call Ramos for you. I'll tell her you'll see her in the morning. You tell Delores you're too sleepy to drive." She found the number on speed dial and hit talk.

She heard it go to voice mail, "Leave a message!" she whispered into his ear.

"A message–right... Delores, it's me, your husband," he sounded more drunk than sleepy, "I'm at the cabin and too tired to drive home. I'll see you in the morning."

She hit the off button before he could say any more. "Now listen to me, Albee, you get a good night's sleep, and all your problems will be gone in the morning."

She got off the couch to let Alberts stretch out and fall into a deep sleep. She immediately put on the latex gloves. She washed both glasses and put them away. She dumped the rest of the wine down the drain and put the empty bottle into her backpack. She wiped down the phone and everything she might have touched. Once she finished inside, she picked up her backpack and headed out.

Alberts' Mercedes wasn't new, but he kept it in excellent condition. *Even a Mercedes' brake line could fail.* She pulled out her trusty knife. It didn't take her long to make four small slits in the brake lines. Just big enough to drain out nice and slowly. She punctured the power steering line too. Might as well make sure he can't negotiate the tight turns as he heads down the mountain. If the ice storm hit after midnight like the weatherman promised, Alberts wouldn't make it home alive in the morning.

She stepped back from the car and surveyed her work. *What about the airbag,* she wondered? *Wouldn't want a silly thing like that getting in the way of a good accident.* She climbed into the car and sat behind the wheel. She pulled the fuse to the airbag and hoped tampering with it wouldn't set off any sensor.

Looking over at the empty passenger's seat, she noticed Alberts' briefcase and laptop. With her gloves still on, she opened the briefcase and rifled through it with mild curiosity. Her idea took on its full form. She closed the briefcase and grabbed the laptop. She flipped it open and pushed the circle to turn it on.

Luckily, Alberts wasn't so paranoid as to demand a password. She went directly to the word processor and began typing.

> *Dear Delores,*
>
> *After so many years, how do I say I'm sorry? Words do not do justice to the tremendous amount of guilt I feel. Please know, I am sorry. I have squandered the life we have built together. I have stolen and cheated for the last twenty years and thought I could get away with it all. I have been unfaithful to you more times, with more women than I care to count. I spent my entire career stealing money from the school district and wasted it on whores and other frivolities.*

When I chose Hector Alverez to be my replacement, I realize now it was a cry for help. Deep down, I knew he would find accounting errors in the budget. I knew he would come to me and demand an explanation. I didn't know how threatened I would feel at finally being exposed. I found an opportunity, and I took it. I shot Alverez and left him for dead.

It would have been okay; I could have lived with my dark secret if it had not been for Detective Ramos. She's been calling me all day, wanting to talk to me about Alverez and the school's accounts. I couldn't put you through the humiliation and torture as I confessed publicly to my crimes and sins.

I am not asking for your forgiveness; I don't deserve any. I just want to set the record straight, so you can live your life in peace. The car accident which I will have in the morning will be no accident. I hope that you can find peace and happiness for the rest of your life without me.

Your husband, Marty

She read her composition and began to laugh–long and loud. This would not only take care of Alberts' big mouth, but it would also put an end to questions concerning Alverez's death.

She turned off the computer and headed back to the cabin. She wanted to leave the laptop in a place where Alberts wouldn't find it, but the police would.

Alberts was asleep on the couch. She looked around. It was too likely he'd putter around the kitchen in the morning. If she left the laptop there, he would take it to the car with him. She needed it found in working condition. Since he was sleeping on the couch, he wouldn't need to go into the bedroom.

She quietly crossed the cabin floor to the bedroom, placed the laptop on a desk in the corner, then turned and left the cabin.

The cabin door clicked closed. The ground was still squishy beneath her feet as she walked to her bike. seven-fifteen her watch read, she'd be home in about an hour. She walked the bike halfway down the drive before revving the engine and driving away.

Chapter 26

THE GIRLS WENT giggling into Ruth's room. Paloma made herself comfortable by kicking off her shoes and sprawling across the bed.

"So, how was Valentine's Day with Scott?" Ruth joined her best friend on the bed.

"We broke up."

"Oh no, Paloma, I'm so sorry!"

Paloma saw the sad look on Ruth's face, "No, don't feel bad for me, Ruth, I'm kinda happy about it, relieved actually. I think I liked the idea of having a boyfriend more than I liked Scott."

The girls sat in silence before Paloma asked, "So, how was your evening with Cowboy?"

"Oh," Ruth perked up, "it was good!" Ruth immediately felt guilty for having a better Valentine's Day than her friend. "I mean fine, you know."

"Tell me everything," Paloma demanded.

"We had dinner with his parents."

"Not very romantic," Paloma commented.

"A little awkward, actually," Ruth admitted.

"But you know his parents. Aren't they friends with your mom and dad?" Paloma questioned.

"Ya, but now that I'm the girlfriend that could potentially ruin their son's life... I don't think they appreciate our relationship," Ruth explained. "After dinner, his mom asked if we wanted to go out to the movies with them, then she said - oh right, you can't."

"Ouch!"

"The rest of the time, they were polite and asked me lots of questions about what I wanted to do in college, but there was a lot of tension."

"What did Cowboy say?"

"He offered to clean up from dinner. I think it was to get them out of the house faster."

"Sorry, Ruth."

"It got better," Ruth assured her.

"Did you give him the slide show you made?" Paloma asked.

"Yes."

"Did he watch it?"

"Ya," Ruth explained, "I gave him the flash drive and told him he could look at it whenever he wanted. He said he wanted to right now, and he had something for me but that it was at his place."

"And they have a guest house?" Paloma recalled.

"So we closed up the house and walked down the drive to his place."

"Oh, what was that like?"

"A little nerve-racking at first. I've never been to a guy's 'place' before. But it's a cute little house. Cowboy said it used to be a bunkhouse for seasonal workers, and his mom turned it into a guest house."

"And then?" Paloma prodded.

"Oh, he gave me these earrings." Ruth pulled up her hair to show off the silver teardrops that hung from her ears.

"They're beautiful," Paloma admired the gift. "But that's not what I mean."

Ruth looked at her blankly.

"Oh, come on, Ruth! You were alone in his place. No one to interrupt you..." Paloma sighed with exasperation, "You're not going to tell me that the evening ended there."

Ruth shifted uncomfortably but remained silent.

"Come on, Ruth, did you or didn't you?"

"Did we or didn't we what?"

Paloma spelled it out, "Did the two of you do...it? Are you still a virgin? Did you have sex?"

Ruth blew out a long breath, "No, Yes, and No."

Paloma gasped, "You're kidding!" She stared at Ruth in shock, "Did you stop him?"

"No, I didn't stop him!" Ruth fired back. "He didn't go far enough to stop." Ruth's head hung low, and she shook it back and forth slowly, "I don't know what's wrong with me. It's only a three-room building, and we never even made it near his bedroom." Ruth looked up at Paloma, "I...I guess... he's not interested in me...like that..."

"I've seen him looking at you when he thinks no one is looking. He's interested like that."

"Oh, you're ridiculous!" Ruth blushed.

"Am I?" Paloma made Ruth look her in the eyes, "Ask him about this." Paloma added reassuringly, "You've only been dating," she quickly counted on her fingers, "five..."

"Six," Ruth corrected her.

"Six weeks, and maybe he has some weird time frame rule."

"No, he's told me he's had one-night stands before."

"Well, I don't know the answer, but he does."

Ruth was happy her phone rang and ended the uncomfortable conversation. She gave Paloma a 'just a minute' gesture when she saw who's number was calling. "Hello... Yes, this is Ruth Willows... You're kidding. You really found it... Oh, I see... yes, I see... Today is fine... Yes, thank you."

Ruth turned to Paloma, "That was the sheriff's office. They found the remains of my laptop."

"The remains?"

Ruth explained, "She said that someone had smashed the screen and keyboard, but the hard drive was still readable; that's how they figured out it belonged to me. Anyway, if I want to copy any files from it, they'll let me."

"That's cool, but you already got a new computer, right?"

"Yeah. But it'll be nice to get my notes back."

Paloma hugged Ruth and then jumped off the bed, "Since school's out for President's Day, I'm going to the paper early. You go ahead and get your laptop. I'll talk to you later." Paloma slipped her shoes back on.

★ ★ ★

Ruth started her truck. The sky had turned velvety grey, and the air had warmed into the forties. *Not the crystal ice world of the last two days,* she thought. Thursday night's ice storm had hit in the wee hours of Friday morning. The temperatures had dipped into the teens and had stayed there until this morning. Now the trees dripped, roads were wet, and Ruth's mind carried her back to Valentine's Day when she and Cowboy drove down the same route in his Jeep. The memory played like a movie in her head.

"Which way are we going, Cowboy?"

A smile spread across his lips, "There's an overlook just after you go through the pass. I bet it looks cool after the ice storm. The roads are clear enough to be safe." He was holding her hand, but he needed to shift. He flipped her hand over and pressed her palm into the gear stick. He kept his hand on top of hers and interlaced his fingers with hers. "That okay with you, Baby Doll?"

"I'm all yours, Cowboy."

They drove up the mountain in relative quiet; Cowboy shifted gears up and down according to the roads' curves, never letting go of her hand. The road was clear, but the ground and all the trees were covered with an inch of ice. It looked like winter in the land of fairy tales.

As they approached the pass and the road leveled off, Ruth announced, "I need a sports car."

"Oh, you do, do you?" Cowboy smirked. "And what kind of sports car do you need?"

"A dark midnight blue with tan leather interior."

"Okay, but what kind?"

"One with a manual transmission. I like shifting gears."

Cowboy chuckled as he pulled into the parking area for the scenic overlook. He thoroughly enjoyed this ditzier side of Ruth. He climbed out of his Jeep and went around to her side "Is that going to be a Ferrari, an Austin-Healey, Lamborghini, or something else?"

"I don't know! What difference does it make?" She answered as they lean against the Jeep's warm engine.

She snuggled into him as they looked out at the view. Trees had refused to grow on the sheer rock face that formed this part of the mountain. The opening gave way to a spectacular view of the valley below, covered in a glistening sheet of ice.

"Shifting gears is fun. So just imagine doing it in a cute little car that can go fast. It's gotta be more fun than a pickup with a horse trailer."

He kissed her, "Since when don't you like pickups and horse trailers?"

"Oh, I do," she defended herself. "I just feel like there's more to me than that."

He held her tighter and looked out at the view, "You'll have to give me a while to save up for a cute one." He kissed her again. "In the meantime, is there anything else you like to put on the wish list?"

When she thought about what happened next, she blushed even now, sitting by herself in her truck. Suddenly she realized that she needed to take the next exit off the highway to get to the sheriff's department. *Dang, I don't even remember getting on the highway.*

By the end of the exit ramp, the movie in her mind played again.

"In the meantime, is there anything else you like to put on the wish list?" Cowboy had just asked.

She wrapped her arms around his neck. She pulled him to her lips and kissed his mouth with as much passion and intensity as she ever had.

He willingly followed the pulsing of her lips and the intertwining of their tongues. She prayed he would get the hint she was trying to send to him, of what she wanted.

He quickened their pace; he intensified the urgency. She thought they were on the same page.

She let her hands slide from his neck down his sides. She dug them under his layers of warm fabric to find skin; warm, firm flesh. She ran them up his abdomen when he pulled away.

"Ow, Baby Doll, your hands are like ice!"

He grabbed both of her hands in his, pressed them against his lips, and blew warm breath onto them.

Let's get back in the car before your fingers fall off," he said as he led her to her side. She climbed in, deflated that her efforts had been for naught.

"Agh, I can't believe that I forgot to tell Paloma about what we found!" she said out loud.

The heater was soon going full force, and Cowboy started the drive down the opposite side of the mountain.

Around a hairpin turn, they spotted the red and blue flashing lights. Her stomach clenched from the memory of those lights flashing in her front yard. Ken slowed to a stop and pulled onto the narrow shoulder behind his Uncle's cruiser.

He rolled down the window as Davis peered in, "What's going on, Uncle Bob?"

We got a report yesterday morning of a broken guard rail. When Tommy came up to check it out, he noticed that whatever busted the guard rail was still down below. Thank God it's only one car and only one person inside."

Ruth shuttered at the thought.

"Do you know who it is?" Ken asked.

"Haven't seen the body yet. The climber just said it was a white male. I have a suspicion it might be the missing person who was just reported."

A man wearing a climbing harness walked up to the sheriff and said they were ready for the tow trucks. Davis thanked him and said goodbye to Ken and Ruth.

Ruth pulled into the municipal parking lot. She concentrated on parking, then put the keys in her bag so she wouldn't absentmindedly leave them in her truck.

As her mind replayed scenes from the weekend, the morning's conversation with Paloma about Ken nagged at her. *What was always stopping them?*

Her mind drifted to the memory of that night:

They stood in the middle of his house, his arms wrapped around her.

"I'll give you the grand tour." Standing behind her, he turned her slightly, "That is the kitchen," turning her again, "and there is the dining room," turning her yet again, "this is the living room," one final turn, "the door on the right is the bathroom, and the one on the left is the bedroom."

"It's charming," she complimented, "I like it."

He kissed her neck as his hand gently caressed her body. "I'm glad you do," he whispered in her ear.

One of his hands moved up from her waist to find her horseshoe pendant. Her breath caught in her throat. He spun her to face him. She thought he was going to kiss her, but he just gazed deep into her eyes.

After a long silence, she softly asked, "Cowboy, you okay?"

As if regaining consciousness, "I been polishing the play with Ellie, but haven't actually written for myself in a long time."

She gave him a puzzled look, but he continued, "I started writing when I was in grade school. Too many thoughts would bombard my brain. I couldn't think straight. A teacher taught me to, I guess you'd call it journaling, to help me organize what was going on in my head. I just realized I can't remember the last time I did that."

All she could say was, "Why haven't you?"

"Too busy, I guess," he shrugged.

"I'm sorry. Is it my fault?" She cautiously asked.. "Do you not want to see me?"

"No! That's not what I meant." He hugged her tight, "We tried that before, and it didn't work." His fingertips grazed the side of her face. "I just got overwhelmed by so many thoughts just now, and I realized that I haven't been writing."

He gazed deeply into her beautiful eyes for another long moment, kissed her softly, and asked her, "You want something to drink?"

Ruth got the unpleasant feeling of being watched. She turned slightly and looked out the side window. A pair of sparkling blue eyes regarded her, Ruth gave a little shriek and jumped, got confined by her seat belt, and she shrieked a second time from that surprise.

A second look out the window settled Ruth's brain. She gasped and laughed. Feeling foolish,she rolled down her window, "Officer Clark!" she giggled while gaining control of herself, "You startled me!"

Tommy Clark took a giant step away from the truck after her initial reaction, "Sorry about that," he looked self-conscious, "I recognized your truck..."

"It's okay; I was just daydreaming... I'm sorry I screamed."

They looked at each other for a moment. Ruth never noticed how alluring Tommy Clark's blue eyes were. *He's kinda cute,* she thought. His black hair had grown in since he'd shaved his head. His build differed from Cowboy. He looked muscular under his county-issued winter jacket. He probably had twenty pounds on Cowboy, all of it muscle.

"Are you coming or going?" Tommy asked.

"Huh?"

"I'm guessing you came here for a reason, or do you just enjoy the beautiful view of the municipal parking lot?" He smiled at her.

"Ha, ha, very funny," she answered dryly. "I got a call about my laptop, and I came to see what I could salvage."

"Oh, right. If you like, I can help you."

"Yeah, that'd be great!" Ruth was relieved to be dealing with someone she kinda knew. The break-in bothered her more than she wanted to admit.

They crossed the parking lot and Tommy signed her into the department's log. He took her to his desk. "If you wait here, I'll get your–um - laptop from the evidence room." He offered her a chair. "Can I get you anything? A soda or something?"

"I'm fine, thanks," she answered.

It took Tommy Clark eight minutes to return, not that Ruth was watching the clock; determined not to get caught up in a daydream again. Tommy returned with a brown bag sealed with red tape. He placed it on his desk, initialed and dated the bag next to the tape, and broke the seal. He carefully reached in and pulled out what looked like the bottom half of a laptop minus the keyboard and placed it down on his desk.

The horror of that night resurfaced. Tommy looked up at Ruth, "Are you all right?" She nodded yes.

"There's not much left to it," he spoke as he hooked up a connection from the laptop to the computer at his desk. "We would have never paid attention to it if the sheriff didn't have us looking for it. They destroyed the screen. What's left of it is in here." He shook the bag and tilted it for Ruth to look into it. All she saw was several dozen large chunks of grey surrounded by shards of plastic. "Whoever smashed it must have done it when it was closed because the hard drive survived. That's how we knew it was yours. It had your math paper on it and school notes."

Ruth asked, "Where did you find it?"

"Oh, um," he was hesitant to answer, "This information isn't being released, but... It was in an alley outside of Rocky's junkyard. Do you know anyone who likes to hang out around there?"

Ruth's mouth had unconsciously formed a small pout as she shook her head no.

Looking at his monitor and moving his mouse around, Tommy said, "I'll need you to look at this and verify this is your hard drive." He looked up at her and rolled his chair out of the way.

She slid her wooden chair around to his side of the desk. She looked at his monitor and clicked around with the mouse. It didn't take long for her to recognize her work. She clicked faster, opened and closed documents, checked programs, and searched for notes on a specific lab that she desperately wanted. She exhaled a deep breath and looked at Tommy, "Yup, this was my laptop. What can I do to get my work back?"

"Did you bring something to copy it onto?" Tommy asked.

She pulled a memory stick out of her bag. "Scoot over a little and let me see what we can do," he told her. She moved her chair back to the other side of the desk, but he stopped her, "You'll have to stay close enough to tell me what you want."

"Do you just want me to do it?" She asked, looking into his handsome blue eyes.

"I can't leave you to handle the evidence alone, but I don't mind helping. It's a slow day so far," he smiled at her.

They went to work, selecting and copying file after file. Ruth got what she needed for upcoming midterms.

Breaking the silence as they waited for an extensive file to copy, Tommy asked, "So, where's the boyfriend today? It surprised me to see you in the parking lot alone."

"He's at school, in-service for teachers," she answered. She looked at her watch, "he should be done soon."

"Guess we need to hurry and get you out of here then."

She looked at him quizzically, "No," she responded slowly, "the university's off today too. I don't have any classes to get to."

"You don't need to hurry home to see him?" he asked wryly.

"You really don't like Cowboy..."

"Cowboy?" he interrupted with a snicker.

"Ken," she corrected herself. "You really don't like him much, do you?"

Tommy blew out a sigh, "It was nicer when Kenny was away at school for the last few years." He made a grimace, "I guess you could say that we rub each other the wrong way."

"Yeah, I heard about that," she admitted.

"He told you?"

She explained. "He told me you liked the same girl in high school, she went back and forth between you, and then she dumped you both for some rich guy."

Tommy couldn't look at Ruth at this point, "Yeah, well, I guess that's a good version of the story."

Just then, a lively pint-sized woman, with long dark hair pulled into a low bun and skin the color of caramel, bounded into the room. She was so focused on Tommy she didn't notice Ruth behind his monitor.

"Hey Tommy," she called with a Native American lilt to her voice, "the M.E. just identified the body that went over the mountain in the Mercedes. The sheriff was right; it was that missing persons, Marty Alberts." She gave a shy laugh as she walked closer to his desk. "It looks like nobody won the pool. It wasn't a student or a teacher that bit the dust."

Tommy glared at the woman. He shook his head and interrupted her, "Sue!"

She looked at him questioningly before Ruth popped her head out from behind the display.

"Oh no, I'm so sorry... I didn't know... I didn't see...I...." Sue trailed off.

Tommy spoke up, "This is Ruth Willows. She's here to identify her recovered laptop."

"Hello Ruth," Sue said, abashed.

Tommy continued the introductions, "This is Sue Chapoose. She works in dispatch."

Ruth smiled back.

"Did you take your lunch break already, Tommy?" Sue asked with a hopeful grin.

"Just got back," he answered. "I'm finishing up my special assignment for the sheriff."

"Oh, well, um, okay," Sue answered, deflated. "Nice to meet you, Ruth." She turned and walked away quickly.

Ruth stared directly at Tommy, "A little office romance?"

"What? Uh... that? Uh...no." Tommy answered as he typed away at his keyboard.

"You sure?" Ruth was still looking at him.

"She's a very friendly girl," he replied, but then thinking that might not sound as polite as he meant, he added, "She's a nice girl, good family."

"Sure." Ruth grinned.

"Look, she shouldn't have said what she did just now. She should have never given out details of an ongoing investigation."

"She didn't know I was here," Ruth said dryly, then added, "but the stuff about the office pool? That's kinda macabre."

"We never bet on people getting hurt," he answered defensively. "Our humor gets a little... dark... sometimes. Day after day, we see people at their worst here. That can wear on you. It shouldn't have been said in front of you," Tommy said apologetically.

"After the break-in at our house, I've been getting creeped out easily."

"I understand, and I'm sorry." He turned his attention back to the computer screen, "Is there anything else you'd like to copy?"

Ruth clicked around for a bit. Tommy finished the last transfer and handed the memory stick back to Ruth.

Tommy escorted Ruth to the lobby and signed her out. She thanked him again for his help.

"You should ask her out. I bet she'd say yes." Ruth grinned at him.

"What? Who?" Tommy looked at her bewildered.

"Sue Chapoose from dispatch? Nice girl, remember."

Tommy smiled shyly, "Yeah, nice girl. She's um... just not my type." He gave Ruth a quick wink and went through the door; a sudden chill went down her spine.

In her car, Ruth had plenty of other subjects to think about other than the inadequacies of her and Cowboy's sexual relationship. No matter how blunderingly the news was delivered, another person from the Golden Valley school district had died. *Too much of a coincidence*, Ruth thought. She'd have to see if Paloma knew anything she didn't know. She thought about the dark humor Tommy tried to explain. She shivered; she understood him intellectually, but this was hitting too close to home. After all, it was her home someone invaded, it was her school in which three people had died; it was her boyfriend who was a teacher and could be next on the list. Or student, Sue had said. *I'm a student, Paloma's a student... who's gonna be next?*

Chapter 27

JOE SAT AT the breakfast table, reading the paper and sipping coffee.

Greater Valley Sentinel–José Pluma

In an eight to one decision on Monday, the Golden Valley School Board agreed to a proposed plan for dealing with employees who possess advanced degrees from non-accredited schools. Last November, eleven employees of the school district, both current and recently retired, were found to be receiving financial benefits from advanced degrees received from non-accredited institutions via the internet.

An ad hoc committee spent the last four months researching the ramifications and contractual obligations the school could be held liable for since the issue of non-accredited degrees had never been addressed in contract negotiations.

Edward Spencer, school board president, said, "I believe that the actions of the committee have been swift and fair. Luckily the representatives from the teachers' union agree with our recommendations. It will be a good thing to have this wrapped up before the school year ends."

The committee found that the current teachers' contract cannot be changed or renegotiated without a public hearing. Teachers' contracts are up for renegotiation this June, but all current contracts must continue to be upheld.

Of the eleven employees in question, only three are directly represented by the teachers' union. Aside from administration, the remaining workers all have contracts directly with the school board, not negotiated by the union. "Of our non-teaching staff who have been benefiting from this loophole," Spencer reported, "we are not obligated to honor their current contract, nor are we obligated to continue their employment till the end of the year." Spencer continued to outline the plan by explaining, "The board has decided to contract out several of the positions that have been run from in house until now. Contracting out services like janitorial and cafeteria staff will not only alleviate present problems but should also save the district approximately $200,000 over the next three years." Spencer added that the employee's immediate supervisor will decide the continued employment of nonunion employees under this investigation.

As for the teachers and staff covered under the union's umbrella, none will be asked to return next year. "We have decided to not renew their contracts in June. We will, however, offer compensation in the form of a severance package," Spencer explained, "the details of which will need to be ratified by the union before June." In addition, all monies currently being held in an escrow fund will be released to the union employees by the end of the year.

Spencer's final comment on the matter was, "Considering all the factors, we believe this to be a fair and just solution and one the taxpayers can live with."

"The taxpayers can live with it my..."

"Joe!" Constance cut him off and gave a warning look.

"Oh Connie," Joe grumbled, "these girls probably know more cuss words than you and I put together."

"Be that as it may," she looked at her daughters eating their breakfast, "and I hope they don't, I don't need to hear that language at the table at six-fifty-seven a.m."

Joe continued his rant, "Spencer thinks he's doing us all some sort of favor. They're all getting off scot-free."

"They're all losing their jobs," Ruth offered.

"Hmm?" Joe grunted.

"None of the teachers with fake degrees are getting their contracts renewed next year. And the employees who aren't teachers are getting canned as soon as they can be replaced. With only eleven weeks left to the school year, that seems fair." Ruth countered her Granddaddy. "To lose teachers so late in the year would put a lot more strain on the budget. The district would end up having to pay substitutes three times more than a regular teacher."

Ruth continued, "Plus, the time it would take to have a series of public hearings and a special election to change the teachers' contract, this school year would be over before and the next one begun before anything would be decided."

"And just how do we know all this?" Joe raised one eyebrow.

"Paloma sent me the unedited article along with her notes," Ruth admitted sheepishly.

Ed and Constance smiled at each other while Ruth and Grace finished their breakfasts. Joe had no argument; silently, he went back to his paper.

Greater Valley Sentinel–José Pluma

Police investigation continues in the death of retired Golden Valley School official Martin Alberts. Alberts, 58, died last month after his late-model Mercedes careened off a cliff on

County Road 210, near National Forest lands. Medical examiner's reports confirm that Alberts died on impact.

Alberts' death sparked suspicion after investigators found his laptop, in the family's cabin, with a suicide note and a confession to the murder of fellow school employee Hector Alverez.

Hector Alverez was found murdered on school property last September.

The written confession surprised officials since they had cleared Alberts of suspicion at the onset of the Alverez murder investigation. Alberts had hired Alverez as his replacement upon his retirement as the high school budget coordinator last spring. Alberts was asked to come out of retirement upon Alverez's death until a suitable replacement could be found.

In his suicide note, Alberts states his motive for the murder as finally being caught by Alverez after a lifetime of embezzlement of school funds and squandering the money on "frivolities."

Golden Valley Sheriff Bob Davis said, "We are required to investigate matters like this fully. We are looking at all the evidence with an objective eye. Hopefully, this will all be wrapped up shortly."

Joe finished his article and looked at Ruth, "You know anything else about Alberts' death that's not in this paper?"

She got up and scanned the article over her Granddaddy's shoulder; he smelled of hot coffee and hay, "That's what Paloma emailed to me too, but she told me she got the feeling that Pluma was playing it close to the cuff. Cowboy and I passed that accident when they were pulling the car up from over the cliff."

Constance perked up at this information, "You never told me that, Ruthie."

"I didn't know who it was when we passed it," Ruth explained. "It was Valentine's Day, and the sheriff said someone had reported a guard-rail break the day before. The ice was so bad it took them a while to get to the car."

"I don't know why we bother anymore!" Joe was a little cranky, having all his thunder stolen.

"What's wrong, Dad?" Ed tried to smooth things over.

"These kids seem to be ready to run the world."

"I just have an in with Paloma, Granddaddy," Ruth wrapped her arms around her Granddaddy's neck and kissed his cheek.

"Maybe if they ran the world for a while, we could all take a vacation," Constance smiled as she sat on Ed's lap and hugged his neck. "I always wanted to go to Hawaii." She kissed her husband.

"Ugh!" Grace watched her parents' embrace and groaned as she took her bowl to the sink. "I'm going to school."

★ ★ ★

It was a two-and-a-half-hour drive to the Denver office of the Colorado Bureau of Investigation on Kipling Street. Officer Clark had been quiet most of the way. Now he and Sheriff Davis sat in a bright, somewhat spacious office.

"What's his name again?" Clark whispered to his boss.

"Saunders, Deputy Director Gary Saunders. He's in charge of the Major Crimes Unit; he's Detective Ramos' boss," Davis responded quietly.

"And we had to drive up here because..."

"Because we're handing over our investigation to them in a cooperative and friendly manner."

Tommy Clark contemplated his boss. Davis wasn't the type of man that shirked his duties. Tommy couldn't understand why he was doing so now.

"I told you before, these crimes require more resources than our department has. We need help, and if the only way to get it is to call in the state... that's what we do."

Davis continued as he studied his young officer, "Tommy, what's more important than catching these criminals and putting them behind bars? We have three people dead. They are not just three people out of a half-million people; we're talking about three members of our community: friends, neighbors, family."

Tommy nodded his head. He knew where Davis was headed, but he still felt he had let his boss down.

"I don't want there to be a next one for the office to bet on."

Tommy looked abashed at the reference to the morbid office pool.

"I don't want another family affected like the Alverez's or the Bowman's or the Willows'. If I have to swallow my pride to see justice done, then my pride be damned..."

"Sorry Bob, there's no crow on the menu here today," Gary Saunders, followed by Pamela Ramos, entered the room and shook Davis' hand. Saunders was both of medium build and height with dark but graying hair. Ramos looked her usual professional self.

"Howdy Gary," Davis smiled and shook Saunders' hand. "Detective Ramos," he shook her hand, "I trust you remember Officer Clark."

Ramos shook Tommy's hand and took a seat at the large wooden table.

"Officer Tommy Clark has been doing most of the work on the cases I wanted to share with you," Davis said.

"Good to meet you, Clark," Saunders greeted Tommy with a firm handshake. "Why don't we all sit down and discuss what you would like us to look into?"

Everyone took a place at the table, and Davis began his tale of the three deaths all involving employees of the Golden Valley High School.

"Now wait a moment there, Bob," Saunders interrupted. "I thought that fellow, what's his name?" He looked towards Ramos, who opened a laptop, hit a few keys, and pushed it towards her boss, "Yes... I thought that fellow Alberts confessed to embezzlement and to killing Alverez before he killed himself."

Davis nudged Tommy, who filled them in, "During our original investigation into Alverez's death, Martin Alberts had an alibi for his whereabouts when Alverez was shot. Furthermore, we've found inconsistencies in Alberts' written confession and physical evidence that someone else was at Alberts' cabin, possibly with him, before he died."

"Go on," Saunders said staunchly.

Tommy opened his own folder and scanned his notes. "When we first investigated Hector Alverez's death, Mr. and Mrs. Alberts had been visiting their son and his family in California when Alverez had been shot. Family and neighbors of their son confirmed this. It would have been very difficult for Mr. Alberts to have shot Alverez from a thousand miles away. He might have had an accomplice, which means there is still someone out there. More recently, phone records show that Martin Alberts made a call from his cell phone to his home phone at six-nineteen p.m. on the Thursday evening preceding his death. We traced the cell tower, and his physical location during the call was the family's cabin near the National Forest. He left a message for his wife saying he was too tired to drive and would drive home in the morning."

Davis added, "I emailed you a copy of the message."

"I heard it," Saunders admitted. "He sounds like he had a few too many."

"We examined his laptop. The suicide note he supposedly wrote was saved at seven-O-seven p.m.. It contained no typos or misspellings. Not that hard to do with a good word processing program, but when you think of the groggy, possibly drunk man who left the message almost an hour before, it is a little hard to believe that his typing skills would be that good."

"Hm, tell me about this evidence that someone was with him at his cabin."

"At his cabin, we found tire tracks belonging to the victim's Mercedes and another set of tracks belonging to what appears to be a motorcycle. We also found several partial boot impressions. Alberts was wearing dress shoes when his body was recovered. These partials are from the tread of a work boot or possibly a bike boot. It looks to be a size eight men's or ten women's boot."

"Interesting, anything else?" Saunders asked

"Your lab down in Pueblo looked at the car after we recovered it. It was a mangled mess, but Mrs. Alberts confirmed that that car was her husband's pride and joy."

"The lab reported all four brake lines had punctures, as well as the power steering line, and the airbag did not deploy because of a missing fuse."

Tommy took a slight pause before he continued, "Why would a guy in a pricey suit and shoes go to a cabin in the woods to check water lines without changing his clothes first? Also, why cut all four brake lines in his favorite toy? If he wanted to kill himself, why not just drive off a cliff? The weather was so bad it's amazing that he made it down the mountain as far as he did."

"I interviewed the Alberts' family and friends. Marty Alberts was a pragmatic and calculating man. He had a half-million-dollar life insurance policy, one that is void if he committed suicide. I can't understand why such a practical man would leave a suicide note knowing it'd stop payment on his policy."

Saunders got up and slowly wandered around the room. "So, let's assume for a minute that your hunch is correct. Alberts didn't kill himself or Alverez. Who did? What's your next lead?"

"I think the file of budget reports is our next lead," Davis answered.

Saunders retook his seat, "Have you looked at Detective Ramos' report?"

"No, we haven't," Davis said coldly. This was another reason Davis agreed to the two-plus hour drive. Ramos had been avoiding his messages.

Yes, he had chewed her out after she questioned Ruth so harshly, but withholding information in an ongoing investigation was childish in his book.

"Why not?" Saunders chastened. "Ramos, print out Bob and Officer Clark each a copy of your report."

She turned the laptop back to face her and hit a few more keys.

Saunders continued, "I'll give you gentlemen the gist of it while Detective Ramos grabs those reports from the printer."

The detective held her tongue as her nostrils flared, and she left for the printer room.

"The girl who brought you that file was right about the school losing money. We had several accountants go over the numbers, and in the last twenty years, eight-hundred-ninety-six-thousand-dollars has gone missing from the high school's budget. It was done very cleverly, I might add. Small amounts, all made to look like accounting mistakes or overused budgets. It started out slowly and only from the cafeteria's budget. But each year, the deficit grew, and the fraud expanded. Somebody must have a tidy little bank account waiting for them."

Saunders looked at the two men, "Any idea who that someone could be?"

Davis spoke, "That's why we're here, Gary. We've looked at the accounts of the deceased and their families, and we've come up with squat."

Saunders nodded and continued. "We've also had the hand-written notes examined by our handwriting analyst. She compared the notes in the file with samples provided by Alverez's wife and has concluded the notes in the folder were written by Hector Alverez."

Pamela Ramos entered the room and handed papers to both Davis and Clark. Tommy added, "Once I've read Detective Ramos' report, I'd like to go back to the school and ask who does their auditing."

Saunders was quick to point out. "I must ask you all to not investigate this on your own. Any information going out or coming in will go through our chief investigator."

Tommy's spine stiffened. He knew this was part of handing the investigation over to the CBI, but it didn't make him happy.

Saunders moved on with the conference. "Bob, you were telling me something about the girl who brought in the file, which we now believe is from Alverez."

"Ruth Willows is her name; nice young lady, very smart," Davis began.

"She was the one who found Alverez's body," Saunders interrupted

"Yes," Davis agreed, "she and a teacher discovered the body."

"And she held on to this file for a long time. Does she know more than she's letting on? Is someone in her family..."

Davis stopped Saunders this time, "She and her family have nothing to do with this, in a nefarious sense. In fact, the family's house was broken into and ransacked after she turned in the file."

Tommy cleared his throat, and Saunders raised an eyebrow towards him. Davis gave Tommy a nod for him to continue.

"The family reported a motorcyclist at the end of their drive the morning of the break-in. A ... friend... of the family," Tommy wasn't sure how to mention Kenny, "reported that he had seen the same cycle on that stretch of road for the past month. No one recognized the cycle or the driver."

"Unfortunately, we don't have the plate number. I've been running the make and model through motor vehicle databases. The closest match I've found is a black ninja registered to a," Tommy referred to his notes again, "Roger Evans at a P.O. Box in Phoenix."

"So, who is he?" Ramos asked.

"No idea," Clark answered. "Name doesn't connect to anyone in the investigation, and it doesn't mean anything to anyone we've interviewed. None of the Roger Evans I found had ever lived near Phoenix. I was ready to let it go when the bike tracks turned up at Alberts' cabin. Your lab in Pueblo confirmed that the cycle tracks at the cabin could belong to several types of bikes, including the ninja."

Ramos typed into her laptop as Saunders mumbled over her shoulder. They had obviously worked together long enough that she understood what grumbles and grunts meant.

"All right, gentlemen," Saunders addressed them formally, "the CBI is prepared to take over the investigation of both the murders of Hector Alverez and Martin Alberts as well as the embezzlement at Golden Valley High School. Detective Ramos will be the lead investigator and will report directly to me. I'll remind you to please refrain from further investigation of these matters on your own. If we need your services, either Ramos or I will contact you."

Saunders slid his chair back from the table when Davis interjected, "Assistant Director, we have more to discuss."

"Really Bob, I read your report, I think this other fellow's death...," he looked at Ramos.

"Bowman," she replied.

"Bowman, that's right, I really don't think his death has anything to do with my cases," Saunders said as his phone started beeping. He looked at it, "I have to take this call. Why don't the two of you grab some lunch in the cafeteria before you head back, my treat. I'll join you, and we'll see what we can do about your other dead guy."

Chapter 28

SHE'D SPENT THE last hour biting her tongue. Her patience was waning. She had barely read past the third paragraph of the contract when she couldn't take any more.

"Blair, honey," she said through clenched teeth, "I believe you've made a mistake on the listing price of my house." She handed the contract back to the bleached blonde real estate agent who was playing with her iPhone.

"No, it's just what I told the secretary," Blair answered, barely perusing the document.

"I thought I made it clear that I wanted to list my house for one hundred sixty-five thousand; this contract only says one hundred forty-five."

"Oh, please," Blair huffed, "it's not that big of a difference. I told you you'd never get one hundred sixty-five thousand for a place with one bathroom in this market. Besides, the lower the price, the quicker we can sell."

She let her calm exterior slip for just a moment to retort, "Two hundred in commission may not be a big difference to you, Ms. Blair Cummings, but twenty thousand in my bank account is a big difference to me!"

The agent finally pulled her eyes away from her toy and gave her client a somewhat startled look.

She continued, "Please don't think that just because I watched you grow up that I'm some old fool and you can pull the wool over my eyes. I'm as capable of looking at comps and market trends as you. I know the name of the game is invest as little of your time as possible for the most amount of money you can get, but we're not playing that way with my money and my house."

Blair adjusted her posture in the old dining room chair, took the unsigned contract from the hands of her new client, and slid it into her opened briefcase, "When I'm the real estate agent, we play by my rules, or we don't play at all."

"I came to you because I thought your youth and intelligence would put you a step above those old boys doing business out there. I guess I was wrong. Don't fool yourself. It's not your game. You're still playing theirs." She got up and began clearing the table of the niceties that she had laid out for her guest. "If you don't want to work with me, I can go talk to Bernie. He'll be glad to sell anything that's not nailed down."

Blair knew her ex-father-in-law Bernie all too well. He had taught her everything she knew about the real estate business and about being a slime ball. Blair hated losing clients to the competition, and she loathed Bernie.

"If that's the type of man you want to deal with..." Blair trailed off.

"It should be obvious that my first choice was you, honey," as she continued to straighten the room, "but I won't be manipulated or taken advantage of either. I'm sure I can hold my own with Bernie. I'm sorry to have wasted your time." She walked to the front door and held it open.

"I'm not trying to take advantage of you..." Blair faltered, "I just wanted to make this as easy for you as possible. You'll eventually have to come down in price. I just wanted to save you time." Blair never lost her plastic smile even when she was backpedaling.

She closed the front door and went through the motions of reconsidering, "Well, I would really hate to start this process all over again... but I just can't sign this contract as it is."

Blair pulled the contract out of the briefcase and scribbled on it. "See if this is more to your satisfaction." She handed the paper over to her.

Blair had crossed one hundred forty-five thousand out and one hundred fifty-nine thousand, nine hundred ninety-nine was in its place. Five thousand less than where she had wanted to start, but then again, she had padded her desired price to accommodate for this. "If you initial by the new price and sign the last page, we'll be good to go," Blair prompted and shoved a pen toward her client.

She read over the rest of the contract, initialed and signed. Blair snatched the paper back, initialed and signed, and stashed the contract quickly away before her new client could change her mind. "I'm sure you'll be thrilled when we close," Blair grinned. "Luckily, I have a For Sale sign in my trunk. I'll put it in the front yard now if you don't mind."

When she opened the front door, they found a visitor just set to knock.

"Betsy, hello, what are you doing here?" she asked.

"I'm sorry, I didn't know where else to go," Elizabeth Gills stammered. "You're busy?"

"Come in Betsy, Blair was just leaving." She said goodbye to Blair Cummings and ushered Betsy into the living room.

"What on earth is the matter with you, Bets?" She sat the teacher down on the couch. "You look like you could use a drink."

Without hesitation, she poured a small glass of dark amber-colored liquor and handed it to her friend. "Drink this," she ordered, "and tell me what's going on. I was going to call you later. What did the sheriff's department want with you today."

"Oh," Gills moaned, "did you notice them?"

"They were kinda hard to miss."

"Do you think anyone else noticed them?" Gills asked.

"It was after three o'clock. Most of the students had left before the cruiser pulled up. Are they why you're in a tizzy?"

"You'll never believe it." Gills took a long sip of the drink, "What is this?"

"Bourbon."

"It's good," Gills took another long sip and almost emptied the glass. "They wanted a DNA sample. They had a warrant. They want to compare my DNA to what they found in Bowman's office. They think I was sleeping with the moron and that I killed him."

She poured herself a bourbon and sat in the chair across from Gills. "Tell me the whole story from the beginning."

The drink relaxed Gills, "That's about all there is to tell. Some officer from the sheriff's department showed up with a lab tech. They showed me a warrant that requested my DNA. They swabbed me and left."

"Why you?" she asked.

"They said they were collecting samples from several of Bowman's closes friends."

"I didn't know you and Bowman were that close."

"We weren't, but they said they had pictures of me entering the building with him a few hours before he died. They showed them to me, and I told them we had been looking for that tuba he'd been bellowing about."

"What did the pictures look like?"

"They were grainy, but it was Bowman and me walking into the back of the theater," Gills explained.

"Where'd they get pictures?" She poured another drink for Gills.

"That's an excellent question! One I'd like to know the answer to myself! I've been racking my brain since they left. I even walked around the school, trying to figure out how the pictures were taken. The school's name is on the side of the building is right above Bowman's head. There's no surveillance camera mounted on that side of the school. Someone had to be in the parking lot taking pictures." Gills took a third long sip. "Someone was spying on Bowman or me. But those fools in the uniforms didn't want to listen to that. No, they just want to accuse me of... killing that fool...."

She knew exactly what the pictures looked like and who took them. They'd been on the laptop she'd taken from the Willows girl's room. She'd run it over with her car.

"Betsy, what are you going to do now?"

"What can I do? Bowman was a pain, but I didn't kill him, and I certainly wasn't sleeping with him! But what if the staff saw them taking a swab of my mouth? You know how fast gossip travels in that school," Gills continued. "It's bad enough; I get no respect from the students or Rodriguez. After the... incident... with that Torres girl, my reputation is gone even after all my years of teaching. Everyone knows we're losing our jobs next year. Derrick is on the five-year plan at the university after his car accident. Now, I'm a murder suspect! I don't think I can take anymore." Gills looked worn out.

"If anyone asks, you can always make an excuse why the sheriff came to see you. I don't think anyone would believe you capable of murder, Bets." Both ladies took a long sip of their drinks, "Is there anything I can do?"

"No... thank you," Gills sighed. "I just needed to get this off my chest. I didn't know who to turn to."

"I'm sure no one even noticed the sheriff." That was a bold-faced lie, but what the hell. "And you can talk to me anytime."

"Thanks," Gills drained her glass. "That girl who was here looked so familiar. Should I know her?"

"You might. She graduated about five or six years ago. Blair Caprice."

"Oh, yes," Gills nodded. "Her face is plastered all over the shopping carts. Isn't she a... real estate agent?"

"Yes, she is.".

"You're not selling your house, are you?" Gills gasped.

"Why not?" she replied. "You said it yourself, we don't have a job next year. Why not sell the house, take an early retirement, live someplace... nice? My son is out of the house. I only have myself to worry about now."

"But where will you go?" Gills sounded a little lost.

"I'm still thinking about it." She changed the subject, "I'm hungry, wanna go out and get something to eat?"

"Sure, why not? But after two bourbons, maybe you should drive."

Chapter 29

UNIVERSITY SPRING BREAK had begun. Unfortunately for Ruth, high school spring break was next week, after university classes resumed.

"So you're telling me you don't have any spring break?" Paloma sounded disbelieving.

"No, I've had a week of break from the University, and we have next week off from here. I just don't have time off from both schools at the same time." Ruth groaned.

"That sucks," whined Paloma. "What are you going to do next week?"

"Just the opposite of what I did this week; go to class in the afternoon," Ruth said.

Before they could say any more, Mr. Silver closed the door to signal the start of class.

Ruth quietly held her phone in her lap and texted Paloma.

Decided.

Paloma felt her phone vibrate and looked at it. She answered with a "?"

College.

Where?!!!

Ruth smiled, *Colorado State Ft. Collins.*

Cool

Ken wandered back to the corner of the classroom, "All phones away, please."

Ruth wanted to continue her conversation, so when Mr. Silver strolled to the other side of the room, she scribbled a note on a sheet of paper and slid it to Paloma: *I want to surprise him one morning next week at his place. I'll tell him and see if he's interested in visiting me. If he says yes, I'll be brave enough to discuss IT.*

It? Paloma mouthed silently.

Ruth rolled her eyes but wrote a second note–*you know. You said I should ask him. I don't know how else to bring it up.*

"Girls, isn't this sophomoric of you?" Ken said disapprovingly as he took the paper and slid it into his pocket.

It mortified Ruth.

Missy chimed in, "Maybe they should share their brilliant ideas with the class."

"That will do Miss Fairchild," Ken continued. "Are there any more questions?"

Missy's hand shot up. Ken assumed it would be another snide remark about Ruth. He motioned her to go ahead, anyway.

Instead, she asked, "What will you be doing next week for spring break, Mr. Silver?"

Ken leaned back on his desk, thought for a moment, and smiled, "Well, I guess it won't hurt to let you all in on my little secret."

The class looked at each other, wondering what it could be. Ruth went blank for one split second. Then her mind raced. *Good God–don't tell me he's going to say something about us! No, he'd never. He'd lose his job. But... he could talk about plans with his girlfriend and only I would know it's me...*

Paloma looked at Ruth, grabbed her arm, and gave it a hard shake. "You okay?" she hissed.

Ruth nodded yes.

"You're white as a sheet," Paloma's whisper was barely audible.

"I'm fine," Ruth whispered, forcing herself to breathe.

Ken was enjoying the murmur he had caused. "I've just found out that a play I've been co-authoring has been selected to be performed at the San Francisco Fringe Festival this summer."

Oh's and Ah's rippled through the class. Missy started the applause. Ruth was so excited she nearly jumped out of her seat. Luckily she banged her knee on the underside of the small desk where she sat; it reminded her to sit back down.

"So," Ken continued, "I'll be on an airplane bright and early Saturday morning bound for SFO." The class looked at him eagerly. "There's a huge casting call, and I need to be there along with the director and my co-author. I've never done anything like this before. I'm very excited!"

Questions and comments erupted from the class; Ruth heard none of it. As quickly as her joy for Cowboy had welled up, the floodgates of her mind opened, and she sat in stunned silence. *He's leaving bright and early Saturday morning? When was he going to tell me? How long has he known about this? He already has a flight out, so he's had enough time to plan... he must have known for weeks. Why didn't he tell me! Where is he going to stay? Is he going to share a room with Ellie? Is that why he hasn't told me anything, he doesn't want me to know he'll be with her? Should it bother me if they're just old friends? Unless something IS going on between them. He doesn't need to sleep with the stupid little virginal me when he can get it from someone who knows what she's doing...*

Tears quickly flooded her eyes, and an involuntary intake of air rushed past her lips; she hadn't realized she'd been holding her breath. There was so much commotion going on with the class no one, except Paloma, noticed her mini-meltdown. Ken still blabbed in front of the room, "...so remember when you write your midterm essay tomorrow, make sure it's interesting enough to keep me awake on the plane."

The bell rang. "Miss Torres, Miss Willows, may I speak to you," Ken held up the slip of paper.

Ruth shot past him and out of the room before Ken could finish his sentence. Paloma approached his desk slowly.

Both Ken and Paloma let the room empty before they looked at the other. Paloma wasn't sure what was going on inside her best friend's head, but something had upset her.

"You and your friend," he said, "pay attention in class."

★ ★ ★

Ruth's cell phone rang–again. Constance stared at it as it vibrated and played music for the fifth time in the last forty-five minutes. She refused to answer someone else's phone. *You would think as much as they love their phones, they would at least remember to take them with them.*

Next, the kitchen phone rang.

"I guess I have no choice now, do I," she said to the irritating machine. "Hello?... Oh, Ken, how are you... oh, that was you? Her cell phone has practically buzzed itself off the counter... she went to check on the North pasture with Joe, she must have left her phone here by accident..."

Ken rolled his eyes at the thought of Ruth doing anything by accident.

"Should I tell her to call you when she gets back?" Constance asked.

"No," he said flatly. "Mrs. Willows," Ken tried to temper his voice. "I'm going out of town for some business. I need to talk to Ruth. Would you mind if I stopped by this evening? I don't want to impose..."

"Ken you're welcome anytime. They should be back soon. They went out right after lunch, and now it's after three... All right... Goodbye." She hung up the phone.

Constance smiled. She liked Ken. She liked how her daughter looked when she was with him, but Ruth had looked strained when she'd gotten home today. *She was more eager to get on that horse of hers than usual.* Constance thought about the edge she'd heard in Ken's voice and all the missed phone calls. *What is going on with that girl of mine?*

Joe burst through the door, halting Constance's train of thought, grinning from ear to ear.

"My Grand-baby has just made me the happiest man on earth! She told me she's going to college in Fort Collins, and she says she wanted me to know first."

Ruth followed Joe in through the kitchen door, "Mom and Dad already know Grandaddy. But I wanted you to be at the top of the list."

"I'm glad you're happy, Dad, we are too," Constance spoke both for herself and Ed.

"You know, that's not the best news of all," Joe said, interrupting Constance.

"Since my Grand-baby here did such a fine job last summer with the rodeo, she's agreed to lead the Spring Carnival Parade. Shep's gonna get a group together from the team, and I'm sure you can get that beau of yours..."

"No, no, no," Ruth cut him off, "you'll have to ask him yourself. I'm not going to make a commitment for anyone but myself."

"Oh, fine Grand-baby," Joe squeezed Ruth tightly with his arm around her shoulder, "I'm sure if you're there, he'll wanna be there too."

Ruth grimaced and mumbled, "Not too sure about that," too low for anyone to hear.

Joe continued, beaming, "And we'll get Gracie in on it too. The organizers decided to have a whaddya call it? Medieval theme this year. You know kings and queens and knights... The whole shebang!"

"What," Ruth protested, "you didn't say anything about dressing up in costume! I don't dress up in costume! I haven't put on a costume since I was twelve years old and went trick-or-treating, and I not going to wear one now!" Ruth stamped her foot like she was twelve years old.

Yes, you will, Grand-baby. And you and your sister will be the prettiest two at the dance," Joe said, and there was no point in disagreeing with him.

"What dance?"

"The masked ball, Friday night after the parade," Joe answered nonchalantly.

"I don't want to go to a dance," Ruth tried to argue.

"Of course you do. Every girl wants to go to a dance." Joe couldn't believe how silly his granddaughter was being.

Constance stood in the counter's crook and laughed to herself. This was one of those times Joe would not take no for an answer.

"You know, this spring carnival is just a vestige of the pagan holiday Beltane..." Ruth began her argument. She knew it was the only way to taunt her grandfather.

"Ruth, please don't start," Constance warned. Joe absolutely hated being told that the Kiwanis would do anything related to the pagans.

Ruth was going to change the subject if she couldn't change her granddaddy's mind. "There's still snow in the North pasture, but with this sun, it won't last too much longer. Hopefully, we can let the herd up there soon."

"We got plenty of time, Grand-baby. It can still snow in April, and I don't want anyone getting stuck if the stream floods or freezes."

Not wanting to return to the subject of the Kiwanis, Ruth resorted to, "Well, I'm gonna shower and change. Thanks for the ride, Granddaddy." Ruth went upstairs with a knit between her brows.

★ ★ ★

Ruth and Grace were in the kitchen preparing dinner with their mother. Ken knocked on the door. When the door opened, Ruth froze.

"May I come in?" He asked from the threshold.

Ruth didn't answer. She no longer wanted to gouge his eyes from their sockets, but she was still plenty mad at him.

"Of course, dear, come in," Constance spoke up. "Ken, will you stay for dinner? We're celebrating Ruth's college choice, but I assume you already know about that."

"I didn't know it was official." Ken had his eyes locked on Ruth. His face was solemn, "Ruth can we speak–alone?"

Ruth said nothing. She handed the carrot she was peeling to Grace.

"I'll have her back before dinner," Ken said to Constance.

Ruth glared at him. He grabbed her jacket from the coat rack by the door and held it out for her to slip on. She huffed, grabbed her cell phone from the counter, slid her arms into her jacket, and shoved her phone into her pocket.

Neither spoke. They walked down the steps of the back porch and across the drive to Ken's Jeep. He waited for her to get in and went around to his side. They drove down the drive and turned toward the mountains.

"Where are you taking me?" she demanded.

"Some place we can discuss your attitude without being interrupted."

"My Attitude?" she shrieked incredulously and added a huff for good measure.

They were both silent as Ken pulled the jeep into the same overlook they'd parked at on Valentine's Day. The wonderful world of ice crystals had vanished. The sun, still above the tops of the distant mountains, set the world below them ablaze.

It would have been beautiful and romantic if they weren't fighting. Part of her wanted to forget that she was so angry and just throw her arms around him and kiss him. She knew she'd miss him next week. She didn't even know when he was coming back. The other part of her wanted to slap him for the "attitude" remark and didn't care if he ever set foot in Colorado again.

"I guess this isn't going to work after all, Ruth," he said flatly.

"What are you talking about?" Her breath whooshed out of her, and she felt like she had just been kicked in the gut.

"Us!" He looked at her with her arms and legs tightly crossed. "First off, your behavior was unacceptable in class today. Texting Paloma like an adolescent and then ignoring me and storming out when I asked you to stay. Second, I can't believe how jealous you are about my success."

"What!"

"Look at you. You're livid, and all because I'm going on a business trip. It's one of the most important things that has ever happened to me, and instead of congratulating me, you're acting like a spoiled brat. Because I won't be here for ONE weekend? You know, I don't plan to spend the rest of my life in this town teaching high school. I took this job for the money. My plans are to travel and write and to take every opportunity that comes my way..."

Ruth had heard enough. She cut him off mid-sentence. "How dare you put words in my mouth and presume to know what I'm thinking!" She slapped her hands on the dashboard, "I am happy for you. I am overjoyed for you. I cracked my knee open on the desk when I heard the news because I wanted to run to you and tell you how excited I was for you. But it's tough for me to express my happiness for you when you don't even tell me about your life!"

They looked at each other for a moment. Ruth decided this would be her opportunity to vent, and she wanted to get started before he had the chance to stop her.

"How long have you known about your play getting accepted? It's had to be for be awhile. I'm not an idiot. It takes time to make arrangements for plane tickets and hotel rooms and everything. In all that time, you couldn't mention it to me, even once? No, I had to hear about it in class? And only because Missy asked you? Were you even going to tell me? Or were you planning on calling me from the airport Saturday morning? Oh, by the way, Baby Doll, I'm getting on a plane to San Fran, have a nice life!" She did a poor imitation of him, but he got the point.

"It makes me feel like I'm unimportant to you when you can tell the entire class something but forget to tell me!" She was furious, and she cut herself off before she said something she really would regret.

"I was planning to tell you tonight. I thought the overlook and the sunset would be romantic. I didn't expect Missy to ask me about my plans during class; quite frankly, I was so excited about it. I couldn't keep it a secret any longer."

"Oh," was all Ruth could reply, but she still had a lot of unanswered questions.

"And I've only known for a few days–Tuesday, actually. Ellie emailed me from California and asked if I was all set to go. Apparently, she's known about it for several weeks and forgot to tell me. Luckily she took it upon herself to make all the arrangements."

"Ha," a sarcastic laugh erupted from Ruth's throat, "isn't that convenient for her."

He looked at her quizzically. "Baby Doll," his tone was softer now, "what is that supposed to mean?"

"Oh Kenny darling," Ruth did an excellent imitation of Ellie and her fake British accent, "our play's been accepted, and I've made all the arrangements, so you don't have to worry about a thing. We'll meet in San Fran. It will be wicked fun." She could see Cowboy's lips beginning to turn up at the corners. "And don't worry darling, I could only book us one hotel room, but there are two beds. That shouldn't be a problem if you only think of me as an older sister?"

His look got serious, and he stared into her eyes for a long moment. Finally, he said, "I'm staying with my buddy Greg. He moved out to Berkley after I moved down here. I finally got a hold of him last night."

"You mean I'm right!" Ruth gasped. "Did she really try to get you to stay with her?"

"I'm not saying anything because you seem to dislike Ellie enough," he reached for Ruth's hand and intertwined their fingers.

Ruth was silent for a while. He held her hands and kissed her fingers. She guessed they were making up.

"I really am happy that your play got chosen. I am proud of you, Cowboy."

"Thank you, Baby Doll. Let me see your knee."

She pulled up the leg of her sweats and show off the slight cut and purple bruise on the top of her knee.

"You need some ice on that," Cowboy bent forward and kissed her knee. His lips were soft against the bruise, but that didn't stop tingles from traveling up and down her leg when he kissed it. He let his head rest in her lap, and she ran her fingers through his hair.

"Do you want to tell me the rest of the details?" she asked.

He sat up, and his hands found hers again. "It goes up at the end of July; I have to check the dates. Ellie's in San Fran now talking to the producers and finding a director. We'll watch auditions on Sunday and Monday. Hopefully, iron out casting choices by Tuesday, and I'll be back by Wednesday."

"That sounds pretty wonderful, Cowboy."

"Yeah, I have to agree with you; it is."

Their fingers intertwined again. "I guess I'm not the only one here with good news." He kissed her forehead and both cheeks, "Congratulations on making your college decision."

"Oh, yeah. It's not really that big of a deal. I had to choose somewhere to go," her words petered out, distracted by his lips.

"Where are you going?"

"CU Fort Collins."

"Good choice." A long, slow kiss interrupted the conversation. "Baby Doll, what was so important that you and Paloma were passing notes in class."

"Nothing, I guess," she could barely keep a thought in her head when his lips caressed her.

Cowboy continued, "Well, what is IT?"

"Huh? I don't know?" She tried to concentrate, "What is what?"

"IT. The IT you were going to ask me about."

She went through the conversation with Paloma in her mind and suddenly realized what Cowboy was talking about. This was not the conversation she felt up to having at the moment.

"Seemed important enough to interrupt my class." Cowboy playfully pushed the matter.

"Are we discussing classroom behavior outside the walls of the school, Mr. Silver? I thought that was against our agreement." Ruth tried to change the subject as Cowboy brushed his lips past her temple and across her forehead.

"You ran out of my classroom Miss Willows. I'm merely trying to be thorough."

She grabbed both his hands. "Cowboy, I'm sorry. It won't happen again."

He accepted her apology by kissing her mouth.

"Cowboy," Ruth cut short the kiss, "Were you really ready to give up... on us?"

"No," he sat up and looked her in the eyes, "I'm sorry. That was not a fair thing to say. I apologize."

She looked at his all too serious face, smirked, and said, "Guys can be such jerks."

"Yeah, we can."

Ruth's phone buzzed and sang in her pocket.

The phone read HOME, "Hello," she answered.

"Mom wants to know if you're still coming home for dinner," Grace asked, "or have you two gone off to your love nest or something disgusting like that?"

In the background, Ruth heard her mother's protest, "I said nothing of the sort! I just want to know how many places to set..."

"We'll be home in..." Ruth looked at Ken's face, "in a few minutes? And set a place for Cowboy," Ken smiled and nodded.

Chapter 30

SHE SAT AT her desk, scanning the news. Elizabeth Gills leaned herself against the edge of the desk. “What are you doing here so late? You’re not one for hanging around after staff meetings.”

“You either,” she replied.

“I just got a call from the sheriff’s department. They’ve taken my name off the suspect list in the ‘wrongful death investigation’ of Bill Bowman,” Elizabeth scoffed.

“Isn’t that good news?”

“My name should have never been on that list in the first place!” Gills shrieked. “I’ve lost a month of my life to worrying and...”

She cut Gills off, “If you knew you had nothing to do with it, why were you worried?”

Gills leaned in close to her friend, “Look at all the things that have gone wrong in my life. First, the you-know-what hits the fan about online degrees - which wasn’t illegal till the school board twisted it all around. Then I get ridiculed by the students, no support from our leader,” she tossed her head, indicating Rodriguez’s door, “and ended up losing my job. Then, there’re pictures of me an’ Bowman, and the next thing I know

I'm a murder suspect. I'm afraid to ask what could happen next." Gills got even closer, "What did I do to deserve all this?"

She gave Elizabeth a looked that said, you've got to be kidding, as Gills resumed an upright stance again.

"Oh, I know I sound paranoid," Gills continued, "but you're not paranoid if someone is really after you."

Rodriguez's door swung open, and Ken emerged. Rodriguez clapped Ken on the shoulder, "I think it will all work out just fine. I appreciate your insights, and I understand your concerns, but I think we've come to an excellent compromise that should make quite a few people happy."

Rodriguez turned back into his office and closed the door. Ken turned and noticed the two ladies staring at him. He flashed them one of his killer smiles; big dimples, white teeth, and a twinkle in his eye. "Good night, ladies," he nodded his head and winked as he strolled out of the office.

"Speaking of a man who looks like he just got all that he wanted," she sneered, "maybe you're looking at the cause of your problems."

"Ken?" Gills said with a soft lilt in her voice. "What would he have to do with my troubles? He's such a good person."

"I think you're going as soft as these lame brain girls do when he flashes that smile of his," she retorted as Gills blushed. "What was the big news at the staff meeting today? Who's replacing us! Who's replacing you, Bets?"

Gills didn't answer.

"Could it be Mister Ken Silver? I believe that's what I heard. From the looks of it, he looks pretty happy about the whole thing."

"I don't care what you say. I've worked with him this whole year, and I just don't think he's the type of person who would do evil things," Gills defended her protégé. "Besides, once I knew that we'd be leaving next year, I've been trying to get him up to speed on all I do here. I would rather Ken took over for me than someone who wouldn't want to continue the work I've started."

"Oh Svengali," she shook her head, "I don't think you know your student, and you think you do."

"So why are you here so late?" Gills changed the subject.

"Oh, no place else to go, I guess," she gave a vacant reply. Gills looked at her questioningly, so she elaborated. "My realtor has an appointment with a couple tonight. She expects them to make an offer on my house."

"Oh, my goodness! Your house sold so quickly! It's only been on the market for a month." Gills added, "Have you decided where you'll go?"

"My son and his family live near Phoenix. Maybe I'll move closer to them." She lied.

"It's Friday night. Let's go out and celebrate," Gills suggested.

She thought for a moment and said, "I'm not quite in the mood for celebrating. Next week when I have a signed contract in my hand, I'll celebrate."

"Well, suit yourself," Gills shrugged and left.

What a dolt, she thought as she watched her go. *If my house sells tonight, guess I could just head out immediately. Will I be able to get the money the school board owes me? May have to stick around till the end of the school year. Maybe stay with Elizabeth for a week or two... If she only knew her little boy toy doesn't need to play with her when he has a sweet young thing. When you think about it, a lot of her problems started once he came on board.*

Now, Willows... I don't trust her. She always seems to be in the thick of it. She found Alverez, she found his files, and those pictures of Bowman were on her laptop! HUH, that little witch is after Betsy... I could keep an eye on her if I stick around. Maybe even find out what she's up to...

The ringing of her cell phone interrupted her thoughts.

"Hey girlfriend, it's Blair!" the annoying agent shouted into the phone, "I've got good news for you! Come on home, and let's sign some papers!"

Chapter 31

"I'VE FINISHED GRACE'S hair. I'll do you next." Constance pulled Ruth into the bedroom, where she'd set up a makeshift salon.

Constance scooted Ruth into a chair in front of the mirror, "You do your makeup while I do your hair. It's supposed to be braided with flowers and ribbons. I won't have time to do anything too complex, but it will hold through the parade." Constance added, "Don't forget the clothes you want to wear to the dance. We're not coming home to change. And don't forget your mask! Your Granddaddy is doorman, and he won't let a soul in without a mask."

Ruth sighed and rolled her eyes.

"Oh, why do you act like that," her mother sighed. "Look what happened at the last dance you went to."

"What?" Ruth mumbled as she painted her lips.

Constance reminded her, "Isn't that when you and Ken started dating?"

Ruth didn't need to be reminded of the last party held at the Kiwanis' lodge–she'd thought of little else all week. She thought of how much their relationship had grown since then. She also thought about all the places their relationship hadn't gone in the last four months–*or should it be counted as nine months? Well, that's one problem right there. It's not like it's a normal relationship. We've never even...*

"Ruth are you?" her mother asked.

"What? I was thinking about... I wasn't paying attention."

"I asked if the two of you were being careful, using protection?"

"With what," Ruth said absentmindedly. She looked at her mother in the mirror, "Oh God... Mother! ... NO! We're not!... I mean, we're not being careful... I mean we're not... we're not doing ... what you think... oh god, I don't want to talk about this!" Ruth stood up to leave, but her mother pushed her back down.

"I'm not done with your hair. Sit still," Constance said with a little ire, "And if you're not capable of having this discussion, I guess you should abstain."

"I am capable of having this discussion - if I want to" ***(not)*** "I just wasn't thinking about that right now." *Oh right, that's almost all you think about.*

"I just assumed that with the amount of time you spend together... it's the natural thing to happen."

"Yeah... well..." Ruth made a face. *I guess you and I have different ideas about natural progression than Cowboy.*

"It's really a choice that the two of you need to make. It doesn't take that much time to put on a condom."

"Ugh, Mother!" Ruth couldn't get away from this conversation fast enough. "Is my hair done?"

Constance pinned two more yellow silk flowers into Ruth's hair and doused it with hair spray. "You're all done, and you're beautiful."

★ ★ ★

After the parade, Ruth and Grace met a masked Paloma at the front entrance of the lodge.

"Wow, you look dramatic, P," Ruth said of the cocktail dress and black-feathered mask.

"You look like you belong in New York instead of here," Grace commented wistfully. Grace had major fantasies about living in NYC.

"I thought a black would be tasteful, but maybe I don't look springy enough." Paloma worried.

"You look perfect!" Ruth assured her as they walked through the door.

Joe stopped the trio before they crossed the threshold, "I have your tickets here, but only one of you may enter."

They all looked at each other, confused.

"My own Granddaughters can't remember to wear a mask to a masked dance?" he complained.

"Sorry, Granddaddy," Ruth and Grace said in almost perfect unison.

Grace had been twirling her mask around her finger by one of the eyeholes, and Ruth had hers tied around her wrist. They tied their masks over their faces and Joe gave them a courtly bow waving them inside.

The lodge was warm and crowded. Ruth surveyed the room. Cowboy was nowhere in sight. She got a sinking feeling that with his old roommate, Greg, popping into town for a visit, they would find an excuse not to make it at all. She saw the guys from the team had already staked claim to a corner of the room. The girls went over to join them.

Ruth introduced Paloma to Larry and his fiancée Michelle, Jeff, and Clayton. She was happy to see Katie was on the other side of the room with Derrick and several other people. Katie had told her Derrick was kicked off the team after getting drunk and crashed the PBR's Viper. The group all seemed familiar, but the masks and dark lighting made it difficult to tell who was who.

Jeff was the first one to pull Ruth onto the dance floor, and Clayton was next. Ed and Constance danced by, and Ed made sure that he got a dance with each of his daughters. The same went for Joe, who made sure everyone knew who his granddaughters were.

The unmasking wasn't till midnight, but by ten o'clock, there was still no Cowboy, and Ruth wanted to go home. She didn't have her car, and no one else wanted to leave. She had been around the dance floor enough times to figure out that the table on the other side of the room included Elizabeth Gills, Lana Laurence, Lezza, Carol Ann, and Louisa Stack, all sitting with Derrick. "Girls' Night Out," Katie had told their table as she flitted between groups.

Just as well Cowboy's not here, Ruth thought as she stayed parked on her chair. She was tired of dancing with everyone except the one person she wanted to be with.

★ ★ ★

"All right, Bro, what's the plan for tonight?" Greg's speech slurred ever so slightly.

Ken bated his friend. "We're going to walk through the door. Then, if you can still keep yourself upright, we're supposed to dance."

"I'm not that far gone, since when can't I handle one or two boilermakers?"

"It was the fourth one you couldn't handle, bro," Ken smirked.

"Man, you are so lame," Greg muttered. His shaggy blonde hair hid his baby face when he shook his head. "You had what one drink?"

"I'm the designated driver."

"So what am I supposed to do when I find someone to hook up with?" Greg flashed a cocky grin.

"Do whatever you want," Ken grumbled.

"You and your lady gonna be rockin' and rollin' in the Jeep? I don't want to walk in on you two. Unless you're both into that..."

"Don't worry about that," Ken sounded dejected.

"What? Your babe won't put out?"

"It's not like that," Ken shook his head.

Greg grabbed Ken by the sleeve, causing him to swing around and face him. "What is going on with you, dude? Where's the man who taught me every move I know? Where's old love 'em and leave 'em Kenny–Hi-Ho Silver and away!"

Ken didn't answer; he simply turned and headed across the lot.

Greg followed, "Come on, man, what's the problem? Can't you get it up anymore? You know they have pills for that now."

Ken glared at him.

"I just don't get it. You don't drink anymore, you don't have sex anymore, you forgot how to have fun, dude! Do you at least still like girls, dude?"

Ken halted and got right Greg's face, "Cool it - DUDE! I'm not living in a frat house." he backed off from Greg, "I don't have to explain myself to you." Ken slowed his pace as he walked on.

"Fine, bro... No explanations necessary."

They had about fifty feet to go when Ken stopped dead in his tracks, "Son-of-a..." He changed course and headed around the side of the building.

"What's up, dude?"

Ken pulled out two black half masks and a ticket to the dance from his shirt pocket. He handed one of each to Greg. "Put this on," he ordered, "and take this ticket. I'm not going."

"Whaddaya talkin' about!" cried Greg.

"The women who just stepped out onto the porch: the one is my boss, the other is a secretary in the front office, and I guarantee you there are more of them inside."

"So... they're not too bad looking, a little long in the tooth but doable," Greg scanned them by stepping out from around the corner.

Ken pulled Greg back by the front of his shirt and growled through clenched teeth, "This is serious, pay attention, will you? I can't be seen with Ruth in public."

"You just rode through the town with her in that lame-ass parade," Greg pointed out.

"Romantically!" Ken corrected him. "I thought I explained all this to you."

"Yeah, yeah... wanna go back to the bar?" Greg looked happy at that prospect.

"No, you are going to go in there and find her. You're going to tell her to meet me in the garden. She'll know where. You got that?"

"Yeah, yeah, I got it," Greg rolled his eyes.

Ken gave Greg a serious look, then turned and walked away. Greg murmured several expletives under his breath as he plodded his way up the stairs.

★ ★ ★

An unfamiliar hand took hold of Ruth's arm and pulled her not only to her feet but to the center of the dance floor. She didn't recognize the touch, and her nose was met with the smell of beer and something more robust. He held her one hand in the typical dance pose, and he wrapped his other arm tight around her waist.

"Greg, what on earth are you doing?" She tried to loosen his grip on her but struggling only made him hold on tighter.

"Trying to get to know my future sister-in-law better," Greg spoke into her ear.

"What are you talking about?" Ruth had only met Cowboy's friend hours earlier, "And how much did you drink?"

"I drank enough to forget the hours upon hours I had to spend wandering around, alone, I might add, at that lame carnival while you guys played with your horses."

"It is not lame!" Even if she agreed with him, she wouldn't let this stranger bash her town's good time.

"Since you were sitting there all alone, presumably pining over your lover-boy, whom I had stolen away from you, I thought I'd be a nice guy and make it up to you with a dance."

"Oh, so that's what you call this–dancing,"

He feigned injury, "I will have you know that in some circles, I am considered a superb dancer."

"Uh, huh."

Greg was tipsy, and he was definitely funny. Before she could ask Greg where Cowboy was, Greg added with a wink, "...in some circles, I'm considered a magnificent lover too."

"Ew - TMI!" She tried to pull away.

"Oh, that's right. You're not interested in sampling my goods; your heart belongs to Kenny." Greg spun Ruth around and then he pulled her in tight to him again, "You sure have done a number on my boy. You know that?" He didn't wait for her to answer, "I lived with Kenny for three years, three happy-go-lucky, wild, fun crazy years!" He sighed, "Then he comes to see me in San Francisco for a few nights and he can't shut up about you."

Ruth just stared at Greg. She didn't know how she was supposed to respond. She didn't have time to say anything before Greg continued.

"So, I figured I better get myself out here and meet my new little sister before anything major takes place..."

"Why do you keep saying that?" Ruth demanded.

"Because that's how far gone he is! I'm telling you, I've never seen this side of him before. I've seen him with a lot of girls–and I mean A LOT."

Ruth flushed red at the thought of her lack of experience.

"He has never been so hung up on one girl before. The man taught me everything I know, and he's not following any of his own rules with you." Then Greg got serious, "He's the best guy in the world–you know that! He is my blood brother–you know what I mean? Promise me you'll take care of him."

Ruth didn't know what to say again. Regardless of the amount of alcohol Greg had consumed, his sentiments were heartfelt. On the other hand, there was no promise of any sort between her and Cowboy. They were dating, and that was a very loose definition of their relationship. But, she looked into Greg's grey eyes, nodded her head, and said, "I will."

She wanted to ask about the rules, but Greg relaxed after her answer, so she laid her head on his shoulder and let the dance finish. She could see what Cowboy meant when he described Greg as rough around the edges but grew on you.

When the music changed, Greg led Ruth through the back door and onto the porch. She remembered standing with Cowboy here only a few months before. It seemed like a lifetime ago.

"Oh yeah, I forgot to tell you," Greg said as he slung his arm over her shoulder, "there's a really good looking guy, well not as good lookin' as me, but he said he'd be waiting for you in that garden out there."

Ruth looked at him in disbelief. "How long has he been waiting?"

"When we walked into the dance, we ran into a couple of people he works with, and he said that it wouldn't be too good if they saw you two getting it on together."

Ruth rolled her eyes - *since when did they get it on?*

"So," Greg continued, "he told me to come in and get you, and he'd be waiting for you in the garden."

Ruth didn't know if she wanted to punch Greg or thank him. She gave him a firm but friendly pat on the cheek before bounding down the wooden steps.

Chapter 32

RUTH STOPPED ABOUT a hundred feet into the garden; *I must look like an idiot–and where is Cowboy, anyway? God, I hope this isn't Greg's idea of a joke...* Her smile turned to a pout, her hands clenched, and her breathing got tense. The spring air was still cold, and she wished she had worn something warmer if she was going to stand outside alone, feeling foolish. It was then that the familiar warm arm slipped around her waist from behind, and she knew it was no joke. He kissed her neck and whispered, "Come with me."

He led her, hand in hand, fingers intertwined, to the far corner of the garden. The moon was bright enough to cast shadows as they walked. Behind a large spruce tree was a bench made from an enormous slab of flagstone.

They had barely made it to the far side of the tree before Ken kissed her. His intensity was stronger than ever before. His powerful energy took her breath away. The fabric of his shirt gathered in her hands as her fingers clung to his back for support.

He tasted similar to how Greg had smelled. *What were they drinking? If he's gonna kiss me like this, maybe he should drink more often.*

His arms held her tight as he leaned her back, further and further, until her back met the cold flagstone. A storm of electrical impulses raged through her body; it reminded her of the first night he'd kissed her. *Whatever he does, he can't stop. If he stops this time, I might suffer some kind of permanent damage.*

His hand slid from her back to her hip and down her thigh. Instinctively she wrapped herself around him. Her legs were bare, and his hand caressed her leg before working its way back to her hips to trace the edge of her small lacy panties.

Heart racing, body pulsing, Ruth was ready to burst from every touch of his fingertips. She clawed at his shirt, pulling at it to get it away from his skin. *Damn buttons,* she thought as her fingers fumbled. Her mind raced to acknowledge each new, incredible sensation. Cowboy was calm, cool, and collected as his fingers danced over her skin, and his lips lingered on her throat. With one hand, he untied her mask and let it fall aside.

She gave up on the shirt buttons. That level of skill was beyond her at present. It was challenging to writhe and undress your lover at the same time for a newbie. She concentrated on what needed to get done. She wore a short skirt-that made things easy; her panties could be off in a nanosecond. His tight black jeans were another matter entirely. There was a belt to undo, then a button, the fly–*oh God, I hope it's a zipper. I can't deal with buttons right now.* Her trembling hands went to his belt buckle, and as she tugged at it, trying to find how it undid without looking. He stopped.

Her heart sunk when he pulled away from her; she tried to hold on to him, but the moment was gone. *What did I do wrong this time?* Her brow furrowed as "Why!" escaped from her lips.

"What?" he breathed heavily.

Tried as she might to stay calm, her pent-up energy needed to be released. Tears of frustration filled her eyes and her voice shook, "Please, Cowboy. Not again."

"What, Baby Doll?"

She couldn't answer. Stifling a sob, "What's wrong with me?"

Cowboy sat up, "Are you all right? Did I hurt you?" Concerned overflowed in his voice as the tears overflowed from her eyes. She sat up, adjusted her skirt, staring into her lap. Waves of heat flashed across her face, and she was glad for the shadows.

"Talk to me, Baby Doll," he pleaded.

Her head hung lower, and she clenched her arms around her body. *It's now or never, and it might as well be now. He probably won't ever want to speak to me again.* She took a deep breath, "Why don't you...want...me?" squeaked out of her throat.

It took him a moment to make out what she'd said, but when he did, he wrapped his arms around her. He held her until her breathing became even again. He didn't want her to be upset. He didn't understand why the outburst of fragile emotions. His eyebrows knitted, he kissed the top of her head, "Baby Doll, I do want you, but we've had this discussion before..."

She pulled away from him and sat up straight. "No, we haven't," she interrupted him.

"Of course, we have..."

"No, we really haven't," she assured him.

He looked at her, dazed and confused. "But I thought... I'm sure we've... I thought we'd..."

She repeatedly and slowly shook her head no.

"I'm sorry, Baby Doll," Cowboy took her hands in his and kissed them. "I guess I've thought about this...you...wanting you and being with you so often. From the first moment you walked into my class, from before that, from the rodeo, no from before that ... I've thought about it so much that I assumed that we had... talked about it."

With drier eyes and a half-smile creeping across her lips, she ventured, "So you do want me? I don't repulse you?"

It was his turn to interrupt, "Repulse? Are you nuts? Where on earth did you come up with that?"

She shrugged her shoulders and looked down at her lap again.

"Do I act like a man that is repulsed by you? Really?" He placed an index finger under her chin and tilted her head back so he could see her eyes.

"Not at first, but then you always stop and take me home. I thought I was doing something wrong or that you're turned off by me..."

"Baby Doll, it takes every ounce of strength I have to stop myself." He held her quietly for a moment before he explained.

"I promised myself, before we began this little arrangement of ours, that I wouldn't have sex with you."

She looked at him, a little horrified and not fully understanding him, "But... why?"

He sighed, "You are still my student. I know that we can both justify why it isn't wrong for us to be together, but I don't enjoy keeping this secret. I hate knowing that getting caught could mean the end of my job and embarrassment or expulsion for you. If Principle Rodriguez asked me if we were seeing each other, I couldn't lie; I'd have to say yes. I could also explain that I've been with you at family gatherings. And if asked, I can still honestly say that we have not had sex."

Ruth tried to hide her grimace. To hear him say it in such a matter a fact way really took the romance out of it.

"Also, since I am in a position of authority, I don't want you to feel pressured into doing something you're not ready and willing to do."

She took a deep breath, and while she fingered the collar of his shirt, she managed a whisper, "But I am ready, and I don't feel any pressure. I wouldn't blame you for making me..."

He stopped her, "Maybe not today, or tomorrow or next week, but I don't want you to look back on us and feel like you had to do something."

Did he understand how much she wanted him? Did he understand this was the first time she had ever wanted to give herself to anyone, and she would give herself to him freely and without guilt or strings attached?

She agreed that the risk of getting caught having sex with a teacher was too great. Ruth let out a long sigh.

"I see your point," she said glumly.

Ken laughed, "Come on, Baby Doll," his fingers traced the outline of her face, "you don't really want our first time together to be out here, do you?" He patted his hand on the cold stone bench. She shrugged her shoulders. "This stone's cold and rough. It wouldn't be as nice as you might think. I can think of a lot nicer places for us to..." he kissed her, "enjoy each other."

She shrugged again. Her fingers had moved from his collar to playing with the waves in his hair. She felt torn; she understood what he said, but the desire that burned within her was so consuming she was wild to quench it.

"In less than a month," he continued, "I will no longer be your teacher. They will record your final grades for posterity, and you'll receive your diploma. After all that, if you're still interested in me... well, we will make it an extraordinary experience–Okay?"

"You know they always say no time like the present," Ruth said with a sly smile.

"They also say good things come to those who wait," Ken reminded her.

"Fine, fine, fine, we wait," she hesitantly agreed. At least he had agreed to do it with her at some point.

He took her face between his hands and kissed her gently and sweetly. Ruth reminded herself that she'd rather be with him like this than not at all.

They didn't hurry back to the dance.

When a big hoot and holler washed down from the dance, they realized that it was midnight and the party-goers must have unmasked themselves.

"I know what you're going to say before you even say it."

"What's that?"

"Time to get back to the party," Ruth sounded gloomy.

"The only girl I know who doesn't like a good party."

"I'm tired of hiding out with you." She climbed into his lap, face to face, and twisted his hair around her fingers, "I'm not tired of being alone with you, you understand. But now, I have even more of a desire to graduate."

He allowed her one more passionate kiss, which was all he could take before he led the way back to the lodge. "You go first, Baby Doll. I'll be in, in a minute to collect Greg."

With a parting peck, Ruth floated down the path and up to the lodge's back porch. A man stepped out of the shadows and onto the steps as Ruth looked back over her shoulder. She ran smack dab into his barrel chest.

"Oh, ouch! I'm sorry, I wasn't... Derrick?"

"Well, lookie here. If it isn't the belle of the ball, returned from where? A midnight tryst? You've been gone quite some time. I wonder who with?"

"I didn't know you were to keep track of me. Excuse me, please."

"Are you gonna tell me that after flouncing around with half the men in that room, you were out here by yourself?"

"I'm not afraid to be alone. Sometimes I prefer it," she said pointedly, "and I don't flounce."

In a swift, unexpected move, Derrick grabbed Ruth and pinned her arms to her sides. He pinned her toes with his feet to slow down any knee action on her part. "Maybe you should be afraid, Willows, maybe you should learn to be very afraid."

She didn't like Derrick, his mauling. or his threats, and she wasn't sure how she would get herself out of this.

"Leave her alone, Derrick!" Ken snapped as he emerged from the building's shadow.

"Oh, look who's here to save the day," Derrick sneered. "Whatcha gonna do, Silver?"

It wasn't much of a distraction, but it was enough. Ruth took full advantage and shoved Derrick away with all her might before she twisted free of his grip. She fled to the top of the stairs. Derrick paid little attention; he had found bigger fish to fry.

"Should have known she was with you," Derrick sneered. "See you're still kowtowing to the little b..."

"Watch your mouth, Gills," Ken cut him off, "and mind your own business."

Derrick spat out a laugh, "I would have thought my little note to that sorry ass excuse of a boss would have done you two in a long time ago. Guess you've charmed that bumbling idiot too. You think you can get away with anything you want."

Ruth bounded down the steps and planted herself on the step above Derrick, "YOU! It was you that wrote that letter to Principal Rodriguez!" She shoved Derrick off the step. "You wrote that slanderous piece of tripe? You jackass! I thought your mother wrote it! Why on earth would you do something so cruel?"

Not knowing what his mother had to do with it, Derrick laughed some more, "Hey, it was funny! I only wish I could have been a fly on the wall when you two found out about it."

Ruth clenched her fist, pulled her arm back, and aimed for Derrick's face.

He didn't see the punch coming. She got in a good crack to his nose. Derrick grabbed his face immediately.

"You stupid Bitch!" Red dripped into his hands, "You broke my nose!"

Before Ken could cross the ten feet to get to Gills, Greg was at Ruth's side.

"Sweet Cakes! There you are!" Greg took Ruth by the waist and hauled her out of Derrick's reach. "Can't a guy go take a leak without some little shrimp trying to steal his girl?" Greg stared Derrick down.

Derrick looked around; Silver had moved up on his right. Some big, unknown blonde dude with his arm around Willows stood in front of him, and now Larry, Clayton, and Jeff flanked this dude from the top of the stairs. They outnumbered him. His nose bleed was already beginning to slow.

"You've got to be kidding," Derrick scoffed at Greg. "You're tellin' me she's with you?"

"She sure is," Greg smiled at Ruth, "aren't you Sweet Cakes? I lost you. I see Kenny found you for me. Now give your Daddy some sugar." With that, Greg planted the biggest, wettest, sloppiest kiss on Ruth's lips.

She went along with it at first; what else could she do. Greg wasn't too bad of a kisser. His lips were soft and squishy, his unshaven stubble was long enough to be soft, his body was broader and less sinewy than Cowboy. He wasn't that much taller than her, but he held her up on her toes, so they were nose to nose without him bending over her. There wasn't the same electricity she felt when Cowboy kissed her, but there was a niceness about his embrace, and she couldn't say she didn't enjoy it more than she would have thought. When he tried to push his tongue past her lips, all she could think was *ew!* Suddenly she felt like she was kissing a brother. She pushed him away, though he still held onto her waist.

"Not in front of others," she complained, "you know I don't like that."

Greg chuckled, "My little Sweet Cakes is so shy."

"My ass she is," Derrick scoffed, "And I don't believe this cock and bull story either."

"Believe what you like, Derrick." Ruth stayed pressed against Greg's side. She looked at Cowboy, who was biting his tongue... hard.

Derrick noticed the look. "So Silver, got dumped by your girl? Guess you had to take up other pastimes like stealing the only income source from a single mother. You feel all manly and proud of yourself?" Derrick accused Ken.

Ken looked at him like he was nuts, "What are you getting at Derrick?"

"Like you don't know, Mister I'm the new head of the English department. A position my mother held for the last fifteen years."

"I didn't take your Mother's job from her Gills. She lost her job when she made the choice to get a fake degree. And I'm not taking over for her."

"Whaddaya call it then?"

"I'm overseeing all the AP programs. That's one of the few things your mother doesn't manage at school."

"Yeah, well, I wouldn't put it past you," Derrick looked over at Ruth still on the steps with Greg, "I wouldn't put it past either of you to be the rats involved with turning her in, in the first place!"

Ruth tried to hide her pang of guilt. She and Paloma had been over this topic numerous times since the news had come out. Ruth felt it was her and Paloma's fault that people lost their jobs. Paloma's view was they might have been the messengers, but it was the employees' own culpability for taking advantage of the system. She'd further reminded Ruth that Gills' treatment of the two of them had been the catalyst for their research.

Elizabeth Gills emerged onto the porch at the top of the stairs, "That will be enough, Derrick. It's time I take you home."

"Come on, Ma, it's early. Thought you and the cougar patrol were on the prowl for a good time tonight." Derrick became a whining child in front of their eyes.

"My friends and I had a good time tonight, but none of us need to take a drug and alcohol test at seven-thirty tomorrow morning. Your parole officer just called. He'll pick you up at seven-fifteen."

Everyone stared, stunned, at Mrs. Gills' casual use of the words parole officer and drug test. She saw their looks and thought embarrassment might serve Derrick well.

"Derrick hasn't bragged about his enviable situation?" She mockingly questioned as she peered at the crowd. "I can't imagine why not? Let me ask you, what do you think happens when a multimillion-dollar corporation lends you a sports car that you wrap around a telephone pole after a night of underage drinking? Well, if you're lucky enough to walk away from the accident, you get placed on probation until your twenty-first birthday. You get put into the custody of your mother, and you get calls from your new best friend, parole officer Smith, to report for random drug tests."

"It's an enjoyable existence knowing that I could lose everything I've ever worked for if my son cannot test negative for drugs and alcohol and the company sues me for the cost of the car he totaled." Mrs. Gills now looked at her son, livid, "You have fifteen seconds to say goodbye before I take you home." She turned to Ken, "Mr. Silver, ah, Ken, may I speak to you for a moment?"

Ken said, "Sure, Elizabeth, what can I do for you?" They stepped away from the others to speak.

Derrick turned and walked away without uttering a word.

Ruth kissed Greg's cheek and said, "Thank you. I'm going to find Paloma."

Larry, Clayton, and Jeff followed Ruth inside, but Greg strolled out into the parking lot, keeping a distant eye on Ken.

★ ★ ★

Greg stood in the parking lot, staring in awe at a bike, when Ruth walked up behind him, "Sweet, isn't it! I love the flames. Whoever did this is a genuine artist."

Ruth's attention was still focused behind her on the conversation she could not hear between Cowboy and Mrs. Gills.

"Where's your girl, Pa-lo-ma?" He over-pronounced the syllables in her name.

"She had a voice mail she wanted to listen to. I told her I'd wait out here," Ruth answered.

She focused on what Greg was ogling. When she saw the black bike and the green flames on the Kawasaki Ninja that had been in her drive nearly four months earlier the morning of the break-in, she went white and froze.

"What, not a fan of cycles? Too dangerous for your delicate disposition?" Greg teased.

She couldn't get enough air in her lungs to speak. She counted to ten and took the biggest breath she could. At the top of her lungs shouted, "Cowboy!"

Greg covered his ears and made a face that showed his annoyance.

She yelled again, "Cowboy!" She didn't dare leave the bike. She had to see who rode it.

Clayton arrived at Ruth's side first. "What's wrong? You sound like you discovered another dead body."

She pointed a condemning finger at the bike.

"Cool bike!" Clayton's eyes lit up as his fingers followed the contour of the seat.

Larry and Jeff joined the trio.

"What's up?" Larry asked. "Ken's still talking to Gills' mother."

A sharp wave of anxiety washed through Ruth. *What if they're talking about me? The months of hiding and being careful could all have been for naught.* She was angry she'd let Granddaddy talk her into participating in this stupid parade and this stupid dance. She was angrier that Cowboy agreed to it so easily. She was mostly angry with herself; for being so selfish. *How on earth could I whine about him not wanting me! He could lose his job, his reputation, even face jail time just to fool around; I'm such an idiot!*

She wasn't interrupted from her wallowing (because Larry and Jeff joined in the gawking of the cycle) until Cowboy sidled up behind her.

"What's up now, Baby Doll?" he asked softly in her ear. "I heard you. You sounded a little panicked."

She would discuss damage control later, now was the time to deal with the bike. She pointed to the guys fluttering around it. It took Cowboy a moment to see precisely what concerned her. When he did, he sucked in a deep breath and let out a long whistle.

"What'll we do? I know it's the same one."

"Yeah, it sure looks like it," Ken agreed.

"Should we call the Sheriff? Should we wait to see who gets on it and make a citizen's arrest? I don't even know how you would do that. Do you have to be strong enough to hold the person down?" She rambled faster and faster.

"Whoa, hold on there, Baby Doll." Cowboy squeezed her arms and tried to think through the situation out loud. "You're right; it looks like the same bike; I'd bet my horse on it. But we don't have any evidence that the person who rides this bike is the same person who broke into your house." He thought for a moment, "And if we are to believe the paper, they solved the Alverez murder when the other guy... Alberts... killed himself. Right?"

She nodded.

"Even if this was his bike, his wife or estate or whatever could have sold it off by now. We don't know who could be driving it."

Ruth nodded again and looked very glum. "It just makes me so mad. I really feel like I want to punch the person who violated my family's privacy, wrecked my room, and took my computer. I know as sure as I'm standing here, the person on this bike that morning had something to do with it!"

"I agree with you, Baby Doll, but how about instead of a fistfight, we take down the plate number and have Uncle Bob run it?"

She clung with both of her hands to Cowboy's arm. His phone was in his other hand, and he took a few quick pictures of the bike and the plate. He kissed her temple reassuringly and was about to look for the VIN when a woman's voice interrupted.

"Well, well, well, seems like we've got quite a commotion going on here. Why does it always seem that the parking lot is where the real fun is?" She chuckled loudly as the entire group turned to see the woman in biker leathers stroll up.

When Ruth saw the woman's face, she realized this was not someone she wanted to be caught holding on to her AP English teacher. But surely this was also not someone who would have come to a town dance on a motorcycle.

Then Ruth noticed the outfit.

She wore biker leathers, but she must have changed in the ladies' room because Ruth had seen her wearing a skirt at the dance. She had a black leather bomber jacket slung over her shoulder and the same shiny silver top that went with her skirt.

Ruth's mouth hung slack-jawed. She took a step away from Ken as she stared wide-eyed.

"You boys enjoying my bike?" She asked coyly. Greg and Clayton were practically sitting on it. All the guys removed their hands from the bike and took a polite step away from it. "It's all right, you can look at her, just be gentle. I love showing her off."

She turned to Ruth and Ken, "Well, hello there, Mr. Silver, looks like you're enjoying yourself too," she snickered at him, then added, "Ruth honey, close your mouth. You'll catch flies."

"C...C... Carol Ann, what are you doing here?" Ruth choked out.

"Well, it's a town dance, ain't everyone invited?" She chuckled again. "It was so nice out this evening I thought I'd take the bike for a spin." Ruth's eyes were locked on Carol Ann. "Is that all right with you, Miss Willows?"

"Yeah, sure, fine." She tried to answer with a smile. Ken's previous words about the bike being recently sold by the Albert's estate popped into her head. "Is that really your bike Carol Ann? I never knew you rode one."

"She's all mine. It's not a side of me I choose to advertise at school. I'm sure you know what I mean." She smirked as her eyes darted from Ruth to Ken and back with the knowledge they, too, had secrets to hide.

Ruth didn't know what to say, but she felt like she had to keep Carol Ann talking. "How did you end up with a motorcycle? I mean, are you like a biker chick?" Carol Ann let out a great laugh, and Ruth tried to amend her question, "Bikes are cool, I guess. I don't know anything about them. You just don't seem like the usual type to go around in a gang."

"I'm not in a gang, Honey."

"I didn't mean that," she apologized again, "I just mean..."

"It's all right. You don't think of your old school secretary as a person who rides a motorcycle," she smiled her familiar warm smile, "but now that you see me in my leathers, your ideas about me have been–shaken?"

Ruth grinned and nodded her head. "I didn't mean to sound rude; I'm fascinated."

"My husband always rode a bike, and I learned how to from him. Now that my son is grown, I decided to do something for myself, so I got myself this bike."

Before anyone could say another word Paloma ran up to the group overflowing with joy, "Ruth I did it, I did it, I can't believe it I actually did it!"

Ruth didn't get the chance to ask, Paloma just launched into her story, "José Pluma left a message on my voice mail; The Sentinel is going to run my story, with my byline, in the paper tomorrow!"

Ruth's attention was now entirely focused on her best friend, and she flung her arms around her in a congratulatory hug.

"It's not a big story, just a few columns on the parade and the carnival, how it all got started, and the preparations involved in setting it all up. They'll bury it in the local interest section, but it's my first published work!"

"All the hard work of the internship paid off. I am more proud of you than you can imagine, P." Ken put a fraternal arm around Paloma's shoulder; he had taken up using her nickname when they weren't in school.

She gushed at him, "There were some nights when after reading hours of copy for Mr. Pluma, I'd have to go home and read some novel for you. I thought my head would burst! I would dream of Mr. Darcy and Mother Courage arguing over the definition of an accredited institution, and I'd wake up in tears. But it all seems so worth it now, knowing that everyone is going to be able to read something I wrote! And it won't just be kids in school, but everyone reading the genuine news. I hope Mrs. Gills gets an eyeful! Especially after she had the nerve to throw me off the paper!"

Ruth was ecstatic for her friend. She suddenly went numb. Ken went quiet too. Paloma noticed other people had been listening to their conversation. She stared at the woman in black leather for a moment before realizing who she was.

"Carol Ann, I'm sorry, I was so excited I didn't even notice you there," Paloma apologized.

"No, you certainly didn't," Carol Ann smiled. "And here I thought I knew everything that went on in our school..."

The guys were losing interest in the bike. It was after one a.m. They were all discussing plans for the rest of the weekend and getting ready to head home. Only Greg leaned against the car parked next to the ninja and took in the conversation.

Carol Ann called out as Elizabeth and Derrick Gills approached their car, "Did you hear that, Bets?"

"Hear what?" Elizabeth Gills sounded agitated.

"I've just been told that you threw Miss Torres here off the school newspaper..."

Gills just huffed.

"... And she went and got herself a job at the Greater Golden Sentinel. And working for, who did you say, honey?" Carol Ann pointed the rhetorical question to Paloma, "Oh, that's right, José Pluma."

Gills huffed again, "Really? Well, looks like I did you a favor then Torres. Maybe you should thank me for jump-starting your career."

"It was Ruth who did me a favor," Paloma retorted.

"Really?" Gills' words were acrid. "I didn't realize that Miss Willows was so well connected. Maybe she could give us all a hand at finding new jobs."

Ruth glared at Gills. Finally, she answered, "Mr. Pluma and I have a mutual friend. I really did nothing special."

Greg jumped into the thick of it, tipsily cutting off the exchange. He squeezed between Ruth and Paloma and wrapped an arm around each of their waists, "Mmmm, mmmm, mmmm. Here I thought I was a lucky man to find my little sweet cakes," He kissed Ruth on the side of the face. "Now

I find this hot mama has something to celebrate too." He gave Paloma a big kiss on the lips while holding on to both girls. "Why don't you ladies take daddy home and show him what you're made of?"

The entire crowd rolled their eyes and groaned; Mrs. Gills turned toward her car, parked two spots down from the ninja, "Get in the car Derrick, we're going home," and left with her son in tow.

Carol Ann looked suspiciously at the foursome, the blonde boy drooling over both girls, and Ken standing to the side. She shook her head, reached for her helmet, and slid it on. Within moments, she was on her bike and left them all in the dust.

"You really enjoy being obnoxious, don't you?" Ruth cocked her head.

"One of my specialties," Greg smiled, took her hand, and kissed the back of it.

The crowd in the parking lot was growing, which meant the dance was officially over. It didn't take long till the dirt lot glowed red from tail lights. Ken suggested, "Let's wait till this crowd clears out."

Ken and Ruth headed over to Paloma's little powder blue Ford parked in the aisle closest to the woods. Ken's jeep was in the same row. He turned to speak to Greg when they reached the Escort, but neither he nor Paloma was around.

Ruth leaned against the Ford. "Oh," she sighed, "what are we gonna do, Cowboy?"

"I guess we'll give them twenty minutes, then give Paloma's cell a call and see if she needs to be rescued."

"What?" Ruth had not noticed the missing pair. Then she realized, "Where'd they go?"

Ken cocked one eyebrow at her and let her answer her own question.

"Ewww."

"Problem, Baby Doll?" He sidled up to her.

She slid her arms around his waist and her fingers into the back pockets of his jeans. "It's a little weird." She wanted to add that it sucked that Paloma would probably lose her virginity before she would. Not that it was a contest, but she was the one with a steady boyfriend, not Paloma. She kept that thought to herself. Instead, she returned to her original question. "What are we gonna do about all this... stuff?"

Ken gave her his attention and waited for further explanation.

"Carol Ann... the bike! Her seeing us together. Then Paloma had to go and announce not only that she was working for Pluma, but that I got her the job - which I didn't!" She took a deep breath then added, "And Gills, what did she want?"

Ken's fingers wandered to the silver charm on Ruth's necklace. He played with it between his fingers. It had become an unconscious habit when he was thinking. He loved the way the light glistened off the diamond cuts in the horseshoes. He also loved that she always wore it.

"Not much we can do, I guess. It's not a crime that P's working at the paper. It's just an uncomfortable situation if everyone now knows. They would have known when her article came out, anyway."

"Yeah," Ruth agreed, "but what about Carol Ann?"

"We weren't doing anything, Baby Doll, and we were in a crowd of people."

"But the bike! We should call your Uncle! Maybe they can pick her up on the way home and... question her or something." Ruth clamored and dug her hands a little deeper into his back pockets looking for his cell.

"It's in the front pocket, but you can keep doing that if you like," he grinned at her. She pulled her hands away, irritated, but he took her wrists and slid her hands back around his hips. "I emailed pictures of the bike to him already. He'll get them when he gets to work."

She protested, but he quieted her, "It's one-thirty in the morning and I'm not calling Uncle Bob right now. He'll throw us both in jail for disturbing his sleep. We'll just have to be careful. Keep our eyes open. Make sure no one's following you. I will call him first thing in the morning."

"First thing?" she looked deep into his beautiful brown eyes.

"First thing."

"So what did Gills want?"

"Oh," his fingers picked up her necklace again, "she wanted to know why I turned down the position as head of the English department. She was upset because she had recommended me for it."

"What did you say?"

"I told her I didn't feel qualified to run a department after only one year on the job and that Ms. Diaz deserved the position more than I did. I also told her that Principal Rodriguez asked me to coordinate all the AP classes. You know the advanced studies in this district has a lot of inconsistencies. It really needs someone to overhaul the whole thing from the ground up..."

Ruth sighed and rolled her eyes. He let his hands drift from the necklace to her waist.

"You're not interested in discussing the finer points of public education right now?" he asked before he kissed her lips.

"Not particularly," she whispered.

He kissed her lips. He always took her breath away, and they both knew that whatever they had been talking about moments before would be lost in their self-induced fog.

"Call Paloma, see if Greg is behaving himself. If she wants to stay, I'll take you home."

Chapter 33

SHE THOUGHT SHE'D seen the movie before. *I hate black and white film.* She knew what would happen next. The girl in the old-fashioned dress would go into the school and start shooting everyone with a paintball gun. The red paint would splatter all over the people and the walls. *The only thing in color is the stupid red paint.*

It all happened as she had predicted. A second little girl wrote down everything with an enormous ostrich feather pen.

She tried to get up and turn the TV off, but she couldn't move. She was so tired.

This time something different happened. Two men entered the scene and began gyrating around the girls. *Now, this is interesting! I don't remember them. I must have fallen asleep the last time I watched this.*

She continued to watch and realized all four were doing modern dance. She was confused. *Did I fall asleep and miss the end of the other movie?*

She got angry; she wanted to see what happened to the girl and all the people who got shot. She knew it was only paintball, *even so, you just can't go into a school and shoot people. Someone has to teach that girl a lesson!*

Just then, the modern dance stopped and shots rang out. She felt the hit to her abdomen and looked down to see red paint splattered across her own body. She knew it was only paint, but it looked like blood, and she was covered in it. The cry of sirens filled the air. She knew the girl was after her and she had to run.

She ran through the never-ending hallways of the school. The sirens pulsed in her ears. *I gotta get outside, where's the door?* Then she saw it, the school's front door. She knew if she got through it, she'd be safe.

The door was mere feet in front of her when the girl in the old-fashioned dress blocked her way. She tried to open her mouth and scream, but nothing came out.

She sat bolt upright to her cell phone screaming at her.

It took her a moment to regain her bearings. She was at home, in her room, on her floor, in her sleeping bag because she was closing on her house in the morning, and everything she was taking with her, she'd packed in the pull behind trailer, including her bike.

She answered her phone, "Hello."

"Ma, it's me. Come get me."

"Denny?" It was her son. "What time is it?"

"I don't know! Four-thirty? You gotta come get me."

"Where are you?"

"I'm here, in Golden Valley!" He yelled into the phone, "What are you doing that you can't come and get me?"

"Sleeping," she answered groggily. "I'm going back to sleep. Goodbye." She pushed the off button. She closed her eyes. It felt like a nanosecond before her phone rang again. This time she looked at the time on her phone before she answered; it said four-forty-five.

"Hello, Denny."

"Don't hang up on me again!" Her son snapped at her.

"Don't speak to me like that," she snapped back.

"All right, all right, I'm sorry." This time he pleaded. "Please don't hang up on me."

She thought for a moment, "What do you need?"

"Like I was trying to tell you, I need you to come and pick me up," he said through clenched teeth.

"And where are you?" she asked.

"I'm downtown." He was quiet for a moment. "I'm at the sheriff's."

"Why'd the sheriff pick you up?"

"I wasn't doing anything..."

"Of course not," she interrupted.

"It wasn't my fault! It was your bike they stopped, not me!"

This got her full attention. "My bike? What does my bike have to do with this?" The last thing she'd done before she'd gone to bed was locked her bike in the back of the trailer; she was sure of it. "What are you doin' with my bike?"

"I borrowed it," he admitted sheepishly.

"You mean you stole it."

"I wasn't gonna keep it! I just need a ride for the night."

"Where's the expensive sports car you bought with my money?"

"Don't bitch to me about that, right now," he shot back defensively.

"That bike was locked up in the back of a trailer. You had no business going in there."

"What's up with the trailer, anyway? Looks like you stuffed the whole house in there," he changed the subject.

"I sold the house. I close in..." she had to think for a moment, "four hours."

"What about me? When were you gonna tell me?"

"I told you six months ago, and I haven't exactly seen much of you since."

"You better come and get me. I'm not spending any more time in here for doin' nothin.' Anyways, the sheriff wants to talk to you about your bike."

Her gut wrenched, "Whadaya mean?"

"They stopped me because they say they've been looking for a black bike with green flames. I told them it was my mother's when they brought me in."

She was dead silent. She knew immediately what the dream meant. One person had seen her on the bike, found the corruption of the school's accounts, and found Alverez's body. It was the girl in the old-fashioned dress. She didn't have a paintball gun, but who needs a paintball gun when you're doing the Sheriff's nephew. It was Ruth Willows, and she was going to have to teach the girl a lesson.

She collected herself and tried to be coy, "What on earth does the sheriff want with my bike? I hardly ever use that old thing."

"How should I know?" Denny's patience was growing thin again. "They said they wanted to question the owner of the bike about a crime they might have witnessed. They ran your plates, and it came up registered to Roger Evans. I told 'em he was my dad but died a long time ago. Then they said it was co-owned by Carlotta Evans. I told them you hadn't gone by that name since my dad died. So they told me to call you and get you down here. They won't give the bike back till you talk to them."

She was quiet again.

"Ma! Are you still there?" Denny yapped.

"Yeah," her mind was spinning. "Nothing better happening to that bike, you hear me! You tell your friends down there in the sheriff's department that it's in pristine condition, and it better be that way when I get there. If you want me to come and get you, I gotta get dressed first. I'll be there as soon as I can." She ended the call.

She laid back on her sleeping bag and glance at her phone; five-O-three. She needed to plan and plan quickly. *What would be the best way to take care of this situation?* She took some time to let the ideas run through her head. She had to hurry, but she had to be thorough. By five-thirty, she was ready to move. She showered and got herself ready for the day. A few minutes after six, she called Blair.

"Blair, I need you to come over to my house with the power of attorney papers. I need you to represent me and let the mortgage company wire the money to my account."

"No problem," she answered lackadaisically, "your closing is at nine. I'll swing by on my way there."

"No, I need you to come over right now," Carol Ann insisted.

"It's six o'clock in the morning!" Blair was affronted. "You're lucky I even answered my phone."

"If you're not here with those papers in twenty minutes, you won't have a closing to go to!"

"Carol Ann, just what is your problem?"

"My problem is that I have been up since four-thirty. My son was critically injured in a motorcycle accident early this morning, and I am trying to get to Phoenix before he dies."

"Oh, My God!" Blair gasped. "Carol Ann, why didn't you say so before? I'll be right there."

By six-forty, Carol Ann locked the front door on her home for the last fifteen years and handed the keys to Blair Cummings. "The money will be in my account by five today?" she re-questioned Blair.

"Yes, it should be."

"Good. And my account numbers are all confidential. You can only give them to the mortgage company?"

"Yes, but they're not withdrawing, just depositing." Blair tried to reassure her.

"I don't care. I don't like giving out my account numbers."

"I've dealt with this company many times. They are very professional."

"All right then. Thank you for coming over so early, Blair. I really appreciate it."

"It's no problem, Carol Ann. I feel terrible about your son. Go do what you can for him. I have your cell. I'll call you to tell you how everything went."

The women shook hands and gave each other a polite hug. Blair climbed into her BMW and sped off. Carol Ann took to the front seat of her CRV and headed down the road.

Carol Ann dialed Ruth's cell as she walked into the main office.

"Hello," Ruth answered.

"Hello Ruth, this is Carol Ann Fitzsimmons."

Ruth was silent on the other end of the phone.

"The school's secretary," Carol Ann clarified. "I'm so sorry to call you so early, but we have a problem you need to take care of immediately."

"Okay," She took Ruth off guard.

"The lab fees for your college classes were never paid. I just got the check from the school board and I need you to sign it so I can deposit it and pay the university. It's only a hundred dollars, but they won't release your grades until it's paid, and you won't be able to graduate from here if your grades aren't released."

Ruth was relieved it was such a simple problem. "It's senior breakfast this morning, but I'll be in class by nine-thirty. I'll stop by the office before I go to class."

"I'm sorry, but that won't do," Carol Ann replied.

"Why not?"

"I'm taking the day off, I shouldn't even be here now, but I came in to finish a few miscellaneous items. If you want me to deposit this check for you, I need you to sign it before I leave."

"Well, can't Lezza deposit the check later?"

"Honey," her voice was tight, and she sounded irritated, "the university wanted this money six months ago. I'm surprised they let you take your final with an outstanding balance. Maybe they realized that the board of Ed is footing your bill, so they let it slide, I don't know. If you would like to graduate with the rest of your classmates, I need to deposit this money today. I will do that if I can be at the bank at eight a.m. By eight-thirty, I will be in a closing on my house, and I cannot call Lezza and remind her to go to the bank and take care of this for you. It's up to you. If I don't see you by seven-thirty, then I'll assume that it's not all that important to you, and I won't worry about it anymore either." She finished her speech with a tone of finality.

"Okay, I didn't realize..." Ruth confessed. "It's a little after seven. I'll be ready to leave in a few minutes. I really will be there."

"Fine," Carol Ann huffed into the phone, "I don't have time to wait for you." She hung up the phone quickly and got to work.

★ ★ ★

Ruth made it to the school in record time. She didn't see any other vehicles in the parking lot. She said a silent prayer that Carol Ann hadn't taken off for the day yet. She shook the main doors, no good. Then she remembered the small blue door to the side of the main entrance. She pulled it and the old worn door swung open. Ruth breathed a sigh of relief.

The halls were dark, and the air was still. Florescent bulbs shone through the large office windows. Ruth opened the office door.

"What happened here?" Ruth exclaimed as she entered the office.

The long narrow counter was littered with at least two dozen gallon bottles. A not so pleasant smell met her nose.

With bunched up, wet paper towels in her yellow gloved hands, Carol Ann popped up from behind the counter. "OSHA," she answered.

"OSHA?" Ruth was perplexed.

"They usually come in the summer," Carol Ann explained, "I got a message they are coming today. Of course, it's the one day I need to take off. They want to inspect the chemicals we keep on the premises."

Ruth perused the bottles; acetone, butane, xylene, toluene, acetic acid, carbon disulfide. "Oh my god, Carol Ann, these are all highly flammable! They shouldn't all be out of their closets at once."

"Thank you for the chemistry lesson, honey," she disappeared behind the counter again.

"What are you doing down there?" Ruth peered around the edge of the counter.

"Oh, I just had a little spill. It should be fine," she answered whimsically. "If you could please sign that check, we can both be out of here. It's on top of Lezza's desk."

Ruth's head was spinning. Nothing about the situation seemed right. As she rounded the counter to Lezza's desk, it looked like every can of paint thinner and mineral spirits the school's shops owned was lined up on the floor.

She headed to Lezza's desk; it had only taken five months for the desk to resume its previously disheveled quality. Ruth let out another long sigh as she fingered through papers on the top layer of the mess.

"Um... Carol Ann," Ruth watched the secretary fiddling around on the floor. "I don't see anything that looks like a check."

"It still must be on my desk then. Just go and sign it," she answered brusquely.

Ruth walked to Carol Ann's immaculate desk. The only paper on it was a yellow legal pad. Without thinking, Ruth bent forward to read the note scribbled on the top sheet:

Hector Alverez

Bill Bowman

Marty Alberts

Ruth Willows

What is this? Those are the three men who… And why is my name…

A tight arm wrapped around her throat. It took just a moment for Ruth's brain to register the hand with the yellow rubber glove attached to the arm, pressing into her carotid. In one brief, fleeting second, she understood everything. It all made sense: the note, and the names, the three men from the school who'd died, the motorcycle with the green flames, the break-in at her home, the missing money... Ruth fought the dimming light, but the smell of all the chemicals made it even more difficult to breathe. Spots twinkled in front of her eyes before everything went black.

Chapter 34

THE FIRE TRUCK screaming down Main Street went unnoticed by the other students crowded into Pat's Pancake House as they inhaled their traditional senior breakfast. The noise set Paloma on edge. Maybe it was the last six months of working at The Sentinel, but she felt poised and waiting for the next big story. She reflexively stood to look out the windows when she ran into her favorite teacher.

"Leaving? You don't look like you're finished," he said, looking over her shoulder at her half-eaten stack of pancakes.

"Oh, Ke... Mr. Silver," she smiled. She would be so glad in three weeks when this charade was finally over. "Sorry. I just heard..." The truck was long gone by now. "Oh, never mind."

"Where's our best friend this morning? She's not skipping out on a senior tradition, is she?" he asked, returning the smile.

"She promised to meet me. I've been holding her a spot since I got here. We were studying for finals last night; I didn't think we stayed up all that late. Guess she must've slept in."

Before Ken could comment, Paloma's cell phone beeped. She pulled it from her jeans pocket and read the screen, "It's from Ruth."

"Go on," he grinned.

She read it aloud, "Have to stop at school, be there by eight."

"Why'd she stop at school?" Paloma looked at Ken for the answer, but he only shrugged his shoulders. "It's after eight." She hit a few buttons on her phone. "It says she sent this message at seven-twenty-three. Where could she be?"

A second and third fire truck went screaming down the street. A few students paused their conversations to let the noise pass. The blood drained from both Ken and Paloma's face.

"Oh My God," Paloma whispered.

Ken grabbed her arm, "Let's go."

★ ★ ★

A sheriff's department cruiser blocked the driveway into the high school. Ken pulled onto the lawn beside it and flung open his door.

"Hey! You can't park here," the officer shouted.

Ken and Paloma jumped out of the Jeep. "John," Ken shouted. "Did they find her?"

The older officer recognized Ken, "Oh, Kenny, it's you. Hey, you can't go up there, authorized personnel only." John tried to bar their way, but he was too slow, and they took off up the small hill of the drive to the school. John immediately radioed the sheriff.

The nearer they got to the school, the thicker the smoke became. Fire trucks poured water into the building. The fire itself looked contained to one section of the large structure, but the smoke hung low around the building and made visibility difficult.

In a full-out run, Ken and Paloma wove their way past the trucks and over the bloated fire hoses to the sidewalk of the burning building. The sheriff grabbed Paloma's arm and free her of Ken's grip.

"Stop right there, Ken!" the sheriff hollered. "Where do you think you're going?"

Ken's pace slowed and came to a halt when he realized he could go no further.

"Did you find her? Is she still in there?" He rounded on his heels and came face to face with his uncle.

"There's no one in there. What are you talking about?" Davis asked as he pulled them both away from the sidewalk.

"Ruth! She came here this morning, and she never showed up at the seniors' breakfast," Ken gasped. "P, keep trying her cell."

"The groundskeeper, Johnston, called the fire in. He was the first one on the scene, just after eight. He was outside the gym when he smelled something. Turned around to see smoke coming through the cracks around the windows," Davis answered reassuringly.

Paloma wandered a few feet away from Ken, the sheriff, and the intense heat and smoke pouring from the building. As she caught her breath, she saw it. Parked in its familiar spot, where it sat five mornings a week, was Ruth's old green Ford Ranger. Her heart sank. Until now, there had been the possibility that Ruth was nowhere near the school. The truck confirmed her worst fears. Ruth was here, somewhere.

Paloma ran back to the sheriff and Ken, and pounded on their arms. She couldn't speak, only point, but they received her message.

Ken made it to the pickup first. It was unlocked, no Ruth in sight. Her backpack and laptop lay on the passenger side floor. Davis got on his radio. He called for a search of the area from his crew. Next, he radioed the fire chief to alert them of a potential victim in the building.

"She's a smart girl. If she couldn't get out, she'd try to get to a safe place. Check the closets, offices, bathrooms, everywhere!" he blasted into the radio.

Paloma sobbed. It was too much for her to take. Ken grabbed her and wrapped his arm around her.

"What the hell was she doing in there?" Davis bellowed at his nephew.

"She texted Paloma she had to stop here before she went to Pat's, but the message didn't go through till after we heard the first firetruck go through town." Ken was trying hard to keep his composure. "We called the Willows on the way here. Grace said Ruth left early. She'd gotten a call she needed to sign some papers, something to do with graduation. Grace thought a secretary called. We've been trying Ruth's cell, but there's no answer."

"We'll call the secretaries. What are their names?" Davis hung his radio back onto his belt and pulled out his cell phone.

"It would have either been Lezza or ..." the thought hit them all at the same time, but Ken said it, "Carol Ann."

Davis had already hit speed dial to dispatch, "Sue, did anyone ever pick up our guest from this morning?"

"Not that I know of Sheriff," Sue answered sweetly in her singsong rhythm. She punched a few buttons on her console, "I've still got video on him in the conference room."

"APB out on his mother Carlotta Evans, AKA Carol Ann Fitzsimmons. Run both of her names and try to pinpoint where she might be."

"Will, do, sir," Chapoose answered.

"Call Baca down in Santa Fe and White up in Denver. Let them know all the details. If she's taking I-25, she'll have to pass one of them."

"Oh my God, Ruth's really in there. She'll never make it," Paloma shook uncontrollably.

"If she's in there, we'll find her," Davis assured Paloma. "Ken," he whispered, "move her away from here and try to get her to calm down."

The next few minutes seemed like hours. Paloma got a paper bag from the first responder van to stop her hyperventilating. Ken paced, each pass taking him closer to the burning building.

A warning shout came from the building, "Clear out, clear out, it's coming down!"

Everyone outside backed up. Several firefighters exited the building empty-handed. "Headcount," someone called out.

"We're missing Darby," another voice called in response.

Like the felling of a giant sequoia, a loud cracking sound resounded from deep inside the building. Ken's heart stopped. His body went numb, and his blood ran cold. This was it, the end. He would never forget his feeling of utter helplessness, uselessness, and failure for as long as he lived. He would never forget the forlorn moan of the collapsing building about to consume the one person could not stand to lose.

Before he drew another breath, a first-floor window exploded and sent shards of glass flying. A large bulky figure in full fire gear appeared in the broken window. Fresh oxygen sucked through the new opening ignited the flames behind the fighter, framing him in an infernal glow.

The figure struggled to extricate himself from the blaze. As Ken stood frozen in place, gawking helplessly at the man, he realized part of his struggle was due to the load he bore in his arms.

Ken's heart jolted to life. It's a person. Ruth! He tried to run toward the firefighter, but his legs were like rubber. With all his will, he forced himself forward.

He'd barely got himself moving when a hand came down on his shoulder and pulled him off balance. The owner of the meat hook sent him reeling in the opposite direction, away from the window, away from the fire, away from what had to be Ruth.

"Back Off Silver!" Tommy Clark's voice was harsh, "You're not dressed for this!"

Ken was livid as his butt hit the wet ground. He watched as the firefighter held a body in his arms like an offering. Tommy threw the blanket over the body, took up the load, and sprinted away from the building with the strength of a Greek hero. Members of his crew whisked the firefighter out of harm's way.

The structure gave way. As it imploded upon itself, a wave of heat washed over Ken, who sat motionless on the wet blacktop. A tower of flames shot overhead as the renewed supply of oxygen fed them. Someone pulled Ken to his feet and dragged him further from the building as the firefighters renewed their efforts with the hoses.

Ken coughed, rolled to his feet, and sprinted after Clark. He flew between the trucks with a boost of energy, then froze. On the pavement, Tommy Clark hovered over the body of a young blonde woman. Ruth!

Tommy had discarded the blanket and his protective coat and helmet. Ruth's T-shirt was sliced down the front from neckline to hem along with her bra. Tommy alternated between chest compressions and giving breaths.

"Twenty-eight, twenty-nine, thirty," Tommy counted quickly and out loud. "Get the AED from the van!" He shouted before he returned to her mouth and gave her two strong breaths. "Ambulance is on its way," he added before returning to her chest and taking up the counting of compressions. Ken ran to the van, grabbed the small plastic case, and kneeled at her head, beside Tommy.

Ruth looked dead. Her lips were pale blue despite the life-saving breaths Tommy pushed into her. Ken was relieved, overjoyed to see her and to know her body existed. Fire hadn't destroyed her. If nothing else, he could still touch her, hold her one more time, even if it was just to say goodbye.

Tommy ripped the AED from Ken's hands, "Two Strong breaths, make sure you tilt the head back and hold her nose."

Ken realized this order was for him. It had been a long time since he had CPR training, but he remembered how to give the kiss of life, so he did.

Tommy reached for Ruth's necklace and tried to rip it from her neck. Ken grab his hand, "I'll do it." Ken pulled the silver rope over her head, and her long blonde hair fanned out like a halo around her face as the chain drew it from behind her.

"Clear," Tommy ordered. He'd applied the two pads of the AED to Ruth, and the machine was set to do its stuff.

After a few brief moments, the machine's monotone female voice requested, "Give shock."

Just as Tommy pushed the red button, Paloma approached the scene. She screamed as she watched the body of her best friend contracting and contorting on the ground. Ken jumped to his feet and grabbed hold of her. He held on tight, as much for her safety as for his own sanity.

The blast of the siren from the incoming ambulance drowned out the machine's next direction to 'resume compressions,' but Tommy had already begun counting as the medics flung open the ambulance's doors.

A woman jumped out and relieved Tommy. Another medic, with a clipboard, took down the information Tommy provided. The third jumped out from behind the wheel and relayed all the information via his cell phone, presumably to the local ER.

"Does anyone know her?" the guy with the clipboard called out.

Both Ken and Paloma resounded with a 'YES.'

He began firing questions at them, "Name?"

"Ruth Willows," Ken was the first to answer.

The medic now directed his questions to Ken, "Age?"

"Eighteen."

"Any previous health problems?"

"No."

"Any allergies?"

"No."

"Is she pregnant?"

Ken was taken aback, but he answered, "No."

"Are you sure?"

"Yes, I'm sure! What the hell kind of question is that?" Ken was losing his temper.

Paloma pulled on his arm, "We always get it."

The medic continued, "Is she on any prescribed medications?"

"NO, I said she was healthy." Ken fired back.

"Is she on any illegal substances?"

"No!"

"Does she smoke?"

"No."

"Is she under the influence of alcohol?"

"No."

"Has she had previous problems with breathing, asthma, emphysema, chronic bronchial infections?"

"No."

"Liver, kidney, gall bladder disease?"

"No."

"Any types of cancer?"

"No," Ken now answered wearily.

The woman working on Ruth called out, "We got a pulse and a steady rhythm. Let's get her in, intubate her and start an IV."

The medic with the clipboard left his questioning, turned to his colleague, and helped hoist Ruth onto a stretcher and into the ambulance. Ken wondered when the stretcher had appeared. He hadn't seen it being taken out of the ambulance.

"We're taking her to Memorial," the one with the clipboard turn and spoke to Ken and Paloma.

Ruth was in the back of the ambulance. One door was closed, and the other about to shut. Ken stepped his foot on the bumper to climb in the back. Clipboard guy stopped him.

"You next of kin?"

Ken wanted to say, yes. He knew that was the only way he would get to be with her. Before he could answer, another hand appeared on his shoulder and again pulled him back.

"Not yet," Sheriff Davis gave the medic a nod. "I'll send Tommy with her. He'll keep an eye on her." Tommy hopped into the back of the ambulance without hesitation. "We'll notify her family. They'll meet you down there."

The door slammed shut, the siren blasted, and the ambulance sped off.

Ken and Paloma stood still in the ambulance's wake. They both slowly sank to the ground and sat on the pavement next to the discarded blanket and a pile of shredded duct tape. Ken slowly opened his clenched fist and found Ruth's silver necklace. He slipped it around his neck and under his shirt for safekeeping.

It was Paloma's turn to support Ken. He said nothing; he just wept. He sunk where he stood, sat with his face buried against bent knees and his arms covering his head. Paloma rested her hands on his shoulders and laid her cheek against his rounded back. She said nothing; tears still fell from her eyes as Ken's tears turned into sobs.

Someone had strung yellow police tape along the parking lot lamp posts closest to the road. The thin strip of plastic was doing an amazing job of holding back students, teachers, and onlookers. Traffic on the two-lane road next to the school was at a standstill.

Ken got control of himself, lifted his head, and asked, "Are you okay, P?" as he eyed the growing crowd.

"Yeah, I guess."

"Let's get out of here."

★ ★ ★

Around one p.m., Paloma made it back to her car. Ken gave her a long hug and a kiss on the top of the head before she climbed into the little blue Ford and headed home.

Instead of driving off, Ken walked to Merchant Street in the center of town, and half sat half fell onto a green park bench. The events of the day played through his mind as he stared blankly at the signs of the businesses that lined the familiar street.

Ken and Paloma's only destination after they left the school was Golden Valley Memorial Hospital. Their repeated questions about Ruth's condition went unanswered. Finally, they found Ed and Joe in the ER's waiting room.

"There you two are," Joe announced when he spotted both Ken and Paloma, "We didn't want to leave before we found you."

"RUTH!" Paloma shouted, "Where is she? How is she? Is she?.."

"She's been life-flighted to Colorado Springs. Connie went with her," Ed answered but Paloma's face sank. "She was in a lot of pain. She took in a good deal of smoke and a lot of bad fumes. She's having a hard time getting enough oxygen into her system."

"Why Colorado Springs?" Paloma asked.

"They have a good treatment facility up there." Then Ed, with tears in his eyes, looked at Ken and took his hand. He put his other arm around Paloma. "The firefighter came in just before they left. He said he found her bound in duct tape and under a desk in the main office. The desk was big enough to protect her from the flames. He said it was you two who came looking for her. If the sheriff hadn't insisted that Ruth was in that building, they would have never found her. Thank you." No one could say anything for quite some time.

Ken felt uncomfortable with the whole situation. He had no desire to be painted as a hero. He'd done nothing. All he could remember was that he had given up hope of ever seeing his Baby Doll again.

It relieved him when Ed and Joe stopped looking at him with grateful expressions and headed off to Colorado Springs. He was also thankful that Paloma was not her usual chatty self as he drove from the hospital to her car. Now he sat on the bench feeling dazed, uncomfortable, and angry.

He saw the occasional passerby in his peripheral vision, but mostly (and thankfully) he felt unnoticed. One figure grew more prominent until it forced him to turn his head and look at her straight on.

"Kenny there you are!" Donna Silver jogged up to her son, sat next to him, and wrapped her arms around him. "My goodness, I just got off the phone with Bob. I heard everything that happened. Are you okay?"

"Yeah, I'm fine."

"What about Ruth?"

"I don't know." His voice cracked slightly.

"You don't know? What is that supposed to mean?" Donna sounded flabbergasted at the nonchalance of her son.

"I haven't seen her since the ambulance pulled away with her this morning," he snapped at his mother. "They took her to Colorado Springs before I could see her."

Donna hugged her son even tighter. Yes, he was a grown man, and he towered over her, but she could tell that he was hurting more than he was letting on. "Should I close the shop early? We can drive up there together," she suggested.

"Ah ... Whatever."

She wasn't used to her son being this emotionally fragile. "Bob wanted me to tell you they got the woman they were after. The one they think set the fire."

"Carol Ann?" His interest perked up a bit. "Where was she? Did she say why she wanted to kill Ruth?" It was the first time he had said it out loud, the first time he had even thought it, really. A lump formed in his throat as he held back tears.

Donna looked at him and then looked across the street to the flower shop she and Frank owned. "Bob said New Mexico State Police came across her in Raton. She was getting gas, and a passing cruiser heard the Be On the Look Out." She glanced at her son. His face showed a modicum of relief, but he still blinked back tears. "I guess some officer from Denver is going down to get her and bring her back. Do you know they think she killed those men from school? Killing and stealing money from the district, how can someone do that?"

"Don't know, Ma."

"What's going to happen with classes for the rest of the year? Bob said the fire destroyed the school."

"Don't know that, either. I'm sure someone will figure it all out."

"Well, thank goodness you're okay." Donna squeezed her son again and stood, "I've gotta get back to the shop. Cindy should be here in a little bit. I'll try calling Connie." Ken was staring at his shoes. "I'd like to go up and give my support. I don't want to drive that far alone."

Since when he would have said if he had the energy to fight her.

"You'll come with me, keep me company." She looked for any type of reaction. "I'll see you in the shop in a few minutes." Donna squeezed her son's shoulder and crossed the street.

Chapter 35

THE LATE JUNE sun shone on the sheriff's wooden desk. Ruth and Ken held hands as they sat on one side. Davis took his seat opposite of them, "The case of Carol Ann Fitzsimmons is officially closed."

Ruth and Ken stared in silence; Davis continued, "Carol Ann wisely accepted the DA's plea deal."

"What was the deal?" Ruth asked.

"She will serve three consecutive life sentences for the three men she killed. She's being charged with embezzlement and has to pay back all the money she took from the district." The sheriff took a long look at Ruth and continued, "In exchange, the DA has agreed to drop the charges of arson and attempted murder. I'm sorry, Ruth. It's nothing personal. It's just the way deals are made."

Ruth blew out a long sigh, "She'll be going away for a long time. I guess that's what's important." She thought for a while. "Did she say anything? Like why?"

"I only spoke to her attorney. I don't know if she'll release any sort of statement to the press," Davis admitted. "If she hadn't taken the deal, we had enough evidence to convict her on all counts."

"Her real estate agent gave us the number to her offshore bank account. It was easy to follow the money. Apparently, Hector Alverez caught on to her when he took over for Alberts. Alberts probably knew about it the whole time. We have her tire and boot treads we picked up at Alberts cabin, and we know someone tampered with his car. Once we got her as the owner of the bike, that all fell into place."

"The hard part was figuring out how Bill Bowman got caught up in the mess. Once we had Carol Ann in custody, we tested her, and her DNA was all over his office and um... him. We assume that Bowman figured out about her money scheme when he tried to find his missing tuba. One of the last deposits made to her account was in the amount of six thousand dollars. I'm told that's a good price for a used tuba."

Ruth stood, walk around the desk, and hugged the sheriff, "Thank you for saving my life."

"Anytime, just don't make me do it again," Davis chuckled. "You two are dressed pretty nice, what are you two up to now?"

Ken rolled his eyes and threw up his hands, "Anything she wants."

Ruth's smile grew extra large, "I'm gonna hold you to that Cowboy. Can we start with lunch?"

"Wanna join us, Uncle Bob?"

"Na, I've got work to do. You kids go have fun." He remembered, "Hey Kenny, you're taking off tomorrow, aren't you?"

"Seven a.m. flight to San Francisco," he answered.

"You be safe out there." He hugged his nephew with a firm slap on the back. "Have fun. Be good!"

"Sure thing, Uncle Bob."

After lunch, Ken and Ruth strolled down the street. He slipped his arm around Ruth's waist. She had lost so much weight in the last month he felt like he could wrap his arm around her twice. "Shall we get you home?"

"Are you trying to welch out of our deal, Cowboy?" she pulled away from him.

"I thought you might be tired," he kissed her temple.

"I'm not tired." She stared him down. "Unless you want to count being tired of hospitals and hyperbaric chamber treatments. Or being tired of doing nothing but watching movies and rereading every book in my house. My lungs are healed up just fine. I don't need to carry that emergency oxygen tank around with me." She looked with disdain at the small blue bag Ken insisted she carry with her today. "I will not pass out from crossing the street. And before you start with your 'You almost died' speech..." She moved closer to him and wrapped her arms around him. "I know you were there while I was in ICU. I know you saw me at my worst. I'm sorry you had to see that. Thank you for being with me, Cowboy."

"I do not allow you to apologize for being hospitalized. I just thank God that you're getting better..."

"I am better," she interrupted.

"You're getting better," he reminded her, "which is why you still have to take it easy."

"You promised to take me out. You're going to San Francisco tomorrow, so this is our last chance, Cowboy."

"We will have lots of other chances Baby Doll," he smiled and kissed her lips. He understood her frustration at being cooped up, but she still looked so frail.

They window-shopped along Merchant Street before stopping at Silver's Flowers to say hello to Donna.

"Your father just went home to pack up some bulbs for shipping, but he left the shipping crates in the back. I tried to call his cell phone, but he never turns the darn thing on. Before you head out, will you throw the crates in the back of your Jeep and drop them off?"

Ken hesitated, but Ruth broke in, "Of course, Mrs. Silver. We're pretty much done here unless there was something else you wanted to do, Cowboy."

Ken shook his head, "I'm just doing whatever I'm told today."

Ruth smiled.

Ken sauntered out the door, "I'll get the car."

★ ★ ★

White smoke billowed from behind the tree line as Ken pulled the Jeep in front of his guesthouse.

"What's with the smoke?" Ruth asked.

"Dad had a pile of old trees. They got infested, so he wanted to burn them. One of the guys must have started it," Ken explained. "I won't be long. I just need to take the crates to the greenhouse. You don't even have to get out of the car if the smoke bothers you."

"It doesn't bother me," Ruth was a little affronted. "I'd like to use the bathroom." She jumped out of the Jeep.

"The door's unlocked," Ken climbed out and walked around to her. He kissed her and unbuttoned his dress shirt.

"Cowboy, right out here in the driveway?" she teased him.

"Those crates are dirty. Since you're going in, will you take this in for me?"

Ruth took the shirt, smiled, and walked into Ken's place.

★ ★ ★

"Hey Baby Doll, where d'you go," Ken called fifteen minutes later from his front door.

"I'm back here," she called from his bedroom. "You're all packed up and ready to go."

"Yeah. I gotta be outta here early," Ken commented as he walked to his bedroom.

Beside the door were two suitcases and his laptop case. A pile of fabric was draped across a chair.

"I realized that I have never been in your bedroom," Ruth smirked. She sat on her knees in the middle of his bed, wearing his dress shirt.

Ken was speechless for a moment. “What are you doing, Baby Doll?”

“Waiting for you to find me.” Her heart pounded a mile a minute. She had never dreamed she could behave like this, but here she was. She was excited and scared and embarrassed and nervous all at the same time. She smiled at him and tried her best to be coy without sounding totally stupid, “You said we’d do whatever I wanted. Well ...” That was the best she was going to do with the pillow talk. Her hands relaxed the death grip they had on the front of the shirt, and it fell open just enough to reveal that all she had on underneath was her silver necklace.

“Baby Doll...” was about all Ken could manage as a response. He kneeled on the mattress in front of her and wrapped his arms around her naked body. The dress shirt fell to the bed as he kissed her more passionately than he had ever done before.

The heat of his bare chest and muscular arms kept her warm, especially when a breeze blew through the open bedroom window. As his warmth penetrated her skin, her nerves disappeared. She felt comfortable and safe in his arms like this was the only place that she could exist from now on.

“Baby Doll,” Ken sighed, “I’m not sure if you’re ready for this.”

“I’m ready, Cowboy.”

“The doctor hasn’t given you the all-clear yet. You aren’t supposed to do anything strenuous. You’re not even allowed to ride Blue yet.”

“It’s six weeks today Cowboy, I’ll be fine. And you’re leaving tomorrow.”

“We’ll have other chances...”

“Don’t you want me?” Ruth’s defenses rose. How mortifying to have worked up this much courage only to feel unwanted.

“I most certainly do want you,” Ken whispered as he laid her head upon the quilt covered pillow. “I just don’t want to hurt you.”

“You won’t, I trust you.”

He kissed her more as he let his hands travel over her skin. It bothered him that he could feel every rib. Her entire body had gone from being slim and healthy-looking to a fragile, breakable skeleton.

His mouth wandered down her throat to her chest and her breasts. She moaned a long sigh. He stopped and pulled away, "Are you okay?"

"I'm sorry, did I do something wrong?" her skin flushed red with embarrassment.

"You groaned. Did I hurt you?"

"No. I didn't mean to. I kinda liked it. Is that okay?"

"Yes, that's okay." Ken berated himself. "I'm the one who should be sorry." He kissed her and ran his finger down her breast to find his talisman charm. "You know you have a red mark." He fingered a small red squiggle at the base of her left breast.

"I know, I guess it will always be a scar."

"What's it from?"

She took the horseshoe charm from his fingers and laid it over the redness. It was a perfect match.

"From the fire?" Ken asked.

"I guess it got so hot the metal burned me."

"I'm sorry, I feel like it's my fault."

"You didn't set the fire." She held his face with one hand and kissed his sweet lips. "Besides, even without the necklace, I'll always have a piece of you close to my heart."

"You'll always have my heart." With that pronouncement, he kissed her long and hard. She knew he still did not say that four-letter L word, but she figured that it might be as close to it as she would ever get from him.

Ken's hands roamed freely to explore every inch of her body. He let his fingers slip inside of her. She was warm and receptive. He checked her breathing. It was heavy, but he thought, maybe she is ready. He knew that he was more than ready, and once he gotten down to business, he wouldn't last very long.

A big gust of wind brought a plume of smoke in through the open window. The smell of burning wood reminded him of campfires.

Ruth was writhing, suddenly gasped, and pulled away. He stopped and sat up. She was choking. "Son of a bitch," he swore. "Where's your oxygen?" he yelled at her.

She gasped again and pointed towards the door. "C..c...car," she croaked out.

Time was of the essence. He scooped her up, wrapped in the quilt from his bed, and carried her to the Jeep. He plopped her down in the passenger seat. "Where!" he demanded.

She reached into the back, but he was quicker. He got the blue canvas bag and extracted the small clear plastic hose. He put the nose piece into her nostrils and turned the valve to start the flow of oxygen. "Breathe through your nose," he ordered. She did.

Ken watched her take several breaths. When he was satisfied that she would not pass out, he slammed the Jeep's door hard and stormed back into the house.

Several minutes passed, Ruth continued to sit and breathe. Finally, Ken stormed back out. He'd changed into a pair of jeans, T-shirt, and cowboy boots. He had her sundress and sandals in one hand, his car keys in the other.

He got behind the wheel and tossed her clothes at her. "I'm taking you to the ER."

"NO," she cried, "I'm fine."

"You are not fine!" he exploded at her. "You couldn't even breathe two minutes ago. You're skinny as a stick, and you don't listen to anything anyone says."

"That's not true. It was the smoke. It made me choke. I was fine as soon as we came outside."

"Fine, then I'll get you away from the smoke. I'm taking you home like I should have done hours ago."

Neither one of them spoke as they drove back to Tall Willows Ranch. Ruth continued to breathe in her oxygen. She didn't feel like she needed it, but she didn't want to get him angrier than he already was. Motionlessly as she could, she slipped on her dress and sandals. She couldn't find her panties and was afraid to ask. She tried to keep her breathing even and slow, but it was hard to breathe when you were also trying to hold back sobs of anger and embarrassment.

The Jeep had barely come to a stop when Ruth flung open the door. She jumped out with the oxygen tank and quilt piled in her arms. Her feet hit the ground in a flat-out run. She flew into the house, up the stairs, and into her bedroom, locking the door behind her.

Ken sat in his Jeep.

When he finally got out, he slammed the door with his foot hard enough to leave a dent. He didn't even bother going to the house; instead, he headed to the field.

Constance, Joe, and Grace were shell-shocked. They'd seen a blur, they presumed to be Ruth, blow past them and up the stairs. They heard a second door slam, but no Cowboy appeared after her.

Ed made it home in time for supper. He saw the Jeep parked in its usual spot and assumed that both his daughter and her beau would be at the table with the rest of the family. He came in the house and looked around, "Where's Ruth and Ken gone off to? Don't they know it's time for supper?"

The three Willows just looked at him. Grace spoke up, "Ruth is upstairs. Her boyfriend is out in the field kicking up a dust storm as far as I can tell. I wanted to go spy on him," she shot a look at her Mother, "but no one will let me."

"Oh," was all Ed replied. They sat down for dinner.

When dinner had almost finished, a knock came from the front door. Everyone at the table looked at each other, but no one moved. The knock came again, this time louder. Grace got up when her mother grabbed her arm. "You stay put," she ordered her youngest daughter.

Constance called to the front of the house, "I'm coming." She stopped at the bottom of the stairs. "Ruth, shall I answer the door, or do you want to?" She got no response, "That's okay, you stay in your room, I'll get the door."

Constance opened the front door to a very dusty, worn-out looking Ken. "Hi Ken, won't you come in?"

"No, thank you, Mrs. Willows. I'd just like to speak to Ruth for a moment."

"Of course." She turned back to the stairs and called to Ruth, "Ruth, Ken would like you to come down so he could speak to you."

She waited for a moment, but there was no reply. "Are you sure you wouldn't like some supper?"

"No, thank you."

"Let me see what's keeping her." Constance headed for the stairs.

"That's all right, ma'am, if she doesn't want to speak with me," Ken turned to leave when Ruth showed up next to her mother.

She had changed to cut-off shorts and an old sweatshirt. Her hair was tied up on the top of her head. The words "What do you want, Cowboy?" stopped him in his tracks.

"I'll leave you two alone," Constance excused herself, closing the front door behind her.

Ruth wandered to the porch railing. She couldn't look at him. All the incredible closeness she had felt, the joy of being alive and being with him, had vanished. She just felt humiliated.

He moved to stand beside her but didn't touch her. That made her feel even worse.

"I'm sorry I got so angry with you, Ruth."

She abhorred it when he called her Ruth. That was what he called her when he needed to feel superior to her, when he wanted to pull away from her. Tears welled up in her eyes.

"I didn't mean to overreact, but you scared me."

She managed one glance at him. Her chest ached, but it wasn't her lungs. It was that hole beginning to rip open again.

"Damn-it," he grabbed her by the arms and turned her toward him. "I watched them pull you out of a burning building, and I thought you were dead. I can't go through that again!"

She attempted a whisper, "I was fine, Cowboy. It was just the smoke..."

"You weren't fine!" His anger was getting the best of him. "All I could think of were headlines reading 'Teacher screws ex-student to death!' I can't just sit around here all the time and take care of you. You're gonna have to learn how to take care of yourself, or you're gonna have problems."

"I never asked you to babysit me. And I can take care of myself, thank you very much," Ruth retorted. "If anyone has problems, maybe it's you. One minute you're boiling hot, the next minute you're ice cold. Maybe you need to decide what exactly it is you want, Cowboy!"

He let go of her arms and took a step back from her. "Yeah, maybe you're right." He walked to the other side of the porch and looked out over Tall Willows. "Maybe it will be good for me to get out of town and clear my head. Let you finish healing in peace."

His words stunned her. If there was any time today she had trouble breathing, it was now.

He walked to her, took her in his arms, and held her tight. "I have to be up and out at the crack of dawn. I'll say goodbye now. I don't want to wake you."

"Sure." she said hesitantly.

He kissed her long and deep, "I'll call you when I get to Greg's."

"Do you still want me to come to see your show?" she asked, not sure if she could handle no as an answer.

"Of course," he was languid in his reply. He kissed her one last time softly on the lips.

She watched him walk down the steps and retreat into his car. She grabbed the porch rail for support and watched him drive slowly down the long drive. His black Jeep dissolved into a cloud of dust, and the cloud disappeared in the wind.

Too many emotions tore through her. She was furious about the things he'd said. The embarrassment of being rejected stung like a poisoned dart in her gut. The old hole in her chest erupted and made her want to curl up and die. She sat on the porch step and hugged her knees.

Is all this worth it? She wondered. She was no fan of the whole "better to have loved and lost" idea right about now. *But I haven't lost*, she reminded herself. *He said he'll call, and I'll fly out to see his show. Focus on the positive, Ruth.*

The sun sank into the horizon, and Constance appeared beside her daughter. "Ken left already?"

"Yeah." After a long pause, Ruth added, "He has to leave for the airport by three a.m."

Constance stepped towards the front door, "I saved a plate of supper for you. Why don't you come in?"

"K," was Ruth's only response.

"Ruthie, you gonna be okay?"

Ruth stood and looked one more time down the drive from where the jeep had vanished. "Yeah." She took a deep breath and decidedly said, "I'm gonna be okay."